ROBERT BLOCH

APPRECIATIONS OF THE MASTER

Photo by Beth Gwinn

ROBERT BLOCH

APPRECIATIONS OF THE MASTER

EDITED BY

RICHARD MATHESON

AND

RICIA MAINHARDT

A TOM DOHERTY ASSOCIATES BOOK / NEW YORK

ROBERT BLOCH: APPRECIATIONS OF THE MASTER

This book is printed on acid-free paper.

A Tor Book
Published by Tom Doherty Associates, Inc.
175 Fifth Avenue
New York, NY 10010

Tor Books on the World-Wide Web:
http://www.tor.com

Tor® is a registered trademark of Tom Doherty Associates, Inc.

Design by Lynn Newmark

Library of Congress Cataloging-in-Publication Data
Robert Bloch : appreciations of the master : a collection of tributes
    to and fiction by Robert Bloch / Richard Matheson and Ricia
    Mainhardt, editors.
        p.   cm.
    "A Tom Doherty Associates book."
    ISBN 0-312-85976-7
    1. Bloch, Robert.   2. Horror tales, American—History
and criticism.   3. Authors, American—20th century—Biography.
4. Horror tales, American.   I. Bloch, Robert.   II. Matheson, Richard.
III. Mainhardt, Ricia.
PS3503.L718Z85   1995
813'.54—dc20   95-30301
                                                                 CIP

First edition: October 1995

Printed in the United States of America

0   9   8   7   6   5   4   3   2   1

COPYRIGHT ACKNOWLEDGMENTS

To the Master, Robert Bloch.
Thank you for the love, laughs, and scares.

CONTENTS

ACKNOWLEDGMENTS

Many thanks to Peter B. Marcus for suggesting this project and for his encouragement, support, and assistance while putting the book together.

Special thanks to Clifford Meth, Todd Cameron Hamilton, and Peder Wagstskjold for their assistance in editing and compiling this volume.

And finally, thanks to Mamma Elly for all her love.

ROBERT BLOCH

APPRECIATIONS OF THE MASTER

INTRODUCTION

In the beginning of September, I spent a couple of weeks with Bob and Elly Bloch at their home in California. This final visit with Bob was to make sure his contracts were in order and his business was on track.

When I was there, the contracts did not seem all that important. Bob had years of fatherly advice and wisdom he wished to impart to me and very little time left to him. Our private moments were far too few. You see, I had to share Bob with others who loved him as much as I. We talked whenever we could find a quiet moment away from the visiting nurses, doctors, and friends.

Once the world learned of Bob's cancer, hundreds of cards and letters poured in. Friends, colleagues, and fans wrote to express their love and appreciation of him and his work.

One afternoon in Bob's office while I helped take care of the day's mail, Bob read me a typical note from one of his fans. The fan wrote to thank Bob for making his life a little better and giving him direction. This was just one of many such letters from countless people whose lives were touched by Robert Bloch.

Often these encounters had been brief and had occurred many years ago. Bob had no reason to remember these meetings. Not because people were unimportant to him, but because kindness was a way of life for him and therefore nothing out of the ordinary or particularly memorable to him.

Whenever approached, Bob would stop and listen to people—really listen. He often gave encouragement or sage advice, or turned tears to smiles. Such encounters, while common to Bob, were anything but common to the recipients of his kindness. These chats often gave fans and struggling young authors the hope they needed to steer their lives in a positive direction.

Bob never asked for this sort of responsibility and he found it a little scary. He worried: if he was able to influence this many people for the good, how many might he have influenced negatively? I found Bob's concern ironic. This kind, gentle, generous man; even while he was wasting away from cancer, he spent precious time being concerned with the well-being of others. This is why so many people quite simply loved Bob Bloch.

In addition to the bundles of cards and letters that arrived spontaneously, Richard Matheson, one of Bob's close friends, solicited letters from some of the many writers Bob knew well, the better for them to convey their love and admiration while Bob could still hear it.

Richard Matheson, like Robert Bloch, is one of those rare individuals who is filled with compassion and insight. He is concerned first about the feelings of others. It is no surprise that he and Robert Bloch were long-time friends.

The responses Richard received were testimonials to a career that spanned more decades than I have been alive. A career that has inspired most of the writers active in speculative fiction today. Richard read these tributes to Bob shortly after I returned to New York.

That night, I received a phone call from Bob's nephew, Peter Marcus. Peter had been present at the reading, and was astounded and moved to hear that his uncle had touched the lives of so many writers. "These famous writers are all fans of Uncle Bob's work. They talk as if he were a god, or at least a saint. Something should be done with these. You're his agent, do something!"

I am always open to ideas, so I asked Peter what he had in mind. He suggested a compilation of the testimonials from these writers, to be printed with their favorite Bloch stories. In this way, the readers of these well-known authors could be introduced to the writings of the man who inspired them, the man they called a master.

I can always see a good idea when it slaps me in the face. I talked to Richard Matheson, who offered his wholehearted support for the project and added some improvements of his own. Then we talked to Melissa Ann Singer, Bob's editor at Tor Books. We quickly struck up a deal, and this book became real.

On September 23, 1994, Robert Bloch died. I was attending my aunt and uncle's fortieth anniversary party in Florida when I received the news. I wanted to go off privately and cry. But I knew Bob would not want that. He would not want any of his friends to be sad. He would much rather we remember his life, his love, and his smile.

So, I invite you to read the stories and the personal remembrances of those who knew and loved Robert Bloch. The tributes will move you and the stories will scare you and delight you. It is a strange dichotomy that such a gentle man could write such intense and sometimes brutal stories. Both the stories and the author changed the way horror and suspense are written, as well as those who write it. As you read these tributes, remember that beneath the blood . . . there is love.

Ricia Mainhardt
March 1995

DOUGLAS E. WINTER

"The real horror is not in the shadows, but in that little twisted world inside our own skulls."

—Robert Bloch

My first great scare came, I like to think, from seeing the motion picture *Invasion of the Body Snatchers* soon after its release in 1956. I didn't sleep very well that night: I dreamed that my parents, my brother, my friends were being replaced by pod people, and that, like poor Kevin McCarthy running through the streets of Santa Mira, no one would believe me when I tried to explain. But the next day, safe and secure in the embrace of daylight, there was no doubt that my nightmare had been fun—I had produced, directed, and starred in my own movie, all at age six.

The appeal of the horror story lies, first and foremost, in that element of fantasy: the vicarious thrill of experiencing the worst that could happen and escaping to live again another day, knowing that the scares were imaginary, but wondering, if only for a moment, what it would be like if they were real.

The time comes for all of us, though, when the fantasy becomes too real—when it crosses that thin borderline from the impossible to the probable or, for the skeptic, when it moves in right next door. Vegetable men from outer space and rubber-suited monsters playing hopscotch on Tokyo are one thing, but what if the creature wears our face, and delivers our mail or fixes our car or . . .

What if he is that nice, soft-spoken fellow who runs the backroads motel?

The reality of horror descended upon me in 1960; I suspect that, upon reflection, many others can point to a similar place, a similar time. I was nine years old, and my Aunt Garnet and Uncle Al had taken my brother and me to the Washington Theater, one of the two indoor movie houses in my hometown of Granite City, Illinois. I was excited; we were going to see a brand-new scary movie with a funny name.

It was called *Psycho*.

Looking back, I wonder just how nervous my aunt must have been, taking two young boys from a good Southern Baptist home to a film whose opening sequence featured a well-proportioned Janet Leigh tossing about on the sack in her skivvies, and soon turned her into a nude pincushion in the shower. Pretty nervous, I suspect; but she was preoccupied, trying to quiet down the two teenage girls sitting behind us. One had seen the film before, and she insisted upon telling her friend, in a loud, gum-popping voice, what was going to happen next. I didn't mind her previews, though—because I, for one, wasn't having a good time. Norman Bates wasn't the kind of monster I had come to love—he was just a man. And I was hunkered down in my seat, scared to even think what might happen next.

Two masters of horror have been immortalized by the motion picture *Psycho*—not simply for that nine-year-old boy, but for the entire popular culture. One, of course, is its director, Alfred Hitchcock; the other is the man who wrote the novel on which it was based. And no one ever said it better than Hitchcock himself: "*Psycho* all came from Robert Bloch's book."

Nearly thirty-five years before my rendezvous with Norman Bates, another nine-year-old boy had also found his first real fear in a motion picture theater. Robert Bloch, born in Chicago, Illinois, on April 5, 1917, and then living in suburban Maywood, had decided to attend his first movie at night alone.

"I knew nothing in particular about what I was going to see; it was just the idea of being able to be on my own at that age. I went to the Lido, and I was a little put off by the fact that the ushers were wearing masks. I was even more disconcerted when the organist began to play some rather discordant notes, and onto the screen came the title *The Phantom of the Opera,* starring Lon Chaney, a gentleman about whom I knew nothing. But I soon learned a great deal about Mr. Chaney: to my surprise, I learned that he wore a mask at all times, that he slept in a coffin because it reminded him of death, that he lived in catacombs five cellars below the Paris Opera House, and that he had some rather antisocial ambitions.

"Then came the unmasking scene: Chaney seated at the organ and Mary Philbin pulling the mask away. And at that point, I paid him the greatest tribute a small child can pay to an actor—I wet my pants.

"I remember running home from that theater and spending the next three years increasing the family's electric bill by sleeping with the lights on."

Even today, at more than seventy years of age, that frightened child lives in Robert Bloch's wide-eyed face. We sit in the poolside office of his home, high in the Hollywood Hills, overlooking Laurel Canyon. The view, he has assured me, was better when he moved in twenty-six years ago, "before the smog." But Bloch isn't looking out across the sunlit scenery; he sits clutching the arms of his easy chair, smiling uneasily, locked in that childhood memory. And for good reason: although the nine-year-old Robert Bloch had earlier read the works of Edgar Allan Poe and other horror stories, this confrontation with *The Phantom of the Opera* was the making of a horror writer.

"I decided, very wisely, that if you can't lick 'em, join 'em. I began to read more and more of this type of material, and to see more films. I had the impression that I was going to find out not only what fear consisted of, but just what it was that frightened me. That way, I could exorcize my own personal demons. About two or three months later, I discovered *Weird Tales* at the newsstand, and from then on, I was home free."

In those times before paperback books, television, and motion pictures with sound, the only regular forum for the horror story was a pulp magazine, *Weird Tales.* Known as "The Unique Magazine," its roster of authors is now a veritable "Who's Who" of fantasy fiction, and it served as the proving grounds for writers from Bloch to Ray Bradbury, Fritz Leiber, Theodore Sturgeon, and Manly Wade Wellman, as well as the creator of Conan the Barbarian, Robert E. Howard. In its pages, and particularly from the hand of its most influential writer, H. P. Lovecraft, the modern American horror story was born.

Bloch was enthralled by *Weird Tales,* and particularly by Lovecraft's fiction of "cosmic dread"; it filled a need in his young life—a need to overcome "feelings of inadequacy or insecurity" that he believes are possessed by most writers of horror fiction:

"Most of us, I think, would be fully qualified as 'loners' for one reason or another. My family was warm and friendly, and far from intimidating, but in those days, education was not all that progressive. There were no so-called special schools for children who seemed precocious. So when I got into grammar school, the teachers, in their infinite wisdom, decided that they didn't want me throwing spitballs at them because I had already done my lessons before class. I ended up, at the age of nine or ten, sitting with classmates who were eleven and twelve. The physical differences were marked, particularly on the playground, where I couldn't compete with my older classmates in body-contact sports and that sort of thing. I couldn't run as fast; I couldn't throw as far. And I felt a little bit discriminated against.

"I was the one who was always organizing the circuses and the plays and the pirate ships and the World War I trenches—and I had a host of eager and willing participants. But when it came to athletic competition, I felt I wasn't really with it. In that sense, I was alienated."

In 1933, Bloch, sixteen years old and living in Milwaukee, wrote a fan letter to H. P. Lovecraft; he was stunned to receive a reply. Lovecraft began regular correspondence with the young enthusaist, and soon encouraged him to write fiction. "After a few letters, he wrote, in effect, 'There's something about the way you write that tells me that perhaps you would like to try your own hand at it. I would be very glad to read whatever you might turn out.' Of course, I was completely enamored of Lovecraft and his writing for *Weird Tales,* so I sat down at once and did a few things in emulation. He didn't criticize; he encouraged me, which was what I needed. And when I got out of high school, I didn't need any encouragement; it was sheer economic necessity.

"I graduated at seventeen. The Depression was in full swing. There were no jobs. You couldn't get a job without experience; you couldn't get experience without a job. I had no alternative but to find something to do. So I bought a secondhand typewriter for fifteen dollars and a secondhand card table for one dollar, put the typewriter on top of the card table in my bedroom, went down to the dime store for some paper and carbons, and started working in earnest—learning to type as I went along. Six weeks later, I sold my first story to *Weird Tales.*

"I still don't know what I want to be when I grow up."

Bloch wrote full time from his high school graduation in 1934 to 1942, when the paper shortage resulting from World War II began to close down the pulp fiction markets. Horror fiction was also in decline; Lovecraft had died in 1937, his brief writing career ending in virtual poverty. Only after his death, with the founding of a small press, Arkham House, by an admiring fellow writer, August Derleth, was Lovecraft's fiction preserved in book form, enabling it to attain the popular success that it continues to hold today.

"In those days," Bloch comments, "you didn't write for posterity, you wrote for a penny a word. Your story had a one-month existence in a magazine, and that was the end of it. There were no paperbacks, there were no collections, there were no anthologies. And no critical attention, of course—no reviews, no academic consideration whatsoever. It was more or less taken for granted that what you wrote for this audience had a thirty-day life on the newsstands and then would disappear forever. Lovecraft himself felt that this was going to be his fate, and only a series of fortunate happenstance after his death rescued him."

It should thus come as no surprise that in 1942, Bloch, with a pregnant wife suffering from tuberculosis of the bone, should become concerned about the dwindling economics of writing short stories. He complained of his plight at a meeting of a Milwaukee writers' group, and one of the members, Gus Marx, offered him an apprenticeship in his advertising agency.

"He said, 'Tell you what. I'll give you an office space of your own and a typewriter. You can do your own writing and you can spend as much time with me as you wish, watching what I do, and at the end of six months you can go on your own way.' He paid nothing. So I decided to take this gamble and see what I could learn.

"At the end of six months, I was writing any and all of the office's copy. We had increased and expanded the agency. He asked me to stay on at a salary. I stayed on for eleven years.

"It was a strange combination. I put my work on the right-hand side of the typewriter, and the layouts and notes for advertising copy on the left-hand side. And when I exhausted what was on the left-hand side, I would put my material in the typewriter."

Those years were also among Bloch's most productive as a writer, because the time restrictions imposed by his advertising work brought him a sense of discipline. He published more than 150 stories in the horror, science fiction, and detective fields, including a series of humorous fantasies that began with "Time Wounds All Heels" (1942). He also produced the most crucial story of his early career, "Yours Truly, Jack the Ripper" (1943), whose adaptation for radio resulted in Bloch's own radio series, *Stay Tuned for Terror* (1945). An Arkham House edition, *The Opener of the Way* (1945), collected the best of his early short fiction. But the 1947 publication of Bloch's first novel, *The Scarf*, signaled his shift away from the traditional supernatural themes of *Weird Tales* to those on which his lasting fame is based. ("Fetish?" it begins. "You name it. All I know is that I've always had it with me . . .")

Bloch explains: "By the mid-1940s, I had pretty well mined the vein of ordinary supernatural themes until it had become varicose. I realized, as a result of what went on during World War II and of reading the more widely disseminated work in psychology, that the real horror is not in the shadows, but in that little twisted world inside our own skulls. And that I determined to explore."

Explore he did, fathering—along with Cornell Woolrich, John Franklin Barden, and Jim Thompson—the psychological horror novel, in which the dark corridors of the human mind supplant the supernatural. His early novels—*The Kidnapper, Spiderweb,* and *The Will to Kill,* all published in 1954—provided the groundwork for his most famous novel, and he left advertising that year, moving to Weyauwega, Wisconsin, to write full time.

In 1957, one of the more bizarre cases in American criminology began to unfold in Plainfield, Wisconsin, less than fifty miles from where Bloch lived. A search for a missing barmaid at the farmhouse of one Edward Gein discovered her corpse hanging by its heels, decapitated and dressed out like a deer. Authorities found preserved human heads, female body parts, a human heart in a coffee can, lampshades fashioned of tanned human skin, and a boarded-up room that had belonged to Gein's mother, who had died twelve years earlier. Intrigued by the case, Bloch wrote the now-classic *Psycho* (1959), with its frightening characterization of Norman Bates.

"I discovered, much to my surprise—and particularly if I was writing in the first person—that I could become a psychopath quite easily. I could think like one and I could devise all manner of unfortunate occurrences. So I probably gave up a flourishing, lucrative career as a mass murderer."

But Bloch feels no affinity for the psychopathic personality: "Again, it's one of those situations—if you can't lick 'em, join 'em. Ever since I was a child, I was unable to explain the callous, casual, careless cruelty of other children, or of adults to one another. My increasing interest in history supplied me with so many thousands of seemingly inexplicable horrors, and I just determined to see what I could learn. I became more and more dissatisfied with the conventional psychiatric explanations.

"I believe that psychotherapy, like meteorology and economics, is an art rather than a science. There are psychiatrists and psychologists who have had some success with a certain type of patient under certain circumstances, but there are an awful lot of impostors, quacks, failures, and just plain incompetents running around in that field, and they exert far too much influence.

"They have become the modern priestcraft. They have supplanted the religious infallibility of previous centuries. A hundred and fifty years ago, phrenologists enjoyed as much status as today's psychiatrists; and yet today, phrenology is dead. I don't know how much longer psychotherapy is going to last."

For many years, Bloch held no religious views, sharing the mechanistic materialism of H. P. Lovecraft:

"My background was German Jewish, without either of my parents or grandparents being devout communicants. They didn't attend temple, they didn't observe the Jewish holidays, they didn't speak or read Hebrew. My mother believed in a Supreme Being, but as a sort of amorphous thing.

"We moved to Maywood when I was five. We found ourselves living in this suburban community outside of Chicago in this friendly neighborhood atmosphere. After a month or so, it was suggested to my mother that a lot of the social life of our neighbors revolved around the Methodist Church. So why didn't we go to the Methodist Church? Why didn't the kids go to Sunday School? So we did. For the next five years, I would careen in the back of a truck with the other kids on the way to the Sunday School picnic, happily singing 'Onward Christian Soldiers.'

"And that's the extent of my formal religious upbringing. I didn't know a word of Hebrew until I got into advertising, and my education was fine-tuned when I got to Hollywood—you can imagine the type of words that I picked up."

But with his increasing dissatisfaction with psychiatric explanations, Bloch has experienced a growing belief in the supernatural:

"Only in recent years have I ceased being quite so much of a pragmatist, because I have encountered enough incidents of what you might call paranormal inexplicabilities to shake my composure. I now feel that I don't know everything that there is to be known about the world, and that the scientists who claim to know by means of mathematics and measurements and the ability to repeat experiments are constantly being confounded as new things come along that force them to revise their so-called laws and expand their horizons. To me, a mechanistic explanation is far too simple.

"I have no spiritual view that would coincide with the dogma of any organized religion. But I do believe that most of us are mindful of our own subjective definitions of good and evil. Most people have, even in the absence of a so-called conscience, knowledge of whether they are doing something that is harmful or helpful. I don't know whether any of the conventional legends and mythologies and superstitions coincide with my notion of what constitutes good or evil, although I've read and heard enough about seemingly inexplicable events in which some of these concepts seem personified. Cases of so-called possession, that sort of thing. I am not saying that I am still window-shopping; but I haven't closed my eyes."

Bloch moved to Hollywood in October 1959, but not because of Alfred Hitchcock's acquisition of the film rights to *Psycho;* he was invited by a friend to attempt writing for television. His first scripts were for the Macdonald Carey vehicle *Lock-Up,* but he soon wrote for a number of classic programs, including *Thriller, Star Trek, Night Gallery*—and indeed, *Alfred Hitchcock Presents.* Ironically, the fact that he had written *Psycho* was not at all helpful to his early screenwriting career.

"When I came out here, *Psycho* was just being filmed. One day I went on the set to look around, and nobody was happy. Paramount, which was to distribute the picture, hated it—they didn't like the title, they didn't like the story, they didn't like anything about it. They put all kinds of obstacles in Hitch's way. He didn't get his usual big budget. He didn't get Technicolor or big stars like Cary Grant or Jimmy Stewart. Then they told him that they had no sound stage for him, and he had to shoot at Universal, using his television cinematographer. But since he had autonomy and he was determined to make his film, they couldn't stop him in the long run.

"At that time, to have announced myself in Hollywood as the author of *Psycho* would have been a negative."

That situation soon changed, of course—to the point that Robert Bloch rarely sees his name in print without the inescapable appendage, "author of *Psycho.*" Does the typecasting concern him?

"At first, I resisted the label very much. But people of much greater stature have faced the problem—Maurice Ravel with his *Bolero,* Serge Rachmaninoff with his Prelude in C Sharp Minor. They used to rail constantly over these things, and in the end, they had to accept them.

"As the years went by, I realized that it was something I couldn't escape, because of the tendency of publishers and publicists to seek some easy identification for the product. And when you've written a book or a teleplay or a motion picture, that's a product. In their minds, it has to be associated with something that is successful.

"Today, the emphasis is entirely on commercial success. You don't talk about the content. You talk about the brand name—this is a Stephen King book or a John Carpenter movie.

"Unfortunately, as the conglomerates take over the film industry and their accountants look more and more at the grosses rather than what goes on the screen, this emphasis is increased. Reliance on the computer to tell you what to do based on mathematical projections is death to the creative impulse. And this is now happening with novels, too. So many publishing houses have been taken over by conglomerates, and there's this terrible intermeshing of film companies and publishing houses and, in some cases, television outlets."

Psycho represented a watershed not only for Bloch but for the horror story. From the Depression heyday of *Weird Tales* and the evocative Universal film adaptations of *Frankenstein* and *Dracula,* the tale of terror had suffered until the mid-1950s, as if the real horrors of World War II had snuffed out the human need for fictional confrontation with death. Not until the Eisenhower era did the monsters reemerge in force: first, in the innocuous science-fictional context of the "big bug" films, then in exuberant American International youth films like *I Was a Teenage Werewolf* (1957), and finally in the serious context of books and films like *Psycho.*

Robert Bloch had evolved as well: after a flurry of books in the early sixties, perfecting the novel of psychological horror—*The Dead Beat* (1960), *Firebug* (1961), *The Couch* (1962)—he devoted most of his time to screenwriting. He penned, among other films, the last great Joan Crawford vehicle, *Strait-Jacket* (1963); *The Night Walker* (1964); and a series of film anthologies based upon his short stories for Britain's Amicus Films, including *Torture Garden* (1967), *The House That Dripped Blood* (1970), and *Asylum* (1972).

He turned to horror fiction rarely and with a growing sense of concern, expressed in novels like *Night-World* (1972), *American Gothic* (1974), *Strange Eons* (1979), and *There Is a Serpent in Eden* (1979). When he wrote his sequel, *Psycho II* (1982) (which bears no relationship to the film of the same name), and *Night of the Ripper* (1984), it was with a recognition that, in the years since Norman Bates first sprang from Robert Bloch's imagination as a transvestite murderer with a handful of victims, the world had changed: even as Boy George O'Dowd serenaded us on television in full drag, a forgettably plain-faced drifter named Henry Lee Lucas claimed to have murdered more than three hundred women and children. And Robert Bloch found that his responsibilities as a horror writer had changed as well.

"Modern horror fiction offers something that present-day society has been seeking for the past twenty years—an abdication of responsibility. It has provided virtually everyone with a Devil theory—as Flip Wilson says, 'The Devil made me do it.' That is the explanation for all of the bad things in the world. No one is individually responsible.

"And it is exactly what we want, because it explains everything from the bomb, the Vietnam War, and corruption in high places, to any individual's actions. What makes such fiction so popular is that it encapsulates this notion and offers a variety of choices, so that the reader may choose from the conventional Devil theory, the psychological Devil theory, and so on.

"We have seen this upsurge of antisocial behavior and, of course, a concomitant abdication of responsibility. The cop-out, the excuse, is that it's all the result of being underprivileged—poor environment, economic circumstances. But I saw those conditions in the Depression, without such drastic consequences in behavior patterns.

"It's the permissiveness of our society and the fact that parents have abdicated their responsibilities that create today's problems. You dump it onto the schools; you dump it onto the law enforcement agencies. And they have their own Devil theory about economics or ethnic inequalities."

Bloch is thus disturbed by the graphic depiction of violence in modern horror film and fiction.

"Violence has become not only a cop-out in terms of being presented as self-explanatory—'This is human nature, that's the way it is, folks'—but it is also a drug. When you dose yourself with it, you find that you need increasingly bigger fixes.

"My generation was the product of the library plus silent films and heavily censored talking films. The next generation saw a little more permissiveness in films and a great deal more graphic violence in comic books; so twenty years later, when their members started to write and make films, this was their frame of reference. The permissiveness that saturated films and television offered even more outlets for a still-younger group who are now entering their twenties. And it's apparent that the end is not yet in sight, although I don't know how much further we can actually go. We have just about reached the limit of visual depiction of violence.

"What's going to come out of those people who think that *Night of the Living Dead* isn't enough?"

But it is not the depiction of violence that so much concerns Bloch; it is the attitudes of the audience and the purveyors of violence.

"It's the kind of people who enjoy that type of material that causes me to cringe a little. I really get turned off when I sit in an audience and see what is supposedly an otherwise sane and normal teenager laughing with joy as someone is being eviscerated on the screen. I would much prefer to see him revert to the old enuresis of my childhood and wet his pants when something like that happens.

"What has changed in my work is that I have increasingly felt a sense of responsibility. I feel that it's necessary to take a position. The chief danger, as I have stated in *Psycho II*, is not so much the violent content of today's fiction and film as it is the lack of any attitude on the part of the creator—or, as I like to think of him, the perpetrator—of the material. This business of saying, 'Here it is, folks, a slice of life, raw and bleeding,' without stating any emotional reaction on the part of the writer or director, seems to imply that there is no such thing as moral responsibility—that these actions have to be judged solely on the basis of an individual's interpretation for his or her own convenience.

"I don't believe in turning what I write into preachments, but if the subject matter deals with events that require some value judgment on the part of the audience, then it is up to the creator to suggest his own views. The audience can accept or reject—that's their privilege. If they don't like the show, they can walk out of the theater or switch the dial on the TV set. If they don't like the book or story, they can close the pages.

"Horror fiction will rapidly reach a dead end unless there is a revision of structure and concept. I don't think it's going to be possible to continue forever basing horror fiction on notions that are more simply handled in comic books.

"As to whether or not all this is of any importance, I don't know. But it being the sort of thing I have wasted my life on, I continue to be interested in its future."

Late in 1989, Bloch celebrated his fifty-fifth year as a professional writer; far from having "wasted" his life, he has become a true legend of the modern horror field, with a staggering output of more than four hundred published short stories, fifty-five books, and twelve produced screenplays. His best short fiction appeared in *The Selected Stories of Robert Bloch* (1989), and his newest novels are *Lori* (1989) and *Psycho House* (1990). What has kept him going?

"Economic necessity." He laughs. "Aided and abetted by a great deal of good luck. I've been fortunate in knowing people like Buster Keaton and Joan Crawford, Boris Karloff and Fritz Lang, and once one has reached a certain degree of intimacy, you realize that ninety percent of everyone's career has been luck. Whatever talent you have means nothing unless it is given an opportunity to flourish.

"I've been very lucky. I've been fortunate in my choice of occupation, fortunate that I've survived physically without undue stress or handicap, fortunate in the quiet life that I lead with my lovely wife, and fortunate in the kind of treatment I have received from my fellow writers and readers and fans. When I came out here, I made the acquaintance of a number of people working quite successfully in television and films; and within ten years, ninety percent of them were out of the business. It's a very fast track, and a lot of people get shoved to one side through no fault of their own—inadvertence, bad breaks, bad timing.

"What would have happened to Boris Karloff if he had not been the fourth or fifth successful candidate for the Frankenstein monster's role?"

But Robert Bloch does not ponder the element of chance; if he has any second thoughts about his career, it is only that he did not become a burlesque comedian. His writing has always been tinged with black humor and outrageous puns, summed up best by his infamous one-liner: "I have the heart of a small boy. I keep it in a jar in my desk."

What is the mutual attraction of humor and horror?

"Comedy and horror are opposite sides of the same coin—a coin that usually ends up in a producer's pocket, by the way. Both deal with the grotesque and the unexpected, but in such a fashion as to provoke two entirely different reactions. Physical comedy is usually fantasy; it's exaggeration, as when W. C. Fields comes out of a small-town pet shop with a live ostrich. There's a willing suspension of disbelief, but we don't generally regard it as fantasy because it's designed to promote laughter rather than tension or fear.

"Comedy is timeless," Bloch says, and notwithstanding his criticism of some aspects of current horror fiction, he is equally certain of its future.

"One of the lures of horror fiction is a constant in the human race—curiosity. It's not fashionable today to speak about emotions except in a knowledgeable way. To confess that one is naive is taboo. But I think that today's youngsters are not much different from those of any previous generation in that they are curious about death and its mysteries, about pain and what happens when one inflicts or undergoes it—about the physiological and psychological symptoms. And the mere fact that it is *verboten* to discuss such matters in ordinary conversation causes them to be even more interested.

"Curiously enough, the attitude toward discussing sex is not as great a barrier to young people as that toward an open, frank discussion of death. It is no longer taboo to avoid all mention of sexual practices. But you still have a hell of a time getting a frank, detailed discussion of the ravages of cancer going in your friendly Sunday afternoon family get-together.

"As long as human beings experience fear, horror will be a timeless emotion. I can scarcely visualize the human being who doesn't have fear, whether it's expressed or secret."

And when I ask Robert Bloch about his darkest fear, he tells me, just as he has written of countless other horrors—with a smile: "I will admit to fear of extinction. I don't like the idea that I am not going to be around any more to complain about how rotten life is. I want to live to the year two thousand, so I can tell everybody, 'See, I told you it was going to be this bad!'"

OUR BOB

FREDERIK POHL

When I think of that very good man, Bob Bloch, I can't help smiling, because so many good things come to memory. They are funny things, mostly; things like, say, the opening line of his Guest of Honor speech at the Toronto Worldcon of 1973. "'Nasty, brutish and short,'" he said, in the familiar quotation; and then went on to say, "This describes either the life of primitive man . . . or Harlan Ellison."

I don't know how Harlan felt about it, but I do know what it did for the rest of us sitting around the tables in the big banquet room of the Royal York Hotel. It brought the house down, just as Bob was in the habit of doing whenever he chose to open his mouth in public. Bob Bloch was a reliably funny man. More than that, he was a *witty* one. That meant that he gave his audiences credit for wits of their own, and so his jokes were sometimes allusive, sometimes cerebral, and always funny as hell.

They often stung—they were meant to sting—but the wounds healed quickly, because, even while the blood was still flowing, the targets of the jokes always knew that somewhere on the other side of the sharp steel point of the wit was an affectionate and kindly regard; for Bob Bloch never *ever* picked on anybody who couldn't fight back.

So—come to think of it—I guess I do know how Harlan felt, after all; he knew perfectly well that behind the needles and the comedy was a large and undepletable well of kindliness and love.

Sadly, there's nothing funny about the present circumstances. The reason for this book is that Bob has died, and that circumstance is not amusing at all. All the same, when I think of Bob Bloch, the sorrow I feel at the loss of a cherished friend has to wait its turn, because the first thing I do is smile. I can't help it. It's an ingrained reflex that is going to be with me as long as I live, because Bob made me smile so many times, in so many parts of the world, for so many years.

PETER STRAUB

When Richard Matheson asked me to write a couple of paragraphs to be included in a gathering of similar statements and presented to Robert Bloch, I sent him the following, essentially intended as no more than a series of in-jokes between myself and Bob, the point being to cheer him up, at least as much as I could, during a very difficult period. I also wanted—very much wanted—Bob to understand how much I really did care for him, how much he meant to me, how great I thought he was. I was pleased to hear that Richard read aloud to Bob all of the statements he had gathered; though I do wonder what Bob Bloch felt about being called a golden giant.

The first time anyone was ever kind enough to give a blurb to a book I had written, that person was Robert Bloch, a matter of considerable pride to me then and now. At the time, I was so dimwitted and unsocialized that it never occurred to me to write a note of thanks—I believe that I could not possibly see how anything I might have to say could matter to a man so much more successful and established than myself. Several years later, I was finally able to atone for this youthful stupidity by giving the Great One a couple of blurbs for books of his own. Of course, I was delighted to do this, especially in the last case, for *Once Around the Bloch*, that marvelous book, in which perhaps the only flaw is an insufficiency of attention given to Bob's crucial role in the local Milwaukee television program *It's a Draw*. My little friends and myself would gather around our woodburning television sets, fasten our beady little eyes upon Mr. Bloch's gangly figure, and say to one another: "You know, some day that guy is going to do something really strange." Really, it was one of our favorite programs, and I cannot understand why Bob did not make more of it in his autobiography.

I think I first saw Bob in person at some otherwise unremarkable convention. I pressed him on the matter of *It's a Draw*, but, having failed to take in the importance of that program to myself, one of his artistic children, he was not terribly responsive. In every other way, he was perfection itself. In fact, he has been perfection itself upon every subsequent meeting—including mere sightings—since then. I wish I'd been able to enjoy many more of these encounters, because I came away every time with the sense of having been with a really remarkable, one-of-a-kind human being. There is the matter of that wonderful blue pin-striped suit and the cigarette holder, which together suggest a combination of the dignified and the rakish; there is the matter of the face, that wry intelligent ironic mask turned toward the world; also the conversation, which is delectable, unsentimental, funny, and wise; above all, the sense of being with someone secretly two or three times the size he appears, and not only that—not only a real giant pretending to be no more than just another tall guy—but in fact made entirely of gold. Golden giants are rare beings, invariably modest, uncommonly brave, impatient with fools but polite, and excellent conversationalists—because they have no reason to feel insecure, they actually do listen to what other people say, they actually do care about others in the deepest, most delighted and delightful way. Naturally, people of this order are just about universally loved, and so it is, I have observed, with Bob "Psycho" Bloch. Certainly I love him, but according to my calculations, he does owe me one more blurb, which I shall eagerly await.

The man to and for whom the above tribute was written provided us with an amazingly lengthy stream of entertainments of various kinds. As far as I know, these culminated in the unpretentious, kind-hearted, funny stroll through his own life which is *Once Around the Bloch*. But that is only as far as I know, and I would not be at all surprised to learn that after the completion of that book, Bob Bloch turned out a new novel, a new screenplay—and twenty or thirty short stories. This man wrote *stories*. The handsome and invaluable Underwood-Miller collection of his stories, three volumes long, is called *The Selected Stories of Robert Bloch*. How long would the *Collected Stories* run, five volumes? Six? I hope we will find out some day.

Unusually in such an extensive output, Bob Bloch's stories are remarkably consistent. Most very prolific writers are uneven: they stray from the main line of their talent to see what they might accomplish in another area, they continue to go to the cupboard even when the only thing in there is shelf paper, they get tired, their level of inspiration rises and falls. I don't see anything like this in Bloch's work, especially the stories. Everything is concentration, focus, detail, economy. There is never, ever any waste or fat. Every time he hits a note, the note is struck squarely in the center, with absolute precision, and it makes exactly the sound he wishes it to make, and no other. His inventiveness is staggering—if the point of most Robert Bloch stories is to entice the main character, the reader, or both, down a pretty path ending in a bear trap, the bear trap seen to be completely inevitable after it slams shut, this author's fecundity is so great that protagonist, path, and trap are freshly imagined every time out. Bloch was an absolute master of this form, and no one will ever write this sort of story any better than he did.

"The Cloak" demonstrates all these virtues in something like their pure form. We have the skeptical, rather misanthropic protagonist, Henderson, who imagines that most real color has been drained from the world—like many in Bloch's gallery of self-deluded grumps, he secretly cherishes his own superiority to the dolts and hypocrites who surround him. On his way to a Halloween party, he purchases a costume deliberately designed to offend the host and his friends, a "society crowd wearing their expensive Elsa Maxwell take-offs." When the costume, a vampire's shabby cloak, proves to be even more effective than Henderson had anticipated, he exults—his morality is already eroding.

From the point at which Henderson first frightens a cab driver and then a group of his fellow guests in the elevator taking them up to the party, we think we can see what Bloch is doing. When Henderson looks in a mirror and fails to see himself, we are sure we can see what he is doing. The point of the story will be Henderson's battle against his own transformation, and the climax, triumph or surrender, will take place in the roof garden where Henderson invites the angelic Sheila. But the bear trap snaps shut on both Henderson and ourselves, and the climax arrives, satisfying, appropriate in every way, and entirely unexpected.

THE CLOAK

𝕤 **The sun was dying, and its blood spattered the sky as it**
crept into a sepulcher behind the hills. The keening wind sent
the dry, fallen leaves scurrying toward the west, as though hastening them to the
funeral of the sun.

"Nuts!" said Henderson to himself, and stopped thinking.

The sun was setting in a dingy red sky, and a dirty raw wind was kicking up
the half-rotten leaves in a filthy gutter. Why should he waste time with cheap imagery?

"Nuts!" said Henderson, again.

It was probably a mood evoked by the day, he mused. After all, this was the
sunset of Halloween. Tonight was the dreaded Allhallows Eve, when spirits
walked and skulls cried out from their graves beneath the earth.

Either that, or tonight was just another rotten cold fall day. Henderson
sighed. There was a time, he reflected, when the coming of this night meant
something. A dark Europe, groaning in superstitious fear, dedicated this Eve to
the grinning Unknown. A million doors had once been barred against the evil
visitants, a million prayers mumbled, a million candles lit. There was something
majestic about the idea, Henderson reflected. Life had been an adventure in
those times, and men walked in terror of what the next turn of a midnight road
might bring. They had lived in a world of demons and ghouls and elementals
who sought their souls—and by Heaven, in those days a man's soul meant something. This new skepticism had taken a profound meaning away from life. Men
no longer revered their souls.

"Nuts!" said Henderson again, quite automatically. There was something
crude and twentieth-century about the coarse expression which always checked
his introspective flights of fancy.

The voice in his brain that said "nuts" took the place of humanity to Henderson—common humanity which would echo the same sentiment upon hearing his secret thoughts. So now Henderson uttered the word and endeavored to forget problems and purple patches alike.

He was walking down this street at sunset to buy a costume for the masquerade party tonight, and he had much better concentrate on finding the costumer's before it closed than waste his time daydreaming about Halloween.

His eyes searched the darkening shadows of the dingy buildings lining the narrow thoroughfare. Once again he peered at the address he had scribbled down after finding it in the phone book.

Why the devil didn't they light up the shops when it got dark? He couldn't make out numbers. This was a poor, run-down neighborhood, but after all—

Abruptly, Henderson spied the place across the street and started over. He passed the window and glanced in. The last rays of the sun slanted over the top of the building across the way and fell directly on the window and its display. Henderson drew a sharp intake of breath.

He was staring at a costumer's window—not looking through a fissure into hell. Then why was it all red fire, lighting the grinning visages of fiends?

"Sunset," Henderson muttered aloud. Of course it was, and the faces were merely clever masks such as would be displayed in this sort of place. Still, it gave the imaginative man a start. He opened the door and entered.

The place was dark and still. There was a smell of loneliness in the air—the smell that haunts all places long undisturbed; tombs, and graves in deep woods, and caverns in the earth, and—

"Nuts."

What the devil was wrong with him, anyway? Henderson smiled apologetically at the empty darkness. This was the smell of the costumer's shop, and it carried him back to college days of amateur theatricals. Henderson had known this smell of moth balls, decayed furs, grease paint and oils. He had played amateur Hamlet and in his hands he had held a smirking skull that hid all knowledge in its empty eyes—a skull, from the costumer's.

Well, here he was again, and the skull gave him the idea. After all, Halloween night it was. Certainly in this mood of his he didn't want to go as a rajah, or a Turk, or a pirate—they all did that. Why not go as a fiend, or a warlock, or a werewolf? He could see Lindstrom's face when he walked into the elegant penthouse wearing rags of some sort. The fellow would have a fit, with his society crowd wearing their expensive Elsa Maxwell take-offs. Henderson didn't greatly care for Lindstrom's sophisticated friends anyway; a gang of amateur Noel Cowards and horsey women wearing harnesses of jewels. Why not carry out the spirit of Halloween and go as a monster?

Henderson stood there in the dusk, waiting for someone to turn on the lights, come out from the back room and gene him. After a minute or so he grew impatient and rapped sharply on the counter.

"Say in there! Service!"

Silence. And a shuffling noise from the rear, then—an unpleasant noise to hear in the gloom. There was a banging from downstairs and then the heavy clump of footsteps. Suddenly Henderson gasped. A black bulk was rising from the floor!

It was, of course, only the opening of the trapdoor from the basement. A man shuffled behind the counter, carrying a lamp. In that light his eyes blinked drowsily.

The man's yellowish face crinkled into a smile.

"I was sleeping, I'm afraid," said the man, softly. "Can I serve you, sir?"

"I was looking for a Halloween costume."

"Oh, yes. And what was it you had in mind?"

The voice was weary, infinitely weary. The eyes continued to blink in the flabby yellow face.

"Nothing usual, I'm afraid. You see, I rather fancied some sort of monster getup for a party—don't suppose you carry anything in that line?"

"I could show you masks."

"No. I meant werewolf outfits, something of the sort. More of the authentic."

"So. The *authentic*."

"Yes." Why did this old dunce stress the word?

"I might—yes. I might have just the thing for you, sir." The eyes blinked, but the thin mouth pursed in a smile. "Just the thing for Halloween."

"What's that?"

"Have you ever considered the possibility of being a vampire?"

"Like Dracula?"

"Ah—yes, I suppose—Dracula."

"Not a bad idea. Do you think I'm the type for that, though?"

The man appraised him with that tight smile. "Vampires are of all types, I understand. You would do nicely."

"Hardly a compliment," Henderson chuckled. "But why not? What's the outfit?"

"Outfit? Merely evening clothes, or what you wear. I will furnish you with the authentic cloak."

"Just a cloak—is that all?"

"Just a cloak. But it is worn like a shroud. It *is* shroud-cloth, you know. Wait, I'll get it for you."

The shuffling feet carried the man into the rear of the shop again. Down the trapdoor entrance he went, and Henderson waited. There was more banging, and presently the old man reappeared carrying the cloak. He was shaking dust from it in the darkness.

"Here it is—the genuine cloak."

"Genuine?"

"Allow me to adjust it for you—it will work wonders, I'm sure."

The cold, heavy cloth hung draped about Henderson's shoulders. The faint odor rose mustily in his nostrils as he stepped back and surveyed himself in the mirror. The lamp was poor, but Henderson saw that the cloak effected a striking transformation in his appearance. His long face seemed thinner, his eyes were accentuated in the facial pallor heightened by the somber cloak he wore. It was a big, black shroud.

"Genuine," murmured the old man. He me must have come up suddenly, for Henderson hadn't noticed him in the glass.

"I'll take it," Henderson said. "How much?"

"You'll find it quite entertaining, I'm sure."

"How much?"

"Oh. Shall we say five dollars?"

"Here."

The old man took the money, blinking, and drew the cloak from Henderson's shoulders. When it slid away he felt suddenly warm again. It must be cold in the basement—the cloth was icy.

The old man wrapped the garment, smiling, and handed it over.

"I'll have it back tomorrow," Henderson promised.

"No need. You purchased it. It is yours."

"But—"

"I am leaving business shortly. Keep it. You will find more use for it than I, surely."

"But—"

"A pleasant evening to you."

Henderson made his way to the door in confusion, then turned to salute the blinking old man in the dimness.

Two eyes were burning at him from across the counter—two eyes that did not blink.

"Good night," said Henderson, and closed the door quickly. He wondered if he were going just a trifle mad.

At eight, Henderson nearly called up Lindstrom to tell him he couldn't make it. The cold chills came the minute he put on the damned cloak, and when he looked at himself in the mirror his blurred eyes could scarcely make out the reflection.

But after a few drinks he felt better about it. He hadn't eaten, and the liquor warmed his blood. He paced the floor, attitudinizing with the cloak—sweeping it about him and scowling in what he thought was a ferocious manner. Damn it, he was going to be a vampire all right! He called a cab, went down to the lobby. The driver came in, and Henderson was waiting, black cloak furled.

"I wish you to drive me," he said in a low voice.

The cab man took one look at him in the cloak and turned pale.

"Whazzat?"

"I ordered you to come," said Henderson gutturally, while he quaked with inner mirth. He leered ferociously and swept the cloak back.

"Yeah, yeah. O.K."

The driver almost ran outside. Henderson stalked after him.

"Where to, boss—I mean, sir?"

The frightened face didn't turn as Henderson intoned the address and sat back.

The cab started with a lurch that set Henderson to chuckling deeply, in character. At the sound of the laughter the driver got panicky and raced his engine up to the limit set by the governor. Henderson laughed loudly, and the impressionable driver fairly quivered in his seat. It was quite a ride, but Henderson was entirely unprepared to open the door and find it slammed after him as the cab man drove hastily away without collecting a fare.

"I must look the part," he thought complacently, as he took the elevator up to the penthouse apartment.

There were three or four others in the elevator, Henderson had seen them before at other affairs Lindstrom had invited him to attend, but nobody seemed to recognize him. It rather pleased him to think how his wearing of an unfamiliar cloak and an unfamiliar scowl seemed to change his entire personality and appearance. Here the other guests had donned elaborate disguises—one woman wore the costume of a Watteau shepherdess, another was attired as a Spanish ballerina, a tall man dressed as Pagliacci, and his companion had donned a toreador outfit. Yet Henderson recognized them all; knew that their expensive habiliments were not truly disguises at all, but merely elaborations calculated to enhance their appearance. Most people at costume parties gave vent to suppressed desires. The women showed off their figures, the men either accentuated their masculinity as the toreador did, or clowned it. Such things were pitiful; these conventional fools eagerly doffing their dismal business suits and rushing off to a lodge, or amateur theatrical, or mask ball in order to satisfy their starving imaginations. Why didn't they dress in garish colors on the street? Henderson often pondered the question.

Surely these society folk in the elevator were fine-looking men and women in their outfits—so healthy, so red-faced, and full of vitality. They had such robust throats and necks. Henderson looked at the plump arms of the woman next to him. He stared, without realizing it, for a long moment. And then, he saw that the occupants of the car had drawn away from him. They were standing in the corner, as though they feared his cloak and scowl, and his eyes fixed on the woman. Their chatter had ceased abruptly. The woman looked at him, as though she were about to speak, when the elevator doors opened and afforded Henderson a welcome respite.

What the devil was wrong? First the cab driver, then the woman. Had he drunk too much?

Well, no chance to consider that. Here was Marcus Lindstrom, and he was thrusting a glass into Henderson's hand.

"What have we here? Ah, a bogy-man!" It needed no second glance to perceive that Lindstrom, as usual at such affairs, was already quite bottle-dizzy. The fat host was positively swimming in alcohol.

"Have a drink, Henderson, my lad! I'll take mine from the bottle. That outfit of yours gave me a shock. Where'd you get the make-up?"

"Make-up? I'm not wearing any make-up."

"Oh. So you're not. How . . . silly of me."

Henderson wondered if he were crazy. Had Lindstrom really drawn back?

Were his eyes actually filled with a certain dismay? Oh, the man was obviously intoxicated.

"I'll . . . I'll see you later," babbled Lindstrom, edging away and quickly turning to the other arrivals. Henderson watched the back of Lindstrom's neck. It was fat and white. It bulged over the collar of his costume and there was a vein in it. A vein in Lindstrom's fat neck. Frightened Lindstrom.

Henderson stood alone in the ante-room. From the parlor beyond came the sound of music and laughter; party noises. Henderson hesitated before entering. He drank from the glass in his hand—Bacardi rum, and powerful. On top of his other drinks it almost made the man reel. But he drank, wondering. What was wrong with him and his costume? Why did he frighten people? Was he unconsciously acting his vampire role? That crack of Lindstrom's about make-up now—

Acting on impulse, Henderson stepped over to the long panel mirror in the hall. He lurched a little, then stood in the harsh light before it. He faced the glass, stared into the mirror, and saw nothing.

He looked at himself in the mirror, and there was no one there!

Henderson began to laugh softly, evilly, deep in his throat. And as he gazed into the empty, unreflecting glass, his laughter rose in black glee.

"I'm drunk," he whispered. "I must be drunk. Mirror in my apartment made me blurred. Now I'm so far gone I can't see straight. Sure I'm drunk. Been acting ridiculously, scaring people. Now I'm seeing hallucinations—or not seeing them, rather. Visions. Angels."

His voice lowered. "Sure, angels. Standing right in back of me, now. Hello, angel."

"Hello."

Henderson whirled. There she stood, in the dark cloak, her hair a shimmering halo above her white, proud face; her eyes celestial blue, and her lips infernal red.

"Are you real?" asked Henderson, gently. "Or am I a fool to believe in miracles?"

"This miracle's name is Sheila Darrly, and it would like to powder its nose if you please."

"Kindly use this mirror through the courtesy of Stephen Henderson," replied the cloaked man, with a grin. He stepped back a ways, eyes intent.

The girl turned her head and favored him with a slow, impish smile. "Haven't you ever seen powder used before?" she asked.

"Didn't know angels indulged in cosmetics," Henderson replied. "But then there's a lot I don't know about angels. From now on I shall make them a special study of mine. There's so much I want to find out. So you'll probably find me following you around with a notebook all evening."

"Notebooks for a vampire?"

"Oh, but I'm a very intelligent vampire—not one of those backwoods Transylvanian types. You'll find me charming, I'm sure."

"Yes, you look like the sure type," the girl mocked. "But an angel and a vampire—that's a queer combination."

"We can reform one another," Henderson pointed out. "Besides, I have a suspicion that there's a bit of the devil in you. That dark cloak over your angel costume; dark angel, you know. Instead of heaven you might hail from my home town."

Henderson was flippant, but underneath his banter cyclonic thoughts whirled. He recalled discussions in the past; cynical observations he had made and believed.

Once, Henderson had declared that there was no such thing as love at first sight, save in books or plays where such a dramatic device served to speed up action. He asserted that people learned about romance from books and plays and accordingly adopted a belief in love at first sight when all one could possibly feel was desire.

And now this Sheila—this blond angel—had to come along and drive out all thoughts of morbidity, all thoughts of drunkenness and foolish gazings into mirrors, from his mind; had to send him madly plunging into dreams of red lips, ethereal blue eyes and slim white arms.

Something of his feelings had swept into his eyes, and as the girl gazed up at him she felt the truth.

"Well," she breathed, "I hope the inspection pleases."

"A miracle of understatement, that. But there was something I wanted to find out particularly about divinity. Do angels dance?"

"Tactful vampire! The next room?"

Arm in arm they entered the parlor. The merrymakers were in full swing. Liquor had already pitched gaiety at its height, but there was no dancing any longer. Boisterous little grouped couples laughed arm in arm about the room. The usual party gagsters were performing their antics in corners. The superficial atmosphere, which Henderson detested, was fully in evidence.

It was reaction which made Henderson draw himself up to full height and sweep the cloak about his shoulders. Reaction brought the scowl to his pale face, caused him to stalk along in brooding silence. Sheila seemed to regard this as a great joke.

"*Pull* a vampire act on them," she giggled, clutching his arm. Henderson accordingly scowled at the couples, sneered horrendously at the women. And his progress was marked by the turning of heads, the abrupt cessation of chatter. He walked through the long room like Red Death incarnate. Whispers trailed in his wake.

"Who is that man?"

"We came up with him in the elevator, and he—"

"His eyes—"

"Vampire!"

"Hello, Dracula!" It was Marcus Lindstrom and a sullen-looking brunette in Cleopatra costume who lurched toward Henderson. Host Lindstrom could scarcely stand, and his companion in cups was equally at a loss. Henderson liked the man when sober at the club, but his behavior at parties had always irritated him. Lindstrom was particularly objectionable in his present condition—it made him boorish.

"M'dear, I want you t' meet a very dear friend of mind. Yes sir, it being Halloween and all, I invited Count Dracula here, t'gether with his daughter. Asked his grandmother, but she's busy tonight at a Black Sabbath—along with Aunt Jemima. Ha! Count, meet my little playmate."

The woman leered up at Henderson.

"Oooh Dracula, what big eyes you have! Oooh, what big teeth you have! Ooooh—"

"Really, Marcus," Henderson protested. But the host had turned and shouted to the room.

"Folks, meet the real goods—only genuine living vampire in captivity! Dracula Henderson, only existing vampire with false teeth."

In any other circumstance Henderson would have given Lindstrom a quick, effencient punch on the jaw. But Sheila was at his side, it was a public gathering; better to humor the man's clumsy jest. Why not be a vampire?

Smiling quickly at the girl, Henderson drew himself erect, faced the crowd, and frowned. His hands brushed the cloak. Funny, it still felt cold. Looking down he noticed for the first time that it was a little dirty at the edges; muddy or dusty. But the cold silk slid through his fingers as he drew it across his breast with one long hand. The feeling seemed to inspire him. He opened his eyes wide and let them blaze. His mouth opened. A sense of dramatic power filled him. And he looked at Marcus Lindstrom's soft, fat neck with the vein standing in the whiteness. He looked at the neck, saw the crowd watching him, and then the impulse seized him. He turned, eyes on that creasy neck—that wobbling, creasy neck of the fat man.

Hands darted out. Lindstrom squeaked like a frightened rat. He was a plump, sleek white rat, bursting with blood. Vampires liked blood. Blood from the rat, from the neck of the rat, from the vein in the neck of the squeaking rat.

"Warm blood."

The deep voice was Henderson's own.

The hands were Henderson's own.

The hands that went around Lindstrom's neck as he spoke, the hands that felt the warmth, that searched out the vein. Henderson's face was bending for the neck, and, as Lindstrom struggled, his grip tightened. Lindstrom's face was turning, turning purple. Blood was rushing to his head. That was good. Blood!

Henderson's mouth opened. He felt the air on his teeth. He bent down toward that fat neck, and then—

"Stop! That's plenty!"

The voice, the cooling voice of Sheila. Her fingers on his arm. Henderson looked up, startled. He released Lindstrom, who sagged with open mouth.

The crowd was staring, and their mouths were all shaped in the instinctive O of amazement.

Sheila whispered, "Bravo! Served him right—but you frightened him!"

Henderson struggled a moment to collect himself. Then he smiled and turned.

"Ladies and gentlemen," he said, "I have just given a slight demonstration to prove to you what our host said of me was entirely correct. I *am* a vampire. Now that you have been given fair warning, I am sure you will be in no further danger. If there is a doctor in the house I can, perhaps, arrange for a blood transfusion."

The O's relaxed and laughter came from startled throats. Hysterical laughter, in part, then genuine. Henderson had carried it off. Marcus Lindstrom alone still stared with eyes that held utter fear. *He* knew.

And then the moment broke, for one of the gagsters ran into the room from the elevator. He had gone downstairs and borrowed the apron and cap of a newsboy. Now he raced through the crowd with a bundle of papers under his arm.

"Extra! Extra! Read all about it! Big Halloween Horror! Extra!"

Laughing guests purchased papers. A woman approached Sheila, and Henderson watched the girl walk away in a daze.

"See you later," she called, and her glance sent fire through his veins. Still, he could not forget the terrible feeling that came over him when he had seized Lindstrom. Why?

Automatically, he accepted a paper from the shouting pseudo-newsboy. "Big Halloween Horror," he had shouted. What was that?

Blurred eyes searched the paper.

Then Henderson reeled back. That headline! It was an *Extra* after all. Henderson scanned the columns with mounting dread.

"Fire in costumer's . . . shortly after 8 P.M. firemen were summoned to the shop of . . . flames beyond control . . . completely demolished . . . damage estimated at . . . peculiarly enough, name of proprietor unknown . . . skeleton found in—"

"No!" gasped Henderson aloud.

He read, reread *that* closely. The skeleton had been found in a box of earth in the cellar beneath the shop. The box was a coffin. There had been two other boxes, empty. The skeleton had been wrapped in a cloak, undamaged by the flames—

And in the hastily penned box at the bottom of the column were eyewitness comments, written up under scareheads of heavy black type. Neighbors had feared the place. Hungarian neighborhood, hints of vampirism, of strangers who entered the shop. One man spoke of a cult believed to have meetings in the place. Superstition about things sold there—love philters, outlandish charms and weird disguises.

Weird disguises—vampires—cloaks—*his eyes!*

"This is an authentic cloak."

"I will not be using this much longer. Keep it."

Memories of these words screamed through Henderson's brain. He plunged out of the room and rushed to the panel mirror.

A moment, then he flung one arm before his face to shield his eyes from the image that was not there—the missing reflection. *Vampires have no reflections.*

No wonder he looked strange. No wonder arms and necks invited him. He had wanted Lindstrom. Good God!

The cloak had done that, the dark cloak with the stains. The stains of earth, grave-earth. The wearing of the cloak, the cold cloak, had given him the feelings of a true vampire. It was a garment accursed, a thing that had lain on the body of one undead. The rusty stain along one sleeve was blood.

Blood. It would be nice to see blood. To taste its warmth, its red life, flowing.

No. That was insane. He was drunk, crazy.

"Ah. My pale friend, the vampire."

It was Sheila again. And above all horror rose the beating of Henderson's heart. As he looked at her shining eyes, her warm mouth shaped in red invitation, Henderson felt a wave of warmth. He looked at her white throat rising above her dark, shimmering cloak, and another kind of warmth rose. Love, desire, and a—hunger.

She must have seen it in his eyes, but she did not flinch. Instead, her own gaze burned in return.

Sheila loved him, too!

With an impulsive gesture, Henderson ripped the cloak from about his throat. The icy weight lifted. He was free. Somehow, he hadn't wanted to take the cloak off, but he had to. It was a cursed thing, and in another minute he might have taken the girl in his arms, taken her for a kiss and remained to—

But he dared not think of that.

"Tired of masquerading?" she asked. With a similar gesture she, too, removed her cloak and stood revealed in the glory of her angel robe. Her blond, statuesque perfection forced a gasp to Henderson's throat.

"Angel," he whispered.

"Devil," she mocked.

And suddenly they were embracing. Henderson had taken her cloak in his arm with his own. They stood with lips seeking rapture until Lindstrom and a group moved noisily into the anteroom.

At the sight of Henderson the fat host recoiled.

"You—" he whispered. "You are—"

"Just leaving," Henderson smiled. Grasping the girl's arm, he drew her toward the empty elevator. The door shut on Lindstrom's pale, fear-filled face.

"Were we leaving?" Sheila whispered, snuggling against his shoulder.

"We were. But not for earth. We do not go down into my realm, but up—into yours."

"The roof garden?"

"Exactly, my angelic one. I want to talk to you against the background of your own heavens, kiss you amidst the clouds, and—"

Her lips found his as the car rose.

"Angel and devil. What a match!"

"I thought so, too," the girl confessed. "Will our children have halos or horns?"

"Both, I'm sure."

They stepped out onto the deserted rooftop. And once again it was Halloween.

Henderson felt it. Downstairs it was Lindstrom and his society friends, in a drunken costume party. Here it was night, silence, gloom. No light, no music, no drinking, no chatter which made one party identical with another; one night like all the rest. This night was individual here.

The sky was not blue, but black. Clouds hung like the gray beards of hovering giants peering at the round orange globe of the moon. A cold wind blew from the sea, and filled the air with tiny murmurings from afar.

This was the sky that witches flew through of their Sabbath. This was the moon of wizardry, the sable silence of black prayers and whispered invocations. The clouds hid monstrous presences shambling in summons from afar. It was Halloween.

It was also quite cold.

"Give me my cloak," Sheila whispered. Automatically, Henderson extended the garment, and the girl's body swirled under the dark splendor of the cloth. Her eyes burned up at Henderson with a call he could not resist. He kissed her, trembling.

"You're cold," the girl said. "Put on your cloak."

Yes, Henderson, he thought to himself. Put on your cloak while you stare at her throat. Then, the next time you kiss her you will want her throat and she will give it in love and you will take it in—hunger.

"Put it on, darling—I insist," the girl whispered. Her eyes were impatient, burning with an eagerness to match his own.

Henderson trembled.

Put on the cloak of darkness? The cloak of the grave, the cloak of death, the cloak of the vampire? The evil cloak, filled with a cold life of its own that transformed his face, transformed his mind, made his soul instinct with awful hunger?

"Here."

The girl's slim arms were about him, pushing the cloak onto his shoulders. Her fingers brushed his neck, caressingly, as she linked the cloak about his throat.

Henderson shivered.

Then he felt it—through him—that icy coldness turning to a more dreadful heat. He felt himself expand, felt the sneer cross his face. This was Power!

And the girl before him, her eyes taunting, inviting. He saw her ivory neck, her warm slim neck, waiting. It was waiting for him, or his lips.

For his teeth.

No—it couldn't be. He loved her. His love must conquer this madness. Yes, wear the cloak, defy its power, and take her in his arms as a man, not as a fiend. He must. It was the test.

"Sheila." Funny, how his voice deepened.

"Yes, dear."

"Sheila, I must tell you this."

Her eyes—so alluring. It would be easy!

"Sheila, please. You read the paper tonight."

"Yes."

"I . . . I got my cloak there. I can't explain it. You saw how I took Lindstrom. I wanted to go through with it. Do you understand me? I meant to . . . to bite him. Wearing this damnable thing makes me feel like one of those creatures."

Why didn't her stare change? Why didn't she recoil in horror? Such trusting innocence! Didn't she understand? Why didn't she run? Any moment now he might lose control, seize her.

"I love you, Sheila. Believe that. I love you."

"I know." Her eyes gleamed in the moonlight.

"I want to test it. I want to kiss you, wearing this cloak. I want to feel that my love is stronger than this—thing. If I weaken, promise me you'll break away and run, quickly. But don't misunderstand. I must face this feeling and fight it; I want my love for you to be that pure, that secure. Are you afraid?"

"No." Still she stared at him, just as he stared at her throat. If she knew what was in his mind!

"You don't think I'm crazy? I went to this costumer's—he was a horrible little old man—and he gave me the cloak. Actually told me it was a real vampire's. I thought he was joking, but tonight I didn't see myself in the mirror, and I wanted Lindstrom's neck, and I want you. But I must test it."

"You're not crazy. I know. I'm not afraid."

"Then—"

The girl's face mocked. Henderson summoned his strength. He bent forward, his impulses battling. For a moment he stood there under the ghastly orange moon, and his face was twisted in struggle.

And the girl lured.

Her odd, incredibly red lips parted in a silvery, chuckly laugh as her white arms rose from the black cloak she wore to circle his neck gently. "I know—I knew when I looked in the mirror. I knew you had a cloak like mine—got yours where I got mine—"

Queerly, her lips seemed to elude his as he stood frozen for an instant of shock. Then he felt the icy hardness of her sharp little teeth on his throat, a strangely soothing sting, and an engulfing blackness rising over him.

GAHAN WILSON

Mulling on how to start this out, I tried to remember when and under what conditions I'd first been lucky enough to meet Robert Bloch and found, to my great surprise and puzzlement, that I couldn't.

I spun through my mental Rolodex, flipping its entries further and further back to more and more ancient conventions, signings, award dinners; conjured up numerous, though sometimes fading, images of Bob signing books, giving speeches, looming benignly over fans, but my brain refused to yield any record of my encountering Robert Bloch as a stranger.

This baffled and confused me no end until I let myself consciously hear the qualifying category I was using, "stranger," and at that point everything suddenly all came clear. There was no Robert Bloch entry under "stranger" in my Rolodex because Bob had never been one.

A large part of it was certainly due to the fact that I'd been not only familiar with, but grateful and loving toward him since I'd read his stories in *Weird Tales* when I was a rather creepy, lonely little boy. I can't tell you how much it helped to know there was a viable, functioning grownup out there as weird as Robert Bloch.

I passed through adolescence hearing various adaptations of those stories on the radio, and enjoyable whiled away many hours of young adulthood watching ghoulish movies about multiple personalities which he'd written, and TV shows beyond counting which he'd also committed.

But all that literary familiarity did not explain the matter. I'd been just as much an avid reader of numerous other authors and I have no trouble recalling the day when I met most of *them*—especially the first ones encountered when I was particularly young and callow—because those initial meetings were usually, to put it frankly, something of an ordeal, a bit of a hurdle, a definite challenge.

The fact is that most authors aren't really all that easy to meet, especially when you're a gibbering fan who is new to such things, and it's certainly no help that the authors are almost always trying—with varying degrees of success—to cope with simultaneously meeting numerous other gibbering fans.

They by no means intend to be unkind—though I must admit there *are* a select few who could be kinder with very little effort—but though their polished prose may suggest that they are perpetually confident and debonair, authors in the flesh are inevitably merely human and very likely to be heavy laden with numerous defensive reflexes and hidden insecurities, and a good many of them are as shy as the most socially inept of the fans they are meeting, truth be told. There is, therefore, often a certain element of strain in the initial contact.

I never saw it to be so with Robert Bloch. I observed him meeting crowds of total strangers on numberless occasions, and he was always so effortlessly friendly, so obviously kindly, and so gently accepting of the fragile souls pressing close about him, that even the most insecure and frightened of them soon found themselves chatting with him as easily as they would have with someone they'd known for years.

He always managed to give you his full attention, did Bob. He'd turn those bulgy eyes on you and hear what you said, then he'd visibly give it serious thought and do his level best to respond to it respectfully and helpfully. Not many people do that.

I treasure all the meetings I've ever had with him, now more so than ever since now I know I'll never *have* another. There are two of them that stand out particularly.

The first was on the opening of the premier World Fantasy Convention. A bunch of us had created the WFC out of thin air because it seemed to us way past high time that somebody held such an event just for fantasy writers, and because it struck us as a long way from fair that while science fiction authors could pile up Hugos and Nebulas galore to brag about on the covers of their paperbacks, fantasy and horror writers got zip so far as official recognition with certificates and statues attached was concerned.

The thing turned out to be altogether magical, but it was busy every moment and when you arrived, you hit the ground running. Bob had barely got his luggage in his room when he was snatched up and thrown into the passenger seat of a Volkswagen with me and my wife Nancy in the back, and Harry Beckwith, the author of *Lovecraft's Providence*—which is the absolute must guidebook for any Lovecraft nut visiting HPL's hometown—doing the driving and creating his guidebook in the flesh as we watched.

It turned out that Bob had never before visited Providence, in spite of his intimate historical association with it *vis-à-vis* his famous correspondence with Lovecraft, or perhaps because of it. I was always too shy to ask him about it, but I wouldn't have been at all surprised to learn he felt that a trip anywhere near close to the event of his beloved mentor's death would only have made him sad.

But now it was years and years since and he was come to Providence at last, and I solemnly swear that little thrills still run through me as I recall watching Bob with combined awe and delight as he sat in the front seat of that Volkswagen and pointed his ski-slope nose this way and then that as Harry Beckwith—his sweet New England accent evoking echoes of how HPL himself must have sounded—first directed his attention to the place where Bloch as Robert Blake in *The Haunter of the Dark* died staring at the "three-lobed, burning eye," and then pointed out the distant dark spire of the brooding old church that once contained the Shining Trapezohedron which had opened the way to Blake/Bloch's awful doom.

Then, after viewing such diverse wonders as the Shunned House and the mansion of Charles Dexter Ward, we drove on to the North Burial Ground where, nearly forty years after the death of his helpful Grandpa, Bob stood in silence by Lovecraft's grave.

The second meeting that looms particularly for me was the last one. I was in Los Angeles in the midst of one of those complicated dances you go through out there trying to get people to let you do something pretty for them, when I heard that Bob was dying.

I called him at once, of course, and I was all set for a low-spoken, funereal kind of exchange over the telephone, but that never happened because Bob immediately launched into a series of hilarious one-liners about his illness and his fast-approaching death. In between laughs—and they *were* laughs—we set up a visit for the next day.

Nancy was with me again, and her son Paul, who is my stepson and a friend of Bob's for years. Bob's wife, Elly, sat us down and gave us drinks and cookies, and Bob came in with a walker, wearing a snappy ascot and smiling that big wide smile he had, and once again he would have nothing to do with gloom but insisted on regaling us with extremely funny stories about the inanities and casual cruelties of the American medical establishment and the various absurd things that were happening to him in the process of dying.

Only once, when I was bending over close to him during the stir of our leaving preparations, did he let it get sad.

"The only thing is," he whispered to me, "it's happening so damn much faster than they told me it would!"

He was heading back to his bedroom as we clustered at the door saying our farewells to Elly, but then I heard a little noise and turned and saw that he'd changed his mind and his direction and snuck up on us with his Ames Walker and his oversize smile, and that's how I remember dear, brave Robert Bloch most of all.

P.S. The editor has pointed out that, wrapped in memories, I neglected an essential point, which is to identify my favorite story and say why. It's

"Beetles," and I am fond of it because it is the first story of Bob's I ever read, and because it managed to gross me out like nothing I had encountered up to then (I imagine passing grownups wondered why that little kid was wearing such a weird expression), and because I think the slammer at the end is maybe the best succinct horror image Bob ever came up with. One of the great pleasures of my life was to do a cover for *Weird Tales* illustrating "Beetles," showing Bob's face exuding ancient scarabs from its mouth, nose, and ears. I am pleased to report he liked it.

BEETLES

🌱 **When Hartley returned from Egypt, his friends said he** had changed. The specific nature of that change was difficult to detect, for none of his acquaintances got more than a casual glimpse of him. He dropped around to the club just once, and then retired to the seclusion of his apartments. His manner was so definitely hostile, so markedly anti-social, that very few of his cronies cared to visit him, and the occasional callers were not received.

It caused considerable talk at the time—gossip rather. Those who remembered Arthur Hartley in the days before his expedition abroad were naturally quite cut up over the drastic metamorphosis in his manner. Hartley had been known as a keen scholar, a singularly erudite fieldworker in his chosen profession of archeology; but at the same time he had been a peculiarly charming person. He had the worldly flair usually associated with the fictional characters of E. Phillips Oppenheim, and a positively devilish sense of humor which mocked and belittled it. He was the kind of fellow who could order the precise wine at the proper moment, at the same time grinning as though he were as much surprised by it all as his guest of the evening. And most of his friends found this air of culture without ostentation quite engaging. He had carried this urbane sense of the ridiculous over into his work; and while it was known that he was very much interested in archeology, and a notable figure in the field, he inevitably referred to his studies as "pottering around with old fossils and the old fossils that discovered them."

Consequently, his curious reversal following his trip came as a complete surprise.

All that was definitely known was that he had spent some eight months on a field trip to the Egyptian Sudan. Upon his return he had immediately severed all connections with the institute he had been associated with. Just what had occurred during the expedition was a matter of excited conjecture among his former intimates. But something had definitely happened; it was unmistakable.

The night he spent at the club proved that. He had come in quietly, too quietly. Hartley was one of those persons who usually made an entrance, in the true sense of the word. His tall, graceful figure, attired in the immaculate evening dress so seldom found outside of the pages of melodramatic fiction; his truly leonine head with its Stokowski-like bristle of gray hair; these attributes commanded attention. He could have passed anywhere as a man of the world, or a stage magician awaiting his cue to step onto the platform.

But this evening he entered quietly, unobtrusively. He wore dinner clothes, but his shoulders sagged, and the spring was gone from his walk. His hair was grayer, and it hung pallidly over his tanned forehead. Despite the bronze of Egyptian sun on his features, there was a sickly tinge to his countenance. His eyes peered mistily from amidst unsightly folds. His face seemed to have lost its mold; the mouth hung loosely.

He greeted no one; and took a table alone. Of course cronies came and chatted, but he did not invite them to join him. And oddly enough, none of them insisted, although normally they would gladly have forced their company upon him and jollied him out of a black mood, which experience had taught them was easily done in his case. Nevertheless, after a few words with Hartley, they all turned away.

They must have felt it even then. Some of them hazarded the opinion that Hartley was still suffering from some form of fever contracted in Egypt, but I do not think they believed this in their hearts. From their shocked descriptions of the man they seemed one and all to sense the peculiar *alien* quality about him. This was an Arthur Hartley they had never known, an aged stranger, with a querulous voice which rose in suspicion when he was questioned about his journey. Stranger he truly was, for he did not even appear to recognize some of the men who greeted him, and when he did it was with an abstracted manner—a clumsy way of wording it, but what else is there to say when an old friend stares blankly into silence upon meeting, and his eyes seem to fasten on far-off terrors that affright him?

That was the strangeness they all grasped in Hartley. He was afraid. Fear bestrode those sagging shoulders. Fear breathed a pallor into that ashy face. Fear grinned into those empty, far-fixed eyes. Fear prompted the suspicion in the voice.

They told me, and that is why I went round to see Arthur Hartley in his rooms. Others had spoken of their efforts, in the week following his appearance at the club, to gain admittance to his apartment. They said he did not answer the bell, and complained that the phone had been disconnected. But that, I reasoned, was fear's work.

I wouldn't let Hartley down..I had been a rather good friend of his—and I may as well confess that I scented a mystery here. The combination proved irresistible. I went up to his flat one afternoon and rang.

No answer. I went into the dim hallway and listened for footsteps, some sign of life from within. No answer. Complete, utter silence. For a moment I thought crazily of suicide, then laughed the dread away. It was absurd—and still, there had been a certain dismaying unanimity in all the reports I had heard of Hartley's mental state. When the stolidest, most hard-headed of the club bores concurred in their estimate of the man's condition, I might well worry. Still, suicide . . .

I rang again, more a gesture than in expectation of tangible results, and then I turned and descended the stairs. I felt, I recall, a little twinge of inexplicable relief upon leaving the place. The thought of suicide in that gloomy hallway had not been pleasant.

I reached the lower door and opened it, and a familiar figure scurried past me on the landing. I turned. It was Hartley.

For the first time since his return I got a look at the man, and in the hallway shadows he was ghastly. Whatever his condition at the club, a week must have accentuated it tremendously. His head was lowered, and as I greeted him he looked up. His eyes gave me a terrific shock. There was a stranger dwelling in their depths—a haunted stranger. I swear he shook when I addressed him.

He was wearing a tattered topcoat, but it hung loosely over his gauntness. I noticed that he was carrying a large bundle done up in brown paper.

I said something, I don't remember what; at any rate, I was at some pains to conceal my confusion as I greeted him. I was rather insistently cordial, I believe, for I could see that he would just as soon have hurried up the stairs without even speaking to me. The astonishment I felt converted itself into heartiness. Rather reluctantly he invited me up.

We entered the flat, and I noticed that Hartley double-locked the door behind him. That, to me, characterized his metamorphosis. In the old days, Hartley had always kept open house, in the literal sense of the word. Studies might have kept him late at the institute, but a chance visitor found his door open wide. And now, he double-locked it.

I turned around and surveyed the apartment. Just what I expected to see I cannot say, but certainly my mind was prepared for some sign of radical alteration. There was none. The furniture had not been moved; the pictures hung in their original places; the vast bookcases still stood in the shadows.

Hartley excused himself, entered the bedroom, and presently emerged after discarding his topcoat. Before he sat down he walked over to the mantel and struck a match before a little bronze figurine of Horus. A second later the thick gray spirals of smoke arose in the approved style of exotic fiction, and I smelt the pungent tang of strong incense.

That was the first puzzler. I had unconsciously adopted the attitude of a detective looking for clues—or, perhaps, a psychiatrist ferreting out psychoneurotic tendencies. And the incense was definitely alien to the Arthur Hartley I knew.

"Clears away the smell," he remarked.

I didn't ask "What smell?" Nor did I begin to question him as to his trip, his inexplicable conduct in not answering my correspondence after he left Khar-

"Since then I've stayed here, alone. Before I decide on any course for the future, I must fight the Curse and win. Nothing else will help."

I started to interject a phrase, but he brushed it aside and continued desperately.

"No, I couldn't go away. They followed me across the ocean; they haunt me in the streets. I could be locked up and they would still come. They come every night and crawl up the sides of my bed and try to get at my face and I must sleep soon or I'll go mad, they crawl over my face at night, they crawl—"

It was horrible to see the words ooze out between his set teeth, for he was fighting madly to control himself.

"Perhaps the insecticide will kill them. It was the first thing I should have thought of, but of course panic confused me. Yes, I put my trust in the insecticide. Grotesque, isn't it? Fighting an ancient curse with insect-powder?"

I spoke at last. "They're beetles, aren't they?"

He nodded. "Scarabæus beetles. You know the curse. The mummies under the protection of the Scarab cannot be violated."

I knew the curse. It was one of the oldest known to history. Like all legends, it has had a persistent life. Perhaps I could reason.

"But why should it affect you?" I asked. Yes, I would reason with Hartley. Egyptian fever had deranged him, and the colorful curse story had gripped his mind. If I spoke logically, I might get him to understand his hallucination. "Why should it affect you?" I repeated.

He was silent for a moment before he spoke, and then his words seemed to be wrung out of him.

"I stole a mummy," he said. "I stole the mummy of a temple virgin. I must have been crazy to do it; something happens to you under the sun. There was gold in the case, and jewels, and ornaments. And there was the Curse, written. I got them—both."

I stared at him, and knew that in this he spoke the truth.

"That's why I cannot keep up my work. I stole the mummy, and I am cursed. I didn't believe, but the crawling things came just as the inscription said.

"At first I thought that was the meaning of the Curse, that wherever I went the beetles would go, too, that they would haunt me and keep me from men forever. But lately I am beginning to think differently. I think the beetles will act as messengers of vengeance. I think they mean to kill me."

This was pure raving.

"I haven't dared open the mummy-case since. I'm afraid to read the inscription again. I have it here in the house, but I've locked it up and I won't show you. I want to burn it—but I must keep it on hand. In a way, it's the only proof of my sanity. And if the things kill me—"

"Snap out of it," I commanded. Then I started. I don't know the exact words I used, but I said reassuring, hearty, wholesome things. And when I finished he smiled the martyred smile of the obsessed.

"Delusions? They're real. But where do they come from? I can't find any cracks in the woodwork. The walls are sound. And yet every night the beetles

ANDRE NORTON

There are always writers whose very name on the jacket of a book, or attached to a magazine story, promises the best in their chosen field of work. Certainly Robert Bloch has a firm place among these. In other times the title "craftsman" was a highly honored one, given only after long years of hard work and by producing wares which were recognized by the public to be outstanding. Certainly that is a term we can apply to Robert and his work.

But he was not only a finished craftsman, he was a generous and helpful friend for many in his field and beyond it. His gentle wit made conversation with him a joy—one need only read that enthralling autobiography of his, *Once Around the Bloch,* to realize that here was someone who had risen over many difficulties in the past and never accepted defeat even when it seemed to face him.

Having had the privilege and pleasure of working directly with him twice, I know how rich such a collaboration could be. We started with a tricky performance in one of the Witch World volumes, telling the very same story, but Robert taking the villainess for his protagonist while I dealt with the force of Light. This gave us such satisfaction that we embarked on a novel—*The Jekyll Legacy*—wherein Robert handled the male members of the company and I labored with the heroine, exchanging chapters as we went.

Both these projects were smoothly carried out and I trust that Robert enjoyed it all as much as I did. Not only these manuscripts but many letters passed from one edge of the country to the other in the following years, and to find one from Robert in the mail brought laughter even into a dark day, for his comments on the dealings of the publishing world were to the point and yet uttered—or written—with wit.

There is this—his work will long continue to be read with enjoyment. He has left a very rich heritage behind him for all of us.

CHRISTOPHER LEE

I was staying with Bob and Elly at their home when they invited me to join them at a party in the Valley. It was sometime in the early 1960s, and I vividly remember the party. There, all around me, was gathered this extraordinary collection of great writers. To my right, Isaac Asimov. To my left, Fritz Leiber. A little further on, Ray Bradbury.

As if conversation with such intellects was not stimulating enough, suddenly there appeared a young man by the name of Dr. Doolittle—not a name one soon forgets. The man stood up in front of this unique gathering and, for more than an hour, kept everybody absolutely spellbound. We all watched as he performed in front of a blackboard, on which he chalked phrases and symbols. His topic was genetic engineering. He explained, with these symbols and equations, that if you wanted to create, say, a blond girl with green eyes, it was entirely possible.

I barely understood a word he said.

When it was over, I approached Bob. Careful, so no one would hear me, I whispered, "Could you please explain what this man was talking about?"

Bob smiled. He whispered back that he only understood a little of it himself.

The reason I recall this particular scene is to illustrate something about Bob Bloch. And that was his exceptional humility. Bob was particularly careful about people's feelings. He would much rather talk about you than himself. In fact, in our thirty years of friendship, I didn't learn much about his life until I read his autobiography.

Knowing Bob, it is likely he gathered with perfect clarity what Dr. Doolittle was illustrating. He may, just as likely, not have understood much at all. Either way, his response would have been the same.

*   *   *

I first met Bob in London in the early 1960s. He and Elly had come to town for a science fiction convention. Instantly, Bob and I established a rapport. Indeed, nobody who knew Bob could *fail* to establish a rapport with him. It's a bit of a cliché, but he was one of those very rare people who, when you met him, made you feel as if you'd known him forever. He was the easiest man in the world to talk to. Like all people who were great in their own field, he was extremely self-effacing. And he was a great writer.

Not just a very good writer. Not just a very amusing or very thrilling writer.

A great writer.

But he never used his greatness to intimidate. The immediate impression I had of Bob was of a gentle man. Two words.

He was *also* a gentleman—something that we set great store by in Britain. And we British are not instantaneous, hail-fellow well-met people.

What I saw in Bob reflected itself in an appreciation—a feeling of here is somebody very special. He was already world famous as the author of *Psycho*. But the fame did not show on him.

Bob was responsible for the first work I ever did in the United States. He had written a story called "Return to the Sabbath," which Alfred Hitchcock retitled "The Sign of Satan" for his television series. I flew to Universal Studios to play in this story. Bob had suggested me for the part.

Later, in the early 1960s, I was making a picture in Hong Kong and was told by my agent to come to Los Angeles for something or other. Having only met Bob once, I nevertheless contacted him and asked him to suggest where I should stay, certain he'd recommend a good place.

Bob said, "Of course you'll stay here." And that was that.

Shortly thereafter, I arrived in the United States and managed to find my way to Bob and Elly's home. There, I received this wonderful, warm welcome from the two of them. I can still see their dog Zander bounding from sofa to sofa; myself relaxing in their pool . . . I was made to feel so welcome—so much a part of their lives. It was truthfully just like being with one's own family. There was never any question of, "When are you going back to England?" It was an immediate feeling of welcome, stay as long as you please, and do make yourself at home.

I have wonderful memories of my stay with Bob and Elly. I'll always remember how quiet Bob was, how gentle. He had this marvelous smile and was terribly wise . . . It sounds as if I'm talking about some kind of saint, doesn't it? But that's how I remember him.

No, not a man who was hail-fellow well-met.

He didn't need to be.

It's funny how one imagines a writer might be after reading his work. Bob was nothing like one might have suspected. Quite the opposite, in fact. He had this wonderful sense of humor.

Of course, I realize now that one couldn't write the way he did *without* a sense of humor. Here was a writer who was so often described as having this "gallows" humor. I suppose that meant he could take the most ghastly situations and frightening circumstances and, in one sentence, inject a form of macabre humor. Personally, I believe this was to prevent people from being completely terrorized. Bob wanted to give us, his readers, a comfortable feeling. It was as if to say, let us always remember that this is a fantasy story with imaginary characters—this isn't the way something *really* happens. Though he'd conjure up these marvelous pictures, there was almost always an interjection of humor somewhere—that Bob Bloch wry twist.

This was very much a part of Bob's own character, too. You would meet him and think this was the *last* man in the world who would ever write such a story. What terrible secret black recesses must he have in his mind from which he dredges up these ghastly tales? But in reading them, you find yourself saying, "Hmmm. Very amusing," and even laughing out loud. Then, you'd suddenly realize the reason these wonderful stories *are* so successful is because of Bob's wonderful humor.

It was this subtle mixture of black humor and great writing that I found most unique in Bob's work. Lots of people can write stories that will shock you and terrify you. But few such stories leave you saying, "That really was scary, *but* it was a lot of fun, too."

This was Bob's hallmark.

And what a wonderful legacy he left for us.

WILLIAM F. NOLAN

I 'm proud to be counted among the many friends and admirers of
Robert Bloch. No one else in the business generated so much good-
will; no one has had such a multitude of good things said about him
down the years. Scores of people loved Bob Bloch. Although he had just
recovered from an operation, he took the time (and energy) to write a very
warm and generous afterword to my latest book of stories. That was typical of him. But he didn't just help his fellow professionals; he was always
there for the beginners, the amateurs, the writers who looked up to him
and had been influenced by his work. And while most pros are too busy
to respond to small-press magazine mailings, Bob could always be
counted on for a postcard of criticism and encouragement, issue to issue.
His support was unwavering.

We all owe him, all of us who were privileged to know him, an im-
mense debt of gratitude. With his wit, his warmth, his wisdom, he brightened our lives.

Robert Bloch was a true role model for us all.

As to a favorite story by Bob, I'll go with his wryly ironic identity cri-
sis tale, "I Do Not Love Thee, Dr. Fell"—the first Bloch story to be printed
in Tony Boucher's *Magazine of Fantasy and Science Fiction*. It appeared in
the March 1955 issue and was promptly selected for reprint in Ted Dikty's
annual *Best Science Fiction* series.

In his preface to the story, Boucher remarked on the fact that Bob "is
an intensive and acute student of psychology and psychiatry." Anyone
who has read *Psycho*, or countless other Blochian fictions, is well aware of
this aspect in his work.

For years, Bob earned his bread-and-circus money in an advertising
agency—before he became a full-time writer—and he drew on this per-

sonal background when he made the protagonist of "I Do Not Love Thee, Dr. Fell" a press agent.

Meet Clyde Bromley, a very troubled gentleman who is rapidly losing his identity.

He may also be losing his mind.

flack in the business . . . get the picture . . . in the bag . . . give him the word . . . flashed me the cue . . . but nothing . . . didn't add up."

Doctor Fell leaned forward. "What do those phrases mean to you, Bromely? What do they really *add up* to, in your mind?"

Bromely tried to think about it. He tried hard. But all he could come out with was, "I don't know. They're all slang expressions I used to use in public relations a few years ago. Come to think of it, they're a little dated now, aren't they?"

Doctor Fell smiled. "Exactly. And doesn't that tie in with your final statement, that you couldn't think like a press agent anymore? Isn't that part of your problem, Mr. Bromely—that you aren't a press agent any more, really? That you're losing your identity, losing your orientation? Let me ask you once again, now: *who are you?*"

Bromely froze up. He couldn't answer because he couldn't think of the answer. He lay there on the couch, and Doctor Fell waited. Nothing happened.

Nothing seemed to happen for a long, long time. How Bromely got through the next two days he couldn't remember. All he recalled were the hours on the couch—and it seemed to him that he shuttled back and forth between his office and Doctor Fell's more than once a day.

It was hard to check, of course, because he didn't talk to anyone. He lived alone in a one-room walkup apartment and he ate at one-arm counter joints. He wasn't talking to his office-girl, Thelma, any more either. There was nothing to talk about—no calls since the unfortunate Harrigan affair—and he owed her for three weeks' back salary. Besides, she almost seemed afraid of him when he appeared in the office. Come to think of it (and it was so hard to come to think of it, or anything else, so very hard) even Doctor Fell's little receptionist looked frightened when he walked in, without a word.

Without a word. That was his problem. He had no words any longer. It was as though his final effort, talking to Harrigan and Hal Edwards, had drained him dry of the ability to communicate. All the clichés had flowed out of him, leaving . . . nothing.

He realized it now, lying on the couch in Doctor Fell's office. Once more Doctor Fell had asked the single question, the only question he ever asked. "Who are you?"

And he couldn't answer. There was nothing. He was nobody. For years, now, he'd been in the process of becoming nobody. It was the only explanation that fitted. But he couldn't seem to explain.

With a start, he realized that it wasn't necessary. Doctor Fell was sitting close to Bromely now, breaking the long silence, whispering confidentially in his ear.

"All right," he was murmuring. "Let's try a different approach. Maybe *I* can tell you who you are."

Bromely nodded gratefully, but somewhere deep within him, fear was rising.

"Your case is quite remarkable in a way," said Doctor Fell, "but only because it's one of the first. I don't believe it will be the last. Within several years, there'll be thousands of men like you. The schizoids and the paranoids will have to move over and make room for a new category."

Bromely nodded, waited.

"You know anything about disease germs, bacteria? These organisms undergo swift mutations. Men invent sulfa drugs and the germs develop tolerance to sulfa. Men use antibiotics—penicillin, streptomycin, a dozen others. And the bugs adapt. They breed new strains of bugs."

He thinks I'm bugs, Bromely told himself, but he listened. Fell went on, his voice rising slightly.

"Bugs change, but still they spawn on men. And aberration changes with the times, too—but still it spawns on men. Five hundred years ago the commonest form of insanity was belief in demoniac possession. Three hundred years ago men had delusions of witchcraft and sorcery. A man who couldn't integrate his personality created a new one—he became a wizard. Because the wizard was the symbol of power, who knew the secrets of Life and Death. The disintegrating personality seeks reaffirmation in Authority. Does that make sense to you?"

Bromely nodded, but actually nothing made sense to him any more. The fear rose within him as Doctor Fell's voice rose without.

"Yes, three hundred years ago, thousands of men and women went to the stake firmly convinced that they were, actually, witches and wizards.

"Times change, Bromely. Look what happened to you. Your personality disintegrated, didn't it? You began to lose touch with reality.

"You lived alone, without personal ties to reaffirm identity. Your work was phony, too—the epitome of all phoniness—manufacturing lies to create artificial press-agent personalities for others. You lived in a phony world, used phony words and phrases, and before you knew it, nothing you did was quite real to you any more. And you got panicked because you felt your sense of identity slipping away. True?"

Bromely felt the fear very close now, because Doctor Fell was closer. But he wanted Doctor Fell to stay, wanted him to solve this problem.

"You're not a fool, Clyde." Doctor Fell used his first name now and it underlined the intimacy of his words. "You sensed something was going wrong. And so you did what others are beginning to do today. You did that which will create, in years to come, a new kind of mania."

The fear was *here,* now. But Bromely listened.

"Some start by seeking the 'self-help' books, just as old-time sorcerers used to study grimoires. Some go further and experiment in all the odd bypaths of parapsychology—ESP, telepathy, occultism. And some go all the way. They cannot conjure up the Devil but they can commune with Freud, with Adler, with Jung and Moll and Stekel and the other archfiends. They don't chant spells any more, but they learn the new Cabala, the new language of Mystery. *Schizophrenia, echolalia, involutional melancholia*—the words come trippingly from the tongue, do they not?

"You should know, Clyde. Didn't you visit the library on those long dull days when business was bad, and read endlessly in psychiatry? Didn't you bury yourself, these past several months, in a completely new world of delusion and hallucination and obsession, of neurosis and psychosis? In other words, when you felt you were going crazy—just as in the past, men felt they were becoming possessed of the Devil—didn't you seek to fight it by studying psychiatry as the ancients studied the black arts?"

Bromely tried to sit up. Doctor Fell's face loomed closer, swung away, loomed closer again.

"You know what happened to those men, Clyde. They became, in their own minds, wizards. And you know now—surely you must have guessed—what has happened to you. During the past week, you couldn't be a press agent any more. You couldn't be a rational human being any more. In an effort to project, to invest in a new identity, you became a psychiatrist. And *you invented me!*

"You've told yourself that this office is something like your own office, my receptionist resembles your girl, I resemble you. Don't you understand? This *is* your office. That *is* your girl. You've been coming in daily and lying down here on your own couch. No wonder she's frightened, hearing you talk to yourself. *Now* do you know who you are?"

Was it Doctor Fell or the fear screaming in his ears?

"This is your last chance, Clyde. You've got to decide once and for all. You can be yourself again, completely, if you have faith in your own identity. If not, you're the first of the new maniacs. Let me ask you once again, once and for all: *who are you?*"

Clyde Bromely lay there on the couch while the room whirled and swirled. He saw pictures, endless pictures: a faded snapshot of a little Clyde, clinging to Mamma's skirt—Bromely, Lt. j.g., U.S.N., in uniform—Speed Bromely, public relations, shaking hands with a top comic at a benefit show—Bromely sitting in the public library, seeking the answer in the ologies and the isms—Bromely lying on the couch, clawing at nothing.

Bromely saw the pictures, shuffled them, sorted them, and made his choice.

Then the fear fell away, and Bromely slept. He slept there on the couch for a long, long time. When he woke up it was dark and he was alone in the room. Somebody was rapping on the door.

It was his girl. He knew that now. He was in his own office, and his own girl came in, timidly and hesitantly, as he rose with a smile of renewed confidence.

"I was worried," she said. "You being in here so long, and—"

He laughed, and laughed again inside as he realized that the sound but dimly conveyed the new security he felt within himself.

"I was sleeping," he told her. "There's nothing to worry about, my dear. From now on, we're going places. I've been in a pretty bad slump for the past month or so—someday I'll tell you all about it—but I'm all right now. Let's go out for dinner and we'll make plans."

The girl smiled. She could sense the change, too. Dark as the room was, it seemed to fill with sudden sunlight.

"All right," she said. "All right, Mr. Bromely."

He stiffened. "Bromely? That patient? Don't you know me, my dear?"

RICHARD MATHESON

*K*indness
It is the word which comes to mind most readily in seeking to recapture the essence of Robert Bloch.

And, with it, inevitably, *thoughtfulness.*

I was witness to a prime example of these two qualities before I even
met him.

I had read his stories, of course, and aspired to achieve some small
measure of his skill and imagination.

Which made what he did for me such a source of total wonderment.

Having read a limited number of my stories—there *were* only a limited number because I was just starting out as a writer—he wrote a long,
carefully delineated, astonishingly generous article about my work, titling
it (this really flabbergasted me) *The Art of Richard Matheson.*

To a novice writer, it was an injection of gratification and excitement
I had never anticipated and which I will never forget.

My wife and I met Robert while on our honeymoon drive back east in
1952. Passing through Chicago, we stopped at the World Science Fiction
Convention which just happened to be taking place then.

There, once again, Robert demonstrated those two wonderfully built-
in qualitites of kindness and thoughtfulness.

My bride and I were absolute newcomers to that world, and Robert,
clearly sensing it, spent extra time with us, making certain that we felt
comfortable and that we met other people there—writers, editors, etc.

This we have never forgotten.

*　　*　　*

In later years, we came to know Robert on a more personal, friendship basis, meeting, as well, his lovely wife Elly and his charming daughter Sally, who lived close by us for a number of years.

To them, on numerous occasions, we saw demonstrations of his kindness and thoughtfulness—in addition to his abiding show of love.

Naturally, one remembers a talented and skillful writer by his body of work. Robert is one of the giants of imaginative literature.

But he was also a warm, perceptive human being.

As a writer myself, I sometimes wonder which of these two personas is the more important in the long run.

Robert's memory is secure in that respect. He achieved greatness in both roles.

One of the regrets of Robert's writing life—and of my reading life for that matter—is the fact that his dream of creating a trilogy devoted to encompassing the history of silent pictures in fictional terms never came to fruition.

He completed the first novel (which I read with great pleasure) but, as far as I know, he never got to complete the two follow-up books.

As I recall, his notion was to call the three novels something like SUPER!—COLOSSAL!—GIGANTIC!—a wry and telling comment on the grandiose pretensions of itself so much of the movie industry promulgates.

Robert knew *so much* about silent pictures.

There seemed to be literally nothing that had to do with them that he couldn't talk about extensively, no conceivable question on the subject he could not readily—and totally—answer.

He was a delightful source of arcana about that most interesting—if short-lived—era of film creativity.

I remember, in particular, him telling me how his viewing of The Phantom of the Opera had literally altered his life.

When that mask was pulled off by the heroine and that ghastly, skull-like face filled the screen, young Robert Bloch's forming creative existence was radically expanded—if not actually jump-started—into that long, amazingly productive period of his writing life. (Three cheers for Lon Chaney!)

Because of all this, I regard it as a literary tragedy that Robert was never given the opportunity to complete this worthy project about silent films.

It is sad enough (I know from personal experience) when a writer does not get the opportunity to shape, polish, and present to the world a particular dream that he or she has loved and nurtured.

When that dream has to do with a subject as close to the heart as silent films were to Bob . . . well, that's *bad*. Unforgivable.

There oughtta be a law.

*　　*　　*

What more can I say in general terms about Robert's writing?

Perhaps that not enough readers are aware of his marvelous sense of humor. Aware of the Dark Horrors in his work, yes. The Black Doings and Keen Insights into the Shadows of The Human Mind.

But humor? Too few readers know about that.

Yet—as I commented about Bob's Lefty Feep stories—saying that Bob had a sense of humor was akin to saying that "Einstein had a good head on his shoulders—the understatement of any desired year."

Robert made his friends laugh—a lot. I just wish that more readers knew how he can make *them* laugh as well.

"Make future generations chortle and enjoy." (My quote)

Finally, a few words about *Psycho*.

I will not go into the details I did in my introduction to the thirty-fifth anniversary edition of that novel. But what I said in essence bears repeating.

Robert Bloch was the fundamental creator of the film *Psycho* as well as of the novel. Even Hitchcock admitted it. Stated that the film "all came from the book."

Still, as with Robert's sense of humor, not enough people know about it.

They *should.*

Bob's blueprint for the story of *Psycho* was absolutely precise. "The building of the Bates Motel with all of its interior horrors (as seen in the movie) was in the book.

"To the detail."

I hope that more people become aware of that. It is only simple justice.

Let me conclude this tribute by repeating the last line of that introduction to *Psycho*.

With admiration and affection to the
Grandest Master of them all.

I find "Enoch" an intriguing story for a number of reasons. Primarily, of course, because it is skillfully written and totally involving—a hallmark of all Robert's work.

But, beyond that, I see in it an interesting forerunner to *Psycho*.

The strange yet sympathetic protagonist with a serious mother complex.

The odd emphasis on head removal. (I once told Bob that I thought it indicated an attitude on his part regarding the separation between mind and body. He found the notion possible but didn't necessarily agree with it.)

The sinking of the car and the young female victim's body in the swamp.

The protagonist's conviction that he is an innocent, that any of his dreadful acts were forced upon him by a power other than himself.

Intriguing parallels. Intriguing story.

ENOCH

It always starts the same way. First, there's the feeling.
Have you ever felt the tread of little feet walking across the top of your skull? Footsteps on your skull, back and forth, back and forth?

It starts like that.

You can't see who does the walking. After all, it's on top of your head. If you're clever, you wait for a chance and suddenly brush a hand through your hair. But you can't catch the walker that way. He knows. Even if you clamp both hands flat to your head, he manages to wriggle through, somehow. Or maybe he jumps.

He is terribly swift. And you can't ignore him. If you don't pay any attention to the footsteps, he tries the next step. He wriggles down the back of your neck and whispers in your ear.

You can feel his body, so tiny and cold, pressed tightly against the base of your brain. There must be something numbing in his claws, because you don't hurt—although later, you'll find little scratches on your neck that bleed and bleed. But at the time, all you know is that something tiny and cold is pressing there. Pressing, and whispering.

That's when you try to fight him. You try not to hear what he says. Because when you listen, you're lost. You have to obey him then.

Oh, he's wicked and wise!

He knows how to frighten and threaten, if you dare to resist. But I seldom try, any more. It's better for me if I do listen and then obey.

As long as I'm willing to listen, things don't seem so bad. Because he can be soothing and persuasive, too. Tempting. The things he has promised me, in that little silken whisper!

He keeps his promises, too.

Folks think I'm poor because I never have any money and live in that old shack on the edge of the swamp. But he has given me riches.

After I do what he wants, he takes me away—out of myself—for days. There are other places besides this world, you know; places where I am king.

People laugh at me and say I have no friends; the girls in town used to call me "scarecrow." Yet sometimes—after I've done his bidding—he brings queens to share my bed.

Just dreams? I don't think so. It's the other life that's just a dream; the life in the shack at the edge of the swamp. That part doesn't seem real any more.

Not even the killing . . .

Yes, I kill people.

That's what Enoch wants, you know.

That's what he whispers about. He asks me to kill people, for him.

I don't like that. I used to fight against it—I told you that before, didn't I?—but I can't any more.

He wants me to kill people for him. Enoch. The thing that lives on the top of my head. I can't see him. I can't catch him. I can only feel him, and hear him, and obey him.

Sometimes he leaves me alone for days. Then, suddenly, I feel him there, scratching away at the roof of my brain. I hear his whisper ever so plainly, and he'll be telling me about someone who is coming through the swamp.

I don't know how he knows about them. He couldn't have seen them, yet he describes them perfectly.

"There's a tramp walking down the Aylesworthy Road. A short, fat man, with a bald head. His name is Mike. He's wearing a brown sweater and blue overalls. He's going to turn into the swamp in about ten minutes when the sun goes down. He'll stop under the big tree next to the dump.

"Better hide behind that tree. Wait until he starts to look for firewood. Then you know what to do. Get the hatchet, now. Hurry."

Sometimes I ask Enoch what he will give me. Usually, I just trust him. I know I'm going to have to do it, anyway. So I might as well go ahead at once. Enoch is never wrong about things, and he keeps me out of trouble.

That is, he always did—until the last time.

One night I was sitting in the shack eating supper when he told me about this girl.

"She's coming to visit you," he whispered. "A beautiful girl, all in black. She has a wonderful quality to her head—fine bones. Fine."

At first I thought he was telling me about one of my rewards. But Enoch was talking about a real person.

"She will come to the door and ask you to help her fix her car. She has taken the side road, planning to go into town by a shorter route. Now the car is well into the swamp, and one of the tires needs changing."

It sounded funny, hearing Enoch talk about things like automobile tires. But he knows about them. Enoch knows everything.

"You will go out to help her when she asks you. Don't take anything. She has a wrench in the car. Use that."

This time I tried to fight him. I kept whimpering, "I won't do it, I won't do it."

He just laughed. And then he told me what he'd do if I refused. He told me over and over again.

"Better that I do it to her and not to you," Enoch reminded me. "Or would you rather I—"

"No!" I said. "No. I'll do it."

"After all," Enoch whispered, "I can't help it. I must be served every so often. To keep me alive. To keep me strong. So I can serve you. So I can give you things. That is why you have to obey me. If not, I'll just stay right here and—"

"No," I said. "I'll do it."

And I did it.

She knocked on my door just a few minutes later, and it was just as Enoch had whispered it. She was a pretty girl—with blonde hair. I like blonde hair. I was glad, when I went out into the swamp with her, that I didn't have to harm her hair. I hit her behind the neck with the wrench.

Enoch told me what to do, step by step.

After I used the hatchet, I put the body in the quicksand. Enoch was with me, and he cautioned me about heelmarks. I got rid of them.

I was worried about the car, but he showed me how to use the end of a rotten log and pitch it over. I wasn't sure it would sink, too, but it did. And much faster than I would have believed.

It was a relief to see the car go. I threw the wrench in after it. Then Enoch told me to go home, and I did, and at once I felt the dreamy feeling stealing over me.

Enoch had promised me something extra special for this one, and I sank down into sleep right away. I could barely feel the pressure leave my head as Enoch left me, scampering off back into the swamp for his reward . . .

I don't know how long I slept. It must have been a long time. All I remember is that I finally started to wake up, knowing somehow that Enoch was back with me again, and feeling that something was wrong.

Then I woke up all the way, because I heard the banging on my door.

I waited a moment. I waited for Enoch to whisper to me, tell me what I should do.

But Enoch was asleep now. He always sleeps—afterwards. Nothing wakes him for days on end; and during that time I am free. Usually I enjoy such freedom, but not now. I needed his help.

The pounding on my door grew louder, and I couldn't wait any longer.

I got up and answered.

Old Sheriff Shelby came through the doorway.

"Come on, Seth," he said. "I'm taking you up to the jail."

I didn't say anything. His beady little black eyes were peeping everywhere inside my shack. When he looked at me, I wanted to hide, I felt so scared.

He couldn't see Enoch, of course. Nobody can. But Enoch was there; I felt him resting very lightly on top of my skull, burrowed down under a blanket of hair, clinging to my curls and sleeping as peaceful as a baby.

"Emily Robbins' folks said she was planning on cutting through the swamp," the Sheriff told me. "We followed the tire tracks up to the old quicksand."

Enoch had forgotten about the tracks. So what could I say? Besides,

"Anything you say can be used agin you," said Sheriff Shelby. "Come on, Seth."

I went with him. There was nothing else for me to do. I went with him into town, and all the loafers were out trying to rush the car. There were women in the crowd too. They kept yelling for the men to "get" me.

But Sheriff Shelby held them off, and at last I was tucked away safe and sound in back of the jailhouse. He locked me up in the middle cell. The two cells on each side of mine were vacant, so I was all alone. All alone except for Enoch, and he slept through everything.

It was still early in the morning, and Sheriff Shelby went out again with some other men. I guess he was going to try and get the body out of the quicksand, if he could. He didn't try to ask any questions, and I wondered about that.

Charley Potter, now, he was different. He wanted to know everything. Sheriff Shelby had left him in charge of the jail while he was away. He brought me my breakfast after a while, and hung around asking questions.

I just kept still. I knew better than to talk to a fool like Charley Potter. He thought I was crazy. Just like the mob outside. Most people in that town thought I was crazy—because of my mother, I suppose, and because of the way I lived all alone out in the swamp.

What could I say to Charley Potter? If I told him about Enoch he'd never believe me anyway.

So I didn't talk.

I listened.

Then Charley Potter told me about the search for Emily Robbins, and about how Sheriff Shelby got to wondering over some other disappearances a while back. He said that there would be a big trial, and the District Attorney was coming down from the County Seat. And he'd heard they were sending out a doctor to see me right away.

Sure enough, just as I finished breakfast, the doctor came. Charley Potter saw him drive up and let him in. He had to work fast to keep some of the oafs from breaking in with him. They wanted to lynch me, I suppose. But the doctor came in all right—a little man with one of those funny beards on his chin—and he made Charley Potter go up front into the office while he sat down outside the cell and talked to me.

His name was Dr. Silversmith.

Now up to this time, I wasn't really feeling anything. It had all happened so fast I didn't get a chance to think.

It was like part of a dream; the Sheriff and the mob and all this talk about a trial and lynching and the body in the swamp.

But somehow the sight of this Dr. Silversmith changed things.

He was real, all right. You could tell he was a doctor who wanted to send me to the Institution after they found my mother.

That was one of the first things Dr. Silversmith asked me—what had happened to my mother?

He seemed to know quite a lot about me, and that made it easier for me to talk.

Pretty soon I found myself telling him all sorts of things. How my mother and I lived in the shack. How she made the philtres and sold them. About the big pot and the way we gathered herbs at night. About the nights when she went off alone and I would hear the queer noises from far away.

I didn't want to say much more, but he knew, anyway. He knew they had called her a witch. He even knew the way she died—when Santo Dinorelli came to our door that evening and stabbed her because she had made the potion for his daughter who ran away with that trapper. He knew about me living in the swamp alone after that, too.

But he didn't know about Enoch.

Enoch, up on top of my head all the time, still sleeping, not knowing or caring what was happening to me . . .

Somehow, I was talking to Dr. Silversmith about Enoch. I wanted to explain that it wasn't really I who had killed this girl. So I had to mention Enoch, and how my mother had made the bargain in the woods. She hadn't let me come with her—I was only twelve—but she took some of my blood in a little bottle.

Then, when she came back, Enoch was with her. And he was to be mine forever, she said, and look after me and help me in all ways.

I told this very carefully and explained why it was I couldn't help myself when I did anything now, because ever since my mother died Enoch had guided me.

Yes, all these years Enoch had protected me, just as my mother planned. She knew I couldn't get along alone. I admitted this to Dr. Silversmith because I thought he was a wise man and and would understand.

That was wrong.

I knew it at once. Because while Dr. Silversmith leaned forward and stroked his little beard and said, "Yes, yes," over and over again, I could feel his eyes watching me. The same kind as the people in the mob. Mean eyes. Eyes that don't trust you when they see you. Prying, peeping eyes.

Then he began to ask me all sorts of ridiculous questions. About Enoch, at first—although I knew he was only pretending to believe in Enoch. He asked me how I could hear Enoch if I couldn't see him. He asked me if I ever heard any other voices. He asked me how I felt when I killed Emily Robbins and whether I—but I won't even think about that question. Why, he talked to me as if I were some kind of—crazy person!

He had only been fooling me all along about not knowing Enoch. He proved that now by asking me how many other people I had killed. And then he wanted to know, where were their heads?

He couldn't fool me any longer.

I just laughed at him, then, and shut up tighter than a clam.

After a while he gave up and went away, shaking his head. I laughed after him because I knew he hadn't found out what he wanted to find out. He wanted to know all my mother's secrets, and my secrets, and Enoch's secrets too.

But he didn't, and I laughed. And then I went to sleep. I slept almost all afternoon.

When I woke up, there was a new man standing in front of my cell. He had a big, fat smiling face, and nice eyes.

"Hello, Seth," he said, very friendly. "Having a little snooze?"

I reached up to the top of my head. I couldn't feel Enoch, but I knew he was there, and still asleep. He moves fast, even when he's sleeping.

"Don't be alarmed," said the man. "I won't hurt you."

"Did that Doctor send you?" I asked.

The man laughed. "Of course not," he told me. "My name's Cassidy. Edwin Cassidy. I'm the District Attorney, and I'm in charge here. Can I come in and sit down, do you suppose?"

"I'm locked in," I said.

"I've got the keys from the Sheriff," said Mr. Cassidy. He took them out and opened my cell; walked right in and sat down next to me on the bench.

"Aren't you afraid?" I asked him. "You know, I'm supposed to be a murderer."

"Why Seth," Mr. Cassidy laughed, "I'm not afraid of you. I know you didn't mean to kill anybody."

He put his hand on my shoulder, and I didn't draw away. It was a nice fat, soft hand. He had a big diamond ring on his finger that just twinkled away in the sunshine.

"How's Enoch?" he said.

I jumped.

"Oh, that's all right. That fool Doctor told me when I met him down the street. He doesn't understand about Enoch, does he, Seth? But you and I do."

"That Doctor thinks I'm crazy," I whispered.

"Well, just between us, Seth, it did sound a little hard to believe at first. But I've just come from the swamp. Sheriff Shelby and some of his men are still working down there.

"They found Emily Robbins' body just a little while ago. And other bodies, too. A fat man's body, and a small boy, and some Indian. The quicksand preserves them, you know."

I watched his eyes, and they were still smiling, so I knew I could trust this man.

"They'll find other bodies too, if they keep on, won't they, Seth?"

I nodded.

"But I didn't wait any longer. I saw enough to understand that you were telling the truth. Enoch must have made you do these things, didn't he?"

I nodded again.

"Fine," said Mr. Cassidy, pressing my shoulder. "You see, we do understand each other now. So I won't blame you for anything you tell me."

"What do you want to know?" I asked.

"Oh, lots of things. I'm interested in Enoch, you see. Just how many people did he ask you to kill—all together, that is?"

"Nine," I said.

"And they're all buried in the quicksand?"

"Yes."

"Do you know their names?"

"Only a few." I told him the names of the ones I knew. "Sometimes Enoch just describes them for me and I go out to meet them," I explained.

Mr. Cassidy sort of chuckled and took out a cigar. I frowned.

"Don't want me to smoke, eh?"

"Please—I don't like it. My mother didn't believe in smoking; she never let me."

Mr. Cassidy laughed out loud now, but he put the cigar away and leaned forward.

"You can be a big help to me, Seth," he whispered. "I suppose you know what a District Attorney must do."

"He's a sort of lawyer, isn't he—at trials and things?"

"That's right. I'm going to be at your trial, Seth. Now you don't want to have to get up in front of all those people and tell them about—what happened. Right?"

"No, I don't, Mr. Cassidy. Not those mean people here in town. They hate me."

"Then here's what you do. You tell me all about it, and I'll talk for you. That's friendly enough, isn't it?"

I wished Enoch was there to help me, but he was asleep. I looked at Mr. Cassidy and made up my own mind.

"Yes," I said. "I can tell you."

So I told him everything I knew.

After a while he stopped chuckling, but he was just getting so interested he couldn't bother to laugh or do anything but listen.

"One thing more," he said. "We found some bodies in the swamp. Emily Robbins' body we could identify, and several of the others. But it would be easier if we knew something else. You can tell me this, Seth.

"Where are the heads?"

I stood up and turned away. "I won't tell you that," I said, "because I don't know."

"Don't know?"

"I give them to Enoch," I explained. "Don't you understand—that's why I must kill people for him. Because he wants their heads."

Mr. Cassidy looked puzzled.

"He always makes me cut the heads off and leave them," I went on. "I put the bodies in the quicksand, and then go home. He puts me to sleep and rewards me. After that he goes away—back to the heads. That's what he wants."

"Why does he want them, Seth?"

I told him. "You see, it wouldn't do you any good if you could find them. Because you probably wouldn't recognize anything anyway."

Mr. Cassidy sat up and sighed. "But why do you let Enoch do such things?"

"I must. Or else he'll do it to me. That's what he always threatens. He has to have it. So I obey him."

Mr. Cassidy watched me while I walked the floor, but he didn't say a word. He seemed to be very nervous, all of a sudden, and when I came close, he sort of leaned away.

"You'll explain all that at the trial, of course," I said. "About Enoch, and everything."

He shook his head.

"I'm not going to tell about Enoch at the trial, and neither are you," Mr. Cassidy said. "Nobody is even going to know that Enoch exists."

"Why?"

"I'm trying to help you, Seth. Don't you know what the people will say if you mention Enoch to them? They'll say you're crazy! And you don't want that to happen."

"No. But what can you do? How can you help me?"

Mr. Cassidy smiled at me.

"You're afraid of Enoch, aren't you? Well, I was just thinking out loud. Suppose you gave Enoch to me?"

I gulped.

"Yes. Suppose you gave Enoch to me, right now? Let me take care of him for you during the trial. Then he wouldn't be yours, and you wouldn't have to say anything about him. He probably doesn't want people to know what he does, anyway."

"That's right," I said. "Enoch would be very angry. He's a secret, you know. But I hate to give him to you without asking—and he's asleep now."

"Asleep?"

"Yes. On top of my skull. Only you can't see him, of course."

Mr. Cassidy gazed at my head and then he chuckled again.

"Oh, I can explain everything when he wakes up," he told me. "When he knows it's all for the best, I'm sure he'll be happy."

"Well—I guess it's all right, then," I sighed. "But you must promise to take good care of him."

"Sure," said Mr. Cassidy.

"And you'll give him what he wants? What he needs?"

"Of course."

"And you won't tell a soul?"

"Not a soul."

"Of course you know what will happen to you if you refuse to give Enoch what he wants," I warned Mr. Cassidy. "He will take it—from you—by force?"

"Don't you worry, Seth."

I stood still for a minute. Because all at once I could feel something move towards my ear.

"Enoch," I whispered. "Can you hear me?"

He heard.

Then I explained everything to him. How I was giving him to Mr. Cassidy. Enoch didn't say a word.

Mr. Cassidy didn't say a word. He just sat there and grinned. I suppose it must have looked a little strange to see me talking to—nothing.

"Go to Mr. Cassidy," I whispered. "Go to him, now."

And Enoch went.

I felt the weight lift from my head. That was all, but I knew he was gone.

"Can you feel him, Mr. Cassidy?" I asked.

"What—oh, sure!" he said, and stood up.

"Take good care of Enoch," I told him.

"The best."

"Don't put your hat on," I warned. "Enoch doesn't like hats."

"Sorry, I forgot. Well, Seth, I'll say good-bye now. You've been a mighty great help to me—and from now on we can just forget about Enoch, as far as telling anybody else is concerned.

"I'll come back again and talk about the trial. That Doctor Silversmith, he's going to try and tell the folks you're crazy. Maybe it would be best if you just denied everything you told him—now that I have Enoch."

That sounded like a fine idea, but then I knew Mr. Cassidy was a smart man.

"Whatever you say, Mr. Cassidy. Just be good to Enoch, and he'll be good to you."

Mr. Cassidy shook my hand and then he and Enoch went away. I felt tired again. Maybe it was the strain, and maybe it was just that I felt a little queer, knowing that Enoch was gone. Anyway, I went back to sleep for a long time.

It was night time when I woke up. Old Charley Potter was banging on the cell door, bringing me my supper.

He jumped when I said hello to him, and backed away.

"Murderer!" he yelled. "They got nine bodies out'n the swamp. You crazy fiend!"

"Why Charley," I said. "I always thought you were a friend of mine."

"Loony! I'm gonna get out of here right now—leave you locked up for the night. Sheriff'll see that nobuddy breaks in to lynch you—if you ask me, he's wasting his time."

Then Charley turned out all the lights and went away. I heard him go out the front door and put the padlock on, and I was all alone in the jail house.

All alone! It was strange to be all alone for the first time in years—all alone, without Enoch.

I ran my fingers across the top of my head. It felt bare and queer.

The moon was shining through the window and I stood there looking out at the empty street. Enoch always loved the moon. It made him lively. Made him restless and greedy. I wondered how he felt now, with Mr. Cassidy.

I must have stood there for a long time. My legs were numb when I turned around and listened to the fumbling at the door.

The lock clicked open, and then Mr. Cassidy came running in.

"Take him off me!" he yelled. "Take him away!"

"What's the matter?" I asked.

"Enoch—that thing of yours—I thought you were crazy—maybe I'm the crazy one—but take him off!"

"Why, Mr. Cassidy! I told you what Enoch was like."

"He's crawling around up there now. I can feel him. And I can hear him. The things he whispers!"

"But I explained all that, Mr. Cassidy. Enoch wants something, doesn't he? You know what it is. And you'll have to give it to him. You promised."

"I can't. I won't kill for him—he can't make me—"

"He can. And he will."

Mr. Cassidy gripped the bars on the cell door. "Seth, you must help me. Call Enoch. Take him back. Make him go back to you. Hurry."

"All right, Mr. Cassidy," I said.

I called Enoch. He didn't answer. I called again. Silence.

Mr. Cassidy started to cry. It shocked me, and then I felt kind of sorry for him. He just didn't understand, after all. I know what Enoch can do to you when he whispers that way. First he coaxes you, and then he pleads, and then he threatens—

"You'd better obey him," I told Mr. Cassidy. "Has he told you who to kill?"

Mr. Cassidy didn't pay any attention to me. He just cried. And then he took out the jail keys and opened up the cell next to mine. He went in and locked the door.

"I won't," he sobbed. "I won't, I won't!"

"You won't what?" I asked.

"I won't kill Doctor Silversmith at the hotel and give Enoch his head. I'll stay here, in the cell, where I'm safe! Oh you fiend, you devil—"

He slumped down sideways and I could see him through the bars dividing our cells, sitting all hunched over while his hands tore at his hair.

"You'd better," I called out. "Or else Enoch will do something. Please, Mr. Cassidy—oh, hurry—"

Then Mr. Cassidy gave a little moan and I guess he fainted. Because he didn't say anything more and he stopped clawing. I called him once but he wouldn't answer.

So what could I do? I sat down in the dark corner of my cell and watched the moonlight. Moonlight always makes Enoch wild.

Then Mr. Cassidy started to scream. Not loud, but deep down in his throat. He didn't move at all, just screamed.

I knew it was Enoch, taking what he wanted—from him.

What was the use of looking? You can't stop him, and I had warned Mr. Cassidy.

I just sat there and held my hands to my ears until it was all over.

When I turned around again, Mr. Cassidy still sat slumped up against the bars. There wasn't a sound to be heard.

Oh yes, there was! A purring. A soft, faraway purring. The purring of Enoch, after he has eaten. Then I heard a scratching. The scratching of Enoch's claws, when he frisks because he's been fed.

The purring and the scratching came from inside Mr. Cassidy's head.

That would be Enoch, all right, and he was happy now.

I was happy, too.

I reached my hand through the bars and pulled the jail keys from Mr. Cassidy's pocket. I opened my cell door and I was free again.

There was no need for me to stay now, with Mr. Cassidy gone. And Enoch wouldn't be staying, either. I called to him.

"Here, Enoch!"

That was as close as I've ever come to really seeing Enoch—a sort of a white streak that came flashing out of the big red hole he had eaten in the back of Mr. Cassidy's skull.

Then I felt the soft, cold, flabby weight landing on my own head once more, and I knew Enoch had come home.

I walked through the corridor and opened the outer door of the jail.

Enoch's tiny feet began to patter on the roof of my brain.

Together we walked out into the night. The moon was shining, everything was still, and I could hear, ever so softly, Enoch's happy chuckling in my ear.

HUGH B. CAVE

L ong before I came face to face with Robert Bloch and shook his hand for the first time, I knew him well. I had been reading and admiring his printed words for years, hearing his tales on radio, and seeing his name on big screen and television dramas that kept me spellbound.

Then in July of 1983, Bob and I were invited to be co-guests at Pulpcon in Dayton, Ohio, and as luck—good luck!—would have it, we arrived at the Dayton airport only moments apart.

Pulpcon, still going strong, is an annual gathering of writers, editors, collectors, and fans who were associated with, or who appreciate, those grand old pulp-paper, all-fiction magazines that made life so colorful from early in this century until about 1940. Magazines bearing titles like *Weird Tales, Strange Tales, Western Story, Detective Story, Adventure, Short Stories, Dime Mystery, Astounding,* and more than a hundred other such in about every genre you can imagine. Bob Bloch wrote for them. So did I.

It so happened that in Columbus, where my lady Peggy and I had changed planes on our journey from Florida, our airline had lost the return portion of my ticket. So, while Peg stood at the counter in the Dayton airport trying to straighten things out (she had worked in public relations for years) and a Pulpcon man who had come to drive us to the convention patiently waited, Bob Bloch and I sat on a bench in the Dayton airport and got acquainted. By the time Peg was finished, some forty-five minutes later, Bob and I had discovered we knew quite a lot about each other and each other's work.

And I had found a warm, witty, wonderful friend with whom I never lost touch thereafter. From cherishing the man's work, I came to love and admire the man himself.

His work? Ah, now, there's something to talk about. Pick up any story Robert Bloch has written and you'll discover certain qualities about it that, especially today, make a deep and lasting impression. First, from the opening line a Bloch tale will hold your attention and keep you reading. Second, when you've finished it, you won't be asking yourself what it was all about and why it was ever published in the first place. Third, it will be a welcome relief from some of the gimmickry, garbage language, and deliberate obscurity that is so often being published in today's magazines and books. Bob Bloch belonged to the old school of writers who believed language was invented as a means of communication. Too many writers today work under the mistaken belief that a story should be some sort of contest between writer and reader. (Of course, the obscurity may be unintentional. Sometimes, obviously, the writer just doesn't do his job well enough to be understood.)

Robert Bloch did the job, always. He had no need of gimmicks, nor did he use garbage language to grab the reader's attention. He was never obscure.

My favorite Bob Bloch story? Oh, Lord, there are so many. Ever so many. Some, like "Yours Truly, Jack the Ripper," have been reprinted time and time again. So let me go to one of the less well known tales that I always enjoy rereading. I refer to a little gem published first in the March 1947 issue of *Weird Tales,* called "Sweets to the Sweet."

It's about an abused little girl, and, so far as I know, is one of the earliest tales ever written about child abuse. And it's about the making of a doll, as in voodoo. Having lived in Haiti for nearly five years, I know a little something about voodoo and have always groaned loudly on reading stories about sticking pins in dolls. But the ending of this little gem is so unexpected, so unpredictable, so—well, so *wonderfully satisfying,* that the story has become one of my all-time favorites.

Thank you, Bob Bloch, for writing it. And for all the other hours of reading pleasure you've given us. And for the even greater pleasure of having known you in person.

SWEETS TO THE SWEET

Irma didn't look like a witch.

She had small, regular features, a peaches-and-cream complexion, blue eyes, and fair, almost ash-blonde hair. Besides, she was only eight years old.

"Why does he tease her so?" sobbed Miss Pall. "That's where she got the idea in the first place—because he calls her a little witch."

Sam Steever bulked his paunch back into the squeaky swivel chair and folded his heavy hands in his lap. His fat lawyer's mask was immobile, but he was really quite distressed.

Women like Miss Pall should never sob. Their glasses wiggle, their thin noses twitch, their creasy eyelids redden, and their stringy hair becomes disarrayed.

"Please, control yourself," coaxed Sam Steever. "Perhaps if we could just talk this whole thing over sensibly—"

"I don't care!" Miss Pall sniffled. "I'm not going back there again. I can't stand it. There's nothing I can do, anyway. The man is your brother and she's your brother's child. It's not my responsibility. I've tried—"

"Of course you've tried." Sam Steever smiled benignly, as if Miss Pall were foreman of a jury. "I quite understand. But I still don't see why you are so upset, dear lady."

Miss Pall removed her spectacles and dabbed at her eyes with a floral-print handkerchief. Then she deposited the soggy ball in her purse, snapped the catch, replaced her spectacles, and sat up straight.

"Very well, Mr. Steever," she said. "I shall do my best to acquaint you with my reasons for quitting your brother's employ."

She suppressed a tardy sniff.

"I came to John Steever two years ago in response to an advertisement for a housekeeper, as you know. When I found that I was to be governess to a motherless six-year-old child, I was at first distressed. I know nothing of the care of children."

"John had a nurse the first six years," Sam Steever nodded. "You know Irma's mother died in childbirth."

"I am aware of that," said Miss Pall, primly. "Naturally, one's heart goes out to a lonely, neglected little girl. And she was so terribly lonely, Mr. Steever—if you could have seen her, moping around in the corners of that big, ugly old house—"

"I have seen her," said Sam Steever, hastily, hoping to forestall another outburst. "And I know what you've done for Irma. My brother is inclined to be thoughtless, even a bit selfish at times. He doesn't understand."

"He's cruel," declared Miss Pall, suddenly vehement. "Cruel and wicked. Even if he is your brother, I say he's no fit father for any child. When I came there, her little arms were black and blue from beatings. He used to take a belt—"

"I know. Sometimes, I think John never recovered from the shock of Mrs. Steever's death. That's why I was so pleased when you came, dear lady. I thought you might help the situation."

"I tried," Miss Pall whimpered. "You know I tried. I never raised a hand to that child in two years, though many's the time your brother has told me to punish her. 'Give the little witch a beating' he used to say. 'That's all she needs—a good thrashing.' And then she'd hide behind my back and whisper to me to protect her. But she wouldn't cry, Mr. Steever. Do you know, I've never seen her cry."

Sam Steever felt vaguely irritated and a bit bored. He wished the old hen would get on with it. So he smiled and oozed treacle. "But just what is your problem, dear lady?"

"Everything was all right when I came there. We got along just splendidly. I started to teach Irma to read—and was surprised to find that she had already mastered reading. Your brother disclaimed having taught her, but she spent hours curled up on the sofa with a book. 'Just like her,' he used to say. 'Unnatural little witch. Doesn't play with the other children. Little witch.' That's the way he kept talking. Mr, Steever. As if she were some sort of—I don't know what. And she so sweet and quiet and pretty!

"Is it any wonder she read? I used to be that way myself when I was a girl, because—but never mind.

"Still, it was a shock that day I found her looking through the Encyclopedia Britannica. 'What are you reading, Irma?' I asked. She showed me. It was the article on Witchcraft.

"You see what morbid thoughts your brother has inculcated in her poor little head?

"I did my best. I went out and bought her some toys—she had absolutely nothing, you know; not even a doll. She didn't even know how to *play!* I tried to get her interested in some of the other little girls in the neighborhood, but it was no use. They didn't understand her and she didn't understand them. There were scenes. Children can be cruel, thoughtless. And her father wouldn't let her go to public school. I was to teach her—

"Then I brought her the modelling clay. She liked that. She would spend hours just making faces with clay. For a child of six Irma displayed real talent.

"We made little dolls together, and I sewed clothes for them. That first year was a happy one, Mr. Steever. Particularly during those months when your brother was away in South America. But this year, when he came back—oh, I can't bear to talk about it!"

"Please," said Sam Steever. "You must understand. John is not a happy man. The loss of his wife, the decline of his import trade, and his drinking—but you know all that."

"All I know is that he hates Irma," snapped Miss Pall, suddenly. "He hates her. He wants her to be bad, so he can whip her. 'If you don't discipline the little witch, I shall,' he always says. And then he takes her upstairs and thrashes her with his belt—you must do something, Mr. Steever, or I'll go to the authorities myself."

The crazy old biddy would at that, Sam Steever thought. Remedy—more treacle. "But about Irma," he persisted.

"She's changed, too. Ever since her father returned this year. She won't play with me any more, hardly looks at me. It is as though I failed her, Mr. Steever, in not protecting her from that man. Besides—she thinks she's a witch."

Crazy. Stark, staring crazy. Sam Steever creaked upright in his chair.

"Oh you needn't look at me like that, Mr. Steever. She'll tell you so herself—if you ever visited the house!"

He caught the reproach in her voice and assuaged it with a deprecating nod.

"She told me all right, if her father wants her to be a witch she'll be a witch. And she won't play with me, or anyone else, because witches don't play. Last Halloween she wanted me to give her a broomstick. Oh, it would be funny if it weren't so tragic. That child is losing her sanity.

"Just a few weeks ago I thought she'd changed. That's when she asked me to take her to church one Sunday. 'I want to see the baptism,' she said. Imagine that—an eight-year-old interested in baptism! Reading too much, that's what does it.

"Well, we went to church and she was as sweet as can be, wearing her new blue dress and holding my hand. I was proud of her, Mr. Steever, really proud.

"But after that, she went right back into her shell. Reading around the house, running through the yard at twilight and talking to herself.

"Perhaps it's because your brother wouldn't bring her a kitten. She was pestering him for a black cat, and he asked why, and she said, 'Because witches always have black cats.' Then he took her upstairs.

"I can't stop him, you know. He beat her again the night the power failed and we couldn't find the candles. He said she'd stolen them. Imagine that—accusing an eight-year-old child of stealing candles!

"That was the beginning of the end. Then today, when he found his hairbrush missing—"

"You say he beat her with his hairbrush?"

"Yes. She admitted having stolen it. Said she wanted it for her doll."

"But didn't you say she has no dolls?"

"She made one. At least I think she did. I've never seen it—she won't show us anything any more; won't talk to us at table, just impossible to handle her.

"But this doll she made—it's a small one, I know, because at times she carries it tucked under her arm. She talks to it and pets it, but she won't show it to me or to him. He asked her about the hairbrush and she said she took it for the doll.

"Your brother flew into a terrible rage—he'd been drinking in his room again all morning, oh don't think I don't know it!—and she just smiled and said he could have it now. She went over to her bureau and handed it to him. She hadn't harmed it in the least; his hair was still in it, I noticed.

"But he snatched it up, and then he started to strike her about the shoulders with it, and he twisted her arm and then he—"

Miss Pall huddled in her chair and summoned great racking sobs from her thin chest.

Sam Steever patted her shoulder, fussing about her like an elephant over a wounded canary.

"That's all, Mr. Steever. I came right to you. I'm not even going back to that house to get my things. I can't stand any more—the way he beat her—and the way she didn't cry, just giggled and giggled and giggled—sometimes I think she is a witch—that he made her into a witch—"

Sam Steever picked up the phone. The ringing had broken the relief of silence after Miss Pall's hasty departure.

"Hello—that you, Sam?"

He recognized his brother's voice, somewhat the worse for drink.

"Yes, John."

"I suppose the old bat came running straight to you to shoot her mouth off."

"If you mean Miss Pall, I've seen her, yes."

"Pay no attention. I can explain everything."

"Do you want me to stop in? I haven't paid you a visit in months."

"Well—not right now. Got an appointment with the doctor this evening."

"Something wrong?"

"Pain in my arm. Rheumatism or something. Getting a little diathermy. But I'll call you tomorrow and we'll straighten this whole mess out."

"Right."

But John Steever did not call the next day. Along about supper time, Sam called him.

Surprisingly enough, Irma answered the phone. Her thin, squeaky little voice sounded faintly in Sam's ears.

"Daddy's upstairs sleeping. He's been sick."

"Well don't disturb him. What is it—his arm?"

"His back, now. He has to go to the doctor again in a little while."

"Tell him I'll call tomorrow, then. Uh—everything all right, Irma? I mean, don't you miss Miss Pall?"

"No. I'm glad she went away. She's stupid."

"Oh. Yes. I see. But you phone me if you want anything. And I hope your Daddy's better."

"Yes. So do I," said Irma, and then she began to giggle, and then she hung up.

There was no giggling the following afternoon when John Steever called Sam at the office. His voice was sober—with the sharp sobriety of pain.

"Sam—for God's sake, get over here. Something's happening to me!"

"What's the trouble?"

"The pain—it's killing me! I've got to see you, quickly."

"There's a client in the office, but I'll get rid of him. Say, wait a minute. Why don't you call the doctor?"

"That quack can't help me. He gave me diathermy for my arm and yesterday he did the same thing for my back."

"Didn't it help?"

"The pain went away, yes. But it's back now. I feel—like I was being crushed. Squeezed, here in the chest. I can't breathe."

"Sounds like pleurisy. Why don't you call him?"

"It isn't pleurisy. He examined me. Said I was sound as a dollar. No, there's nothing organically wrong. And I couldn't tell him the real cause."

"Real cause?"

"Yes. The pins. The pin that little fiend is sticking into the doll she made. Into the arm, the back. And now heaven only knows how she's causing *this*."

"John, you mustn't—"

"Oh what's the use of talking? I can't move off the bed here. She has me now. I can't go down and stop her, get hold of the doll. And nobody else would believe it. But it's the doll all right, the one she made with the candle-wax and the hair from my brush. Oh—it hurts to talk—that cursed little witch! Hurry, Sam. Promise me you'll do something—anything—get that doll from her—get that doll—"

Half an hour later, at four-thirty, Sam Steever entered his brother's house.

Irma opened the door.

It gave Sam a shock to see her standing there, smiling and unperturbed, pale blonde hair brushed immaculately back from the rosy oval of her face. She looked just like a little doll. A little doll—

"Hello, Uncle Sam."

"Hello, Irma. Your Daddy called me, did he tell you? He said he wasn't feeling well—"

"I know. But he's all right now. He's sleeping."

Something happened to Sam Steever; a drop of ice-water trickled down his spine.

"Sleeping?" he croaked. "Upstairs?"

Before she opened her mouth to answer he was bounding up the steps to the second floor, striding down the hall to John's bedroom.

John lay on the bed. He was asleep, and only asleep. Sam Steever noted the regular rise and fall of his chest as he breathed. His face was calm, relaxed.

Then the drop of ice-water evaporated, and Sam could afford to smile and murmur "Nonsense" under his breath as he turned away.

As he went downstairs he hastily improvised plans. A six-month vacation for his brother; avoid calling it a "cure." An orphanage for Irma; give her a chance to get away from this morbid old house, all those books . . .

He paused halfway down the stairs. Peering over the banister through the twilight he saw Irma on the sofa, cuddled up like a little white ball. She was talking to something she cradled in her arms, rocking it to and fro.

Then there was a doll, after all.

Sam Steever tiptoed very quietly down the stairs and walked over to Irma. "Hello," he said.

She jumped. Both arms rose to cover completely whatever it was she had been fondling. She squeezed it tightly.

Sam Steever thought of a doll being squeezed across the chest—

Irma stared up at him, her face a mask of innocence. In the half-light her face did resemble a mask. The mask of a little girl, covering—what?

"Daddy's better now, isn't he?" lisped Irma.

"Yes, much better."

"I knew he would be."

"But I'm afraid he's going to have to go away for a rest. A long rest."

A smile filtered through the mask. "Good," said Irma.

"Of course," Sam went on, "you couldn't stay here all alone. I was wondering—maybe we could send you off to school, or to some kind of a home—"

Irma giggled. "Oh, you needn't worry about me," she said. She shifted about on the sofa as Sam sat down, then sprang up quickly as he came close to her.

Her arms shifted with the movement, and Sam Steever saw a pair of tiny legs dangling down below her elbow. There were trousers on the legs, and little bits of leather for shoes.

"What's that you have, Irma?" he asked. "Is it a doll?" Slowly, he extended his pudgy hand.

She pulled back.

"You can't see it," she said.

"But I want to. Miss Pall said you made such lovely ones."

"Miss Pall is stupid. So are you. Go away."

"Please, Irma. Let me see it."

But even as he spoke, Sam Steever was staring at the top of the doll, momentarily revealed when she backed away. It was a head all right, with wisps of hair over a white face. Dusk dimmed the features, but Sam recognized the eyes, the nose, the chin—

He could keep up the pretense no longer.

"Give me that doll, Irma!" he snapped. "I know what it is. I know *who* it is—"

For an instant, the mask slipped from Irma's face, and Sam Steever stared into naked fear.

She knew. She knew he knew.

Then, just as quickly, the mask was replaced.

Irma was only a sweet, spoiled, stubborn little girl as she shook her head merrily and smiled with impish mischief in her eyes.

"Oh Uncle Sam," she giggled. "You're so silly! Why, this isn't a *real* doll."

"What is it, then?" he muttered.

Irma giggled once more, raising the figure as she spoke. "Why, it's only— candy!" Irma said.

"Candy?"

Irma nodded. Then, very swiftly, she slipped the tiny head of the image into her mouth.

And bit it off.

There was a single piercing scream from upstairs.

As Sam Steever turned and ran up the steps, little Irma, still gravely munching, skipped out of the front door and into the night beyond.

ON ROBERT BLOCH

PHILIP KLASS
(WILLIAM TENN)

Robert Bloch's path and mine crossed several times, although I actually met him on only two occasions. To begin with, of course, he was a many-times-published professional way back when I was just an aspiring and perspiring beginner.

And I do mean perspiring! I would read and reread his stories, analyze and reanalyze them exhaustively, searching for the wonderful secret that made editors select and buy them. What did he do that I should do, just how did he take ideas that were so very similar to ideas that I had had and somehow transmute them into full narrative flower?

His publication in Street & Smith's *Unknown* particularly interested me. This most remarkable fantasy magazine, which John W. Campbell edited as a sister magazine to *Astounding* (then, in the 1940s, entering upon its Golden Age), was where I most wanted a piece of mine to achieve print.

Robert Bloch's stories in *Weird Tales* I could appreciate—but publication in *Unknown* was, so far as I was concerned then, on another level entirely. An appearance in *Unknown* was for me a sort of pulp-magazine version of some Nobel Prize for Fantasy.

Later, at the end of World War II, when I had become a professional myself, my good friend and very first agent was another *Unknown* writer, Theodore Sturgeon. Ted had been following Bloch's work for years and had read some of his stories that had seen first publication only in the fan magazines. One or two of them he had read and reread so often that he knew them almost by heart. He could recite them damn close to verbatim.

I remember being particularly impressed at the time by a Sturgeonian recitation of a piece of Bloch juvenilia entitled "The Laughter of a Ghoul." The tale had appeared originally in a fan magazine, and described a child-birth in which the newborn infant set itself to murder its own mother.

Years later, as I typed the last words in my science fiction story "Wednesday's Child," I realized that I was still being influenced by Bloch: the ending of "Wednesday's Child" had been precipitated in my mind by the ending of "The Laughter of a Ghoul." And when I was putting together my 1953 anthology, *Children of Wonder*, I found myself rereading one of my favorite selections, Ray Bradbury's "The Small Assassin," and suddenly becoming aware of how much the young Bradbury too had been enormously influenced by that early Bloch story.

I once described science fiction and science fantasy as a kind of literary jazz, where each writer listens closely to a predecessor blowing riffs and then works out his own variations on the themes he has heard. In modern fantasy especially, Robert Bloch was a kind of intellectual Bunk Johnson or King Oliver. He showed the very strange places into which the trumpet solos could go. He was a leader and very noticeably one of a kind.

He was certainly hard to classify. Where do you place a writer, I wondered—as I encountered more and more of his achievements and began to meet him personally—who had his range stylistically and psychologically? Upon what literary shelf—top, bottom, or middle—do you place his work?

Take, for example, a hilarious musing like "The Seven Ages of Fan," which doubled me up when I encountered it in the back pages of a *Thrilling Wonder* or *Startling Stories* of 1948 or 1949. Try to relate that to a piece as pointedly grisly as the classic "Yours Truly, Jack the Ripper," from *Weird Tales* of July 1943. Or consider *Psycho,* Bloch's smash-hit novel of 1959, with all of its abnormal psychology horrifics, and then look at the delicacy and overflowing tenderness of a story like "The Movie People," which first appeared in *Fantasy and Science Fiction* for October 1969.

They hardly seem to be capable of coming from the same personality.

That personality! It could show up on the platform of a science fiction convention and deliver a talk in which pun was piled on outrageous pun, in which imitations of well-known actors and parodies of fellow writers left his audience widely grinning or helplessly gasping—or it could conduct an intense private conversation in which the issue was the fundamental problem of man's relationship with man. But his preoccupation with ethics was just the outer edge of his spiritual side.

Robert Bloch was the only writer I ever met, after I'd read the works of Mark Twain, who seemed also to manage both a jocular and a deeply committed relationship with God.

(And to his credit let it be added that, like Twain, he was warmly tolerant of Satan as well!)

Finally and above all, Robert Bloch was a gentleman. I, Philip Klass (William Tenn), have a special reason to say that.

Let me tell you why. But be patient: you'll have to bear with me for a bit of history.

After Anthony Boucher retired from *The Magazine of Fantasy and Science Fiction* in early 1958, Cyril Kornbluth was invited to substitute for him until Bob Mills, the managing editor, could find his feet and operate alone. But there was a freak heavy snowstorm the day that Cyril was to show up at the magazine's office and begin his duties—and Cyril, who suffered from very high blood pressure, made the tragic mistake of trying to get at his car by shoveling his driveway in a frantic hurry. His death from the resulting heart attack (at the age of thirty-five!) was perhaps the greatest single loss science fiction experienced in that decade.

Mills and Joe Ferman asked me to come on board as consulting editor in Cyril's place. I took time off from my own work and served for three issues. I enjoyed the experience immensely.

One thing I didn't entirely enjoy, however, was emptying the inventory. Over the years, Boucher—and before Boucher alone, Boucher and McComas as coeditors—had bought a number of stories from name writers that, upon later consideration, did not seem to be good enough to be published as they stood. They had piled up in the inventory, in almost every case with a little sticker on the first page, signed by Tony Boucher or Francis McComas, saying something like "the beginning has to be cleared up," or "needs a better ending."

My primary job as consulting editor, I was told, was to figure some way of getting those stories out of inventory and into the magazine. I did what I could, with a deletion here or a buffing there, but almost every time I asked the writers to make necessary improvements themselves, they told me that the story was long ago sold and was therefore yesterday's news. As professionals, they were not interested in rewriting stories that had been completed and bought five or six years before. And, as a professional myself, I couldn't quite argue with them.

A story by Bloch was one of the most agonizing problems I faced. It was a delightful piece—I loved his picture of a trainload of "the drunks and the sinners, the gambling men and the grifters, the big-time spenders, the skirt-chasers, and all the jolly crew" rumbling down to Hell, but I couldn't see it as publishable in its present form. I agreed with the note Tony had paper-clipped to the piece: "It just can't go without a better ending. A very fine story, but somehow it doesn't generate a conclusion."

I got in touch with Bloch—hopelessly, miserably, because, after all, the story had been purchased a couple of years ago and was probably ice-cold in his mind by now—and asked him to do a fairly nonprofessional thing: take back the piece and rewrite it, somehow provide it with a better ending. By that time, I had had enough experience asking writers to do that sort of thing, and I knew exactly what to expect.

But I forgot I was dealing with Bob Bloch. He was a professional, yes, but first and foremost he was an artist. "Give me some suggestions," he said. "Point out a direction or two. I'll be happy to rewrite it. I want to make it *good*."

He took one of my several suggestions and wonderfully expanded it—turned a little seed, so to speak, into a whole bouquet of flowers—and returned it to me as almost a new story with a magnificent new ending.

But that wasn't all.

When "That Hell-Bound Train" won a Hugo in 1959, Bloch went out of his way, in public and private, to thank me for my contribution. It did me no good to reiterate that that contribution had been most minor, one of a group of suggestions, of a hand-waving miscellany almost. Bob Bloch drowned out my very real, very truthful protests with his thanks.

In the course of a lifetime spent in publishing, I've helped a lot of other writers an awful lot more, but I've rarely had the appreciation that Bloch showed me for what was, after all, only my job, and only the tiniest smidgin of assistance.

He was a gentleman, a very talented gentleman, and a monument of decency.

THAT HELL-BOUND TRAIN

𝄢 **When Martin was a little boy, his Daddy was a Railroad** Man. He never rode the high iron, but he walked the tracks for the *CB&Q* and he was proud of his job. And when he got drunk (which was every night) he sang this old song about *That Hell-Bound Train.*

Martin didn't quite remember any of the words, but he couldn't forget the way his Daddy sang them out. And when Daddy made the mistake of getting drunk in the afternoon and got squeezed between a Pennsy tank-car and an *AT&SF* gondola, Martin sort of wondered why the Brotherhood didn't sing the song at his funeral.

After that, things didn't go so good for Martin, but somehow he always recalled Daddy's song. When Mom up and ran off with a traveling salesman from Keokuk (Daddy must have turned over in his grave, knowing she'd done such a thing, and with a *passenger,* too!) Martin hummed the tune to himself every night in the Orphan Home. And after Martin himself ran away, he used to whistle the song at night in the jungles, after the other bindlestiffs were asleep.

Martin was on the road for four-five years before he realized he wasn't getting anyplace. Of course he'd tried his hand at a lot of things—picking fruit in Oregon, washing dishes in a Montana hash-house—but he just wasn't cut out for seasonal labor or pearl-diving, either. Then he graduated to stealing hub-caps in Denver, and for a while he did pretty well with tires in Oklahoma City, but by the time he'd put in six months on the chain-gang down in Alabama he knew he had no future drifting around this way on his own.

So he tried to get on the railroad like his Daddy had, but they told him times were bad; and between the truckers and the airlines and those fancy new fintails General Motors was making, it looked as if the days of the highballers were just about over.

But Martin couldn't keep away from the railroads. Wherever he traveled, he rode the rods; he'd rather hop a freight heading north in sub-zero weather than lift his thumb to hitch a ride with a Cadillac headed for Florida. Because Martin was loyal to the memory of his Daddy, and he wanted to be as much like him as possible, come what may. Of course, he couldn't get drunk every night, but whenever he did manage to get hold of a can of Sterno, he'd sit there under a nice warm culvert and think about the old days.

Often as not, he'd hum the song about *That Hell-Bound Train*. That was the train the drunks and the sinners rode; the gambling men and the grifters, the big-time spenders, the skirt-chasers, and all the jolly crew. It would be fun to take a trip in such good company, but Martin didn't like to think of what happened when that train finally pulled into the Depot Way Down Yonder. He didn't figure on spending eternity stoking boilers in Hell, without even a Company Union to protect him. Still, it would be a lovely ride. If there *was* such a thing as a Hell-Bound Train. Which, of course, there wasn't.

At least Martin didn't *think* there was, until that evening when he found himself walking the tracks heading south, just outside of Appleton Junction. The night was cold and dark, the way November nights are in the Fox River Valley, and he knew he'd have to work his way down to New Orleans for the winter, or maybe even Texas. Somehow he didn't much feel like going, even though he'd heard tell that a lot of those Texas automobiles had solid gold hub-caps.

No sir, he just wasn't cut out for petty larceny. It was worse than a sin—it was unprofitable, too. Bad enough to do the Devil's work, but then to get such miserable pay on top of it! Maybe he'd better let the Salvation Army convert him.

Martin trudged along, humming Daddy's song, waiting for a rattler to pull out of the Junction behind him. He'd have to catch it—there was nothing else for him to do.

Too bad there wasn't a chance to make a better deal for himself, somewhere. Might as well be a rich sinner as a poor sinner. Besides, he had a notion that he could strike a pretty shrewd bargain. He'd thought about it a lot, these past few years, particularly when the Sterno was working. Then his ideas would come on strong, and he could figure a way to rig the setup. But that was all nonsense, of course. He might as well join the gospel-shouters and turn into a working-stiff like all the rest of the world. No use dreaming dreams; a song was only a song and there was no Hell-Bound Train.

There was only *this* train, rumbling out of the night, roaring towards him along the track from the south.

Martin peered ahead, but his eyes couldn't match his ears, and so far all he could recognize was the sound. It *was* a train, though; he felt the steel shudder and sing beneath his feet.

And yet, how could it be? The next station south was Neenah-Menasha, and there was nothing due out of there for hours.

The clouds were thick overhead, and the field-mists roll like a cold fog in a November midnight. Even so, Martin should have been able to see the headlights as the train rushed on. But there were no lights.

There was only the whistle, screaming out of the black throat of the night. Martin could recognize the equipment of just about any locomotive ever built, but he'd never heard a whistle that sounded like this one. It wasn't signalling; it was screaming like a lost soul.

He stepped to one side, for the train was almost on top of him now, and suddenly there it was, looming along the tracks and grinding to a stop in less time than he'd ever believed possible. The wheels hadn't been oiled, because they screamed too, screamed like the damned. But the train slid to a halt and the screams died away into a series of low, groaning sounds, and Martin looked up and saw that this was a passenger train. It was big and black, without a single light shining in the engine cab or any of the long string of cars, and Martin couldn't read any lettering on the sides, but he was pretty sure this train didn't belong on the Northwestern Road.

He was even more sure when he saw the man clamber down out of the forward car. There was something wrong about the way he walked, as though one of his feet dragged. And there was something even more disturbing about the lantern he carried, and what he did with it. The lantern was dark, and when the man alighted, he held it up to his mouth and blew. Instantly the lantern glowed redly. You don't have to be a member of the Railway Brotherhood to know that this is a mighty peculiar way of lighting a lantern.

As the figure approached, Martin recognized the conductor's cap perched on his head, and this made him feel a little better for a moment—until he noticed that it was worn a bit too high, as though there might be something sticking up on the forehead underneath it.

Still, Martin knew his manners, and when the man smiled at him, he said, "Good evening, Mr. Conductor."

"Good evening, Martin."

"How did you know my name?"

The man shrugged. "How did you know I was the Conductor?"

"You *are,* aren't you?"

"To you, yes. Although other people, in other walks of life, may recognize me in different roles. For instance, you ought to see what I look like to the folks out in Hollywood." The man grinned. "I travel a great deal," he explained.

"What brings you here?" Martin asked.

"Why, you ought to know the answer to that, Martin. I came because you needed me."

"I did?"

"Don't play the innocent. Ordinarily, I seldom bother with single individuals any more. The way the world is going. I can expect to carry a full load of passengers without soliciting business. Your name has been down on the list for several years already—I reserved a seat for you as a matter of course. But then, tonight, I suddenly realized you were backsliding. Thinking of joining the Salvation Army, weren't you?"

"Well—" Martin hesitated.

"Don't be ashamed. To err is human, as somebody-or-other once said. *Reader's Digest,* wasn't it? Never mind. The point is, I felt you needed me. So I switched over and came your way."

"What for?"

"Why, to offer you a ride, of course. Isn't it better to travel comfortably by train than to march along the cold streets behind a Salvation Army band? Hard on the feet, they tell me, and even harder on the ear-drums."

"I'm not sure I'd care to ride your train, sir," Martin said. "Considering where I'm likely to end up."

"Ah, yes. The old argument." The Conductor sighed. "I suppose you'd prefer some sort of bargain, is that it?"

"Exactly," Martin answered.

"Well, I'm afraid I'm all through with that sort of thing. As I mentioned before, times have changed. There's no shortage of prospective passengers any more. Why should I offer you any special inducements?"

"You must want me, or else you wouldn't have bothered to go out of your way to find me."

The Conductor sighed again. "There you have a point. Pride was always my besetting weakness, I admit. And somehow I'd hate to lose you to the competition, after thinking of you as my own all these years." He hesitated. "Yes, I'm prepared to deal with you on your own terms, if you insist."

"The terms?" Martin asked.

"Standard proposition. Anything you want."

"Ah," said Martin.

"But I warn you in advance, there'll be no tricks. I'll grant you any wish you can name—but in return, you must promise to ride the train when the time comes."

"Suppose it never comes?"

"It will."

"Suppose I've got the kind of a wish that will keep me off forever?"

"There is no such wish."

"Don't be too sure."

"Let me worry about that," the Conductor told him. "No matter what you have in mind, I warn you that I'll collect in the end. And there'll be none of this last-minute hocus-pocus, either. No last-hour repentances, no blonde *frauleins* or fancy lawyers showing up to get you off. I offer a clean deal. That is to say, you'll get what you want, and I'll get what I want."

"I've heard you trick people. They say you're worse than a used-car salesman."

"Now wait a minute—"

"I apologize," Martin said, hastily. "But it *is* supposed to be a fact that you can't be trusted."

"I admit it. On the other hand, you seem to think you have found a way out."

"A sure-fire proposition."

"Sure-fire? Very funny!" The man began to chuckle, then halted. "But we waste valuable time, Martin. Let's get down to cases. What do you want from me?"

"A single wish."

"Name it and I shall grant it."

"Anything, you said?"

"Anything at all."

"Very well, then." Martin took a deep breath. "I want to be able to stop Time."

"Right now?"

"No. Not yet. And not for everybody. I realize that would be impossible, of course. But I want to be able to stop Time for myself. Just once, in the future. Whenever I get to a point where I know I'm happy and contented, that's where I'd like to stop. So I can just keep on being happy forever."

"That's quite a proposition," the Conductor mused. "I've got to admit I've never heard anything just like it before—and believe me, I've listened to some lulus in my day." He grinned at Martin. "You've really been thinking about this, haven't you?"

"For years," Martin admitted. Then he coughed. "Well, what do you say?"

"It's not impossible, in terms of your own *subjective* time-sense," the Conductor murmured. "Yes, I think it could be arranged."

"But I mean *really* to stop. Not for me just to *imagine* it."

"I understand. And it can be done."

"Then you'll agree?"

"Why not? I promised you, didn't I? Give me your hand."

Martin hesitated. "Will it hurt very much? I mean, I don't like the sight of blood, and—"

"Nonsense! You've been listening to a lot of poppycock. We already have made our bargain, my boy. No need for a lot of childish rigamarole. I merely intend to put something into your hand. The ways and means of fulfilling your wish. After all, there's no telling at just what moment you may decide to exercise the agreement, and I can't drop everything and come running. So it's better if you can regulate matters for yourself."

"You're going to give me a Time-stopper?"

"That's the general idea. As soon as I can decide what would be practical." The Conductor hesitated. "Ah, the very thing! Here, take my watch."

He pulled it out of his vest-pocket; a railroad watch in a silver case. He opened the back and made a delicate adjustment; Martin tried to see just exactly what he was doing, but the fingers moved in a blinding blur.

"There we are," the Conductor smiled. "It's all set, now. When you finally decide where you'd like to call a halt, merely turn the stem in reverse and unwind the watch until it stops. When it stops, Time stops, for you. Simple enough?"

"Sure thing."

"Then here, take it." And the Conductor dropped the watch into Martin's hand.

The young man closed his fingers tightly around the case. "That's all there is to it, eh?"

"Absolutely. But remember—you can stop the watch only once. So you'd better make sure that you're satisfied with the moment you choose to prolong. I caution you in all fairness; make very certain of your choice."

"I will," Martin grinned. "And since you've been so fair about it, I'll be fair, too. There's one thing you seem to have forgotten. It doesn't really matter *what* moment I choose. Because once I stop Time for myself, that means I stay where I am forever, I'll never have to get any older. And if I don't get any older, I'll never die. And if I never die, then I'll never have to take a ride on your train."

The Conductor turned away. His shoulders shook convulsively, and he may have been crying. "And you said *I* was worse than a used-car salesman," he gasped, in a strangled voice.

Then he wandered off into the fog, and the train-whistle gave an impatient shriek, and all at once it was moving swiftly down the track, rumbling out of sight in the darkness.

Martin stood there, blinking down at the silver watch in his hand. If it wasn't that he could actually see it and feel it there, and if he couldn't smell that peculiar odor, he might have thought he'd imagined the whole thing from start to finish—train, Conductor, bargain, and all.

But he had the watch, and he could recognize the scent left by the train as it departed, even though there aren't many locomotives around that use sulphur and brimstone as fuel.

And he had no doubts about his bargain. Better still, he had no doubts as to the advantages of the pact he'd made. That's what came of thinking things through to a logical conclusion. Some fools would have settled for wealth, or power, or Kim Novak. Daddy might have sold out for a fifth of whiskey.

Martin knew that he'd made a better deal. Better? It was foolproof. All he needed to do now was choose his moment. And when the right time came, it was his—forever.

He put the watch in his pocket and started back down the railroad track. He hadn't really had a destination in mind before, but he did now. He was going to find a moment of happiness . . .

Now young Martin wasn't altogether a ninny. He realized perfectly well that happiness is a relative thing; there are conditions and degrees of contentment, and they vary with one's lot in life. As a hobo, he was often satisfied with a warm handout, a double-length bench in the park, or a can of Sterno made in 1957 (a vintage year). Many a time he had reached a state of momentary bliss through such simple agencies, but he was aware that there were better things. Martin determined to seek them out.

Within two days he was in the great city of Chicago. Quite naturally, he drifted over to West Madison Street, and there he took steps to elevate his role in life. He became a city bum, a panhandler, a moocher. Within a week he had risen to the point where happiness was a meal in a regular one-arm luncheon joint, a two-bit flop on a real army cot in a real flophouse, and a full fifth of muscatel.

There was a night, after enjoying all three of these luxuries to the full, when Martin was tempted to unwind his watch at the pinnacle of intoxication. Then he remembered the faces of the honest johns he'd braced for a handout today. Sure, they were squares, but they were prosperous. They wore good clothes, held good jobs, drove nice cars. And for them, happiness was even more ecstatic; they ate dinner in fine hotels, they slept on innerspring mattresses, they drank blended whiskey.

Squares or no, they had something there. Martin fingered his watch, put aside the temptation to hock it for another bottle of muscatel, and went to sleep determining to get himself a job and improve his happiness-quotient.

When he awoke he had a hangover, but the determination was still with him. It stayed long after the hangover disappeared, and before the month was out Martin found himself working for a general contractor over on the South Side, at one of the big rehabilitation projects. He hated the grind, but the pay was good, and pretty soon he got himself a one-room apartment out on Blue Island Avenue. He was accustomed to eating in decent restaurants now, and he bought himself a comfortable bed, and every Saturday night he went down to the corner tavern. It was all very pleasant, but—

The foreman liked his work and promised him a raise in a month. If he waited around, the raise would mean that he could afford a second-hand car. With a car, he could even start picking up a girl for a date now and then. Lots of the other fellows on the job did, and they seemed pretty happy.

So Martin kept on working, and the raise came through and the car came through and pretty soon a couple of girls came through.

The first time it happened, he wanted to unwind his watch immediately. Until he got to thinking about what some of the older men always said. There was a guy named Charlie, for example, who worked alongside him on the hoist. "When you're young and don't know the score, maybe you get a kick out of running around with those pigs. But after a while, you want something better. A nice girl of your own. That's the ticket."

Well, he might have something there. At least, Martin owed it to himself to find out. If he didn't like it better, he could always go back to what he had.

It was worth a try. Of course, nice girls don't grow on trees (if they did, a lot more men would become forest rangers) and almost six months went by before Martin met Lillian Gillis. By that time he'd had another promotion and was working inside, in the office. They made him go to night school to learn how to do simple bookkeeping, but it meant another fifteen bucks extra a week, and it was nicer working indoors.

And Lillian *was* a lot of fun. When she told him she'd marry him, Martin was almost sure that the time was now. Except that she was sort of—well, she was a *nice* girl, and she said they'd have to wait until they were married. Of course, Martin couldn't expect to marry her until he had a little more money saved up, and another raise would help, too.

That took a year. Martin was patient, because he knew it was going to be worth it. Every time he had any doubts, he took out his watch and looked at it. But he never showed it to Lillian, or anybody else. Most of the other men wore expensive wristwatches and the old silver railroad watch looked just a little cheap.

Martin smiled as he gazed at the stem. Just a few twists and he'd have something none of these other poor working slobs would ever have. Permanent satisfaction, with his blushing bride—

Only getting married turned out to be just the beginning. Sure, it was wonderful, but Lillian told him how much better things would be if they could move into a new place and fix it up. Martin wanted decent furniture, a TV set, a nice car.

So he started taking night courses and got a promotion to the front office. With the baby coming, he wanted to stick around and see his son arrive. And when it came, he realized he'd have to wait until it got a little older, started to walk and talk and develop a personality of its own.

About this time the company sent him out on the road as a trouble-shooter on some of those other jobs, and now he was eating at those good hotels, living high on the hog and the expense-account. More than once he was tempted to unwind his watch. This was the good life. And he realized it could be even better if he just didn't have to work. Sooner or later, if he could cut in on one of the company deals, he could make a pile and retire. Then everything would be ideal.

It happened, but it took time. Martin's son was going to high school before he really got up there into the chips. Martin got the feeling that it was now or never, because he wasn't exactly a kid any more.

But right about then he met Sherry Westcott, and she didn't seem to think he was middle-aged at all, in spite of the way he was losing hair and adding stomach. She taught him that a *toupee* could cover the bald spot and a cummerbund could cover the potgut. In fact, she taught him quite a number of things, and he so enjoyed learning that he actually took out his watch and prepared to unwind it.

Unfortunately, he chose the very moment that the private detectives broke down the door of the hotel room, and then there was a long stretch of time when Martin was so busy fighting the divorce action that he couldn't honestly say he was enjoying any given amount.

When he made the final settlement with Lil he was broke again, and Sherry didn't seem to think he was so young, after all. So he squared his shoulders and went back to work.

He made his pile, eventually, but it took longer this time, and there wasn't much chance to have fun along the way. The fancy dames in the fancy cocktail lounges didn't seem to interest him any more, and neither did the liquor. Besides, the Doc had warned him about that.

But there were other pleasures for a rich man to investigate. Travel, for instance—and not riding the rods from one hick burg to another, either. Martin went around the world *via* plane and luxury liner. For a while it seemed as though he would find his moment after all. Visiting the Taj Mahal by moonlight, the moon's radiance was reflected from the back of the battered old watch-case, and Martin got ready to unwind it. Nobody else was there to watch him—

And that's why he hesitated. Sure, this was an enjoyable moment, but he was alone. Lil and the kid were gone, Sherry was gone, and somehow he'd never had time to make any friends. Maybe if he found a few congenial people, he'd have the ultimate happiness. That must be the answer—it wasn't just money or power or sex or seeing beautiful things. The real satisfaction lay in friendship.

So on the boat trip home, Martin tried to strike up a few acquaintances at the ship's bar. But all these people were so much younger, and Martin had nothing in common with them. Also, they wanted to dance and drink, and Martin wasn't in condition to appreciate such pastimes. Nevertheless, he tried.

Perhaps that's why he had the little accident the day before they docked in San Francisco. "Little accident" was the ship's doctor's way of describing it, but Martin noticed he looked very grave when he told him to stay in bed, and he'd called an ambulance to meet the liner at the dock and take the patient right to the hospital.

At the hospital, all the expensive treatment and expensive smiles and the expensive words didn't fool Martin any. He was an old man with a bad heart, and they thought he was going to die.

But he could fool them. He still had the watch. He found it in his coat when he put on his clothes and sneaked out of the hospital before dawn.

He didn't have to die. He could cheat death with a single gesture—and he intended to do it as a free man, out there under a free sky.

That was the real secret of happiness. He understood it now. Not even friendship meant as much as freedom. This was the best thing of all—to be free of friends or family or the furies of the flesh.

Martin walked slowly beside the embrankment under the night sky. Come to think of it, he was just about back where he'd started, so many years ago. But the moment was good, good enough to prolong forever. Once a bum, always a bum.

He smiled as he thought about it, and then the smile twisted sharply and suddenly, like the pain twisting sharply and suddenly in his chest. The world began to spin and he fell down on the side of the embankment.

He couldn't see very well, but he was still conscious, and he knew what had happened. Another stroke, and a bad one. Maybe this was it. Except that he wouldn't be a fool any longer. He wouldn't wait to see what was still around the corner.

Right now was his chance to use his power and save his life. And he was going to do it. He could still move, nothing could stop him.

He groped in his pocket and pulled out the old silver watch, fumbling with the stem. A few twists and he'd cheat death, he'd never have to ride that Hell-Bound Train. He could go on forever.

Forever.

Martin had never really considered the word before. To go on forever—but *how?* Did he want to go on forever, like this; a sick old man, lying helplessly here in the grass?

No. He couldn't do it. He wouldn't do it. And suddenly he wanted very much to cry, because he knew that somewhere along the line he'd outsmarted himself. And now it was too late. His eyes dimmed, there was this roaring in his ears . . .

He recognized the roaring, of course, and he wasn't at all surprised to see the train come rushing out of the fog up there on the embankment. He wasn't surprised when it stopped, either, or when the Conductor climbed off and walked slowly towards him.

The Conductor hadn't changed a bit. Even his grin was still the same.

"Hello, Martin," he said. "All aboard."

"I know," Martin whispered. "But you'll have to carry me. I can't walk. I'm not even really talking any more, am I?"

"Yes you are," the Conductor said. "I can hear you fine. And you can walk, too." He leaned down and placed his hand on Martin's chest. There was a moment of icy numbness, and then, sure enough, Martin could walk after all.

He got up and followed the Conductor along the slope, moving to the side of the train.

"In here?" he asked.

"No, the next car," the Conductor murmured. "I guess you're entitled to ride Pullman. After all, you're quite a successful man. You've tasted the joys of wealth and position and prestige. You've known the pleasures of marriage and fatherhood. You've sampled the delights of dining and drinking and debauchery, too, and you travelled high, wide and handsome. So let's not have any last-minute recriminations."

"All right," Martin sighed. "I guess I can't blame you for any mistakes. On the other hand, you can't take credit for what happened, either. I worked for everything I got. I did it all on my own. I didn't even need your watch."

"So you didn't," the Conductor said, smiling. "But would you mind giving it back to me now?"

"Need it for the next sucker, eh?" Martin muttered.

"Perhaps."

Something about the way he said it made Martin look up. He tried to see the Conductor's eyes, but the brim of his cap cast a shadow. So Martin looked down at the watch instead, as if seeking an answer there.

"Tell me something," he said, softly. "If I give you the watch, what will you do with it?"

"Why, throw it into the ditch," the Conductor told him. "That's all I'll do with it." And he held out his hand.

"What if somebody comes along and finds it? And twists the stem backwards, and stops Time?"

"Nobody would do that," the Conductor murmured. "Even if they knew."

"You mean, it was all a trick? This is only an ordinary, cheap watch?"

"I didn't say that," whispered the Conductor. "I only said that no one has ever twisted the stem backwards. They've all been like you, Martin—looking ahead to find that perfect happiness. Waiting for the moment that never comes."

The Conductor held out his hand again.

Martin sighed and shook his head. "You cheated me after all."

"You cheated yourself, Martin. And now you're going to ride that Hell-Bound Train."

He pushed Martin up the steps and into the car ahead. As he entered, the train began to move and the whistle screamed. And Martin stood there in the swaying Pullman, gazing down the aisle at the other passengers. He could see them sitting there, and somehow it didn't seem strange at all.

Here they were; the drunks and the sinners, the gambling men and the grifters, the big-time spenders, the skirt-chasers, and all the jolly crew. They knew where they were going, of course, but they didn't seem to be particularly concerned at the moment. The blinds were drawn on the windows, yet it was light inside, and they were all sitting around and singing and passing the bottle and laughing it up, telling their jokes and bragging their brags, just the way Daddy used to sing about them in the old song.

"Mighty nice traveling companions," Martin said. "Why, I've never seen such a pleasant bunch of people. I mean, they seem to be really enjoying themselves!"

"Sorry," the Conductor told him. "I'm afraid things may not be quite so enjoyable, once we pull into that Depot Way Down Yonder."

For the third time, he held out his hand. "Now, before you sit down, if you'll just give me that watch. I mean, a bargain's a bargain—"

Martin smiled. "A bargain's a bargain," he echoed. "I agreed to ride your train if I could stop Time when I found the right moment of happiness. So, if you don't mind, I think I'll just make certain adjustments."

Very slowly, Martin twisted the silver watch-stem.

"No!" gasped the Conductor. "No!"

But the watch-stem turned.

"Do you realize what you've done?" the Conductor panted. "Now we'll never reach the Depot. We'll just go on riding, all of us, forever and ever!"

Martin grinned. "I know," he said. "But the fun is in the trip, not the destination. You taught me that. And I'm looking forward to a wonderful trip."

The Conductor groaned. "All right," he sighed, at last. "You got the best of me, after all. But when I think of spending eternity trapped here riding this train—"

"Cheer up!" Martin told him. "It won't be that bad. Looks like we have plenty to eat and drink. And after all, these are your kind of folks."

"But I'm the Conductor! Think of the endless work this means for me!"

"Don't let it worry you," Martin said. "Look, maybe I can even help. If you were to find me another one of those caps, now, and let me keep this watch—"

And that's the way it finally worked out. Wearing his cap and carrying his battered old silver watch, there's no happier person in or out of this world—now and forever—than Martin. Martin, the new Brakeman on That Hell-Bound Train.

DAVID J. SCHOW

One of the first topics Robert Bloch ever spoke about personally to me, as an audience of one, was dying. He did so while sunning on a poolside deck in Tucson, Arizona, in the wake of a convention, noting that the best and brightest among us still only have a set number of years, and that the clock is always ticking. It never stops. We do.

Prior to that sobering observation came others, over cocktails on a cool desert evening. Bob bought beer and lugged it over. He spoke of his love for and closeness to his wife, Elly, and his daughter, Sally; he always carried their photographs in his wallet. I admired his gentle patience with insensitive fans and their never-ending, too-repeated questions. Bob was always too gracious to let on, but he hated signing one shopping bag after another of books and such for a single person. He detested the notion that some so-called collector had paid more for an ancient, crumbling pulp magazine than Bob had been paid to write the story that *made* the damned thing a so-called collector's item in the first place.

When Bob declared a moratorium on the glut of "signed limited" editions that required his autograph hundreds of times per project, it was a reasoned response to another kind of insensitivity. But he relented, after about a year off, because it was also forever in his nature to be as accommodating as possible to the demands—however greedy or unthinking—of his formidable public.

Right now, in an evil backspin on phototropism, it is the very darkness of Bob Bloch's passing that has cued the drool reflex, magnetizing the remoras and necrophages who will slither forth to exploit the Dear Departed. By their ethical stench, crocodile tears, and inflated prices for collector's editions, you shall know them.

Ever since I first met Bob, I've been asked to write him up—for program books, encyclopedias, and appreciations. Now that he's dead, I'm still being asked to write him up . . . which may be as good a barometer as any of some kind of cheap immortality.

How long after you're gone will anyone care?

Bob died on the evening of Friday, September 23, 1994, from complications due to esophagal and liver cancer, after devoting six decades of his seventy-seven years on the planet to writing of *all* types—not merely "sci-fi," as *Variety* headlined its notice of his death.

Bob was so mordantly wry that he composed his *own* obituary notes for the fourth estate, once he knew he was dying. With him, an entire era of horror, suspense, and fantasy has passed into record. "I can't tell you who first came up with the term *psychological suspense,*" Bob wrote in 1979. "But I'm forever grateful to him." Likewise, anyone interested in present-day scary stuff has Bob Bloch to thank for the modern popular nomenclature for the form: *psychological horror.* This was his specialty, whether he was writing supernatural fantasy or the *conte cruel.* Hannibal Lecter could never have become Oscar bait without the precedent of Norman Bates, just as many people who earn their living making up scary stuff today could not call themselves professionals were it not for an early and telling exposure to what Gahan Wilson aptly termed "Blochian horrors."

Icon, mentor, friend, colleague . . . you should be fortunate enough to meet a person who functions as all these things in *your* life.

Bob collated his ruminations on his own imminent demise into an article published in *Omni* magazine, titled "The Other Side of the Bloch," as a sort of black valentine to friends and fans. He concluded this almost clinically detached sign-off by writing: ". . . you and I, somewhere or someplace, may meet again. Anyway, it's nice to think so.

"See you later.

"I hope."

"I am completely out of touch with the modern world," Bob once told me. "I've never been into a McDonald's, and I've never eaten a pizza. I have never touched a computer, not even to turn it on or off or sideways, and hopefully, I never will. I permitted such a device to invade my home—once—because I needed a secretary. I dictated to the secretary, the secretary dictated to the computer, the computer dictated to the printer, then I corrected the whole thing, and so in that way I was able to write four books in the time it would normally take me to write two. The minute I got those four books done, the secretary went, the printer went, and the computer went, and I restored the room to abnormal, and got back to my Olympia Standard typewriter, which I feel very comfortable with."

One advantage to being a writer of stature—if you can call it that—is that academic institutions are easily conned into storing your papers, drafts, correspondence and ephemera, all in the mistaken belief that this might lend students and seekers some unspecified future insight to the process of putting words on paper for a living. Bob was happy to ship off box after box of stuff, leaving more room for books . . . whereupon he divested himself of the majority of his books as well. Quite apart from most writers I've known, who are content to live the cliché of an existence choked to the rafters with books of all sizes and shapes stuffed between joists and piled red-line high, Bob expressed a very sane, though contrary sentiment: "I absolutely will not keep a book, unless I've read it at least twice."

Think about that for a minute. It certainly helped me to clean my shelves of a lot of garbage.

Then Bob died, and now I'm supposed to select a favorite story for a memorial chrestomathy of his short work.

The emotions, they do conflict.

For one thing, I admire certain values in Bob's short work, and quite a different set when it comes to his many novels. In the stories, what distinguishes this writer as confusable with no other is the set-up, the pay-off, and the snap in the tail—a black play on words, not so often a pun as a gruesome double entendre, such as *Louise was decorating the Christmas tree,* or, *Ronnie—what's the matter? Has the cat got your tongue—?*

Or, as in the case of my selection for this book . . . no. Can't be a spoiler just yet. You have to read it.

Several years ago I was contracted to script several dramatic pieces for a proposed legit stage revival of the *Théâtre du Grand Guignol.* The first of these was an adaptation of a Bob Bloch story, the rights to which had been acquired by Douglas Cramer, who had produced several of Bob's made-for-TV movies, such as *The Cat Creature* and *The Dead Don't Die,* in the early 1970s.

Quickly, "The Final Performance" centers on a defunct vaudevillian, slowly losing his marbles in the middle of the desert. He is prone to alcohol-fogged reminiscences about the good old days; more than that, I need not disclose.

But picture what the concept meeting must have been like: *"Hmm— this story has to be convincing in terms of classic vaudeville. Let's have David Schow do it!"*

The fun part was getting to attend vaudeville primary school, as a class of one, with Bob as the tutor. He gave me access to his voluminous reference collection (and let there be no doubt—he had definitely read each of these books many more times than twice). He patiently corrected my various idiocies through notes, phone calls, and more notes. The final revised submission draft (circa November 1990) was amended and rinsed free of the few remaining vaude boners by Bob; thus did I evade the dunce cap and squeak past on the grade curve. The project as an entity collapsed for the same reasons most Hollywood development deals turn to sludge. Bob liked the script. The closest we came to an actual performance was two staged read-throughs of the material before live audiences. In the first one, Lea Thompson played Rosie.

Structurally, "The Final Performance" is kin to Bob's own "The Man Who Knew Women," with resonances of his more modern, and more comic (though little-reprinted) story, "Memo to a Movie Maker." While perhaps not a classic on the order of "A Toy for Juliette" (my second choice), I've chosen it for the personal memories associated with my work on it—events that encapsulate, for me, my friendship with its author.

They've remodeled the Hollywood Hamburger Hamlet. The bar is no longer a high-ceilinged chamber crowded with chairs and booths of red leatherette (or whatever it really was), as it was when Bob and I met, from time to time, to pound down ice cream across from a whole wall of sketches and drawings of the Barrymores. Bob would blitz down from the hills in his fire engine red Pontiac with the sheepskin seat covers. That was before all the corneal procedures, when he could still see well enough to drive.

Courtesy of Richard Matheson, I got to thank Bob for a lot of things once it was common knowledge that his condition had become terminal. I don't think I ever got to thank him for introducing me to the joys of Oscar Levant, via those sessions at the Hamlet. As you can perhaps glean from all the foregoing, one of Bob's capacities was the ability to explain, regardless of whether it annoyed him, remembrances of things past, to assist in the evocation of times and places and eras and styles that frequently predated the listener. If you could ask, Bob could answer . . . and without playing that dismissive game known as *my-nostalgia-can-beat-up-your-nostalgia*.

Beyond the indisputable importance of his canon and his knowledge, Bob could serve as a model for the present-day horror writer in other ways, too. Yes—I'm talking about *wardrobe* here.

When I first met Bob, he still affected the cigarette holder (though mostly as a stage prop); the operative word was *dapper*. Effortlessly, he could play to a slovenly audience of adipose-stressed *Star Trek* T-shirts and pizza-fouled Reeboks while clad in sixties finery that somehow still looked classy, yet dignified, on him. He still wore hats, with the suits. It was a shock, therefore, when he greeted me at his home one time clad in his outrageous, bright orange terrycloth jumpsuit (it made him look like Milton Selzer, newly escaped from *Sesame Street*).

Only after repeated exposure could one begin to gain a sense of the sheer *breadth* of Bob's accumulation of strange sports coats, from the red plaid one to my absolute favorite, a kind of off-white creation with little quilts and bumps; sort of tuck-and-roll for the fashion-conscious. Bob had style by the ton. Maybe that's why so many of his contemporaries had none; he got it all.

Most horror writers, after all, seek to impress upon the world at large what ordinary joes they are, while insisting that yes, they really, truly *do* write "edge" fiction. Not only is this boring beyond belief, but if you stab through that authorial tweed, nine times out of ten you'll find a heart and soul of purest Naugahyde. In Bob's case, he was not only different, but typically unpretentious; at conventions that made a big loud deal over how they were actually "conferences" for "professional writers," Bob never considered himself to be one of those pros. "Remember, you're talking to an amateur," he said to me. "I've never approached writing as a professional."

One of the best times we shared at a convention together was an occasion where Bob attended as *fan* guest of honor.

It's no mistake that Bob was the World Horror Convention's first acknowledged Grand Master. Here was a case where the accolade was not only convenient (because Bob was still alive), but appropriate (because it was an appellation he deserved). It was a gentlemanly way, I think, to address the problem of how to distinguish the debut convention *without* inaugurating yet another needless rack of stupid awards. Just one prize, no competition.

Sadly, if the most recent World Horror affair was any weathervane, *that* distinction got flushed toot-sweet.

At the time of the first one, in 1991, Bob said, "I think awards and trophies become meaningless, and lose their value, if they are something political, for people who actively campaign for them. In recent years, it seems to me, there's been an underground industry in the acquisition and accumulation of trophies. But if an award is something that is given spontaneously, without any premeditation on the part of the recipient, then I think the spirit and intention behind that is a wonderful thing. In many cases it is the most lasting and satisfying reward one can acquire, because of the memories associated with a convention, and the people that gave it to you."

Of course, I'm saying this as one of the guys who conspired to "award" Bob with a shellacked piece of toast on a dinner plate—as a "toastmaster" prize—if for no other reason than to compete with the absurd "Gray Mauser" award I'd seen in his trophy room (Sic, isn't it?).

Bob attended hundreds of conventions since his first Pacificon in 1926, where the banquet cost one dollar. Apart from the fan horror stories related in Harlan Ellison's survey of same, "Xenogenesis" (which addressed individual wrongdoers, not fans as a group entity), here is Bob's more-or-less final word on dealing with his public:

"I've never gone to a convention where I felt ill at ease, or disappointed in the least. Sometimes the accommodations were better than other times. The purpose of going to a convention is to talk to people, to see people, to find out who your readers are—if any—and to speak to artists and editors and publishers and, sometimes, in desperation, even to your fellow writers."

Of course, I'm not *nearly* as polite as Bob.

To all the leeches and emotional vampires and masturbators of tragedy, to all the usurious scumbags who would exploit Bob's death for selfish reasons and skate without ever picking up the karma check . . . Uncle Bob has already Explained It All to You, and you would do the world good by trying to emulate his example.

None of us needs posthumous fireworks, brouhaha, panel discussions, or even pieces like this one to denote how vital Bob was, because it's too late for him to appreciate the effort now, and dammit, we should *know* this stuff, and not have to be railroaded, or lectured to.

For all the rest, not a warning, here, to remember Bob's life and work, but a reminder: Don't forget him. At your peril, don't forget.

THE FINAL PERFORMANCE

🌱 ***The neon intestines had been twisted to form the word***
EAT.

I squinted up at it, the sand stinging my eyes, and shifted my overnight bag to the left hand. As I opened the sagging screen door a trickle of perspiration ran down my arm.

Two flies accompanied me into the restaurant. One of them headed for a pile of crullers on the counter and the other alighted on the bald head of an elderly fat man who leaned behind it. The man looked up and the fly buzzed away.

"Evening," he said. "What'll it be?"

"Are you Rudolph?" I asked.

He nodded.

I slid onto a stool. "Fellow named Davis sent me."

"From the garage?"

"That's right—the place up the highway. My car conked out on me coming through the mountains. He had to phone Bakersfield for a new connecting rod. They're bringing it out first thing tomorrow morning, and he figures he can get it installed before evening. But tonight I'm looking for a place to stay. He told me to try here—said you used to run a motel."

"Not any more. Isn't enough traffic along this route."

"I noticed a couple of cabins out in back."

"Closed up." The fat man reached under the counter and came up with a half-empty bottle of beer. He took a long gulp; when he set the bottle down again it was empty. "Look, you could hitch a ride into Bakersfield and come back to-morrow."

"I thought of that, but I hate to leave all my belongings. Everything I own is in that car—guess it broke down because it was overloaded. You see, I'm moving to Hollywood, and I packed all my books and—"

"Hollywood?" The fat man blinked. "You in show biz?"

"I'm a writer."

"Television?"

"Short stories and books."

He blinked again. "That's better. TV is lousy, I can't understand what they think they're doing out there. Now you take a guy like that Ed Sullivan—" He broke off abruptly and stared at me. "Book writer, you say. Ever run into Arnie Pringle?"

"No, I can't say that I have."

"Before your time, I guess. Probably dead by now. He used to write my act."

"You were in show business?"

"Are you kidding? Rudolph the Great. Twenty years top billing, Pantages, Albee, Keith-Orpheum time. Why, I've got three press books full of—"

I rose from the stool.

"Here, where you going?"

I shrugged. "Sorry, but if I'm hitching a ride into Bakersfield I'd better get out there on the highway before dark."

"Never mind that. Guess we can fix up a cabin for you. Put some clean sheets on the bed." He swayed along behind the counter, and it suddenly occurred to me that he was just a little bit drunk.

"Look, I wouldn't want to put you to any trouble," I told him.

"No trouble. My pleasure." He jerked his head toward the swinging door behind him. "Rosie!" he yelled.

Rosie came into the room.

She was a tall girl, blonde and amply proportioned, her hair done up in a ponytail. She wore a blue sleeveless smock and her legs were bare.

"Rose, this is Mr.—"

"Chatham. Jim Chatham." I nodded at her and she wrinkled up her nose at me. It took a moment before I realized she was smiling.

"Had a little trouble with his car," Rudolph said. "Davis is fixing it up at the crossroads. He needs a place to stay overnight. You think you can find some clean bedclothes for Number One?"

She nodded at him, still looking at me.

"Better take him out with you. Let him have a look."

"All right." Her voice was soft, deeper than I'd expected.

"Keys in my desk, right-hand drawer."

"I know. I'll get them."

She turned and left the room. Rudolph reached under the counter into the cooler and brought out another bottle of beer, a full one this time. "Care for a brew?" he asked.

"Later, perhaps. Let me get settled and then I'll come back for dinner."

"Suit yourself." He bent to open the bottle, then raised it to his lips.

Rosie came back into the room; she carried a bundle of sheets wrapped around a pillow. "All set?" she asked.

I picked up my bag and followed her outside. The sun was setting and the desert wind was cool. Joshuas cast their shadows along the path leading to the cabins in the rear, striping the sand and the backs of her bare calves as she walked along before me.

"Here we are." She halted and opened the door of the tiny cabin. The interior of the little shack was dark and stifling hot. She switched on the light. "It'll cool off in a minute with the door open," she said. "I'll make up the bed for you."

I put down the suitcase and slumped into the single chair next to the gray-filmed window. She went to work, bending over the bed. She had fine breasts. As she moved around to tuck in the sheet, her leg brushed mine.

All at once, for no reason at all, my mind was filled with corny dialogue. *What's a nice girl like you doing in such a godforsaken hole? Let me take you away from all this . . .*

Suddenly I noticed she had stopped working. She stood there with the pillow in her arms, staring at me.

"I heard you talking to him," she said. "About being a writer. What are you going to do out in Hollywood, work for the movies?"

"I doubt it. Probably just keep turning out stories the same as usual. But the climate's better."

"Yes, the climate." She nodded and wrinkled her nose at me. "Take me with you."

"What?"

"I said, take me with you."

"But Mrs. Rudolph—"

"His *first* name is Rudolph. Bitzner."

"Mrs. Bitzner, then—"

"I'm not Mrs. Bitzner either."

"Oh, I just thought—"

"I know what you thought. Never mind that. Just take me with you. All I'd do is ride along. There wouldn't be any trouble." She let the pillow fall on the bed and moved closer. "I wouldn't be any bother at all. I promise."

I stood up, and I didn't reach for her. I didn't have to reach for her, because she came right into my arms, and she said, "Please, please, say you'll take me. You've got to. You don't know what it's like all alone out here. You don't know what he's like. He's crazy—"

She had this trick of talking without opening her mouth, keeping her lips puckered up, waiting to be kissed, and she wrinkled her nose and I could see the tiny freckles on the bridge, and her skin was marble-cool in all this heat. And it's one thing to sit back and make sophisticated remarks about cheap waitresses named Rosie (*Rosie, for God's sake!*) and another thing entirely to feel a waiting, willing woman stirring hard against you and whispering. "Please . . . promise me you will . . . I'll do anything. . . ."

So I opened my mouth to answer, then let it remain open in bewilderment as she stepped back quickly and picked up the pillow again. Then I heard him scuffling along the path and understood.

"Rosie!" he yelled. "You almost finished? Customers!"

"Be right in," she called.

I stepped over to the doorway and waved at Rudolph.

"Everything all right?" he asked.

"Everything's fine."

"Come and eat, then. You can wash up inside."

I glanced back at Rosie. She was bending over the bed and she didn't look at me. But she whispered, "I'll see you later. Wait for me."

That's what kept me going through the long evening.

I followed Rudolph, and I cleaned myself up a bit in the filthy washroom, and I shared a steak and french fries with the two flies and their cousins. The customers were in and out for the next couple of hours, and there was no chance to talk to Rudolph or even catch a glimpse of Rosie out in back. Then, finally, it was nine o'clock and the place was empty again. Rudolph yawned and walked over to the door, switching off the EAT sign.

"This concludes the evening's performance," he said. "Thanks for the use of the hall." He went over to the swinging door. "You fixing yourself something?" he yelled.

"Yes, just a hamburger. How about you?" Rosie asked.

"Never mind. I'll have myself another beer." He looked at me. "You ready for one now?"

I shook my head and stood up. "No, thanks, It's about time I turned in."

"What's your hurry? Stick around. We'll go in back and chew that fat awhile. To hell with the beer—I've got some hard stuff here."

"Well, I—"

"Come on. Got some things that might interest you. Man doesn't get much chance to talk to anybody halfway intelligent around here."

"All right."

He ran his wrist across the gray stubble around his mouth.

"Tell you what, I'll check the register first. You go right on back, through that door on the end. I'll be along."

So I went back, into the little room on the side of the restaurant which served as a parlor. I saw the overstuffed couch and the easy chair and the desk, the lamp, the TV set, but I didn't do any more than glance at them.

Because I was staring at the walls—the walls of another world.

It was the world of the Twenties and the early Thirties, a world that belonged to the half-forgotten faces which peered out at me from a thousand photographs reaching from floor to ceiling. Some of the pictures had peeled and faded, just as my memories had peeled and faded in the long years since early childhood. But I could still remember the familiar countenances, and I had at least heard of most of the names scrawled in autograph fashion beneath the unfamiliar ones. I moved around the room, moved around the mementos of what had once been a world called vaudeville.

Here was a skinny, gangling kid called Milton Berle and a buxom young woman named Sophie Tucker. Here was a youthful Bert Wheeler holding an apple and a smiling Joe Cook holding an Indian club and explaining why he would not imitate the Four Hawaiians. There was an entire section of faces in burnt cork—Cantor, Jolson, Lou Holtz in the pre–Sam Lapidus days, Frank Tinney (way before my time), and one mournfully humorous countenance which needed no spurious blackface; the signature read, "To Rudolph from Bert Williams."

And there were the teams and the acts—Moran and Mack, Gallagher and Shean, Cross and Dunn, Phil Baker and Ben Bernie, Smith and Dale (Dr. Kronkheit, I presume), and a surprisingly handsome young couple who signed themselves "George and Gracie." And there was an incredible Jimmy Durante—with hair—and Clayton and Jackson.

"See? It's like I told you, I knew 'em all." Rudolph had come up behind me, carrying a bottle and glasses. "Here, let me fix you a snort and I'll show you my press books."

He made me a drink, but he didn't get around to the press books. Instead he sprawled out on the sofa, uncorked the bottle again, and uncorked himself.

I don't know how long he rambled on about the old days and the old ways; about the Six Brown Brothers and Herman Timberg and Walter C. Kelly and Chic Sale. At another time, under other circumstances, I might have hung on to his every word. But right now I was hanging on to other words—"I'll see you later. Wait for me."

So I really didn't listen to him, to Rudolph the Great who used to do Orpheum Time until vaudeville died and then wandered out here into the desert to do a twenty-year layoff as Rudolph Bitzner. Twenty years—why, Rosie couldn't be much over twenty herself! And here was this fat old man wheezing away on the couch, drinking out of the bottle now and slobbering. He was getting ready to pass out. He had to pass out soon, he *had* to. . . .

"Have 'nother drink?" He sat up, blinking at the bottle. "Oh, 's empty, well whaddya know?"

"That's all right," I told him. "I've had enough."

"Well, I haven'. Got more 'round here someplace. Rosie!" He yelled her name, then lowered his voice as he turned to me. "She's out front. Told her to clean up the joint. Won't come near me when I'm drinking, anyhow, you know?" He chuckled. "Don't matter—I locked the door before I came back. Got the key ri' here, so she can't get away. Never get away, not from me."

He swayed to his feet. "Know what you're thinkin'—just an old lush, that's all, just an old lush. But wait till I show you the press books. Then you'll see who I was. Who I *am*." He stumbled back against the sofa. "Rudolph the Great. Tha's me. Keep in practice. Jus' as good as I ever was. Better. Why, I could go on Sullivan's show nex' week. . . ."

Then the color drained from his face and he fell back on the couch. I never did get to see those press books. By the time I put his feet up on the sofa he'd started to snore. I took the keys from his pocket and went back into the restaurant. She was waiting for me in the dark. And we went out through the dark to my cabin, and she clung to me in the dark, and that's the one thing I want to remember, *have* to remember now.

Afterward she told me about herself. She'd been ten when she'd come to

Rudolph—her parents stopped by on their way to Texas and dropped her off while they filled a fair date. They were a couple of ex-vaudevillans themselves: the Flying Keenos. They knew Rudolph from the old days and they accepted his suggestion to leave her in his care while they traveled on, because they were down on their luck.

"Only they never came back," she said. "They never came back. And he tried to find them. He wrote to *Billboard* and everything, but they just disappeared. So I stayed on. Rudolph—he wasn't so bad then, you know. I mean, he didn't drink so much or anything. He sent me to school on the bus, bought me clothes and things. Treated me just like he was my father—until I was sixteen."

She started to cry, very softly. "He isn't even in love with me, not really. It's because of living out here all alone in this crazy desert and knowing he's getting old. Before it started he used to talk about making a comeback on TV. He said it was just like vaudeville, he'd always known there'd be a revival. Then, that summer when I was sixteen, he decided the time was right and he took me with him out to L.A. He went around and saw some agents, had a few auditions. I never did find out what really happened. But when we came back here in the fall he started to drink right away, and that's when—"

That's when she tried to sneak off, and he caught her, and he closed up the motel so she couldn't see anyone or attempt to hitch a ride. He kept her inside the restaurant, didn't even allow her to go up to the crossroads for supplies, wouldn't let anyone come near her.

There were times when she thought of running away in the night, but something always stopped her. She realized she owed him something for all the years he'd taken care of her, and he needed her now. He was just an old man, not quite right in the head, and he seldom bothered her any more. Most nights he just drank and passed out. She'd resigned herself to putting up with it until this evening. Then, when she saw me—

"I know. You figured you *could* get a ride, and maybe I'd even take care of you out on the Coast for a week or so, long enough for you to find a job. That's it, isn't it?"

"No!" She dug her nails into my arms. "Maybe I *did* think something like that at first. But not *now*. Believe me, not *now*."

I believed her. I believed her voice and I believed her body, even though it was incredible and I should be lying here in the desert night with this stranger whom I'd known forever.

"It's all right," I said. "We'll go away. But I'd feel better if we told him. Maybe if I talked things over with him, explained, I could make him understand."

"Oh no—you can't do that! He's crazy jealous. I didn't want to tell you, but one time he caught this truckdriver talking to me outside—just talking is all— and he took after him with that big butcher knife. He would have killed him if he caught him, I know he would! And he beat me up so that I couldn't even get out of bed for three days. No, he mustn't even suspect. Tomorrow afternoon, when the car is fixed. . . ."

We made our simple plans. The restaurant was closed on Sundays, and it would be better if I didn't attempt to take a meal there—just went straight to the garage and saw to it that Davis got the car fixed as soon as possible. Meanwhile Rosie would have her suitcase packed and ready. She'd encourage Rudolph to drink—not that he generally needed any encouragement from her. Maybe he'd even pass out. If not, she'd go so far as to cut the phone wire, if necessary; just so she could slip out to me with the assurance of getting a head start.

So we talked it all over, calmly and sensibly, and she slipped out of the cabin, and I lay there and tried to sleep. It was almost dawn when I closed my eyes, and the bats were out, flying against the gaudy desert sunrise.

I slept for a long time. When I left the cabin and cut across to the highway, it was almost two o'clock. I walked the mile to the crossroads garage and found Davis working with the car up on the rack. We talked for a while, but I didn't listen to what he said, or to what I said either. From time to time somebody drove up for gas and Davis would have to stop and give them service. The car wasn't ready until a little after five; it was already getting dark.

I paid him and drove off. The motor hummed smoothly, but I almost stripped gears as I shifted. I was nervous, that's all, just nervous. I didn't feel any guilt and I didn't feel any fear. Certainly I didn't feel any horror.

That came later.

That came when I parked in the deepening shadows on the side of the darkened restaurant and went up to the door. This was it. If something had gone wrong—

But nothing could go wrong. I squared my shoulders and took a deep breath, then rattled the doorknob. That was the signal; she'd be waiting to hear me.

Nothing happened. A few flies buzzed against the glass awaiting entry. I rattled the door again softly. It was locked.

Then the figure emerged from the back room.

I recognized Rudolph.

He moved briskly; there was no shuffle in his gait and no stagger either. His face was gray and puffy, but his red-rimmed eyes weren't blinking. He stooped and unlocked the door, motioning for me to come inside.

"Good afternoon," I said. There was nothing else I *could* say, not yet, not until I knew what had happened.

He nodded, moving behind me to lock the door again. I could hear the click of the key and I didn't bother to look around.

That's when the horror came.

Horror is something cold and sharp, biting against the back of your neck.

"Let's go into the other room," Rudolph said. "Rosie has something to say to you."

"What have you done to her?"

"Nothing. She just wants to talk to you. You'll see."

We went down the aisle past the counter, the flies buzzing in our wake. Then we were in the back room and they were all waiting for me there—George and Gracie, Frank Tinney, Lou Holtz. They were all staring, as I stared, at the open torn heap. For a moment, in the dim light, I thought it was Rosie lying there.

But no, Rosie was sitting on the sofa and she was looking at the suitcase too. She didn't say a word when I came in because there was nothing to say now.

I could feel Rudolph's breath on my neck, right behind me. And I could feel the coldness, too, the sharpness, the horror. All at once it went away. I heard the knife clatter to the floor.

"You can thank her for that," Rudolph murmured. "I could have killed you, you know. I wanted to kill you. But she talked me out of it. And now she has something to say to you. Go ahead, Rosie, tell him."

He left me standing there in the doorway and walked over to where Rose was sitting. He slid down on the sofa beside her and put his arm around her, smiling. Rosie looked up then, but she didn't smile.

The shadows crept across the walls, across the faces of Williams and Bernie and Jolson, across his face and hers. But I wasn't watching the shadows. I was listening to the girl.

"You see how it happened," she murmured. "He walked in while I was packing. He found out."

"All right," I said. "So he found out. I wanted to tell him in the first place. And now that he knows, he can let us go."

I was already moving before I finished my last sentence, crossing the room in two strides and scooping up the big, broad-bladed butcher knife from the floor.

"Look," I said. "I've got the knife now. He can't hurt us and he'd better not try. We can walk out of here whenever we please."

She sat there, turning her head to stare at the knife. And he stared, too, tightened his arm around her and stared and smiled while she said, "No. I've changed my mind. I'm not going with you."

"But I don't understand—"

"We talked it all over before you came. I can't go. He needs me so. It's right that I should stay. I belong with him. Can't you see that?"

I shook my head. There was something wrong with her words, something wrong with the way she stared and he smiled. And all at once it came to me as I looked into his fat face off in the shadows. "Maybe I can see," I said. "Rudolph the Great. You were a hypnotist, weren't you? That's the answer, isn't it? You've hypnotized her, that's what you've done—"

He started to laugh.

"You're wrong, mister," he said. "Tell him how wrong he is, darling."

And then she was laughing, too, in a high, hysterical titter. But there was no laughter in her face, and her words, when they came, were soft and somber.

"He's no hypnotist. I know what I'm doing, believe me. I'm telling you to get out. Just get out, do you hear me? Go away and don't come back. I don't want to go the Coast with you. I don't want you pawing me in some dirty cabin. I know what you are. You're a—"

She began to curse me then; the filth and the foulness poured out of her mouth and he bobbed her head at me in rage, while he just sat there and smiled.

Finally she was finished. "All right," he said. "Have you heard enough?"

"I've heard enough," I said. "I'll go." And I dropped the knife again. It rolled across the floor, and a thin ray of light from the dying sunset streaked the dulled and darkened blade.

I turned to go, and neither of them rose. They just sat there, arms entwined, and stared at me. The shadows blotted out their faces, then pursued me all the way down the hall.

The car stood waiting for me in the twilight. I climbed in, switched on the ignition, pulled away. I must have driven two or three miles before I remembered to turn on my lights. I was in a daze. There was nothing but the shadows, the strange shadows. Shadows in the room, on their faces, on the dulled and darkened knife. *The dulled and darkened knife. . . .*

Then it hit me, and I speeded up. I found a phone just ahead in a filling station outside Pono and put in my call.

The state troopers arrived in fifteen minutes, and I told my story as we roared back to the restaurant in their patrol car.

"He must have done *something* to her," I said. "That knife blade was dark with dried blood."

"We'll see," the sergeant told me.

But at first we didn't see, because Rudolph must have heard us coming, and that's when he used the knife on himself. We found it sticking out of his chest there on the floor in the back room, and he was quite dead.

Rosie still sat there on the sofa, staring at us. It was the sergeant who discovered she'd been strangled.

"Must have happened a couple of hours ago," he told me. "The body's getting stiff."

"Strangled? A couple of hours? But I was just here. We were talking—"

"See for yourself."

I walked over and touched her shoulder. She was stiff and cold and there were purple marks on her neck. Suddenly she toppled forward, and that's when I saw how the knife had been used—saw the huge, foot-long gash extending from the back of her neck down across the shoulders. The wound was incredibly deep; I couldn't understand why. Not even when the sergeant called my attention to the blood on Rudolph's right hand.

It wasn't until I saw the press books that I really knew. Yes, we found his press books, and I finally saw them there at the last, finally found out what must have happened in his dark room, in his dark mind, when he walked in and discovered her getting ready to leave.

That's when he'd strangled her, of course, strangled her to death in a crazy rage. But he was sane enough to realize I'd be coming by to get her and that he'd have to find a way to get rid of me.

So he used the knife then and cut the hole, cut it wide and deep. Wide and deep enough so that she could bow and nod and turn her head when he had his hand behind her. Of course I'd heard her talking to me, but the press books explained all that.

He wasn't lying about his notices; they were raves.

And he wasn't lying about hypnotism either. Rudolph the Great hadn't been a hypnotist. He was just one of the best damned ventriloquists in the business.

ROBERT BLOCH—
A PERSONAL APPRECIATION

RANDALL D. LARSON

My first encounter with Robert Bloch came in 1970 as a seventeen-year-old high school sophomore eager to produce my first fanzine. Bob was one of a few people whose names I found in fanzine letter columns and to whom I sent interview requests, accompanied by a list of unknowingly naive questions. At this point, all I knew about Robert Bloch was that he had written some articles in *Famous Monsters of Filmland* and had written *Psycho,* a book which had scared the bellbottoms off of me a few years earlier. Bob's friendly and informative response really made an impression, and one that remained throughout twenty-five ensuing years of correspondence.

Reflecting back now, at the middle age of forty, I feel extremely fortunate to have known the man behind the words. In many ways, Bob Bloch became a role model for me. His perceptive outlook impressed me, as did his way of expressing himself on paper, and I learned a great deal from him. Bob encouraged my own writing endeavors, even supported them with information, enduring dozens of questions and interviews and requests when I decided to compile a series of fanzines and, finally, books about his work and his words. He generously supplied me with all the information I needed, answered my voluminous lists of questions, even allowed me to inspect and photograph in his home the rarest pulps and fanzines that had published his work.

But Bob's kindness went far beyond giving a young and eager bibliographer a helping hand. His continual reassurance as much as the influence of his own writing really had an impact on my own literary efforts, and he helped me develop and mature as a writer. He and Elly both treated me and my family with warmth and friendship, welcoming me into their home during my rare visits to Los Angeles. They took the time to care, and it's difficult to describe how extraordinary it is to connect, in friendship and mutual respect, with someone you hold in such high regard.

When I first met Bob, through the mail, I knew next to nothing about him. But as I got to know him, through letters, through his novels and stories and articles, through the many interviews he granted to journalists over the years, I developed a strong respect for him. The man behind the menacing stories was one of the kindest and most sincere gentlemen I've ever encountered, and I feel exceedingly grateful for being allowed to share a small part of his world.

Robert Bloch was far more than just a fictioneer. Although his novels and short stories ran the gamut from science fiction to crime, humor to psychological horror, speculative to traditional, they all share a common perception about humanity, about good and evil. Considering humor and horror flip sides of the same coin, Bob constantly set the nickel edgewise and revealed the mutual absurdity and terror that he saw in the world. It is this quality—this sense of perceptive examination—that characterizes Bob's fiction. He did far more than simply weave a neat tale with a shock ending. Robert Bloch was a perceptive observer of humanity, never compromising his own values or his commitment to the idea of personal responsibility, and his stories reflected the world he saw. Through a variety of grotesqueries, ironies, ghoulish comeuppances and horrible puns, Bob took a look at the world and tried to figure out what made it shriek. And he did it with more insight and style than he has often been given credit for.

Bob Bloch touched a lot of people in many ways, and I am extraordinarily grateful to have been one of them. He spoke to us through his stories, his essays, his interviews, his letters, his deliciously humorous convention speeches. And while he maintained an unassuming modesty throughout his life, his influence had a great deal to do with how many of us turned out.

I think we must all be grateful for having been allowed to share just a little bit of his world, his personality and his friendship. We will all keep his memory burning brightly for decades to come.

Selecting a single favorite Robert Bloch story is like choosing a favorite wine. There are simply too many preferred choices. There are too many flavors, from earthy rum to classic Amontillado, and each is to be savored and its aftertaste cherished.

Do I choose one of Bob's early Lovecraftian stories—vintage whisky, full of flavor and packing a pungent bite? Or how about one of his clever science fiction tales of the fifties, dry sherry with a most unusual sparkle? Maybe one of his mystery and crime stories—smooth spirits with a firewater chaser—or even one of his humorous fantasies from the pulp era, simple yet intoxicating moonshine? Bob wrote in too many fields, concocted too many treasures. True, not all of it was literary champagne, but that was all right. A good hit of wordsmithed gin, well-authored vermouth, or just plain old typewritten hooch had magic when it flowed from his mind.

Reacquainting myself with sixty years' worth of Bob's shriek-inducing stories, I resolved it simply impossible to settle on a single story as "my favorite." I have several dozen favorites, yet even through a process of elimination I couldn't come up with a single story that I liked better than the others. If I chose this one for its superbly funny irony, I slighted that one with its unique psychological portrait, or if I selected this one for its remarkable wordplay, then I neglected that one with its hauntingly subtle denouement. I didn't think I cadaver decide on a suitable tale.

Ultimately, I chose a story that in its sum as well as in its parts seemed to represent much of what Bob Bloch felt and conveyed in his multitude of stories and novels. "The Pin" isn't Bloch's spookiest story, and it doesn't have one of the cleverly mounted punch-line endings that characterized a lot of his efforts. Yet it is a serious, powerful work, capturing the same premise that punctuates the majority of Bob's examinations of horror. "The Pin" is a return to that oft-appearing theme of *death* that has frequented his work since the very beginning. In this remarkable short story, Bob personifies Death not as a shrouded, skull-faced figure swinging a scythe, but as a little fat man who sits in a condemned office building wielding his own sharp instrument of death. The story is both a quirky and pointedly frightening look at the aimlessness of death over which humankind has no control. As Barton Stone climbs the stairs into the abandoned loft, he descends into the inevitability of dying, of disease, of unwanted tragedy. Themes that Bloch examined frequently in his fiction.

Bob once told me that the things that *really* frightened him weren't the eldritch creatures or malevolent entities or compulsive vampires and werewolves that peopled his fantasy fiction, nor even the sociopathic killers who lurked among his psychological thrillers, no matter how disturbingly real they may have been. Instead, Bob's personal fears had to do with things *beyond* his control—beyond his ability to dispatch the werewolf with a silver bullet or banish the ancient gods with a well-turned verse, to close the book or walk out of the darkened theater. Beneath the surface, Bob was continuously asserting his uneasiness with the prevalence toward cruelty that exists in people, and conveying his apprehension toward the frailty of human beings who lie at the mercy of such ambivalent Lovecraftian entities as disease and age—those very same terrible gods that ultimately succeeded in taking him from us. "The Pin" personifies this fear perhaps better than any of his other stories. Familiarity breeds insight, and if nothing else Robert Bloch spent three score years examining the cruel scythe-bearer and gaining an understanding that perhaps left him better prepared to live in its shadow. It's a poignant thought, now that the little fat man has stolen him from us.

Bob used to describe himself as an entertainer—and there is no denying his work has been very, very entertaining. "The Pin" is full of the kind of wordplays that make Bloch's work so effective and enjoyable to read. The *way* he wrote was often just as interesting as what he had to say. Yet there's much more to Bob's creative output than that. Beneath the surface, beyond the amiable narration, the carefully crafted character portraits and the skillfully launched punch lines, Robert Bloch is quite often expressing his own personal sense of anxiety. It's this private sense of horror, more than the fanciful tales of crimes both natural and supernatural, that reveals the themes in Bob's fiction. Robert Bloch found the horrors of real life, fancifully exaggerated as they are in "The Pin," far more frightening than the supernatural monstrosities of his earlier days. Read it, and you'll never look at a telephone book—or a pin—quite the same way again.

THE PIN

Somehow, somewhere, someone would find out.
It was inevitable.

In this case the *someone* was named Barton Stone. The *somewhere* was an old loft over a condemned office building on Bleecker Street.

And the *somehow* . . .

Barton Stone came there early one Monday morning as the sun shone yellow and cold over the huddled rooftops. He noted the mass of the surrounding buildings, rearranged them into a more pleasing series of linear units, gauged his perspective, evaluated the tones and shadings of sunlight and shadow with his artist's eye. There was a picture here, he told himself, if only he could find it.

Unfortunately he wasn't looking for a picture. He had plenty of subjects in mind. Right now he was looking for a place in which to paint. He wanted a studio, wanted it quickly. And it must be cheap. Running water and north light were luxuries beyond his present consideration. As for other aesthetic elements, such as cleanliness—Stone shrugged as he mounted the stairs, his long fingers trailing dust from the rickety railing.

There was dust everywhere, for this was the domain of dust, of darkness and desertion. He stumbled upward into the silence.

The first two floors of the building were entirely empty, just as Freed had told him. And the stairs to the loft were at the end of the hall on the second floor.

"You'll have it all to yourself," the rental agent had promised. "But remember to stay in the loft. Nobody'd ever bother looking up there. Damned inspectors come around—they keep telling us to raze the building. But the floor's safe enough. All you got to do is keep out of sight—why, you could hide out there for years without being caught. It's no palace, but take a look and see what you think. For twenty bucks a month you can't go wrong."

Stone nodded now as he walked down the debris-littered hall toward the loft stairs. He couldn't go wrong. He sensed, suddenly and with utter certainty, that this was the place he'd been searching for during all of these frustrating futile weeks. He moved up the stairs with inevitable—

Then he heard the sound.

Call it a thud; call it a thump; call it a muffled crash. The important thing was that it sounded from above, from the deserted loft.

Stone paused on the second step from the top. There was someone in the loft. *For twenty bucks a month you can't go wrong*—but *you could hide out there for years without being caught.*

Barton Stone was not a brave man. He was only a poor artist, looking for a cheap loft or attic to use as a studio. But his need was great, great enough to impel him upward, carry him to the top of the loft stairs and down the short corridor leading to the entry.

He moved quietly now, although there was thunder in his chest. He tiptoed delicately toward the final door, noted the overhead transom, noted, too, the small crate in the corner against the wall.

There was silence beyond the door and silence in the hall now as he carefully lifted the crate and placed it so that he could mount the flat top and peer over the open transom.

No sense in being melodramatic, he told himself. On the other hand, there was no sense rushing in—Barton Stone was not a fool and he didn't want to become an angel.

He looked over the transom.

The loft was huge. A dusty skylight dominated the ceiling, and enough light filtered through to bathe the room in sickly luminance. Stone could see everything, everything.

He saw the books, stacked man-high, row after row of thick books. He saw the sheaves bulked between the books, pile after pile of sheaves. He saw the papers rising in solid walls from the floor. He saw the table in the center of the loft—the table, bulwarked on three sides of books and sheaves and papers all tossed together in toppling towers.

And he saw the man.

The man sat behind the table, back to the wall, surrounded on three sides by the incredible array of printed matter. He sat there, head down, and peered at the pages of an opened book. He never looked up, never made a sound, just sat there and stared.

Stone stared back. He understood the source of the noise now; one of the books had fallen from its stack. But nothing else made sense to him. His eyes sought clues; his mind sought meaning.

The man was short, fat, middle-aged. His hair was graying into white, his face lining into wrinkles. He wore a dirty khaki shirt and trousers and he might have been an ex-GI, a tramp, a fugitive from justice, an indigent bookdealer, an eccentric millionaire.

Stone moved from the realm of might-have-been to a consideration of what he actually saw. The little fat man was riffling through the pages of a fat, paper-bound book which could easily be mistaken for a telephone directory. He turned the pages, apparently at random, with his left hand. Very well, then; he was left-handed.

Or was he? His right hand moved across the table, raised and poised so that the sunlight glittered in a thin line of silver against the object he held.

It was a pin, a long, silver pin. Stone stared at it. The man was staring at it too. Stone's gaze held curiosity. The little fat man's gaze held utter loathing and, more than that, a sort of horrified fascination.

Another sound broke the stillness. The little man sighed. It was a deep sigh that became, with abrupt and hideous clarity, a groan.

Eyes still intent on the pin, the little man brought it down suddenly upon the opened pages of his book. He stabbed at random, driving the point home. Then he hurled the book to the floor, sat back, buried his face in his hands, and his shoulders shook with silent sobbing.

A second sped. Stone blinked. And beyond the door, in the loft, the little man straightened up, reaching for a long sheet of paper that might have been a polling list, and scanned its surface. The pin poised itself over the center of the sheet. Again the sigh, the stab, the sob.

Now the little man rose, and for a frantic moment Stone wondered if he'd been detected. But no, the pin wielder merely wandered down the row of books and pulled out another thick volume. He carried it back to the table and sat down, picking up the pin with his right hand as his left turned page after page. He scanned, scrutinized, then sighed, stabbed, sobbed.

Barton Stone descended from the top of the crate, replaced it carefully in the corner, and tiptoed down the stairs. He moved carefully and silently, and it was an effort to do so, because he wanted all the while to run.

His feeling was irrational, and he knew it, but he could not control himself. He had always experienced that sudden surge of fear in the presence of the de-mented. When he saw a drunk in a bar, he was afraid—because you never know what a drunk will do next, what will enter his mind and how he will act. He shied away from arguments, because of what happens to a man's reaction pattern when he sees red. He avoided the mumblers, the people who talk to themselves or to the empty air as they shuffle down the street.

Right now he was afraid of a little fat man, a little fat man with a long, sharp, silver needle. The needle was crooked at one end, Stone remembered—and he could see that needle sinking into his own throat, right up to the crooked angle. The fat man was crazy and Stone wanted no part of him. He'd go back to the rental agency, see Mr. Freed, tell him. Freed could evict him, get him out of there in a hurry. That would be the sensible way.

Before he knew it, Stone was back in his own walk-up flat, resting on the bed and staring at the wall. Although it wasn't the wall he was seeing. He was seeing the little fat man and studying him as he sat at his big table. He was seeing the books and the sheaves and the long rolls and scrolls of paper.

He could group them in the background, so. Just sketch them in lightly, in order to place the figure. The khaki shirt hung thusly—and the open collar draped in this fashion. Now the outlines of the head and shoulders; be sure to catch the intent intensity, the concentrated concentration of the pose.

Stone had his sketchpad out now, and his hands moved furiously. The sunlight would serve as a high light over the shoulder. It would strike the silver pin and the reflection would fleck the features of the face.

The features—the face—most important. He began to rough it in. If he could only capture the instant before the sob, if he could only fathom the secret of the eyes as the pin stabbed down, he'd have a painting.

What *was* that look? Stone had unconsciously catalogued and categorized the features. The proportions of nose to forehead, ears to head, chin to jaw; the relationship of brow and cheekbone to the eyes—he knew them and reproduced them. But the expression itself—particularly that look around the eyes—that was the key to it all.

And he couldn't get it down. He drew, erased, drew again. He made a marginal sketch and rubbed it out. The charcoal smeared his palm.

No, it was wrong, all wrong. He'd have to see him again. He was afraid to go, but he wanted that painting. He wanted to do it; he *had* to do it. There was a mystery here, and if he could only pin it down on canvas he'd be satisfied.

Pin it down. The pin was what frightened him, he knew it now. It wasn't the man so much. Granted, he was probably insane—without the pin he'd be harmless, deprived of weapons.

Stone stood up. He went out, down the stairs, walked. He should have gone to the rental agency first, he told himself, but the other need was greater. He wanted to see his subject once more. He wanted to stare into the face of the little fat man and read the secret behind the planes and angles.

And he did. He climbed the stairs silently, mounted the crate quietly, directed his soundless gaze over the transom.

The fat man was still at work. New books, new papers bulked high on the big table. But the left hand turned the pages, the right hand poised the pin. And the endless, enigmatic pantomime played on. Sigh, stab, sob. Stop and shudder, shuffle through fresh pages, scan and scrutinize again, and then—sigh, stab, sob.

The silver pin glared and glistened. It glowed and glittered and grew. Barton Stone tried to study the face of the fat man, tried to impress the image of his eyes.

Instead he saw the pin. The pin and only the pin. The pin that poised, the pin that pointed, the pin that pricked the page.

He forced himself to concentrate on the little man's face, forced himself to focus on form and features. He saw sorrow, read resignation, recognized revulsion, found fear there. But there was neither sorrow nor resignation, revulsion nor fear in the hand that drove the pin down again and again. There was only a mechanical gesture, without pattern or meaning that Barton Stone could decipher. It was the action of a lunatic, the antic gesture of aberration.

Stone stepped down from the crate, replaced it in the corner, then paused before the loft door. For a moment he hesitated. It would be so simple merely to walk into the loft, confront the little man, ask him his business. The little man would look up, and Stone could stare into his eyes, single out and scrutinize the secrets there.

But the little man had his pin, and Stone was afraid. He was afraid of the pin that didn't sob or sigh but merely stabbed down. And made its point.

The point—what was it?

Well, there was another way of finding out, the sensible way. Stone sidled softly down the stairs, padded purposefully up the street.

Here it was, ACME RENTALS. But the door was locked. Barton Stone glanced at his watch. Only four o'clock. Funny he'd be gone so early, unless he'd left with a client to show some property or office space.

Stone sighed. Tomorrow, then. Time enough. He turned and strode back down the street. He intended to go to his flat and rest before supper, but as he rounded the corner he saw something that stopped him in his tracks.

It was only a brownish blur, moving very fast. His eye caught a glimpse of khaki, a suggestion of a bowed back, a white-thatched head disappearing into the doorway of a local restaurant. That was enough; he was sure now. His little fat man had taken time out to eat.

And that meant . . .

Stone ran the remaining blocks, clattered up the rickety stairs. He burst into the loft, raced over to the table. Then, and then only, he stopped. What was he doing here? What did he hope to find out? What was he looking for?

That was it. He was looking for something. Some clue, some intimation of the little fat man's perverted purpose.

The books and papers billowed balefully all about him. There were at least half a hundred presently on the table. Stone picked up the first one. It was a telephone directory, current edition, for Bangor, Maine. Beneath it was another— Yuma, Arizona. And below that, in a gaudy cover, the city directory of Montevideo. At one side a long list of names, sheet after sheet of them, in French. The town roll of Dijon. And over at one side the electoral rolls of Manila, P.I. Another city directory—Stone guessed it must be in Russian. And here was the phone book from Leeds, and the census sheets from Calgary, and a little photostat of the unofficial census of Mombasa.

Stone paged through them, then directed his attention to another stack on the right-hand side of the table. Here were opened books aplenty, piled one upon the other in a baffling miscellany. Stone glanced at the bottom of the collection. Another phone book, from Seattle. City directory of Belfast. Voting list from Bloomington, Illinois. Precinct polling list, Melbourne, Australia. Page after page of Chinese ideographs. Military personnel, USAF, Tokyo base. A book in Swedish or Norwegian—Stone wasn't sure which, but he recognized that it contained nothing but names; and like all the others it was recent or currently published and in use.

And here, right on top, was a Manhattan directory. It was open, like the others, and apparently the choice of page had been made on random impulse. Barton Stone glanced at the heading: FRE. Was there a pin mark? He stared, found it.

Freed, George A. And the address.

Wait a minute! Wasn't that *his* rental agency man? Something began to form and fashion, and then Stone pushed the book away and ran out of the room and down the stairs, and he rounded the corner and found the newsstand and bought his paper and clawed it open to the death notices, and then he read the name again.

Freed, George A. And the address. And on another page—Stone's hands were trembling, and it took him a while to find it—was the story. It had happened this morning. Accident. Hit by a truck crossing the street. Survived by blah, blah, blah.

Yes, blah, blah, blah, and this morning (perhaps while Stone has been watching him the first time) the pin had pointed and stabbed and a name in the directory was marked for destruction. For death.

For *Death!*

Nobody'd ever bother looking up there. You could hide out there for years without being caught. Yes, you could gather together all the lists, all the sources, all the names in the world and put them into that deserted loft. You could sit there, day after day and night after night, and stick pins into them the way the legends said witches stuck pins into effigies of their victims. You'd sit there and choose book after book at random, and the pin would point. And wherever it struck somebody died. You could do that, and you *would* do that. If you were the little fat man. The little fat man whose name was *Death.*

Stone almost laughed, although the sound didn't come out that way. He'd wondered why he couldn't get the little man's eyes right, wondered why he couldn't search out their secret. Now he knew. He'd encountered the final mystery—that of Death itself. Death *himself.*

And where was Death now? Sitting in a cheap restaurant, a local hash house, taking a breather. Death was dining out. Simple enough, wasn't it? All Stone need do now was find a policeman and take him into the joint.

"See that little fat guy over there, Officer? I want you to arrest him for murder. He's Death, you know. And I can prove it. I'll show you the pin point."

Simple. *Insanely* simple.

Maybe he was wrong. He *had* to be wrong. Stone riffled back to the death notices again. Kooley, Leventhaler, Mautz. He had to make sure.

Kooley, Leventhaler, Mautz.

Question: How long does it take for Death to dine?

Question: Does Death care to linger over a second cup of coffee?

Question: Does one dare to back and search that directory to find the pin points opposite the names of Kooley, Leventhaler, and Mautz?

The first two questions couldn't be answered. They constituted a calculated risk. The third question could be solved only by action.

Barton Stone acted. His legs didn't want to move; his feet rebelled every step of the way, and his hands shook as he climbed the stairs once more.

Stone almost fell as he peered over the transom. The loft was still empty. And it was shrouded now in twilight. The dusk filtering through the skylight provided just enough illumination for him to read the directory. To find the names of Kooley, Leventhaler, and Mautz. And the pin points penetrating each, puncturing the *o,* the *v,* the *u.* Puncturing their names, puncturing their lives, providing punctuation. The final punctuation—period.

How many others had died today, in how many cities, towns, hamlets, crossroads, culverts, prisons, hospitals, huts, kraals, trenches, tents, igloos? How many times had the silver pin descended, forced by fatal fancy?

Yes, and how many times would it descend tonight? And tomorrow, and the next day, and forever and ever, time without end, amen?

They always pictured Death wielding a scythe, didn't they? And to think that it was really just a pin—a pin with a curve or a hook in it. A long, sharp, silver pin, like *that one there.*

The last rays of the dying sunset found it, set its length ablaze in a rainbow glow. Stone gasped sharply. It was here, right here on the table, where the little fat man had left it when he went out to eat—the silver pin!

Stone eyed the sparkling instrument, noted the hooked end, and gasped again. It *was* a scythe after all! A little miniature scythe of silver. The weapon of Death which cut down all mankind. Cut down mankind without rhyme or reason, stabbed senselessly to deprive men forever of sensation. Stone could picture it moving in frantic rhythm over the names of military personnel, pick, pick, picking away at lives; point, point, pointing at people; stick, stick, sticking into human hearts. The fatal instrument, the lethal weapon, smaller than any sword and bigger than any bomb.

It was *here,* on the table.

He had only to reach out and take it. . . .

For a moment the sun stood still and his heart stopped beating and there was nothing but silence in the whole wide world.

Stone picked up the pin.

He put it in his shirt pocket and stumbled out of the room, stumbled through darkness and tumbled down the flights of the night.

Then he was out on the street again and safe. He was safe, and the pin was safe in his pocket, and the world was safe forever.

Or was it? He couldn't be sure.

He couldn't be sure, and he wouldn't be sure, and he sat there in his room all night long, wondering if he'd gone completely mad.

For the pin was only a pin. True, it was shaped like a miniature scythe. True, it was cold and did not warm to the touch, and its point was sharper than any tool could ever grind.

But he couldn't be sure. Even the next morning there was nothing to show. He wondered if Death read the papers. He couldn't read *all* the papers. He couldn't attend *all* the funerals. He was too busy. Or, rather, he *had* been too busy. Now he could only wait, as Stone was waiting.

The afternoon editions would begin to provide proof. The home editions. Stone waited, because he couldn't be sure. And then he went down to the corner and bought four papers and he knew.

There were death notices still; of course there would be. Death notices from yesterday. Only from yesterday.

And the front pages carried further confirmation. The subject matter of the stories was serious enough, but the treatment was still humorous, quizzical, or, at best, speculative and aloof. Lots of smart boys on the wire services and the city desks; too hard-boiled to be taken in or commit themselves until they were certain. So there was no editorial comment yet, just story after story, each with its own "slant."

The prisoner up at Sing Sing who went to the chair last night—and was still alive. They'd given him plenty of juice, and the power worked all right. The man had fried in the hot seat. Fried, literally, but lived. Authorities were investigating. . . .

Freak accident up in Buffalo—cables snapped and a two-ton safe landed squarely on the head and shoulders of Frank Nelson, forty-two. Broken back, neck, arms, legs, pelvis, skull completely crushed. But in Emergency Hospital, Frank Nelson was still breathing and doctors could not account for. . . .

Plane crash in Chile. Eighteen passengers, all severely injured and many badly burned when engines caught fire, but no fatalities were reported and further reports. . . .

City hospitals could not explain the sudden cessation of deaths throughout Greater New York and environs. . . .

Gas-main explosions, automobile accidents, fires and natural disasters; each item isolated and treated as a freak, a separate phenomenon.

That's the way it would be until perhaps tomorrow, when the hard-boiled editors and the hard-headed medical men and the hard-shelled Baptists and the hard-nosed military leaders and the hard-pressed scientists all woke up, pooled their information, and realized that Death had died.

Meanwhile, the torn and the twisted, the burned and the maimed, the tortured and the broken ones writhed in their beds—but breathed and lived, in a fashion.

Stone breathed and lived in a fashion too. He was beginning to see the seared body of the convict, the mangled torso of the mover, the agonized forms that prayed for the mercy of oblivion all over the world.

Conscience doth make cowards of us all and *no man is an island.* But on the other hand, Stone breathed and lived after a fashion. And as long as he had the pin, he'd breathe and live forever. Forever!

So would they all. And more would be born, and the earth would teem with their multitude—what then? Very well, let the editors and the doctors and the preachers and the soldiers and the scientists figure out solutions. Stone had done his part. He'd destroyed Death. Or at the least, disarmed him.

Barton Stone wondered what Death was doing right now. Death, in the afternoon. Was he sitting in the loft, pondering over his piles of useless papers, lingering over his lethal ledgers? Or was he out, looking for another job? Couldn't very well expect to get unemployment compensation, and he had no social security.

That was *his* problem. Stone didn't care. He had other worries.

The tingling, for example. It had started late that morning, around noon. At first Stone ascribed it to the fact that he hadn't eaten or slept for over twenty-four hours. It was fatigue. But fatigue gnaws. Fatigue does not bite. It doesn't sink its sharp little tooth into your chest.

Sharp. Chest. Stone reached up, grabbed the silver pin from his pocket. The little scythe was cold. Its sharp, icy point had cut through his shirt, pricked against his heart.

Stone laid the pin down very carefully on the table, and he even turned the point away from himself. Then he sat back and sighed as the pain went away.

But it came back again, stronger. And Stone looked down and saw that the pin pointed at him again. He hadn't moved it. He hadn't touched it. He hadn't even looked at it. But it swung around like the needle of a compass. And he was its magnetic pole. He was due north. North, cold and icy like the pains that shot through his chest.

Death's weapon had power—the power to stab him, stab his chest and heart. It couldn't kill him, for there was no longer any dying in the world. It would just stab him now, forever and ever, night and day for all eternity. He was a magnet, attracting pain. Unendurable, endless pain.

The realization transfixed him, just as the point of the pin itself transfixed him.

Had his own hand reached out and picked up the pin, driven it into his chest? Or had the pin itself risen from the table and sought its magnetic target? Did the pin have its own powers?

Yes. That was the answer, and he knew it now. Knew that the little fat man was just a man and nothing more. A poor devil who had to go out and eat, who slept and dozed as best he could while he still stabbed ceaselessly away. He was only a tool. *The pin itself was Death.*

Had the little man once looked over a transom or peered through a window in New York or Baghdad or Durban or Rangoon? Had he stolen the silver pin from yet another poor devil and then been driven by it, driven out into the street by the pin that pricked and pricked at his heart? Had he returned to the place where all the names in the world awaited their final sentencing?

Barton Stone didn't know. All he knew was that the pin was colder than arctic ice and hotter than volcanic fire and it was tearing at his chest. Every time he tore it free the point inexorably returned and his hand descended with it, forcing the pin into his chest. Sigh, stab, sob—the power of Death was in the pin.

And the power of Death animated Barton Stone as he ran through the nighted streets, panted up the midnight stairs, staggering into the loft.

A dim light burned over the table, casting its glow over the waiting shadows. The little fat man sat there, surrounded by his books, and when he saw Barton Stone he looked up and nodded.

His stare was impersonal and blank. Stone's stare was agonized and intent. There was something Stone had to find out, once and for all, a question which must be answered. He recognized its nature and the need, sought and found his solution in the little fat man's face.

The little fat man *was* a man and nothing more. He *was* merely the instrument, and the pin held all the power. That was enough for Barton Stone to know. It was all he could know, for the rest was only endless pain. He had to be relieved of the pain, had to be released from it, just as the poor devils all over the world had to be relieved and released. It was logic, cold logic, cold as the pin, cold as Death.

Stone gasped, and the little fat man stood up and moved around from behind the table.

"I've been waiting for you," he said. "I knew you'd come back."

Stone forced the words out. "I stole the pin," he panted. "I've come to give it back."

The little fat man looked at him, and for the first time Stone could read his eyes. In them he saw infinite compassion, limitless understanding, and an endless relief.

"What is taken cannot be returned," murmured the little man. "I think you know that. When you took the pin you took it forever. Or until—"

The little man shrugged and indicated the seat behind the table.

Silently Stone sat down. The books bulked before him; the books, the directories, the papers and scrolls and lists that contained all the names in the world.

"The most urgent are on top," whispered the little man. "I sorted them while I waited."

"Then you knew I'd be back?"

The little fat man nodded. "I came back once too. And I found—as you will find—that the pain goes away. You can remove the pin now and get to work. There's so much work to do."

He was right. There was no longer any stabbing sensation in Stone's chest. The little scythe-shaped pin came away quite easily and balanced in Stone's right hand. His left hand reached for the topmost book. A small piece of paper, bearing a single scribbled name, rested on the opened volume.

"If you don't mind," breathed the little fat man, "this name first, please."

Stone looked at the little fat man. He didn't look down at the scribbled name—he didn't have to, for he knew. And his right hand stabbed down, and the little man sighed and then he fell over and there was only a wisp of dust.

Old dust, gossamer-light dust, soon blows away. And there was no time to look at the dancing, dissipating motes. For Barton Stone was sighing, stabbing, shuddering, sobbing.

And the pin pointed and pricked. Pricked the convict up in Sing Sing and Frank Nelson in Buffalo Emergency and the crash victims in Chile. Pricked Chundra Lal of Bombay, Ramona Neilson of Minneapolis, Barney Yates in Glasgow, Igor Vorpetchzki in Minsk, Mrs. Minnie Haines and Dr. Fisher and Urbonga and Li Chan and a man named John Smith in Upper Sandusky.

It was day and it was night and it was summer and it was autumn and it was winter and it was spring and it was summer again, but you could hide out there for years without being caught.

All you did was keep shuffling the books, picking at random. That was the best you could do, the only fair way. Sometimes you got mad and took a lot from one place; sometimes you just kept going, plodding along and leaving it up to the pin.

You sighed, you stabbed, you shuddered, and you sobbed. But you never stopped. Because the pin never stopped; the scythe was always swinging.

Thus it was, and thus it would be forever. Until the day came, inevitably, when somehow, somewhere, someone would find out. . . .

JOE R. LANSDALE

I suppose I should talk about "The Animal Fair," as that's the story I've chosen as a favorite, but I'd rather talk about Robert Bloch.

I must admit, right up front, that I hardly knew the man. He and I had met, exchanged a few letters, and I had the honor of asking him for, and receiving, the rights to have a comic adaptation done of his marvelous "That Hell-Bound Train" for *Weird Business,* a comic book collection I'm coediting with Rick Klaw. But that was pretty much the extent of our personal relationship.

Our card and letter exchanges were brief and simple, but even in those, he was witty and fun. I will admit, too, that Robert Bloch is the only author, with the possible exception of Richard Matheson, who I've met and was so in awe of that I could not speak. Speak intelligently, anyway. He was just too important and influential a person in my life, and I hardly knew him. But I knew his books and stories, and loved them.

I first met him, briefly, at a convention in St. Louis, Missouri. He was on a panel, and he looked out at the audience, spied my baby son, Keith, and while most everyone else on the panel was absorbed in being self-important, he pointed at Keith and called him a "beautiful infant."

This right after one of horror's younger biggies had refused to shake hands with me for no reason I could ever determine other than the fact that I wasn't famous, having only published a handful of stories and a novel at the time. Maybe it wasn't intentional, this refusing to shake my hand, just a moment where the writer was self-absorbed, but I've not forgotten it. I've forgiven, but not forgotten.

I think Robert Bloch took note of this incident, and commented on my son, not only because Keith was a beautiful infant, but because he saw I had been snubbed and wanted to make me feel human again, if in an indirect manner.

And you know what? I think he would have done it anyway, because that's just the kind of man he was.

Bloch never lost the human touch. Never gave the impression that he thought so highly of himself he couldn't consider others. He was one of that handful of writers who actually was as wonderful in person as their work.

Recently, when Robert Bloch agreed to let Rick and me option rights to his story, "That Hell-Bound Train," I had no idea that he was dying, or that he knew he was dying. His notes to me and to Rick and our publisher gave no indication of this, except that they were a little slow in coming.

When I found out a short time later that he was very ill, I was stunned. In one sense, I expected it. He was elderly, and I'd heard rumors off and on that he had not been in the best of health; but still, it was a shock.

But again he was, as always, a class act. He even handled dying with dignity—or as much as is humanly possible—and went out the way he lived his life: Laughing at himself and death. You can see this in his last published piece, an article in the October 1994 issue of *Omni*, where he writes about dying, sort of does his own obituary, and leaves us all with a bit of his courage to cling to.

Finally, all I can say is this: He was a hero to me. I would not have written the horror stories I've written without Robert Bloch, and neither would a large number of the horror/suspense/mystery writers working today.

He was a literary uncle for so many of us. He showed us how to be scary. How to tap into the terrors of the mind, and how to laugh at ourselves, as well as at the horrors of the world. And yet, he was always, somehow, compassionate and gentle.

Keep in mind, though I say with the greatest of pride that Robert Bloch influenced me, I in no way consider myself his equal, by half. Frankly, I wouldn't make a pimple on the great man's ass. But I hope I learned something from the master.

Not only about writing.

But about living.

And finally, about dying.

All right, something about "The Animal Fair." This is just the sort of Robert Bloch story I love. It's scary, creepy, offbeat, and the horror is of a realistic nature—meaning no supernatural elements. Just plain old twisted meanness. And yet, it's funny. Not in the "I just heard a good joke" kind of way, but in a deeper, more biting manner. Bloch makes you laugh, but makes you feel bad for laughing, while at the same time giving you a certain insight into human nature. Not always an insight you appreciate, but a truthful insight, nonetheless.

But you know what I love best about this story, about all of Robert Bloch's fiction, for that matter?

The simplicity with which he leads you into the tale, nails you to it, proceeds with a deceptively simple style, and won't let you go until the tale is told.

Wonderful.

"The Animal Fair," like so many of his stories, is caviar.

Enjoy.

But I needn't suggest that. You won't be able to do otherwise.

THE ANIMAL FAIR

🦢 *It was dark when the truck dropped Dave off at the de-*
serted freight depot. Dave had to squint to make out the lettering on the weather-faded sign. MEDLEY, OKLAHOMA—POP. 1,134.

The trucker said he could probably get another lift on the state highway up
past the other end of town, so Dave hit the main drag. And it was a drag.

Nine o'clock of a hot summer evening, and Medley was closed for the night.
Fred's Eats had locked up, the Jiffy SuperMart had shut down, even Phil's Phill-
Up Gas stood deserted. There were no cars parked on the dark street, not even
the usual cluster of kids on the corners.

Dave wondered about this, but not for long. In five minutes he covered the
length of Main Street and emerged on open fields at the far side, and that's when
he saw the lights and heard the music.

They had a carnival going in the little county fairgrounds up ahead—canned
music blasting from amplifiers, cars crowding the parking lot, mobs milling
across the midway.

Dave wasn't craving this kind of action, but he still had eight cents in his
jeans and he hadn't eaten anything since breakfast. He turned down the sideroad
leading to the fairgrounds.

As he figured, the carnival was a bummer. One of those little mud shows,
traveling by truck; a couple of beat-up rides for the kids and a lot of come-ons
for the local yokels. Wheel o' Fortune, Pitch-a-Winner, Take a Chance on a Blanket, that kind of jive. By the time Dave got himself a burger and coffee at one of
the stands he knew the score. A big fat zero.

But not for Medley, Oklahoma—Pop. 1,134. The whole damn town was here
tonight and probably every redneck for miles around, shuffling and shoving himself to get through to the far end of the midway.

And it was there, on the far end, that he saw the small red tent with the tiny platform before it. Hanging limp and listless in the still air, a sunbleached banner proclaimed the wonders within.

CAPTAIN RYDER'S HOLLYWOOD JUNGLE SAFARI, the banner read.

What a Hollywood Jungle Safari was, Dave didn't know. And the wrinkled cloth posters lining the sides of the entrance weren't much help. A picture of a guy in an explorer's outfit, tangling with a big snake wrapped around his neck—the same joker prying open the jaws of a crocodile—another drawing showing him wrestling a lion. The last poster showed the guy standing next to a cage; inside the cage was a black, furry question mark, way over six feet high. The lettering underneath was black and furry too. WHAT IS IT? SEE THE MIGHTY MONARCH OF THE JUNGLE ALIVE ON THE INSIDE!

Dave didn't know what it was and he cared less. But he'd been bumping along those corduroy roads all day and he was wasted and the noise from the amplifiers here on the midway hurt his ears. At least there was some kind of a show going on inside, and when he saw the open space gaping between the canvas and the ground at the corner of the tent he stooped and slid under.

The tent was a canvas oven.

Dave could smell oil in the air; on hot summer nights in Oklahoma you can always smell it. And the crowd in here smelled worse. Bad enough that he was thumbing his way through and couldn't take a bath, but what was their excuse?

The crowd huddled around the base of a portable wooden stage at the rear of the tent, listening to a pitch from Captain Ryder. At least that's who Dave figured it was, even though the character with the phony safari hat and the dirty white riding breeches didn't look much like his pictures on the banners. He was handing out a spiel in one of those hoarse, gravelly voices that carries without a microphone—some hype about being a Hollywood stunt man and African explorer—and there wasn't a snake or a crocodile or a lion anywhere in sight.

The two-bit hamburger began churning up a storm in Dave's guts, and between the body heat and the smells he'd just about had it in here. He started to turn and push his way through the mob when the man up on the stage thumped the boards with his cane.

"And now friends, if you'll gather around a little closer—"

The crowd swept forward in unison, like the straws of a giant broom, and Dave found himself pressed right up against the edge of the square-shaped canvas-covered pit beside the end of the platform. He couldn't get through now if he tried; all the rednecks were bunched together, waiting.

Dave waited, too, but he stopped listening to the voice on the platform. All that jive about Darkest Africa was a put-on. Maybe these clowns went for it, but Dave wasn't buying a word. He just hoped the old guy would hurry and get the show over with; all he wanted now was out of here.

Captain Ryder tapped the canvas covering of the pit with his cane and his harsh tones rose. The heat made Dave yawn loudly, but some of the phrases filtered through.

"—about to see here tonight the world's most ferocious monster—captured at deadly peril of life and limb—"

Dave shook his head. He knew what was in the pit. Some crummy animal picked up secondhand from a circus, maybe a scroungy hyena. And two to one it wasn't even alive, just stuffed. Big deal.

Captain Ryder lifted the canvas cover and pulled it back behind the pit. He flourished his cane.

"Behold—the lord of the jungle!"

The crowd pressed, pushed, peered over the rim of the pit.

The crowd gasped.

And Dave, pressing and peering with the rest, stared at the creature blinking up at him from the bottom of the pit.

It was a live, full-grown gorilla.

The monster squatted on a heap of straw, its huge forearms secured to steel stakes by lengths of heavy chain. It gaped upward at the rim of faces, moving its great gray head slowly from side to side, the yellow-fanged mouth open and the massive jaws set in a vacant grimace. Only the little rheumy, red-rimmed eyes held a hint of expression—enough to tell Dave, who had never seen a gorilla before, that this animal was sick.

The matted straw at the base of the pit was wet and stained; in one corner a battered tin plate rested untouched, its surface covered with a soggy slop of shredded carrots, okra and turnip greens floating in an oily scum beneath a cloud of buzzing blowflies. In the stifling heat of the tent the acrid odor arising from the pit was almost overpowering.

Dave felt his stomach muscles constrict. He tried to force his attention back to Captain Ryder. The old guy was stepping offstage now, moving behind the pit and reaching down into it with his cane.

"—nothing to be afraid of, folks, as you can see he's perfectly harmless, aren't you, Bobo?"

The gorilla whimpered, huddling back against the soiled straw to avoid the prodding cane. But the chains confined movement and the cane began to dig its tip into the beast's shaggy shoulders.

"And now Bobo's going to do a little dance for the folks—right?" The gorilla whimpered again, but the point of the cane jabbed deeply and the rasping voice firmed in command.

"Up, Bobo—up!"

The creature lumbered to its haunches. As the cane rose and fell about its shoulders, the bulky body began to sway. The crowd oohed and aahed and snickered.

"That's it! Dance for the people, Bobo—dance—"

A swarm of flies spiraled upward to swirl about the furry form shimmering in the heat. Dave saw the sick beast shuffle, moving to and fro, to and fro. Then his stomach was moving in responsive rhythm and he had to shut his eyes as he turned and fought his way blindly through the murmuring mob.

"Hey—watch where the hell ya goin', fella—"

Dave got out of the tent just in time.

Getting rid of the hamburger helped, and getting away from the carnival grounds helped too, but not enough. As Dave moved up the road between the open fields he felt the nausea return. Gulping the oily air made him dizzy and he knew he'd have to lie down for a minute. He dropped in the ditch beside the road, shielded behind a clump of weeds, and closed his eyes to stop the whirling sensation. Only for a minute—

The dizziness went away, but behind his closed eyes he could still see the gorilla, still see the expressionless face and the all-too-expressive eyes. Eyes peering up from the pile of dirty straw in the pit, eyes clouding with pain and hopeless resignation as the chains clanked and the cane flicked across the hairy shoulders.

Ought to be a law, Dave thought. There must be some kind of law to stop it, treating a poor dumb animal like that. And the old guy, Captain Ryder—there ought to be a law for an animal like him, too.

Ah, to hell with it. Better shut it out of his mind now, get some rest. Another couple of minutes wouldn't hurt—

It was the thunder that finally woke him. The thunder jerked him into awareness, and then he felt the warm, heavy drops pelting his head and face.

Dave rose and the wind swept over him, whistling across the fields. He must have been asleep for hours, because everything was pitch-black, and when he glanced behind him the lights of the carnival were gone.

For an instant the sky turned silver and he could see the rain pour down. See it, hell—he could feel it, and then the thunder came again, giving him the message. This wasn't just a summer shower, it was a real storm. Another minute and he was going to be soaking wet. By the time he got up to the state highway he could drown, and there wouldn't be a lift there for him, either. Nobody traveled in this kind of weather.

Dave zipped up his jacket, pulled the collar around his neck. It didn't help, and neither did walking up the road, but he might as well get going. The wind was at his back and that helped a little, but moving against the rain was like walking through a wall of water.

Another flicker of lightning, another rumble of thunder. And then the flickering and the rumbling merged and held steady; the light grew brighter and the sound rose over the hiss of wind and rain.

Dave glanced back over his shoulder and saw the source. The headlights and engine of a truck coming along the road from behind him. As it moved closer Dave realized it wasn't a truck; it was a camper, one of those two-decker jobs with a driver's cab up front.

Right now he didn't give a damn what it was as long as it stopped and picked him up. As the camper came alongside of him Dave stepped out, waving his arms.

The camper slowed, halted. The shadowy silhouette in the cab leaned over from behind the wheel and a hand pushed the window vent open on the passenger side.

"Want a lift, buddy?"

Dave nodded.

"Get in."

The door swung open and Dave climbed up into the cab. He slid across the seat and pulled the door shut behind him.

The camper started to move again.

"Shut the window," the driver said. "Rain's blowing in."

Dave closed it, then wished he hadn't. The air inside the cab was heavy with odors—not just perspiration, but something else. Dave recognized the smell even before the driver produced the bottle from his jacket pocket.

"Want a slug?"

Dave shook his head.

"Fresh corn likker. Tastes like hell, but it's better'n nothing."

"No, thanks."

"Suit yourself." The bottle tilted and gurgled. Lightning flared across the roadway ahead, glinting across the glass of the windshield, the glass of the upturned bottle. In its momentary glare Dave caught a glimpse of the driver's face, and the flash of lightning brought a flash of recognition.

The driver was Captain Ryder.

Thunder growled, prowling the sky, and the heavy camper turned onto the slick, rain-swept surface of the state highway.

"—what's the matter, you deaf or something? I asked you where you're heading."

Dave came to with a start.

"Oklahoma City," he said.

"You hit the jackpot. That's where I'm going."

Some jackpot. Dave had been thinking about the old guy, remembering the gorilla in the pit. He hated this bastard's guts, and the idea of riding with him all the way to Oklahoma City made his stomach churn all over again. On the other hand it wouldn't help his stomach any if he got set down in a storm here in the middle of the prairie, so what the hell. One quick look at the rain made up his mind for him.

The camper lurched and Ryder fought the wheel.

"Boy—sure is a cutter!"

Dave nodded.

"Get these things often around here?"

"I wouldn't know," Dave said. "This is my first time through. I'm meeting a friend in Oklahoma City. We figure on driving out to Hollywood together—"

"Hollywood?" The hoarse voice deepened. "That goddamn place!"

"But don't you come from there?"

Ryder glanced up quickly and lightning flickered across his sudden frown. Seeing him this close, Dave realized he wasn't so old; something besides time had shaped that scowl, etched the bitter lines around eyes and mouth.

"Who told you that?" Ryder said.

"I was at the carnival tonight. I saw your show."

Ryder grunted and his eyes tracked the road ahead through the twin pendulums of the windshield wipers. "Pretty lousy, huh?"

Dave started to nod, then caught himself. No sense starting anything. "That gorilla of yours looked like it might be sick."

"Bobo? He's all right. Just the weather. We open up north, he'll be fine." Ryder nodded in the direction of the camper bulking behind him. "Haven't heard a peep out of him since we started."

"He's traveling with you?"

"Whaddya think, I ship him airmail?" A hand rose from the wheel, gesturing. "This camper's built special. I got the upstairs, he's down below. I keep the back open so's he gets some air, but no problem—I got it all barred. Take a look through that window behind you."

Dave turned and peered through the wire-meshed window at the rear of the cab. He could see the lighted interior of the camper's upper level, neatly and normally outfitted for occupancy. Shifting his gaze, he stared into the darkness below. Lashed securely to the side walls were the tent, the platform boards, the banners, and the rigging; the floor space between them was covered with straw, heaped into a sort of nest. Crouched against the barred opening at the far end was the black bulk of the gorilla, back turned as it faced the road to the rear, intent on the roaring rain. The camper went into a skid for a moment and the beast twitched, jerking its head around so that Dave caught a glimpse of its glazed eyes. It seemed to whimper softly, but because of the thunder Dave couldn't be sure.

"Snug as a bug," Ryder said. "And so are we." He had the bottle out again, deftly uncorking it with one hand.

"Sure you don't want a belt?"

"I'll pass," Dave said.

The bottle raised, then paused. "Hey, wait a minute." Ryder was scowling at him again. "You're not on something else, are you, buddy?"

"Drugs?" Dave shook his head. "Not me."

"Good thing you're not." The bottle tilted, lowered again as Ryder corked it. "I hate that crap. Drugs. Drugs and hippies. Hollywood's full of both. You take my advice, you keep away from there. No place for a kid, not any more." He belched loudly, started to put the bottle back into his jacket pocket, then uncorked it again.

Watching him drink, Dave realized he was getting loaded. Best thing to do would be to keep him talking, take his mind off the bottle before he knocked the camper off the road.

"No kidding, were you really a Hollywood stunt man?" Dave said.

"Sure, one of the best. But that was back in the old days, before the place went to hell. Worked for all the majors—trick riding, fancy falls, doubling fight scenes, the works. You ask anybody who knows, they'll tell you old Cap Ryder was right up there with Yakima Canutt, maybe even better." The voice rasped on, harsh with pride. "Seven-fifty a day, that's what I drew. Seven hundred and fifty, every day I worked. And I worked a lot."

"I didn't know they paid that kind of dough," Dave told him.

"You got to remember one thing. I wasn't just taking falls in the long shots. When they hired Cap Ryder they knew they were getting some fancy talent. Not many stunt men can handle animals. You ever see any of those old jungle pictures on television—Tarzan movies, stuff like that? Well, in over half of 'em I'm the guy handling the cats. Lions, leopards, tigers, you name it."

"Sounds exciting."

"Sure, if you like hospitals. Wrestled a black panther once, like to rip my arm clean off in one shot they set up. Seven-fifty sounds like a lot of loot, but you should have seen what I laid out in medical bills. Not to mention what I paid for costumes and extras. Like the lion skins and the ape suit—"

"I don't get it." Dave frowned.

"Sometimes the way they set a shot for a close-up they need the star's face. So if it was a fight scene with a lion or whatever, that's where I came in handy—I doubled for the animal. Would you believe it, three grand I laid out for a lousy monkey suit alone! But it paid off. You should have seen the big pad I had up over Laurel Canyon. Four bedrooms, three-car garage, tennis court, swimming pool, sauna, everything you can think of. Melissa loved it—"

"Melissa?"

Ryder shook his head. "What'm I talking about? You don't want to hear any of that crud about the good old days. All water over the dam."

The mention of water evidently reminded him of something else, because Dave saw him reach for the bottle again. And this time, when he tilted it, it gurgled down to empty.

Ryder cranked the window down on his side and flung the bottle out into the rain.

"All gone," he muttered. "Finished. No more bottle. No more house. No more Melissa—"

"Who was she?" Dave said.

"You really want to know?" Ryder jerked his thumb toward the windshield. Dave followed the gesture, puzzled, until he raised his glance to the roof of the cab. There, fastened directly above the rear-view mirror, was a small picture frame. Staring out of it was the face of a girl; blonde hair, nice features, and with the kind of a smile you see in the pages of high school annuals.

"My niece," Ryder told him. "Sixteen. But I took her when she was only five, right after my sister died. Took her and raised her for eleven years. Raised her right, too. Let me tell you, that girl never lacked for anything. Whatever she wanted, whatever she needed, she got. The trips we took together—the good times we had—hell, I guess it sounds pretty silly, but you'd be surprised what a kick you can get out of seeing a kid have fun. And smart? President of the junior class at Brixley—that's the name of the private school I put her in, best in town, half the stars sent their own daughters there. And that's what she was to me, just like my own flesh-and-blood daughter. So go figure it. How it happened I'll never know." Ryder blinked at the road ahead, forcing his eyes into focus.

"How what happened?" Dave asked.

"The hippies. The goddam sonsabitching hippies." The eyes were suddenly alert in the network of ugly wrinkles. "Don't ask me where she met the bastards, I thought I was guarding her from all that, but those lousy freaks are all over the place. She must of run into them through one of her friends at school—Christ knows, you see plenty of weirdos even in Bel Air. But you got to remember, she was just sixteen and how could she guess what she was getting into? I suppose at that age an older guy with a beard and a Fender guitar and a souped-up cycle looks pretty exciting.

"Anyhow they got to her. One night when I was away on location—maybe she invited them over to the house, maybe they just showed up and she asked them in. Four of 'em, all stoned out of their skulls. Dude, that was the oldest one's name—he was like the leader, and it was his idea from the start. She wouldn't smoke anything, but he hadn't really figured she would and he came prepared. Must have worked it so she served something cold to drink and he slipped the stuff into her glass. Enough to finish off a bull elephant, the coroner said."

"You mean it killed her—"

"Not right away. I wish to Christ it had." Ryder turned, his face working, and Dave had to strain to hear his voice mumbling through the rush of rain.

"According to the coroner she must have lived for at least an hour. Long enough for them to take turns—Dude and the other three. Long enough after that for them to get the idea.

"They were in my den, and I had the place all fixed up like a kind of trophy room—animal skins all over the wall, native drums, voodoo masks, stuff I'd picked up on my trips. And here were these four freaks, spaced out, and the kid, blowing her mind. One of the bastards took down a drum and started beating on it. Another got hold of a mask and started hopping around like a witch doctor. And Dude—it was Dude all right, I know it for sure—he and the other creep pulled the lion skin off the wall and draped it over Melissa. Because this was a trip and they were playing Africa. Great White Hunter. Me Tarzan, You Jane.

"By this time Melissa couldn't even stand up any more. Dude got her down on her hands and knees and she just wobbled there. And then—that dirty rotten son of a bitch—he pulled down the drapery cords and tied the stinking lion skin over her head and shoulders. And he took a spear down from the wall, one of the Masai spears, and he was going to jab her in the ribs with it—

"That's what I saw when I came in. Dude, the big stud, standing over Melissa with that spear.

"He didn't stand long. One look at me and he must have known. I think he threw the spear before he ran, but I can't remember. I can't remember anything about the next couple of minutes. They said I broke one freak's collarbone, and the creep in the mask had a concussion from where his head hit the wall. The third one was almost dead by the time the squad arrived and pried my fingers loose from his neck. As it was, they were too late to save him.

"And they were too late for Melissa. She just lay there under that dirty lion skin—that's the part I do remember, the part I wish I could forget—"

"You killed a kid?" Dave said.

Ryder shook his head. "I killed an animal. That's what I told them at the trial. When an animal goes vicious, you got a right. The judge said one to five, but I was out in a little over two years." He glanced at Dave. "Ever been inside?"

"No. How is it—rough?"

"You can say that again. Rough as a cob." Ryder's stomach rumbled. "I came in pretty feisty, so they put me down in solitary for a while and that didn't help. You sit there in the dark and you start thinking. Here am I, used to traveling all over the world, penned up in a little cage like an animal. And those animals—the ones who killed Melissa—they're running free. One was dead, of course, and the two others I tangled with had maybe learned their lesson. But the big one, the one who started it all, he was loose. Cops never did catch up with him, and they weren't about to waste any more time trying, now that the trial was over.

"I thought a lot about Dude. That was the big one's name, or did I tell you?" Ryder blinked at Dave, and he looked pretty smashed. But he was driving OK and he wouldn't fall asleep at the wheel as long as he kept talking, so Dave nodded.

"Mostly I thought about what I was going to do to Dude once I got out. Finding him would be tricky, but I knew I could do it—hell, I spent years in Africa, tracking animals. And I intended to hunt this one down."

"Then it's true about you being an explorer?" Dave asked.

"Animal-trapper," Ryder said. "Kenya, Uganda, Nigeria—this was before Hollywood, and I saw it all. Things these young punks today never dreamed of. Why, they were dancing and drumming and drugging over there before the first hippie crawled out from under his rock, and let me tell you, they know how to do this stuff for real.

"Like when this Dude tied the lion skin on Melissa, he was just freaked out, playing games. He should have seen what some of those witch doctors can do.

"First they steal themselves a girl, sometimes a young boy, but let's say a girl because of Melissa. And they shut her up in a cave—a cave with a low ceiling, so she can't stand up, has to go on all fours. They put her on drugs right away, heavy doses, enough to keep her out for a long time. And when she wakes up her hands and feet have been operated on, so they can be fitted with claws. Lion claws, and they've sewed her into a lion skin. Not just put it over her—it's sewed on completely, and it can't be removed.

"You just think about what it's like. She's inside this lion skin, shut away in a cave, doped up, doesn't know where she is or what's going on. And they keep her that way. Feed her on nothing but raw meat. She's all alone in the dark, smelling that damn lion smell, nobody talking to her and nobody for her to talk to. Then pretty soon they come in and break some bones in her throat, her larynx, and all she can do is whine and growl. Whine and growl, and move around on all fours.

"You know what happens, boy? You know what happens to someone like that? They go crazy. And after a while they get to believing they really are a lion.

The next step is for the witch doctor to take them out and train them to kill, but that's another story."

Dave glanced up quickly. "You're putting me on—"

"It's all there in the government reports. Maybe the jets come into Nairobi airport now, but back in the jungle things haven't changed. Like I say, some of these people know more about drugs than any hippie ever will. Especially a stupid animal like Dude."

"What happened after you got out?" Dave said. "Did you ever catch up with him?"

Ryder shook his head.

"But I thought you said you had it all planned—"

"Fella gets a lot of weird ideas in solitary. In a way it's pretty much like being shut up in one of those caves. Come to think of it, that's what first reminded me—"

"Of what?"

"Nothing." Ryder gestured hastily. "Forget it. That's what I did. When I got out I figured that was the best way. Forgive and forget."

"You didn't even try to find Dude?"

Ryder frowned. "I told you. I had other things to think about. Like being washed up in the business, losing the house, the furniture, everything. Also I had a drinking problem. But you don't want to hear about that. Anyway, I ended up with the carny and there's nothing more to tell."

Lightning streaked across the sky and thunder rolled in its wake. Dave turned his head, glancing back through the wire-meshed window. The gorilla was still hunched at the far end, peering through the bars into the night beyond. Dave stared at him for a long moment, not really wanting to stop, because then he knew he'd have to ask the question. But the longer he stared, the more he realized that he had no choice.

"What about him?" Dave asked.

"Who?" Ryder followed Dave's gaze. "Oh, you mean Bobo. I picked him up from a dealer I know."

"Must have been expensive."

"They don't come cheap. Not many left."

"Less than a hundred." Dave hesitated. "I read about it in the Sunday paper back home. Feature article on the national preserves. Said gorillas are government-protected, can't be sold."

"I was lucky," Ryder murmured. He leaned foward and Dave was immersed in the alcoholic reek. "I got connections, understand?"

"Right." Dave didn't want the words to come but he couldn't hold them back. "What I don't understand is this lousy carnival. With gorillas so scarce, you should be with a big show."

"That's my business." Ryder gave him a funny look.

"It's business I'm talking about." Dave took a deep breath. "Like if you were so broke, where'd you get the money to buy an animal like this?"

Ryder scowled. "I already said. I sold off everything—the house, the furni-ture—"

"And your monkey suit?"

The fist came up so fast Dave didn't even see it. But it slammed into his fore-head, knocking him back across the seat, against the unlocked side door.

Dave tried to make a grab for something but it was too late, he was falling. He hit the ditch on his back, and only the mud saved him.

Then the sky caught fire, thunder crashed, and the camper slid past him, dis-appearing into the dark tunnel of the night. But not before Dave caught one final glimpse of the gorilla, squatting behind the bars.

The gorilla, with its drug-dazed eyes, its masklike, motionless mouth, and its upraised arms revealing the pattern of heavy black stitches.

BOB, WE BEARLY KNEW YE . . . THE HOKAS, HOLLYWOOD, AND DEVELOPMENT HELL

JEFF WALKER

I didn't know Robert Bloch well, but I did have the pleasure of working with him as a producer on a screenplay based on Poul Anderson and Gordon R. Dickson's classic Hoka stories—the zany adventures of a couple of humans trying to control a race of intelligent, anarchistic Teddy Bears whose entire civilization is a pastiche of Earth's great fiction.

I've been a fan of science fiction (and all of its related genres) as long as I can remember. I subscribed to F&SF and joined the SF Book Club at the still impressionable (in those days, anyway) age of eleven. I read the classic novels as well as the new writers; the old pulps and current comics. I consumed and collected everything I could get my hands on (all of which was eventually thrown out by, yes, my mother) and saw just about every genre film every made, in spite of her dire warnings.

I loved short stories and satire. Stan Freberg, Richard Armour, Robert Benchley, *MAD* magazine; and especially enjoyed several unique writers who managed to find a special place in my consciousness with their combination of science fiction, fantasy, horror, irony, social satire, and terrible puns—particularly Fredric Brown, Charles Beaumont, and Robert Bloch.

During this same time, a number of the Hoka tales were made available once again in the delightful collection *Earthman's Burden*, where I first encountered them. Little did I know that almost twenty-five years later, I would somehow manage to bring together, for a short time, a few of the most wondrous voices of my youth.

By the early 1980s, in the midst of a career spanning the publishing, film, and music industries, as a writer, critic, and occasional executive, the Hokas seemed to me to be an ideal vehicle for a series of comic films—a kind of ET meets Monty Python, starring a group of Ursanoid Marx Bros.

Along with my brother, Michael, and our executive producer, Eddie

Rissien, we managed to secure the motion picture rights to all of the Hoka stories. Oscar-winning makeup effects genius Rick Baker agreed to create the animatronic Hokas based on character designs by multiple Hugo Award–winning artist Michael Whelan. We were off to a good start.

The first piece we commissioned was essentially a movie poster approach, featuring Hoka versions of a cowboy, space cadet, pirate, pith-helmeted British explorer, and Sherlock Holmes surrounding the exasperated Earthman who has crash-landed on their planet.

Armed with this wonderful painting, an elaborate presentation, and the original source material, we caught the attention of the director Sydney Pollack, who was at that time helping to set up a new movie studio with the late Gary Hendler. They fell in love with the Hokas at first sight and our film became the first announced project of Tri-Star Pictures. Now all we needed was a script.

We subsequently had meetings with a number of hot young comedy writers on the studio's "acceptable" list, including Chris Columbus (*Gremlins*) and [Peter S.] Seaman and [Jeffrey] Price (*Who Framed Roger Rabbit?*). But even with the lure of a new studio, Sydney Pollack's involvement, and the genuine interest of several top directors, none of the writers seemed to be able to (or even want to) rein the rambunctious Hokas into something coherent. It was usually simply dismissed as "too episodic" or "just a kid's movie."

I was convinced that the Hokas needed an edge to appeal to a wider audience and wanted to find a pro in the genre who was familiar with these characters; someone who would be enthusiastic enough to devote the time necessary to it. My first phone calls were to Harlan Ellison and Robert Bloch. Harlan's reaction was "Great idea . . . the Hokas could make a terrific movie. But why on earth are you calling *me*?" I told him about our dilemma and my crazy thoughts about structure, satire, and dark humor. I also mentioned we were approaching Robert Bloch as well. Harlan instantly said, "If you can get Bob Bloch, you don't need me. He's the best." Well, if there's one thing I'd learned about Harlan over the years, it's that I could trust him. Thus validated, we called Robert Bloch out of the blue and broached our beloved bears. Not only was Bob enamored of the little beasts himself, he also counted Poul and Gordy among his closest friends.

We set up a meeting at Bob's office to get acquainted and throw a few ideas around. The Blochs lived in an unassuming home high in one of L.A.'s canyons. Bob greeted us at the door and warmly ushered us into his house. As we entered his studio, I immediately noticed that, true to his reptuation, Robert Bloch indeed had the heart of a small boy, and, yes, it was pickled in a jar on his desk. With his back framed by a view of his patio in the sunset, Bob sat at a desk that looked as if it belonged in the Dean's Office at Miskatonic University. We were seated in the midst of a library that became a constant distraction and delight—the first edition

Lovecrafts; the definitive collection of literature devoted to Jack the Ripper; the *Psycho* shelf; a first edition of the Bible (autographed by the author); and the massive *World Conspiracy Against Robert Bloch* that formed the centerpiece of his bookshelf. By dusk we knew we had our man.

Our next step was convincing the studio. No easy task. By this time, Sydney Pollack was halfway around the world filming *Out of Africa,* and we found ourselves being bounced around between development executives who hadn't been there when the project came on board and had never heard of Robert Bloch. Just try to convince genre-ignorant (not to mention film history) middle-management types why the creator of *Psycho* would be a good choice to write a movie about Teddy Bears in Space. After much exasperation, they finally said yes because, if nothing else, it would give us a first draft, Bob was available, and, best of all, he was willing to try.

Thus began our sojourn into development hell, with Bob joining us at the oars of our leaky ferry across the river Styx (you know, where the Hix Nix Pix). For the first few weeks we were living out a film buff's fantasy. We took full advantage of studio perks and set up a series of private screenings of movies in every genre the Hokas might parody, with Bob joining us daily. We basically had our own revival house. Our procedure for sifting through the source material became quite efficient very quickly. If Bob fell asleep during a film, we'd cross it off our list. Needless to say, Bob was well rested by the time we were ready to go to script. We then huddled together for story conferences in Bob's den of iniquity, while script pages would emerge from his vintage typewriter every few days.

Earthman's Burden was probably among Bob Bloch's last efforts as a screenwriter, and this seems like the perfect forum to allow his fans a glimpse of something that will likely never see the light of day. The following are a couple of scenes from late in Bob's first revised draft, when our human castaways have been reunited and are trying to get back to Earth.

We had just been through weeks of haggling with various development execs and had to deal with an inane reader's coverage of the first draft that actually suggested we add "robot sidekicks" and an "arch-villain, like Darth Vader." But all the trademark Bloch traits were there—dry wit, slapstick, bad puns, and an acute awareness of the power and appeal of popular culture. I think you can tell it would have been a fun ride of a movie.

By the way, as you read this, bear in mind that Bob used profanity reluctantly and rarely. He was quite bemused by the fact that all a film had to do to avoid the then-dreaded "G" rating was to use a four-letter word. With that mandate in mind, in this climactic scene, Bob basically sums up the whole damn universe with one such well-placed bon mot.

SCENES FROM A SCREENPLAY

EARTHMAN'S BURDEN

Note: Wingate is an Earthman who has been stranded among the Hokas for many years. Alex and Tanni are two fellow humans who have recently stumbled on him. The remaining cast are all Hokas playing twisted versions of their favorite Earth characters.

EXT.—COURTYARD BEHIND PALACE—NIGHT

Led by Moriarity and flanked by the two pike-bearing Hoka Guards who stood outside the chamber, the three captives MOVE OUT from a side doorway into a walled courtyard—then HALT as Moriarity gestures toward

WINGATE'S SPACE-SHIP

A crumpled, battered metal craft resting on a rocky slab in the silvery moonlight. A stone pedestal stands before it, draped with a tapestry emblazoned with a huge staring eye.

ALEX

Gazes at the craft in startled recognition.
(to Moriarity)
He made a crash landing here
—at the palace?

WIDER ANGLE—FEATURING MORIARITY
Moving to the stone pedestal before the ship.

MORIARITY
There was no palace when he landed. The fools who found him built Shaggy-La after they nursed him back to health.

ALEX

I remember a place like this in an old, old movie called *Lost Horizon*. But how
would the Hokas know about it?

MORIARITY

The same way they learned English.
(*yanks tapestry off*)
With this.

Revealed atop the pedestal is a portable television set.

ALEX

Television—

MORIARITY

We have another name for it.

ALEX

The Monitor!

INT.—WINGATE'S CELL—NIGHT

*Motley removes one of the keys on the metal loop from the lock of the now-open cell door
as Tanni and Wingate converse inside, in guarded tones.*

WINGATE

—I installed it on my ship to pass time. After the crash I discovered that by
some fluke its batteries still functioned.

TANNI

You picked up signals from Earth?

WINGATE

Only a single frequency that took fifty years to reach here. A cable channel,
broadcasting nothing but old movies.

TANNI

(*nods*)
So the Hokas learned about Earth from watching films. Amazing!

WINGATE

The Hokas are an amazing species, with even more amazing talents. Not only
did they believe everything they saw on the screen—they could also imitate and
duplicate it.

TANNI

Like western towns—English taverns—knights in armor?

WINGATE

Anything they wished. They came here from all over the planet to monitor
what was shown. I didn't realize the danger.

TANNI
What danger?

WINGATE
Not all Hokas modeled themselves after the heroes in old films. Some chose to become villains.

TANNI
So you had to be careful what you showed them.

WINGATE
One day I caught a particularly intelligent Hoka watching an old science fiction serial. I cut off reception immediately—but it was too late. He and his followers caught *me*.

EXT.—COURTYARD BEHIND PALACE—NIGHT

As Rowdy and Holmes listen, Moriarity addresses Alex.

MORIARITY
I'm told you are a repairman.

ALEX
(*his ego is showing*)
You're looking at the best in the business.

MORIARITY
(*gestures toward TV set*)
Then repair this.

ALEX
So that's why you wanted me here!

MORIARITY
The Monitor has taught me a great deal. But I need to learn more to carry out my plans.

HOLMES
(*to Alex*)
I told you he was a super-criminal! He won't stop until he takes over the whole planet!

MORIARITY
(*nods*)
My people have already taken over Shaggy-La. Others are preparing the way elsewhere.

ROWDY
Like the ones who burned down my ranch an' stole my cattle?

MORIARITY

I need those cattle for my own purposes. Those stupid cowboys aren't allowed to use them for food.

WIDE ANGLE—FEATURING WINGATE'S SHIP

As the reunited group turns to descend slab, Holmes lights his pipe, puffing contentedly as he nods at Wingate.

HOLMES

Jolly good show that ray didn't harm your ship!

WINGATE
(smiling)
Never touched us.

A SUDDEN CRACKING SOUND. Wingate looks up quickly: he and his companions stare at

ANOTHER ANGLE—FEATURING WINGATE'S SHIP

As a FISSURE WIDENS along its tail—and, with a SCREECH OF METAL, the entire rear of the craft SPLITS OFF and crashes to the pavement, amidst a CLOUD OF DEBRIS—while Hokas scamper off, SHOUTING

AT BASE OF SLAB

Alex steadies Tanni as the debris settles: Motley, Rowdy, and Wingate look up dazedly. Holmes has been knocked on his butt—and now Rowdy moves to help him rise. He grips Holmes' arm.

ROWDY
You hurt?

HOLMES

I'm afraid I broke my calabash.

He reaches down and produces the two halves of his pipe from underneath, then rises.

ALEX
(unhappily)
Well, there goes our last chance. I was hoping perhaps we could repair this ship for a return to Earth.

TANNI
It doesn't matter now. By this time the vortex has closed.

ALEX
You mean we're stuck here forever?

                    WINGATE
                There are worse fates.

                    TANNI
            Wouldn't you like to see Earth again?

                    WINGATE
I'm too old. Here in Toka's pure atmosphere I've aged very slowly. If I returned
    to Earth I'd become a ninety-year-old man.
                    (to Tanni)
            You can keep your youth here.

                    TANNI
Our misson comes first. If we can prove it's possible to travel faster than light,
    the space program would open the way to the stars.

                    ALEX
                Sorry, Tanni. You tried.
                    (to Wingate)
If you'd shown the Hokas some science fiction movies, they could have built a
            new space ship for you.

                    WINGATE
You saw what science fiction did to Moriarity. I couldn't risk having a bunch of
            Hokas playing *Star Wars* for real.

                    ALEX
            I'd be willing to take that chance.
                    (glances down)
                What is it, Motley?

ANOTHER ANGLE

We see Motley tugging at Alex's leg with one paw.
His other paw grasps a plastic box.

                    MOTLEY
    I dunno. I found it in some stuff that fell out of the ship.

Alex takes the box—opens it. Startled, he holds
the open box out for Wingate's inspection.

                    ALEX
            Is this what I think it is?

                    WINGATE
                    (stunned)
        Good God—I forgot I had them!

> TANNI
> *(peers in box)*
> What are they?

> ALEX
> Spare batteries—for the TV set.

INT.—HIGH LAMA'S CHAMBER—NIGHT

REAR ANGLE ON TOP OF DAIS shows Alex beside portable TV on stand. He fiddles with controls. Suddenly the room is filled with the theme from Star Trek. *Now CAMERA PULLS OUT and we see the room crowded with shadowy HOKAS staring up into the tube. The darkness is pierced by MYRIAD PAIRS of wide, GLOWING YELLOW EYES.*

EXT.—COURTYARD—DAY

FEATURING A NEW SPACECRAFT, glittering in the bright sunlight. It bears a vague resemblance to the Enterprise. *Shaven-headed "good" Hokas carry various cartons into a side hatch opening near tail. CAMERA TO Alex, Tanni, Wingate, and Holmes, moving OUT from side entrance to palace. Wingate stares up at the ship, dazzled.*

> WINGATE
> Incredible!

> ALEX
> A brand new model—bigger, roomier, faster—

> WINGATE
> *(frowns)*
> I still don't understand about the power source.

> TANNI
> *(glancing o.s.)*
> There it is—right under your nose.

CAMERA PANS TO a GROUP OF HOKAS lugging huge buckets balanced on their shoulders, Chinese fashion, up an inclined ramp to the open hatchway.

> WINGATE

Sniffs, then holds his nose.

> WINGATE
> Phew! Where's you get that stuff?

WIDER, INC. TANNI

> TANNI
> From them.

She gestures and CAMERA PULLS OUT so that we see Rowdy and Motley herding a half-dozen of the blue, three horned cattle up the ramp and INTO hatchway.

TANNI

I can't explain it, but my analysis of the fuel system the Hokas installed shows a thrust-factor exceeding the speed of light.

ANGLE ON GROUP

WINGATE
(shakes head)
With all due respect, that sounds like a lot of crap to me.

HOLMES
(nods)
Exactly! When Rowdy told me how Moriarity took over the cattle, I deduced they must be an energy source.

ALEX
This is the most powerful propulsion volatility I've ever seen! With cattle aboard to keep us supplied, we'll be home in no time flat.

TANNI
We should have guessed. Without electricity here, this is the source of power for all of Toka's industries.

WINGATE
(aghast)
You mean this whole planet is run on *bullshit*?

ALEX
Yeah. Just like on Earth.

JEFF WALKER

Bob talks a bit about his struggles with Hollywood studios in his "Un-official Autobiography," *Once Around the Bloch,* and he was right. We were all terribly disappointed by the turn of events that would cause *Earthman's Burden*—a wonderful (and quite commercial) project, sur-rounded by some very talented people—to fall victim to studio politics. Yet it happens all the time. Sometimes, such projects even come back to life and ultimate success. This is Hollywood. Anything's possible. If noth-ing else, the experience is a precious memory and Robert Bloch was a major contributor. Harlan was right. Bob was the best.

The story I would like to introduce is "The Plot Is the Thing." In all honesty, it's not really my favorite Bloch story, but its basic premise—that a recipe of couch potatoes, frontal lobotomies, and old celluloid monsters could somehow combine to create a new reality—seems downright ap-propriate for the subject at hand.

THE PLOT IS THE THING

𝓎 When they broke into the apartment, they found her
sitting in front of the television set, watching an old movie.

Peggy couldn't understand why they made such a fuss about that. She liked to watch old movies—the Late Show, the Late, Late Show, even the All Night Show. That was really the best, because they generally ran the horror pictures. Peggy tried to explain this to them, but they kept prowling around the apartment, looking at the dust on the furniture and the dirty sheets on the unmade bed. Somebody said there was green mold on the dishes in the sink; it's true she hadn't bothered to wash them for quite a long time, but then she hadn't eaten for several days, either.

It wasn't as though she didn't have any money; she told them about the bank accounts. But shopping and cooking and housekeeping was just too much trouble, and besides, she really didn't like going outside and seeing all those *people*. So if she preferred watching TV, that was her business, wasn't it?

They just looked at each other and shook their heads and made some phone calls. And then the ambulance came, and they helped her dress. Helped her? They practically *forced* her.

In the end it didn't do any good, and by the time she realized where they were taking her it was too late.

At first they were very nice to her at the hospital, but they kept asking those idiotic questions. When she said she had no relatives or friends they wouldn't believe her, and when they checked and found out it was true it only made things worse. Peggy got angry and said she was going home, and it all ended with a hypo in the arm.

There were lots of hypos after that, and in between times this Dr. Crane kept after her. He was one of the heads of staff and at first Peggy liked him, but not when he began to pry.

She tried to explain to him that she'd always been a loner, even before her parents died. And she told him there was no reason for her to work, with all that money. Somehow, he got it out of her about how she used to keep going to the movies, at least one every day, only she liked horror pictures and of course there weren't quite that many, so after a while she just watched them on TV. Because it was easier, and you didn't have to go home along dark streets after seeing something frightening. At home she could lock herself in, and as long as she had the television going she didn't feel lonely. Besides, she could watch movies all night, and this helped her insomnia. Sometimes the old pictures were pretty gruesome and this made her nervous, but she felt more nervous when she didn't watch. Because in the movies, no matter how horrible things seemed for the heroine, she was always rescued in the end. And that was better than the way things genrally worked out in real life, wasn't it?

Dr. Crane didn't think so. And he wouldn't let her have any television in her room now, either. He kept talking to Peggy about the need to face reality, and the dangers of retreating into a fantasy world and identifying with frightened heroines. The way he made it sound, you'd think she *wanted* to be menaced, *wanted* to be killed, or even raped.

And when he started all that nonsense about a "nervous disorder" and told her about his plans for treatment, Peggy knew she had to escape. Only she never got a chance. Before she realized it, they had arranged for the lobotomy.

Peggy knew what a lobotomy was, of course. And she was afraid of it, because it meant tampering with the brain. She remembered some mad doctor— Lionel Atwill, or George Zucco?—saying that by tampering with the secrets of the human brain one can change reality. "There are some things we were not meant to know," he had whispered. But that, of course, was in a movie. And Dr. Crane wasn't mad. *She* was the mad one. Or was she? He certainly looked insane—she kept trying to break free after they strapped her down and he came after her—she remembered the way everything gleamed. His eyes, and the long needle. The long needle, probing into her brain to change reality—

The funny thing was, when she woke up she felt fine. "I'm like a different person, Doctor."

And it was true. No more jitters; she was perfectly calm. And she wanted to eat, and she didn't have insomnia, and she could dress herself and talk to the nurses, even kid around with them. The big thing was that she didn't worry about watching television any more. She could scarcely remember any of those old movies that had disturbed her. Peggy wasn't a bit disturbed now. And even Dr. Crane knew it.

At the end of the second week he was willing to let her go home. They had a little chat, and he complimented her on how well she was doing, asked her about her plans for the future. When Peggy admitted she hadn't figured anything out yet, Dr. Crane suggested she take a trip. She promised to think it over.

But it wasn't until she got back to the apartment that Peggy made up her mind. The place was a mess. The moment she walked in she knew she couldn't stand it. All that dirt and grime and squalor—it was like a movie set, really, with clothes scattered everywhere and dishes piled in the sink. Peggy decided right then and there she'd take a vacation. Around the world, maybe. Why not? She had the money. And it would be interesting to see all the *real* things she'd seen represented on the screen all these years.

So Peggy dissolved into a travel agency and montaged into shopping and packing and faded out to London.

Strange, she didn't think of it that way at the time. But looking back, she began to realize that this is the way things seemed to happen. She'd come to a decision, or go somewhere and do something, and all of a sudden she'd find herself in another setting—just like in a movie, where they cut from scene to scene. When she first became aware of it she was a little worried; perhaps she was having blackouts. After all, her brain *had* been tampered with. But there was nothing really alarming about the little mental blanks. In a way they were very convenient, just like in the movies; you don't particularly want to waste time watching the heroine brush her teeth or pack her clothing or put on cosmetics. The plot is the thing. That's what's *real*.

And everything was real, now. No more uncertainty. Peggy could admit to herself that before the operation there had been times when she wasn't quite sure about things; sometimes what she saw on the screen was more convincing than the dull gray fog which seemed to surround her in daily life.

But that was gone, now. Whatever that needle had done, it had managed to pierce the fog. Everything was very clear, very sharp and definite, like good black and white camera work. And she herself felt so much more capable and confident. She was well-dressed, well-groomed, attractive again. The extras moved along the streets in an orderly fashion and didn't bother her. And the bit players spoke their lines crisply, performed their functions, and got out of the scene. Odd that she should think of them that way—they weren't "bit players" at all; just travel clerks and waiters and stewards and then, at the hotel, bellboys and maids. They seemed to fade in and out of the picture on cue. All smiles, like in the early part of a good horror movie, where at first everything seems bright and cheerful.

Paris was where things started to go wrong. This guide—a sort of Eduardo Ciannelli type, in fact he looked to be an almost dead ringer for Ciannelli as he was many years ago—was showing her through the Opera House. He happened to mention something about the catacombs, and that rang a bell.

She thought about Erik. That was his name, Erik—The Phantom of the Opera. *He* had lived in the catacombs underneath the Opera House. Of course, it was only a picture, but she thought perhaps the guide would know about it and she mentioned Erik's name as a sort of joke.

That's when the guide turned pale and began to tremble. And then he ran. Just ran off and left her standing there.

Peggy knew something was wrong, then. The scene just seemed to dissolve— that part didn't worry her, it was just another one of those temporary blackouts she was getting used to—and when Peggy gained awareness, she was in this bookstore asking a clerk about Gaston Leroux.

And this was what frightened her. She remembered distinctly that *The Phantom of the Opera* had been written by Gaston Leroux, but here was this French bookstore clerk telling her there was no such author.

That's what they said when she called the library. No such author—and no such book. Peggy opened her mouth, but the scene was already dissolving. . . .

In Germany she rented a car, and she was enjoying the scenery when she came to this burned mill and the ruins of the castle beyond. She knew where she was, of course, but it couldn't be—not until she got out of the car, moved up to the great door, and in the waning sun of twilight, read the engraved legend on the stone. FRANKENSTEIN.

There was a faint sound from behind the door, a sound of muffled, dragging footsteps, moving closer. Peggy screamed, and ran. . . .

Now she knew where she was running to. Perhaps she'd find safety behind the Iron Curtain. Instead there was another castle, and she heard the howling of a wolf in the distance, saw the bat swoop from the shadows as she fled.

And in an English library in Prague, Peggy searched the volumes of library biography. There was no listing for Mary Wollstonecraft Shelley, none for Bram Stoker.

Of course not. There wouldn't be, in a *movie* world, because when the characters are real, their "authors" do not exist.

Peggy remembered the way Larry Talbot had changed before her eyes, metamorphosing into the howling wolf. She remembered the sly purr of the Count's voice, saying, "I do not drink—wine." And she shuddered, and longed to be far away from the superstitious peasantry who draped wolfbane outside their windows at night.

She needed the reassurance of sanity in an English-speaking country. She'd go to London, see a doctor immediately.

Then she remembered what was *in* London. Another werewolf. And Mr. Hyde. And the Ripper. . . .

Peggy fled through a fadeout, back to Paris. She found the name of a psychiatrist, made her appointment. She was perfectly prepared to face her problem now, perfectly prepared to face reality.

But she was not prepared to face the baldheaded little man with the sinister accent and the bulging eyes. She knew him—Dr. Gogol, in *Mad Love*. She also knew Peter Lorre had passed on, knew *Mad Love* was only a movie, made the year she was born. But that was in another country, and besides, the wench was dead.

The wench was dead, but Peggy was alive. *"I am a stranger and afraid, in a world I never made."* Or had she made this world? She wasn't sure. All she knew was that she had to escape.

Where? It couldn't be Egypt, because that's where *he* would be—the wrinkled hideous image of the Mummy superimposed itself momentarily. The Orient? What about Fu Manchu?

Back to America, then? Home is where the heart is—but there'd be a knife waiting for that heart when the shower curtains were ripped aside and the creature of *Psycho* screamed and slashed. . . .

Somehow she managed to remember a haven, born in other films. The South Seas—Dorothy Lamour, John Hall, the friendly natives in the tropical paradise. There *was* escape.

Peggy boarded the ship in Marseilles. It was a tramp steamer but the cast—crew, rather—was reassuringly small. At first she spent most of her time below deck, huddled in her berth. Oddly enough, it was getting to be like it had been *before*. Before the operation, that is, before the needle bit into her brain, twisting it, or distorting the world. *Changing reality,* as Lionel Atwill had put it. She should have listened to them—Atwill, Zucco, Basil Rathbone, Edward Van Sloan, John Carradine. They may have been a little mad, but they were good doctors, dedicated scientists. They meant well. "There are some things we were not meant to know."

When they reached the tropics, Peggy felt much better. She regained her appetite, prowled the deck, went into the gallery and joked with the Chinese cook. The crew seemed aloof, but they all treated her with the greatest respect. She began to realize she'd done the right thing—this *was* escape. And the warm scent of tropic nights beguiled her. From now on, this would be her life; drifting through nameless, uncharted seas, safe from the role of heroine wth all its haunting and horror.

It was hard to believe she'd been so frightened. There were no phantoms, no werewolves in this world. Perhaps she didn't need a doctor. She was facing reality, and it was pleasant enough. There were no movies here, no television; her fears were all part of a long-forgotten nightmare.

One evening, after dinner, Peggy returned to her cabin with something nagging at the back of her brain. The captain had put in one of his infrequent appearances at the table, and he kept looking at her all through the meal. Something about the way he squinted at her was disturbing. Those little pig-eyes of his reminded her of someone. Noah Berry? Stanley Fields?

She kept trying to remember, and at the same time she was dozing off. Dozing off much too quickly. Had her food been drugged?

Peggy tried to sit up. Through the porthole she caught a reeling glimpse of land beyond, but then everything began to whirl and it was too late. . . .

When she awoke she was already on the island, and the woolly-headed savages were dragging her through the gate, howling and waving their spears.

They tied her and left her and then Peggy heard the chanting. She looked up and saw the huge shadow. Then she knew where she was and what *it* was, and she screamed.

Even over her own screams she could hear the natives chanting, just one word, over and over again. It sounded like, "Kong."

HARLAN ELLISON

Of his endless kindness you've heard paeans. Litanies of the stories that shaped and enriched half a dozen genres are pandemic. What he said at this convention, what he did at that roast . . . passed into legend. It seemed as if he had always been with us; and the world of fantastic literature is inconceivable without him. He was a nexus. There are those who judge their worth in this life by the sole fact that he was their friend.

How many times I've been asked to write "just a few words of appreciation" of Bob Bloch! And no matter how many trips to that well, there is always one more bucketful of whimsy to pull up. Here's one of the most bizarre.

Dreams. How we live in them. How they make the days of keeping appointments, of drudgework, of spending time in the company of people who say things we've heard, in just those same words, a thousand times . . . just a little more bearable. Without them, what an utter desolation of predictability and frustration. Bloch knew this. He'd spent most of his life spading up those potato dreams, mashing and serving them with a rich country gravy of mischievous wickedness. He knew that without the dreams, the suicide stats would be cataclysmic.

And yet, the best dreams of all are not the ones we carry with us for years; or the ones that come true; or the ones that stay always just out of reach. The best dreams are the ones that come upon us suddenly, startling us like Bambi in the forest.

The ones we never knew we had, till we're suddenly living them. I'll tell you one that happened to Bloch and me.

We'd been lots of places together. Ohio, New York, even exotic Milwaukee. But the most interesting trip we ever took was to Brazil. Rio in the primeval blistering cauldron of March 1969. A country ruled ruthlessly by a military *junta* that decorated the street corners every night with tanks and machine gun emplacements. To Rio journeyed Bloch and Ellison.

The Trylon and Perisphere of the realm phantasmagoric.

It was 1969. Bob and I had been invited—along with such luminaries as Agnes Varda, Roman Polanski, Josef von Sternberg, Roger Corman, and Diane Varsi—as well as a gaggle of fantasists that included Heinlein, Bester, Harrison, Sheckley, Van Vogt, and Farmer—to be guests of the 2nd International Film Festival of Rio de Janeiro. Despite the depressing realities of life in that glittering, jungle-bordered metropolis baking in the lee of Sugar Loaf—for the abyss that lies between the obscenely wealthy and the grindingly poor in Brazil is a thousand times more pronounced and heartbreaking than here in the States—being treated like princes from a far land took our breath away.

And the dream came to Bob and me like this:

As "notables," we received invitations to endless embassy receptions. Rio had lost its senses, gone ga-ga, over this contingent of famous film and fantasy folk. Everywhere we went, we were cheered as though we had somehow contributed to the advancement of Western Culture when, in fact, we were only a *divertissement* for the Léblon billionaires. We were that hot season's incarnation of bread and circuses. Bloch was the bread; I was the chicken fat.

Have I mentioned the women? Oh, my friends, the women of Rio! Gleaming black sweeps of hair hanging to the small of their backs. Toasted a thousand shades of golden treasure. In the day, barely clothed as they languished on the beaches; by night, whispering in white silk at the embassy parties. Oh, my friends, the forbidden conversations Bloch and I shared!

But after the first three or four of such social orgies, staged with incredible opulence in settings of art and grandeur (and very quickly painful to me, when matched against the awful sights that burned in my mind: the *peons* in their hillside *favellas,* feeding a dozen family members, children, animals, from one big kettle in the front "yard" of their tin-roofed hovels . . . going without food so they could buy candles to burn on the balustrades of the thousand-step stoneways that climb to the glorious Catholic cathedrals . . . the young women wearing themselves down to premature middle age working in the factories so their shark-thin young men have the free time to hustle wealthy American and German tourist widows on the Copacabana beach), I found myself being sickened by the profligacy. Both Bob and I resolved to attend no more of these charades.

Yet our hideous sense of gallows humor compelled us to make one special exception. We had received an invitation to the reception at the Polish Embassy. This was 1969, remember.

We confess to an ugliness of nature that demanded we see what the Polish Embassy was like.

We were advised it was black tie, and that we should assemble in front of our hotel at 5:00 to be transported by limousines. It was 120 degrees in Rio that summer, and even the joke that passed for air conditioning in the hotel was suffering from Cheyne-Stokes respiration. So at quarter to five we found ourselves decked out in elegance (Bloch looked *smashing* in a tux), standing on the restaurant patio, waiting for the limos that had been promised.

In Rio, time comes slathered with molasses. When they say 5:00 they mean 5:30 if you're lucky; 6:00 if they're on time; 6:30 if they're running true to form; and 7:00 if they're a little behind schedule. By 7:30 we were drenched and redolent, thoroughly wilted and swimming in our tuxedos. And finally, the "limousines" arrived: four old and incredibly swaybacked buses.

Soggily, we climbed aboard, like brutalized *mestizos* being chivvied back to the castor-bean plantations for another fifteen hours of back-breaking labor under that assassin oven, the open sky. Shortly after 8:00 we rolled out to the Polish Embassy.

Understand this: in Rio the embassies outdo one another for sumptuousness. The Spanish Embassy is in a renovated villa, festooned with ancient tapestries, reeking of history and *Droit de Seigneur*. Harry Harrison told me about it. He went, I didn't. The American reception was held in an art museum, with three rock bands, light shows, and old movies flashed on the walls, champagne flowing, beluga and osetra in tureens filled to surface tension, all free-form and glass walls. One could expect no less from the Polish Embassy. Unless, like Bloch and Ellison, one had a gallows sense of humor.

The Polish Embassy was like a bad Polack joke. It was on the third floor (walk-up) of a nondescript apartment building: a huge, empty series of rooms utterly devoid of furniture. No air conditioning. No music. No chairs, we stood or leaned. The refreshments consisted solely of cornucopial flowings of *slivovitz* and an extraterrestrially mutated species of *vodka* Brian Aldiss assured me could be used to launch a Soyuz rocket into Lunar orbit. (Not being a drinker, I have to rely on the opinions of experts in these matters.)

As the humidity was 100 percent and the heat was bubbling well over a hundred and twenty *outdoor* degrees, with everyone schvitzing like malamutes, within an hour the crowded "embassy" was ass-deep in drunken dignitaries, babbling at one another in a dozen tongues, making no sense, sweat-stinking and jammed belly-to-backside like slaves in the hold of a privateer, everyone demented as fruit-bats and beginning to look like characters out of one of Bloch's most hallucinogenic stories.

Bob and I clung together for protection like a couple of Spartans at the

Hot Gates. Like Eliza and Little Eva on an ice floe. Like the last two survivors at Fort Zinderneuf.

The Polish attachés were, how shall I put it, *sensational!* To a man they were all squat, hemispherical, cherubic, and clad in heavy wool suits (with vests) that may well have been out of fashion even when soldered together in 1938. Miraculously, even in the oily, dripping atmosphere of that gulag apartment, vacuum-packed with several hundred gibbering eye-rolling aliens, our own little dungeon of Babel, with droplets of moisture condensing on the walls 'neath a stillatitious ceiling . . . even in those grotesque woolen suits . . . not one of them perspired!

Bob and I wandered around the empty rooms looking for a couple of feet of untenanted space where we could draw a breath of air that hadn't been recycled through laboring lungs. We found our way into what might have been the living room, had it contained even a stick of furniture. And it was there that the dream took root.

As we came into that huge, empty space, we found our eyes drawn to the only non-human item in the room. (Or perhaps we were hasty in our judgement of some affinity with humanity, non- or otherwise.) There was an enormous painting on the wall. Bob looked at it; I looked at it; then we looked at each other. Bob shivered. I felt a centipede traverse my spine.

"Does that look to you like what it looks to me?" I asked. Bob nodded. He *kept* nodding; like he couldn't stop; as if he were having a seizure.

The painting was a hideous green and yellow smash of unparallelled ghastliness. Disreputably alien, disturbingly suggestive, distressingly nauseating, it looked like some soft wet thing fallen out of a Lovecraft nightmare. Something unnameable and unspeakable, one of those Elder Gods, with a name like Yog-Sothoth, or maybe Yig, or at least a close relative that not even the rest of that icky family would acknowledge. This was genuine puke art. Bloch was now mumbling.

I took him by the elbow as his eyes glazed over and, shuddering, we turned away; and neither of us strayed back into that room during the entire reception. We pressed our way swiftly, perhaps a trifle hysterically, into the farthest corner of the farthest room from that portrait, what might have been the "dining room," trying with equal vigor to get as far away from the nasty thing as we could, while positioning ourselves next to the one open window in the apartment.

Now the dream comes to full flower.

I tell it *precisely* as it happened, sans comment, sans embellishment. This one needs no flourishes; it is true.

I was looking out the window, mired in sweat and ennui, tasting the spice of oblivion, when my eyes traveled across the narrow street to the apartment building across from us. One floor above us, across the way, the curtains were parted, revealing the interior of an apartment. Windows wide open in hopes of a vagrant cooling breeze. Absolute clarity of view.

I stared into that apartment for almost a minute before my brain would accept what I was seeing:

On the wall was an enormous blood-red flag with the Nazi swastika emblazoned in the center in glossy black, as if it had been painted with lacquer over the original print. The flag was torn and frayed at the edges, as if it had possibly been ripped, suddenly, from the wall of a building going up in flames. But perhaps I dramatize. It may just have been old and weathered.

On another wall, there was a huge, framed photograph of Adolf Hitler.

And marching back and forth in front of the window was a gentleman whose face I could not see, dressed in the black leather and livery of an SS *Oberstgruppenfuehrer.* He was marching stiffly, as if his limberness had decreased with age, in what newsreels have always advised me was a "goose-step."

I stared, dumbfounded, for a couple of minutes. Deep in the dream. Suffocating in the nightmare. Then, in that time-lapse state of dreaming, I slowly reached over and touched Bob's hand. "Take a look out the window," I said softly, trying to keep my voice level as concerns for my sanity presented themselves. "Take a look, that apartment across the street. Tell me if I'm seeing what I think I'm seeing, Bob."

He bent around me and looked. He was silent for some time. Then he looked around at me and tried several times to say something. When he finally got it out, it was a breathy kind of "Oh my god."

We stood silently, side by side, and just stared.

After a while, we called several other people's attention to the tableau; and they all seemed chilled by the sight. But they all saw it. Not too long after, the fellow in the other apartment saw us staring, and he pulled the curtains closed.

Further, deponent sayeth not; save to comment that this was, remember, 1969. It had been less than ten years since an agent of the Israeli Mossad had walked up to Adolf Eichmann, thirty years a fugitive of Holocaust justice, on Garibaldi Street in Buenos Aires, and said, "*Un momentito, señor.*" Mengele, Muller, and Martin Bormann were still out there, rumored to be living comfortably in Venezuela, Argentina, Ecuador. We knew nothing of Kurt Waldheim's odious past. We could not have suspected that the vile Klaus Barbie, "the butcher of Lyon," had been provided escape, succor, and decades-long cover by Western intelligence agencies.

Bob Bloch had written of realized horrors unceasingly for years; but now he stood staring wordlessly as the dream that was pure nightmare produced its rotting blossoms. We have spoken often of the aroma of fear and evil that permeated the ludicrous Polish "embassy" that evening in Rio de Janeiro. And of all the moments I might have recounted by way of "appreciation," this has been the one that most deeply touched us not only as friends, not only as fellow writers, but as part of the human wad that never ever really escapes the terrors that are of our own making.

In 1943 Robert Bloch published a story titled "Yours Truly, Jack the Ripper." The number of times it has been reprinted, anthologized, translated into radio and TV scripts, and most of all plagiarized, are staggering. I read it in 1953, and the story stuck with me always. When I *heard* its dramatization on the Mollé Mystery Theater, it became a recurring favorite memory. The story idea was simply that Jack the Ripper, by killing at specific times, made his peace with the dark gods and was thus allowed to live forever. Jack was immortal, and Bloch traced with cold methodical logic a trail of similar Ripper-style murders in almost every major city of the world, over a period of fifty or sixty years. The concept of Jack—who was never apprehended—living on, from era to era, caught my imagination. As my favorite Bloch, I introduce it here.

It's chillier here, now. The light to read by, it's too dim.

We talked many times between the day he learned he was going to die, and the night of 23 September 1994, when he left. Face to face, and over the phone, I knew him since I was sixteen years old; in May of 1951, at Beatley's On-the-Lake Hotel just outside of Bellefontaine, Ohio; we stayed friends for forty-three years. Not once in a while friends, or I'll call you when I get to town friends, or We really must get together for dinner one night soon friends, but close and regular chums. He was the examplar of what my father told me a man should always strive to be: a *mensch.* There is no higher accolade. He was a *mensch.* His photo in the dictionary under the definition of a class act.

I sat on the stairs and spoke his name, and I cried for myself because I had lost another friend.

Three nights before he left, I called to check in, and Elly said he wanted to talk to me. I hadn't expected that. The day before, he had been in bad shape, couldn't speak, sat propped up on pillows on the bed, terribly thin and pale, his head down, eyes closed. I hadn't expected him to be able to talk to me. But he got on, and it was twenty years ago! No huskiness, no hesitation, no rambling sentences, it was Bob, back again. And we talked for twenty minutes. We talked about his typewriters, the Olympia office standard machine he hadn't been able to get repaired because the world was intent on converting everyone to electronic junkware. We often talked about how annoying it was that commercial interests brainwashed everyone into believing they had to have this or that new toot'n'whistle, when the technology we already used was perfect for us . . . and the concomitant need of those who had been so mercilessly conned, to belittle those who chose not to go along with the game. And I told Bob I had a guy who did great repairs, and I'd come over and pick up the three Olympias, and I'd take them along with one of my own six, when I went to see Jésus Silva this week. He said that would be grand. Too soon, he died. He told Elly to give me his typewriters. I've had them refurbished. I wrote a new story on one of them this week, just this week. Does my pal, Bob, know the work goes on?

Never to see his face again, that grin. It's hard, it's really tough.

There is a picture of us together, on that street in Ohio in 1951. He is three times my height, and a thousand times my presence. I am a kid, and he has his arm around my shoulders. And we are friends. It is tough, boy, you just don't know.

YOURS TRULY, JACK THE RIPPER

I looked at the stage Englishman. He looked at me.
"Sir Guy Hollis?" I asked.

"Indeed. Have I the pleasure of addressing John Carmody, the psychiatrist?"

I nodded. My eyes swept over the figure of my distinguished visitor. Tall, lean, sandy-haired—with the traditional tufted mustache. And the tweeds. I suspected a monocle concealed in a vest pocket, and wondered if he'd left his umbrella in the outer office.

But more than that, I wondered what the devil had impelled Sir Guy Hollis of the British Embassy to seek out a total stranger here in Chicago.

Sir Guy didn't help matters any as he sat down. He cleared his throat, glanced around nervously, tapped his pipe against the side of the desk. Then he opened his mouth.

"Mr. Carmody," he said, "have you ever heard of—Jack the Ripper?"

"The murderer?" I said.

"Exactly. The greatest monster of them all. Worse than Springheel Jack or Crippen. Jack the Ripper. Red Jack."

"I've heard of him," I said.

"Do you know his history?"

"I don't think we'll get any place swapping old wives' tales about famous crimes of history."

He took a deep breath.

"This is no old wives' tale. It's a matter of life or death."

He was so wrapped up in his obsession he even talked that way. Well—I was willing to listen. We psychiatrists get paid for listening.

"Go ahead," I told him. "Let's have the story."

Sir Guy lit a cigarette and began to talk.

"London, 1888," he began. "Late summer and early fall. That was the time. Out of nowhere came the shadowy figure of Jack the Ripper—a stalking shadow with a knife, prowling through London's East End. Haunting the squalid dives of Whitechapel, Spitalfields. Where he came from no one knew. But he brought death. Death in his blade.

"Six times that blade descended to slash the throats and bodies of London's women. Drabs and alley sluts. August 7th was the date of the first butchery. They found her lying there with thirty-nine stab wounds. A ghastly murder. On August 31st, another victim. The press became interested. The slum inhabitants were more deeply interested still.

"Who was this unknown killer who prowled in their midst and struck at will in the deserted alleyways of nighttown? And what was more important—when would he strike again?

"September 8th was the date. Scotland Yard assigned special deputies. Rumors ran rampant. The atrocious nature of the slayings was the subject for shocking speculation.

"The killer used a knife—expertly. He cut throats and removed—certain portions—of the bodies after death. He chose victims and settings with fiendish deliberation. No one saw him or heard him. But watchmen making their gray rounds in the dawn would stumble across the hacked and horrid thing that was the Ripper's handiwork.

"Who was he? What was he? A mad surgeon? A butcher? An insane scientist? A pathological degenerate escaped from an asylum? A deranged nobleman? A member of the London police?

"Then the poem appeared in the newspapers. The anonymous poem, designed to put a stop to speculations—but which only aroused public interest to a further frenzy. A mocking little stanza:

> I'm not a butcher, I'm not a Yid
> Nor yet a foreign skipper,
> But I'm your own true loving friend,
> Yours truly—Jack the Ripper.

"And on September 30th, two more throats were slashed open. There was silence, then, in London for a time. Silence, and a nameless fear. When would Red Jack strike again? They waited through October. Every figment of fog concealed his phantom presence. Concealed it well—for nothing was learned of the Ripper's identity, or his purpose. The drabs of London shivered in the raw wind of early November. Shivered, and were thankful for the coming of each morning's sun.

"November 9th. They found her in her room. She lay there very quietly, limbs neatly arranged. And beside her, with equal neatness, were laid her breasts and heart. The Ripper had outdone himself in execution.

"Then, panic. But needless panic. For though press, police, and populace alike waited in sick dread, Jack the Ripper did not strike again.

"Months passed. A year. The immediate interest died, but not the memory. They said Jack had skipped to America. That he had committed suicide. They said—and they wrote. They've written ever since. But to this day no one knows who Jack the Ripper was. Or why he killed. Or why he stopped killing."

Sir Guy was silent. Obviously he expected some comment from me.

"You tell the story well," I remarked. "Though with a slight emotional bias."

"I suppose you want to know why I'm interested?" he said.

"Yes. That's exactly what I'd like to know."

"Because," said Sir Guy Hollis, "I am on the trail of Jack the Ripper now. I think he's here—in Chicago!"

"Say that again."

"Jack the Ripper is alive, in Chicago, and I'm out to find him."

He wasn't smiling. It wasn't a joke.

"See here," I said. "What was the date of these murders?"

"August to November, 1888."

"But if Jack the Ripper was an able-bodied man then, he'd surely be dead today? Why look, man—if he were merely born in that year, he'd be fifty-seven years old here in 'forty-three."

"Would he?" smiled Sir Guy Hollis. "Or should I say, 'Would she?' Because Jack the Ripper may have been a woman. Or any number of things."

"Sir Guy," I said. "You came to the right person when you looked me up. You definitely need the services of a therapist.

"Perhaps. Tell me, Mr. Carmody, do you think I'm crazy?"

I looked at him and shrugged. But I had to give him a truthful answer.

"Frankly—no."

"Then you might listen to the reasons I believe Jack the Ripper is alive today."

"I might."

"I've studied these cases for thirty years. Been over the actual ground. Talked to officials. Talked to friends and acquaintances of the poor drags who were killed. Visited with men and women in the neighborhood. Collected an entire library of material touching on Jack the Ripper. Studied all the wild theories or crazy notions.

"I learned a little. Not much, but a little. I won't bore you with my conclusions. But there was another branch of inquiry that yielded more fruitful return. I have studied unsolved crimes. Murders.

"I could show you clippings from the papers of half the world's greatest cities. San Francisco. Shanghai. Calcutta. Omsk. Paris. Berlin. Pretoria. Cairo. Milan. Adelaide.

"The trail is there, the pattern. Unsolved crimes. Slashed throats of women. With the peculiar disfigurations and removals. Yes, I've followed a trail of blood. From New York westward across the continent. Then to the Pacific. From there to Africa. During the World War of 1914–18 it was Europe. After that, South America. And since 1930, the United States again. Eighty-seven such murders— and to the trained criminologist, all bear the stigma of the Ripper's handiwork.

"Recently there were the so-called Cleveland torso slayings. Remember? A shocking series. And finally, two similar deaths in Chicago. Within the past six months. One out on South Dearborn. The other somewhere up in Halsted. Same type of crime, same technique. I tell you, there are unmistakable indications in all these affairs—indications of the work of Jack the Ripper!"

"A very tight theory," I said. "I'll not question your evidence at all, or the deductions you draw. You're the criminologist, and I'll take your word for it. Just one thing remains to be explained. A minor point, perhaps, but worth mentioning."

"And what is that?" asked Sir Guy.

"Just how could a man of, let us say, eighty-five years commit these crimes? For if Jack the Ripper was around thirty in 1888 and still lived, he'd be eighty-five today."

"*Suppose he didn't get any older?*" whispered Sir Guy.

"What's that?"

"Suppose Jack the Ripper didn't grow old? Suppose he is still a young man today?

"It's a crazy theory, I grant you," he said. "All the theories about the Ripper are crazy. The idea that he was a doctor. Or a maniac. Or a woman. The reasons advanced for such beliefs are flimsy enough. There's nothing to go by. So why should my notion be any worse?"

"Because people grow older," I reasoned with him. "Doctors, maniacs, and woman alike."

"What about—*sorcerers?*"

"Sorcerers?"

"Necromancers. Wizards. Practicers of Black Magic."

"What's the point?"

"I studied," said Sir Guy. "I studied everything. After a while I began to study the dates of the murders. The pattern those dates formed. The rhythm. The solar, lunar, stellar rhythm. The sidereal aspect. The astrological significance.

"Suppose Jack the Ripper didn't murder for murder's sake alone? Suppose he wanted to make—a sacrifice?"

"What kind of sacrifice?"

Sir Guy shrugged. "It is said that if you offer blood to the dark gods they grant boons. Yes, if a blood offering is made at the proper time—when the moon and the stars are right—and with the proper ceremonies—they grant boons. Gifts of youth. Eternal youth."

"But that's nonsense!"

"No. That's—Jack the Ripper."

I stood up. "A most interesting theory," I told him. "But why do you come here and tell it to me? I'm not an authority on witchcraft. I'm not a police official or criminologist. I'm a practicing psychiatrist. What's the connection?"

Sir Guy smiled.

"You are interested, then?"

"Well, yes. There must be some point."

"There is. But I wished to be assured of your interest first. Now I can tell you my plan."

"And just what is that plan?"

Sir Guy gave me a long look.

"John Carmody," he said, "you and I are going to capture Jack the Ripper."

2

That's the way it happened. I've given the gist of that first interview in all its intricate and somewhat boring detail, because I think it's important. It helps to throw some light on Sir Guy's character and attitude. And in view of what happened after that—

But I'm coming to those matters.

Sir Guy's thought was simple. It wasn't even a thought. Just a hunch.

"You know the people here," he told me. "I've inquired. That's why I came to you as the ideal man for my purpose. You number amongst your acquaintance many writers, painters, poets. The so-called intelligentsia. The lunatic fringe from the near north side.

"For certain reasons—never mind what they are—my clues lead me to infer that Jack the Ripper is a member of that element. He chooses to pose as an eccentric. I've a feeling that with you to take me around and introduce me to your set, I might hit upon the right person."

"It's all right with me," I said. "But just how are you going to look for him? As you say, he might be anybody, anywhere. And you have no idea what he looks like. He might be young or old. Jack the Ripper—a Jack of all trades? Rich man, poor man, beggar man, thief, doctor, lawyer—how will you know?"

"We shall see." Sir Guy sighed heavily. "But I must find him. At once."

"Why the hurry?"

Sir Guy sighed once more. "Because in two days he will kill again."

"Are you sure?"

"Sure as the stars. I've plotted this chart, you see. All of the murders correspond to certain astrological rhythm patterns. If, as I suspect, he makes a blood sacrifice to renew his youth, he must murder within two days. Notice the pattern of his first crimes in London. August 7th. Then August 31st. September·8th. September 30th. November 9th. Intervals of twenty-four days, nine days, twenty-two days—he killed two this time—and then forty days. Of course there were crimes in between. There had to be. But they weren't discovered and pinned on him.

"At any rate, I've worked out a pattern for him, based on all my data. And I say that within the next two days he kills. So I must seek him out, somehow, before then."

"And I'm still asking you what you want me to do."

"Take me out," said Sir Guy. "Introduce me to your friends. Bring me to parties."

"But where do I begin? As far as I know, my artistic friends, despite their eccentricities, are all normal people."

"So is the Ripper. Perfectly normal. Except on certain nights." Again that far-away look in Sir Guy's eyes. "Then he becomes an ageless pathological monster, crouching to kill."

"All right," I said. "All right. I'll take you."

We made our plans. And that evening I took him over to Lester Baston's studio.

As we ascended to the penthouse roof in the elevator I took the opportunity to warn Sir Guy.

"Baston's a real screwball," I cautioned him. "So are his guests. Be prepared for anything and everything."

"I am." Sir Guy Hollis was perfectly serious. He put his hand in his trousers pocket and pulled out a gun.

"Watch it—" I began.

"If I see him I'll be ready," Sir Guy said. He didn't smile, either.

"But you can't go running around at a party with a loaded revolver in your pocket, man!"

"Don't worry, I won't behave foolishly."

I wondered. Sir Guy Hollis was not, to my way of thinking, a rational man.

We stepped out of the elevator, went toward Baston's apartment door.

"By the way," I murmured, "just how do you wish to be introduced? Shall I tell them who you are and what you are looking for?"

"I don't care. Perhaps it would be best to be frank."

"But don't you think that the Ripper—if by some miracle he or she is present—will immediately get the wind up and take cover?"

"I think the shock of the announcement that I am hunting the Ripper would provide some kind of betraying gesture on his part," said Sir Guy.

"It's a fine theory. But I warn you, you're going to be in for a lot of ribbing. This is a weird bunch."

Sir Guy smiled.

"I'm ready," he announced. "I have a little plan of my own. Don't be shocked at anything I do."

I nodded and knocked on the door.

Baston opened it and poured out into the hall. His eyes were as red as the maraschino cherries in his Manhattan. He teetered back and forth regarding us very gravely. He squinted at my square-cut homburg hat and Sir Guy's mustache.

"Aha," he intoned. "The Walrus and the Carpenter."

I introduced Sir Guy.

"Welcome," said Baston, gesturing us inside with over-elaborate courtesy. He stumbled after us into the garish parlor.

I stared at the crowd that moved restlessly through the fog of cigarette smoke.

It was the shank of the evening for this mob. Every hand held a drink. Every face held a slightly hectic flush. Over in one corner the piano was going full blast, but the imperious strains of the *March* from *The Love for Three Oranges* couldn't drown out the profanity from the crap game in the other corner.

Prokofiev had no chance against African polo, and one set of ivories rattled louder than the other.

Sir Guy got a monocle-full right away. He saw LaVerne Gonnister, the poet-ess, hit Hymie Kralik in the eye. He saw Hymie sit down on the floor and cry until Dick Pool accidentally stepped on his stomach as he walked through to the dining room for a drink.

He heard Nadia Vilinoff, the commercial artist, tell Johnny Odcutt that she thought his tattooing was in dreadful taste, and he saw Barclay Melton crawl under the dining room table with Johnny Odcutt's wife.

His zoological observations might have continued indefinitely if Lester Bas-ton hadn't stepped to the center of the room and called for silence by dropping a vase on the floor.

"We have distinguished visitors in our midst," bawled Lester, waving his empty glass in our direction. "None other than the Walrus and the Carpenter. The Walrus is Sir Guy Hollis, a something-or-other from the British Embassy. The Carpenter, as you all know, is our own John Carmody, the prominent dispenser of libido liniment."

He turned and grabbed Sir Guy by the arm, dragging him to the middle of the carpet. For a moment I thought Hollis might object, but a quick wink reassured me. He was prepared for this.

"It is our custom, Sir Guy," said Baston, loudly, "to subject our new friends to a little cross-examination. Just a little formality at these very formal gatherings, you understand. Are you prepared to answer questions?"

Sir Guy nodded.

"Very well," Baston muttered. "Friends—I give you this bundle from Britain. Your witness."

Then the ribbing started. I meant to listen, but at that moment Lydia Dare saw me and dragged me off into the vestibule for one of those Darling-I-waited-for-your-call-all-day routines.

By the time I got rid of her and went back, the impromptu quiz session was in full swing. From the attitude of the crowd, I gathered that Sir Guy was doing all right for himself. Then Baston himself interjected a question that upset the apple-cart.

"And what, may I ask, brings you to our midst tonight? What is your mission, oh Walrus?"

"I'm looking for Jack the Ripper."

Nobody laughed.

Perhaps it struck them all the way it did me. I glanced at my neighbors and began to *wonder.*

LaVerne Gonnister. Hymie Kralik. Harmless. Dick Pool. Nadia Vilinoff. Johnny Odcutt and his wife. Barclay Melton. Lydia Dare. All harmless.

But what a forced smile on Dick Pool's face! And that sly, self-conscious smirk that Barclay Melton wore!

Oh, it was absurd, I grant you. But for the first time I saw these people in a new light. I wondered about their lives—their secret lives beyond the scenes of parties.

How many of them were playing a part, concealing something?

Who here would worship Hecate and grant that horrid goddess the dark boon of blood?

Even Lester Baston might be masquerading.

The mood was upon us all, for a moment. I saw questions flicker in the circle of eyes around the room.

Sir Guy stood there, and I could swear he was fully conscious of the situation he'd created, and enjoyed it.

I wondered idly just what was *really* wrong with him. Why he had this odd fixation concerning Jack the Ripper. Maybe he was hiding secrets, too. . . .

Baston, as usual, broke the mood. He burlesqued it.

"The Walrus isn't kidding, friends," he said. He slapped Sir Guy on the back and put his arm around him as he orated. "Our English cousin is really on the trail of the fabulous Jack the Ripper. You all remember Jack the Ripper, I presume? Quite a cut-up in the old days, as I recall. Really had some ripping good times when he went out on a tear.

"The Walrus has some idea that the Ripper is still alive, probably prowling around Chicago with a Boy Scout knife. "In fact"—Baston paused impressively and shot it out in a rasping stage whisper—"in fact, he has reason to believe that Jack the Ripper might even be right here in our midst tonight."

There was the expected reaction of giggles and grins. Baston eyed Lydia Dare reprovingly. "You girls needn't laugh," he smirked. "Jack the Ripper might be a woman, too, you know. Sort of a Jill the Ripper."

"You mean you actually suspect one of us?" shrieked LaVerne Gonnister, simpering up to Sir Guy. "But that Jack the Ripper person disappeared ages ago, didn't he? In 1888?"

"Aha!" interrupted Baston. "How do you know so much about it, young lady? Sounds suspicious! Watch her, Sir Guy—she may not be as young as she appears. These lady poets have dark pasts."

The tension was gone, the mood was shattered, and the whole thing was beginning to degenerate into a trivial party joke. The man who had played the *March* was eyeing the piano with a *scherzo* gleam in his eye that augured ill for Prokofiev. Lydia Dare was glancing at the kitchen, wanting to make a break for another drink.

Then Baston caught it.

"Guess what?" he yelled. "The Walrus has a gun."

His embracing arm had slipped and encountered the hard outline of the gun in Sir Guy's pocket. He snatched it out before Hollis had the opportunity to protest.

I stared hard at Sir Guy, wondering if this thing had carried far enough. But he flicked a wink my way and I remembered he had told me not to be alarmed.

So I waited as Baston broached a drunken inspiration.

"Let's play fair with our friend the Walrus," he cried. "He came all the way from England to our party on this mission. If none of you is willing to confess, I suggest we give him a chance to find out—the hard way."

"What's up?" asked Johnny Odcutt.

"I'll turn out the lights for one minute. Sir Guy can stand here with his gun. If anyone in this room is the Ripper he can either run for it or take the opportunity to—well, eradicate his pursuer. Fair enough?"

It was even sillier than it sounds, but it caught the popular fancy. Sir Guy's protests went unheard in the ensuing babble. And before I could stride over and put in my two cents' worth, Lester Baston had reached the light switch.

"Don't anybody move," he announced, with fake solemnity. "For one minute we will remain in darkness—perhaps at the mercy of a killer. At the end of that time, I'll turn up the lights again and look for bodies. Choose your partners, ladies and gentlemen."

The lights went out.

Somebody giggled.

I heard footsteps in the darkness. Mutterings.

A hand brushed my face.

The watch on my wrist ticked violently. But even louder, rising above it, I heard another thumping. The beating of my heart.

Absurd. Standing in the dark with a group of tipsy fools. And yet there was real terror lurking here, rustling through the velvet blackness.

Jack the Ripper prowled in darkness like this. And Jack the Ripper had a knife. Jack the Ripper had a madman's brain and a madman's purpose.

But Jack the Ripper was dead, dead and dust these many years—by every human law.

Only there are no human laws when you feel yourself in the darkness, when the darkness hides and protects and the outer mask slips off your face and you sense something welling up within you, a brooding shapeless purpose that is brother to the blackness.

Sir Guy Hollis shrieked.

There was a grisly thud.

Baston put the lights on.

Everybody screamed.

Sir Guy Hollis lay sprawled on the floor in the center of the room. The gun was still clutched in his hand.

I glanced at the faces, marveling at the variety of expressions human beings can assume when confronting horror.

All the faces were present in the circle. Nobody had fled. And yet Sir Guy Hollis lay there.

LaVerne Gonnister was wailing and hiding her face.

"All right."

Sir Guy rolled over and jumped to his feet. He was smiling.

"Just an experiment, eh? If Jack the Ripper *were* among those present, and thought I had been murdered, he would have betrayed himself in some way when the lights went on and he saw me lying there.

"I am convinced of your individual and collective innocence. Just a gentle spoof, my friends."

Hollis stared at the goggling Baston and the rest of them crowding in behind him.

"Shall we leave, John?" he called to me. "It's getting late, I think."

Turning, he headed for the closet. I followed him. Nobody said a word.

It was a pretty dull party after that.

3

I met Sir Guy the following evening as we agreed, on the corner of Twenty-Ninth and South Halsted.

After what had happened the night before, I was prepared for almost anything. But Sir Guy seemed matter-of-fact enough as he stood huddled against a grimy doorway and waited for me to appear.

"Boo!" I said, jumping out suddenly. He smiled. Only the betraying gesture of his left hand indicated that he'd instinctively reached for his gun when I startled him.

"All ready for our wild-goose chase?" I asked.

"Yes." He nodded. "I'm glad that you agreed to meet me without asking questions," he told me. "It shows you trust my judgment." He took my arm and edged me along the street slowly.

"It's foggy tonight, John," said Sir Guy Hollis. "Like London."

I nodded.

"Cold, too, for November."

I nodded again and half-shivered my agreement.

"Curious," mused Sir Guy. "London fog and November. The place and the time of the Ripper murders."

I grinned through the darkness. "Let me remind you, Sir Guy, that this isn't London, but Chicago. And it isn't November, 1888. It's over fifty years later."

Sir Guy returned my grin, but without mirth. "I'm not so sure, at that," he murmured. "Look about you. Those tangled alleys and twisted streets. They're like the East End. Mitre Square. And surely they are as ancient as fifty years, at least."

"You're in the black neighborhood of South Clark Street," I said shortly. "And why you dragged me down here I still don't know."

"It's a hunch," Sir Guy admitted. "Just a hunch on my part, John. I want to wander around down here. There's the same geographical conformation in these streets as in those courts where the Ripper roamed and slew. That's where we'll find him, John. Not in the bright lights, but down here in the darkness. The darkness where he waits and crouches."

"Isn't that why you brought a gun?" I asked. I was unable to keep a trace of sarcastic nervousness from my voice. All this talk, this incessant obsession with Jack the Ripper, got on my nerves more than I cared to admit.

"We may need a gun," said Sir Guy, gravely. "After all, tonight is the appointed night."

I sighed. We wandered on through the foggy, deserted streets. Here and there a dim light burned above a gin-mill doorway. Otherwise, all was darkness and shadow. Deep, gaping alleyways loomed as we proceeded down a slanting side street.

We crawled through that fog, alone and silent, like two tiny maggots floundering within a shroud.

"Can't you see there's not a soul around these streets?" I said.

"He's bound to come," said Sir Guy. "He'll be drawn here. This is what I've been looking for. A *genius loci*. An evil spot that attracts evil. Always, when he slays, it's in the slums.

"You see, that must be one of his weaknesses. He has a fascination for squalor. Besides, the women he needs for sacrifice are more easily found in the dives and stewpots of a great city."

"Well, let's go into one of the dives or stewpots," I suggested. "I'm cold. Need a drink. This damned fog gets into your bones. You Britishers can stand it, but I like warmth and dry heat."

We emerged from our sidestreet and stood upon the threshold of an alley.

Through the white clouds of mist ahead, I discerned a dim blue light, a naked bulb dangling from a beer sign above an alley bar.

"Let's take a chance," I said. "I'm beginning to shiver."

"Lead the way," said Sir Guy. I led him down the alley passage. We halted before the door of the dive.

"What are you waiting for?" he asked.

"Just looking in," I told him. "This is a rough neighborhood, Sir Guy. Never know what you're liable to run into. And I'd prefer we didn't get into the wrong company. Some of these places resent white customers."

"Good idea, John."

I finished my inspection through the doorway. "Looks deserted," I murmured. "Let's try it."

We entered a dingy bar. A feeble light flickered above the counter and railing, but failed to penetrate the further gloom of the back booths.

A gigantic black lolled across the bar. He scarcely stirred as we came in, but his eyes flicked open quite suddenly and I knew he noted our presence and was judging us.

"Evening," I said.

He took his time before replying. Still sizing us up. Then, he grinned.

"Evening, gents. What's your pleasure?"

"Gin," I said. "Straight-up. It's a cold night."

"That's right, gents."

He poured, I paid, and took the glasses over to one of the booths. We wasted no time in emptying them.

I went over to the bar and got the bottle. Sir Guy and I poured ourselves another drink. The big man went back into his doze, with one wary eye half-open against any sudden activity.

The clock over the bar ticked on. The wind was rising outside, tearing the shroud of fog to ragged shreds. Sir Guy and I sat in the warm booth and drank our gin.

He began to talk, and the shadows crept up about us to listen.

He rambled a great deal. He went over everything he'd said in the office when I met him, just as though I hadn't heard it before. Those who suffer from obsessions are like that.

I listened very patiently. I poured Sir Guy another drink.

But the liquor only made him more talkative. How he did run on! About ritual killings and prolonging the life unnaturally—the whole fantastic tale came out again. And of course, he maintained his unyielding conviction that the Ripper was abroad tonight.

I suppose I was guilty of goading him.

"Very well," I said, unable to keep the impatience from my voice. "Let us say that your theory is correct—even though we must overlook every natural law and swallow a lot of superstition to give it any credence.

"But let us say, for the sake of argument, that you are right. Jack the Ripper was a man who discovered how to prolong his own life through making human sacrifices. He did travel around the world as you believe. He is in Chicago now and is planning to kill. In other words, let us suppose that everything you claim is gospel truth. So what?"

"What do you mean, 'so what'?" said Sir Guy.

"Suppose you tell me," I replied. "If all this is true, it still doesn't prove that by sitting down in a dingy gin-mill on the South Side, Jack the Ripper is going to walk in here and let you kill him, or turn him over to the police. And come to think of it, I don't even know now just what you intend to *do* with him if you ever did find him."

Sir Guy gulped his gin. "I'd capture the bloody swine," he said. "Capture him and turn him over to the government, together with all the papers and documentary evidence I've collected against him over a period of many years. I've spent a fortune investigating this affair. I tell you, a fortune! His capture will mean the solution of hundreds of unsolved crimes, of that I am convinced."

In vino veritas. Or was all this nonsense the result of too much gin? It didn't matter. Sir Guy Hollis had another. I sat there and wondered what to do with hm. The man was rapidly working up to a climax of hysterical drunkenness.

"That's enough," I said, putting out my hand as Sir Guy reached for the half-emptied bottle again. "Let's call a cab and get out of here. It's getting late and it doesn't look as though your elusive friend is going to put in his appearance. Tomorrow, if I were you, I'd plan to turn all those papers and documents over to the FBI. If you're so convinced of the truth of your theory, they are competent to make a very thorough investigation, and find your man."

"No." Sir Guy was drunkenly obstinate. "No cab."

"But let's get out of here anyway," I said, glancing at my watch. "It's past midnight."

He sighed, shrugged, and rose unsteadily. As he started for the door, he tugged the gun free from his pocket.

"Here, give me that!" I whispered. "You can't walk around the street brandishing that thing."

I took the gun and slipped it inside my coat. Then I got hold of his right arm and steered him out of the door. The black man didn't look up as we departed.

We stood shivering in the alleyway. The fog had increased. I couldn't see either end of the alley from where we stood. It was cold. Damp. Dark. Fog or no fog, a little wind was whispering secrets to the shadows at our backs.

Sir Guy, despite his incapacity, still stared apprehensively at the alley, as though he expected to see a figure approaching.

Disgust got the better of me.

"Childish foolishness," I snorted. "Jack the Ripper, indeed! I call this carrying a hobby too far."

"Hobby?" He faced me. Through the fog I could see his distorted face. "You call this a hobby?"

"Well, what is it?" I said. "Just why else are you so interested in tracking down this mythical killer?"

My arm held his. But his stare held me. "In London," he whispered. "In 1888 . . . one of those nameless drabs the Ripper slew . . . was my mother."

"What?"

"Later I was recognized by my father, and legitimized. We swore to give our lives to find the Ripper. My father was the first to search. He died in Hollywood in 1926—on the trail of the Ripper. They said he was stabbed by an unknown assailant in a brawl. But I knew who that assailant was.

"So I've taken up his work, do you see, John? I've carried on. And I will carry on until I do find him and kill him with my own hands."

I believed him then. He wouldn't give up. He wasn't just a drunken babbler anymore. He was as fanatical, as determined, as relentless as the Ripper himself.

Tomorrow he'd be sober. He'd continue the search. Perhaps he'd turn those papers over to the FBI. Sooner or later, with such persistence—and with his motive—he'd be successful. I'd always known he had a motive.

"Let's go," I said, steering him down the alley.

"Wait a minute," said Sir Guy. "Give me back my gun." He lurched a little. "I'd feel better with the gun on me."

He pressed me into the dark shadows of a little recess.

I tried to shrug him off, but he was insistent.

"Let me carry the gun, now, John," he mumbled.

"All right," I said.

I reached into my coat, brought my hand out.

"But that's not a gun," he protested.

"I know."

I bore down on him swiftly.

"John!" he screamed.

"Never mind the 'John,'" I whispered, raising the knife. "Just call me . . . Jack."

THE GOOD OLD DAYS

JULIUS SCHWARTZ

I can never reminisce about "the good old days" without bringing up my friend Bob Bloch. Bob's personality—his charm, his sense of humor—personified the period many of us remember as the Golden Age.

Somewhere along the map of that period falls the year 1938. Among other milestones of historical significance, that was the year I turned twenty-three. And, being twenty-three, I decided it was time to get serious about seeking my fortune.

At the time, my friend Mort Weisinger was editing *Thrilling Wonder Stories, Startling Stories,* and *Strange Stories.* Mort had recently resigned as my partner in our literary agency, Solar Sales Service, due to the conflict of interest his editorial position placed him in. But the agency was still going strong. And I was still on the lookout for new talent.

I had read a number of stories in *Weird Tales* by a promising young fantasy writer named Robert Bloch. Now, with the Great Depression finally winding down and prosperity poking its nose over the horizon, I decided to try and snare Bob as a client. I had already netted his California-based pal, Henry Kuttner.

So, in the summer of 1938, I shanghaied Mort and his Buick, invested a dozen or so tankfuls of 16-cent-a-gallon gas, and went on a recruitment junket.

Along for the ride with Mort and me was science fiction writer Otto Binder. First we drove out to Chicago to see Otto's family, then we detoured to Milwaukee to drop in on the family of the late Stanley G. Weinbaum. After all, we had nothing better to do—we were a trio of free and easy bachelors. And these were the good old days.

Weinbaum had belonged to a group of pulp writers who called themselves the Milwaukee Fictioneers. At the time, the club included Ralph Milne Farley, Ray Palmer, and their youngest member, Bob Bloch.

I saw my opening.

Sporting our irresistible Bronx accents, Mort and I showed up at a meeting of the Milwaukee Fictioneers and sprung the good news on Bob—that I was inviting him to join my stable of writers.

I don't think Bob knew what to make of the news. I think he was impressed by the fellas I represented, which included such pros as Manly Wade Wellman, Edmond Hamilton, and David H. Keller. He was also awed when I revealed I had sold H. P. Lovecraft's *Weird Tales* reject "At the Mountains of Madness" to *Astounding Stories*. Lovecraft was Bob's mentor.

Finally, I made Bob an offer he couldn't refuse. I let it slip that Mort was standing by to pick up any of his *Weird Tales* rejects.

When he thought about it, it was a proverbial gold mine. There were no other markets for the material Bob was writing at that time, and he was sitting on rejected scripts with nowhere to go.

Being twenty-one and in a mood to get serious about seeking his own fortune, Bob caved in.

Before long, Bob's scripts began arriving in the mail. He was truly one of the most interesting writers of that era—always an easy, enjoyable read. Within two months, I banged out a double. On October 4, I sold two of Bob's yarns to *Strange Stories*.

Bob was thrilled. Unlike *Weird Tales,* which paid upon publication—a policy that could leave a poor writer waiting a year or more for a much-needed check—*Strange Stories* paid upon acceptance. Okay, it only paid 1/2 cent per word, which was, incidentally, half of *Weird Tales'* rate. But these were the good old days. People were happy to be working.

As it turned out, both of Bob's stories were slated to appear in the same February 1939 issue of *Strange Stories.* But everyone agreed that two tales with the same by-line looked strange on a table of contents. So Bob was asked to invent an entirely new writer.

The one he picked was Tarleton Fiske. He used the pseudonym on "The Sorcerer's Jewel," while "The Curse of the House" was by-lined Robert Bloch.

Why Tarleton Fiske? How the hell am I supposed to remember? That was fifty-five years ago.

But one thing I *do* recall is selling literally every story Bob ever sent me. All told, that's about seventy-five stories to a dozen different markets before closing the doors on Solar Sales Service. It was 1944, and I had accepted a position at DC Comics (then National Periodical Publications).

Of course, it wasn't long before fate had Bob and me working together again.

In the early postwar years—which still qualify as good old days as far as I'm concerned—it was a little slippery for fantasy writers. Consequently, I tried to persuade Bob to write a story for *Flash Comics*. At first, Bob was hesitant. He wasn't much of a comics aficionado. But I described the characters, gave him some background, and he banged out a script.

What Bob turned in was "The Flash and the Black Widow" (*Flash Comics*, August–September 1945). It's the one and only superhero story he ever wrote. And it was really weird, come to think of it. But years later, when we did a collection called *The Greatest Flash Stories Ever Told* (DC Comics, 1991), I insisted it be included. And everybody agreed.

There was only one other occasion when I had a chance to publish Bob's work—DC Comics' adaptation of his story "Hell On Earth." I had originally sold it for Bob in 1941 to *Weird Tales* for $200. Now, in 1986, DC was paying Bob a $1500 advance! Forty-five years later, Bob was learning to appreciate comics.

Of the many stories I moved for Bob, my proudest sale was "Yours Truly, Jack the Ripper." Thinking back, my only regret is not having considered it for a better market. I wish I could go back in time and submit it to *Harper's* or *The Saturday Evening Post*.

But *Weird Tales* bought the 8,000-word story and ran it in its July 1943 issue. And they sent Bob a check for eighty dollars.

That's a penny a word. And both Bob and I were happy to make the sale.

The good old days. Go figure.

LESSONS

MELISSA ANN SINGER

I had the distinction of working with Bob Bloch on his last few novels: *Lori, Psycho House,* and *The Jekyll Legacy* (Bob's collaboration with Andre Norton, and a fascinating synthesis of writing styles). I also was able to bring some of my favorite Bloch novels back into print: *American Gothic, Firebug,* and the two earlier *Psycho* novels.

Yes, I was Robert Bloch's editor.

It wasn't a difficult task. Bob was, after all, a gentleman, in business no less than in his personal life. But I didn't know that at first.

When I learned that I was going to be editing Robert Bloch, I'd been working in publishing for seven or eight years. I'd met a number of the writers who had shaped my path through literary life. I didn't think I could still be reduced to a quivering mass of hero-worshipping shock.

Wrong-o.

See, this was (fanfare of trumpets) ROBERT BLOCH.

Never mind all that "author of *Psycho*" stuff. I'd seen the movie, read the book, all right, and been plenty scared. But to me, Robert Bloch was the guy who'd written "That Hell-Bound Train," *American Gothic,* and "Yours Truly, Jack the Ripper."

He was a god.

I was a goner.

I imagine that Bob was fairly amused at the waves of unworthiness that emanated from me the night we first met face to face. But Bob, being Bob, eventually discovered that I loved old radio—"The Lone Ranger," "The Shadow," "Inner Sanctum"—and that subject made up most of our conversation.

It was the beginning of a beautiful friendship.

As an author, Bob was a dream to work with—always willing to listen to suggestions made by his editors; always gracious, even when he was telling people their ideas stank; rarely throwing his weight around, yet managing to get what he wanted. Editing Bob was fun—I looked forward to each novel or short story, each introduction or biographical note.

Reading Bob never felt like work. It was fun—there were always surprises, bad jokes, and scenes and characterizations that would make me catch my breath or make the hair on the back of my neck stand up.

The best thing about editing Bob, though, was being his friend.

He was a great conversationalist. We talked a fair bit by phone, and though he traveled rarely, I tried to attend the same conventions he did, so that we could share a meal and a really good talk.

One of my favorite lunches with Bob took place at a convention in the southern United States in the mid-1980s. We spent a good portion of the meal discussing ways to kill someone and dispose of the body without leaving evidence behind. We were fairly graphic (and, by the end of the meal, fairly outrageous) in our plotting. Later that day, an artist who was also attending the convention approached me. It turned out he had been sitting at the booth behind Bob and me while we were discussing burial pits and limestone and hacksaws—and that we'd made it impossible for the poor fellow to enjoy his meal. I'm afraid I wasn't very sympathetic. When I told Bob about my artistic encounter, he just grinned. A cat-who-ate-the-canary grin. A heart-of-a-small-boy grin.

I had a lot of fun with Bob, and I'll always remember how he could make me laugh. But more than that, I treasure the way he and his wife, Elly, opened their hearts to me. I felt like they were part of my family, because they made me feel like part of theirs. Though I only managed a single visit to their home, it was clearly a place filled with love—something obvious to anyone who ever saw the Blochs together.

When Elly's back went bad, Bob felt it. He was never more worried than when she was ill or in pain. He rarely traveled without her, and when he did attend conventions on his own, she was always in his thoughts. And I know she felt the same way about him.

I felt lucky to be part of the charmed circle that was their extended, nonbiological family.

Robert Bloch had a great impact on me, as he did on many people, through his writings. He dealt with two of the extremes of life, laughter and terror, and handled both with consummate ease.

But through himself, Bob taught me even more important lessons.

(1) Enjoy life.
(2) Work hard, but not so hard that you lose sight of (1).
(3) Love as many people (and cats) as possible.

And of course:

(4) There is no such thing as an unspeakable pun.

The first Robert Bloch story I remember reading was "A Toy for Juliette."
I was about nine years old, and had borrowed my father's copy of *Dangerous Visions* (I had free run of my folks' SF collection). A lot of the stories in the book went over my head. But "A Toy for Juliette" stuck, and became a story I reread at least once a year for more than a decade.

Ah, that catalog of instruments of torture! Thanks to numerous movies, I could visualize the items in Juliette's cabinets—but the delight she took in her tools was new to me. I've felt an echo of that delight many times since, in hardware stores, at auto shows . . .

And when I opened my dissecting kit for the first time.

There's a little of Juliette—and her last toy—in all of us.

Bob knew that.

A TOY FOR JULIETTE

Juliette entered her bedroom, smiling, and a thousand Juliettes smiled back at her. For all the walls were paneled with mirrors, and the ceiling was set with inlaid panes that reflected her image.

Wherever she glanced she could see the blonde curls framing the sensitive features of a face that was a radiant amalgam of both child and angel; a striking contrast to the rich, ripe revelation of her body in the filmy robe.

But Juliette wasn't smiling at herself. She smiled because she knew that Grandfather was back, and he'd brought her another toy. In just a few moments it would be decontaminated and delivered, and she wanted to be ready.

Juliette turned the ring on her finger and the mirrors dimmed. Another turn would darken the room entirely; a twist in the opposite direction would bring them blazing into brilliance. It was all a matter of choice—but then, that was the secret of life. To choose, for pleasure.

And what was her pleasure tonight?

Juliette advanced to one of the mirror panels and passed her hand before it. The glass slid to one side, revealing the niche behind it; the coffin-shaped opening in the solid rock, with the boot and thumbscrews set at the proper heights.

For a moment she hesitated; she hadn't played *that* game in years. Another time, perhaps. Juliette waved her hand and the mirror moved to cover the opening again.

She wandered along the row of panels, gesturing as she walked, pausing to inspect what was behind each mirror in turn. Here was the rack, there the stocks with the barbed whips resting against the dark-stained wood. And here was the dissecting table, hundreds of years old, with its quaint instruments; behind the next panel, the electrical prods and wires that produced such weird grimaces and contortions of agony, to say nothing of screams. Of course the screams didn't matter in a soundproofed room.

Juliette moved to the side wall and waved her hand again; the obedient glass slid away and she stared at a plaything she'd almost forgotten. It was one of the first things Grandfather had ever given her, and it was very old, almost like a mummy case. What had he called it? The Iron Maiden of Nuremberg, that was it—with the sharpened steel spikes set inside the lid. You chained a man inside, and you turned the little crank that closed the lid, ever so slowly, and the spikes pierced the wrists and the elbows, the ankles and the knees, the groin and the eyes. You had to be careful not to get excited and turn too quickly, or you'd spoil the fun.

Grandfather had shown her how it worked, the first time he brought her a real *live* toy. But then, Grandfather had shown her everything. He'd taught her all she knew, for he was very wise. He'd even given her her name—Juliette—from one of the old-fashioned printed books he'd discovered by the philosopher de Sade.

Grandfather had brought the books from the Past, just as he'd brought the playthings for her. He was the only one who had access to the Past, because he owned the Traveler.

The Traveler was a very ingenious mechanism, capable of attaining vibrational frequencies which freed it from the time-bind. At rest, it was just a big square boxlike shape, the size of a small room. But when Grandfather took over the controls and the oscillation started, the box would blur and disappear. It was still there, Grandfather said—at least, the *matrix* remained as a fixed point in space and time—but anything or anyone within the square could move freely into the Past to wherever the controls were programed. Of course they would be invisible when they arrived, but that was actually an advantage, particularly when it came to finding things and bringing them back. Grandfather had brought back some very interesting objects from almost mythical places—the great library of Alexandria, the Pyramid of Cheops, the Kremlin, the Vatican, Fort Knox—all the storehouses of treasure and knowledge which existed thousands of years ago. He liked to go to *that* part of the Past, the period before the thermonuclear wars and the robotic ages, and collect things. Of course books and jewels and metals were useless, except to an antiquarian, but Grandfather was a romanticist and loved the olden times.

It was strange to think of him owning the Traveler, but of course he hadn't actually created it. Juliette's father was really the one who built it, and Grandfather took possession of it after her father died. Juliette suspected Grandather had killed her father and mother when she was just a baby, but she could never be sure. Not that it mattered; Grandfather was always very good to her, and besides, soon he would die and she'd own the Traveler herself.

They used to joke about it frequently. "I've made you into a monster," he'd say. "And someday you'll end up by destroying me. After which, of course, you'll go on to destroy the entire world—or what little remains of it."

"Aren't you afraid?" she'd tease.

"Certainly not. That's my dream—the destruction of everything. An end to all this sterile decadence. Do you realize that at one time there were more than three billion inhabitants on this planet? And now, less than three thousand! Less than three thousand, shut up inside these Domes, prisoners of themselves and sealed away forever, thanks to the sins of the fathers who poisoned not only the outside world but outer space by meddling with the atomic order of the universe. Humanity is virtually extinct already; you will merely hasten the finale."

"But couldn't we all go back to another time, in the Traveler?" she asked.

"Back to *what* time? The continuum is changeless; one event leads inexorably to another, all links in a chain which binds us to the present and its inevitable end in destruction. We'd have temporary individual survival, yes, but to no purpose. And none of us are fitted to survive in a more primitive environment. So let us stay here and take what pleasure we can from the moment. My pleasure is to be the sole user and possessor of the Traveler. And yours, Juliette—"

Grandfather laughed then. They both laughed, because they knew what *her* pleasure was.

Juliette killed her first toy when she was eleven—a little boy. It had been brought to her as a special gift from Grandfather, from somewhere in the Past, for elementary sex play. But it wouldn't co-operate, and she lost her temper and beat it to death with a steel rod. So Grandfather brought her an older toy, with brown skin, and it co-operated very well, but in the end she tired of it and one day when it was sleeping in her bed she tied it down and found a knife.

Experimenting a little before it died, Juliette discovered new sources of pleasure, and of course Grandfather found out. That's when he'd christened her "Juliette"; he seemed to approve most highly, and from then on he brought her the playthings she kept behind the mirrors in her bedroom. And on his restless rovings into the Past he brought her new toys.

Being invisible, he could find them for her almost anywhere on his travels—all he did was to use a stunner and transport them when he returned. Of course each toy had to be very carefully decontaminated; the Past was teeming with strange micro-organisms. But once the toys were properly antiseptic they were turned over to Juliette for her pleasure, and during the past seven years she had enjoyed herself.

It was always delicious, this moment of anticipation before a new toy arrived. What would it be like? Grandfather was most considerate; mainly, he made sure that the toys he brought her could speak and understand Anglish—or "English," as they used to call it in the Past. Verbal communication was often important, particularly if Juliette wanted to follow the precepts of the philosopher de Sade and enjoy some form of sex relation before going on to keener pleasures.

But there was still the guessing beforehand. Would this toy be young or old, wild or tame, male or female? She'd had all kinds, and every possible combination. Sometimes she kept them alive for days before tiring of them—or before the subtleties of which she was capable caused them to expire. At other times she wanted it to happen quickly; tonight, for example, she knew she could be soothed only by the most primitive and direct action.

Once Juliette realized this, she stopped playing with her mirror panels and went directly to the big bed. She pulled back the coverlet, groped under the pillow until she felt it. Yes, it was still there—the big knife with the long, cruel blade. She knew what she would do now: take the toy to bed with her and then, at precisely the proper moment, combine her pleasures. If she could time her knife thrust—

She shivered with anticipation, then with impatience.

What kind of toy would it be? She remembered the suave, cool one—Benjamin Bathurst was his name, an English diplomat from the time of what Grandfather called the Napoleonic Wars. Oh, he'd been suave and cool enough, until she beguiled him with her body, into the bed. And there'd been that American aviatrix from slightly later on in the Past, and once, as a very special treat, the entire crew of a sailing vessel called the *Marie Celeste*. They had lasted for *weeks!*

Strangely enough, she'd even read about some of her toys afterwards. Because when Grandfather approached them with his stunner and brought them here, they disappeared forever from the Past, and if they were in any way known or important in their time, such disappearances were noted. And some of Grandfather's books had accounts of the "mysterious vanishing" which took place and was, of course, never explained. How delicious it all was!

Juliette patted the pillow back into place and slid the knife under it. She couldn't wait, now; what was delaying things?

She forced herself to move to a vent and depress the sprayer, shedding her robe as the perfumed mist bathed her body. It was the final allurement—but why didn't her toy arrive?

Suddenly Grandfather's voice came over the auditor.

"I'm sending you a little surprise, dearest."

That's what he always said; it was part of the game.

Juliette depressed the communicator-toggle. "Don't tease," she begged. "Tell me what it's like."

"An Englishman. Late Victorian Era. Very prim and proper, by the looks of him."

"Young? Handsome?"

"Passable." Grandfather chuckled. "Your appetites betray you, dearest."

"Who is it—someone from the books?"

"I wouldn't know the name. We found no identification during the decontamination. But from his dress and manner, and the little black bag he carried when I discovered him so early in the morning, I'd judge him to be a physician returning from an emergency call."

Juliette knew about "physicians" from her reading, of course; just as she knew what "Victorian" meant. Somehow the combination seemed exactly right.

"Prim and proper?" She giggled. "Then I'm afraid it's due for a shock."

Grandfather laughed. "You have something in mind, I take it."

"Yes."

"Can I watch?"

"Please—not this time."

"Very well."

"Don't be mad, darling. I love you."

Juliette switched off. Just in time, too, because the door was opening and the toy came in.

She stared at it, realizing that Grandfather had told the truth. The toy was a male of thirty-odd years, attractive but by no means handsome. It couldn't be, in that dark garb and those ridiculous side whiskers. There was something almost depressingly refined and mannered about it, an air of embarrassed repression.

And of course, when it caught sight of Juliette in her revealing robe, and the bed surrounded by mirrors, it actually began to *blush*.

That reaction won Juliette completely. A blushing Victorian, with the build of a bull—and unaware that this was the slaughterhouse!

It was so amusing she couldn't restrain herself; she moved forward at once and put her arms around it.

"Who—who are you? Where am I?"

The usual questions, voiced in the usual way. Ordinarily, Juliette would have amused herself by parrying with answers designed to tantalize and titillate her victim. But tonight she felt an urgency which only increased as she embraced the toy and pressed it back toward the waiting bed.

The toy began to breathe heavily, responding. But it was still bewildered. "Tell me—I don't understand. Am I alive? Or is this heaven?"

Juliette's robe fell open as she lay back. "You're alive, darling," she murmured. "Wonderfully alive." She laughed as she began to prove the statement. "But closer to heaven than you think."

And to prove *that* statement, her free hand slid under the pillow and groped for the waiting knife.

But the knife wasn't there any more. Somehow it had already found its way into the toy's hand. And the toy wasn't prim and proper any longer; its face was something glimpsed in nightmare. Just a glimpse, before the blinding blur of the knife blade, as it came down, again and again and again—

The room, of course, was soundproof, and there was plenty of time. They didn't discover what was left of Juliette's body for several days.

Back in London, after the final mysterious murder in the early morning hours, they never did find Jack the Ripper. . . .

ARTHUR C. CLARKE

Bob and I were born in the same year—1917—and we first met at the 1952 Midwestercon in Bellefontaine, Ohio. So we knew each other for half a lifetime, and although we probably met on no more than a dozen occasions in that period, there never seemed to be any gaps between our meetings—we resumed our acquaintanceship just where it had left off.

It was therefore with great sadness that I received a handwritten letter from Bob dated August 2, saying: "I'll not impose more than these few last lines on you, and last they may be, since I'm not up to typing (or thinking) properly nowadays. Within the past few months I've come down with an incurable, terminal duodenal cancer, and am told it may be only a short while before it's all over. . . . Meanwhile, there's far too much to do, or attempt to do, but it seemed important to say farewell, and fondly, to a dear colleague-in-arms. . . . It was with this thought in mind that I tottered over to the desk to set down these notions—only to have the trip interrupted by a phone call from Andre Norton—telling of seeing you just last week, a heartening bit of news under the circumstances. Maybe we are not as coincidental as we sometimes believe ourselves to be.

"I, for one, shall soon know. Meanwhile, do take care, accept my advanced 77th birthday greetings. As always—or, all time being relative, forever, Bob."

His letter was actually posted on August 25 and I wrote back instantly, crying a good deal, and saying how much I appreciated his taking the time and energy to think of me. I added, "I too have nothing but happy memories of the (too few) times we met. You must have great satisfaction from knowing how much enjoyment you gave to millions of readers and viewers. (I'm looking forward very much to your autobiography, which I have on order.)"

I do hope that Bob lived long enough to receive this letter: meanwhile, I'm still waiting for *Once Around the Bloch: The Unauthorized Autobiography.* The title is typical of Bob's wry sense of humor: He really was one of the funniest men I have ever met. For years I've been fond of quoting his claim that his hobby was "Breeding pedigree vultures," and that he has the heart of a little child—"in a jar on my desk."

The last time we met was during the premiere of *2010,* and I am indebted to Neil McAleer's *Odyssey: The Authorized Biography of Arthur C. Clarke* for this:

> The morning after the premiere, Arthur invited Ray Bradbury and Bob Bloch to breakfast, but Bob couldn't make it that early. He did arrive just before they finished, however, and the threesome left the hotel together and were photographed out front by the doorman.
>
> "Then Ray pedalled away," recalls Bloch, "and Arthur said, 'Come with me, I've got something to show you.' So he popped me into a limo, and we went down to a place in Culver City, about a mile away from MGM. This was where all the special effects had been done for *2010.* He, as always, was fascinated with the technology. We went through the whole place, and he showed me what they had done and how they had done it.
>
> "What he wanted to show me particularly was the space child, the baby, operated by remote control, some kind of wind pressure. It was rubberised, a beautifully done thing, and he was fascinated by it, and he knew I would be too. I looked at it, and I said, 'Arthur, it looks just like you!'"

I have often wondered if Bob ever felt annoyed by the fact that despite his large body of excellent fiction, he was identified almost exclusively with *Psycho.* In a 1989 interview he commented: "At one time it did, but then I began to realize it's the audience, the reading audience or the viewing audience that pastes the label on your forehead to identify you, and you might as well wear it! Without any comparisons in mind, I know of several related instances—composer Maurice Ravel with *Bolero,* and another composer, Rachmaninoff, with his *Prelude in C Sharp Minor.* Both men wrote some excellent music in a variety of other forms, but each had to live with that identification. . . . I think I can't complain."

And talking of *Psycho*—in 1984, Bob sent me *Psycho II,* with the inscription: "For Arthur Clarke, may the next thirty years of our friendship be as pleasant as the first thirty years have been!"

Alas, we managed only a third of the second triad, but I am grateful for the time we did share together.

MORE THAN MOST

PHILIP JOSÉ FARMER

I first knew Robert Bloch, the writer, when I read in *Weird Tales* magazine his first published story. He was seventeen years old and a published writer. I was a little over a year younger and had never submitted any fiction. I was jealous of him, though not very much. If he could get started so young, so could I. Someday, I thought, someday soon, I, too, will be published. But that "someday soon" was a long way off.

I first met Bob Bloch, the man, when my wife, Bette, and I attended our first science fiction convention. This was the World Convention in Chicago in 1952. Like most people, we were both charmed and much amused by Bloch. His wide knowledge, his deep intelligence, and his photon-fast wit, ranging from the deep to the trivial, bowled us over. His wit was Voltairean rather than Rabelaisian (though he was not above making really corny puns).

But threaded with all this was a genuine warmth and caring. After forty-two years of knowing him, I can say that the warmth and caring are what I feel the most when I think of him, and that's often.

Bette and Bob Bloch resonated on the same frequency from the moment we met. They understood one another. They corresponded quite often and always managed to get together at conventions. When we moved to Los Angeles, we saw Bob Bloch and his wife, Elly, frequently. Since Bob and Bette were both born on April 5, they always exchanged cards and, if possible, greetings by phone on that day. And Bette was the first person Bob told that he had cancer. That devastated her.

And recently, after a long-distance conversation, Bob signed off with, "Happy Birthday, Bette!" He knew he wouldn't be here next April 5.

As for me, I was numbed when I heard about the cancer. Bad news usually does that to me. It wasn't until Bob's death was absolutely certain that the long-suppressed tears broke out.

We've been fortunate in keeping many of his letters. Reading them over brings him back, and we can see the twinkle in his eyes. They're personal, but I think he'd give his permission for us to quote from some of them. For instance, here are some lines from a letter of June 9, 1990:

> I did a couple of TV sound bites (Entertainment Today and Inside Edition) but would have gotten a lot more exposure if I'd recorded a dirty rap-album instead. Live and learn. If I were writing *Psycho* today, I'd put the motel in South Central Los Angeles and change Norman Bates' name to Bubba.

A postcard sent by Bob, dated September 26, 1992:

> Dear Phil:
> Let this be our secret. Don't tell anybody!

There was no secret. He tossed this off just for fun.
From a postcard, November 4, 1992:

> Dear Bette:
> . . . But hope you two survived the election. I voted for Harlan, but he didn't make it.

From a card to both of us:

> Hope you can get some rest and have a happy Easter. Elly just gave me a chocolate Jesus.

From a letter dated August 7 1/2, 1986, re Bette's dissatisfaction with a doctor:

> Tell the orthopedist that if he wants to live cheap he should move to Peking and make his living repairing bone china.

There are so many quotable lines, but I'll not pursue them. His conversation was even better, and his insight into society in general and individuals in particular was very penetrating and sometimes angry. Usually, though, he tempered his criticisms with a wry and witty comment. He was, however, not politically correct. I'm glad, because I would have thought the less of him if he had been. No writer worth his or her salt is politically correct. To be that means that the writer is following the party line. But being apolitically correct doesn't mean that the writer isn't compassionate or understanding. It means that the writer makes his own judgments based on the facts. That was the kind of writer Bob was.

Rereading the above, I see that it's almost hopeless to portray him or, for that matter, anybody, unless you go to novelistic lengths or compress him into a sonnet. All I can say, really, is that Bob Bloch, the man, will always live in my memory and in Bette's. He won't fade away in there. And we can say truly that we'll miss him. There's nobody to replace him, never will be.

"All On a Golden Afternoon" is not the best short story Bob Bloch wrote. I don't know what his best was, perhaps "Yours Truly, Jack the Ripper." But "All on a Golden Afternoon" sticks most in my memory, is my favorite, and the one I most reread.

One of the reasons is probably that I have loved Lewis Carroll's *Alice* stories and *The Hunting of the Snark* since I first read them when I was nine. But that wouldn't be enough for me unless Bob Bloch had incorporated the Carrollian spirit in the story. At the same time, he satirizes Hollywood types. Which was something he often did in his fiction and so is truly Blochian.

He also makes fun of the psychiatrists (licensed and would-be) who have tried so hard to psychoanalyze Carroll through the *Alice* books. They are sometimes very clever, but they haven't so far convinced me that their findings are valid. They're so grave, unlike fun-loving Carroll (and fun-loving Bloch). Yet, all their seriousness, gravity, and ludicrousness only make the perceptive reader laugh.

I suppose that, sometime in the future, the psychoanalytically inclined critic will tackle Bloch's works. He or she or they should have a field day. Will they conclude that Bloch was a psychopath who somehow sublimated his craving to kill and to mutilate through writing? Will they decide that Yog-Sothoth was a thinly disguised symbol for his mother? Do his Cthulhu Mythos stories reveal a deep fear of those dark, mysterious, and menacing forces which control us as if we were robots and to which no appeal is ever granted? Like the government in general, the Mafia, the IRS?

Bloch would enjoy analyses of himself, though he would poke fun at them.

So, enjoy this story. It's one of the very few Bloch stories in which good triumphs over evil. It sometimes does, you know, and that may be one more reason why this is my favorite story.

ALL ON A GOLDEN AFTERNOON

The uniformed man at the gate was very polite, but he didn't seem at all in a hurry to open up. Neither Dr. Prager's new Cadillac nor his old goatee made much of an impression on him.

It wasn't until Dr. Prager snapped, "But I've an appointment—Mr. Dennis said it was urgent!" that the uniformed man turned and went into the little guard booth to call the big house on the hill.

Dr. Saul Prager tried not to betray his impatience, but his right foot pressed down on the accelerator and a surrogate of exhaust did his fuming for him.

Just how far he might have gone in polluting the air of Bel Air couldn't be determined, for after a moment the man came out of the booth and unlocked the gate. He touched his cap and smiled.

"Sorry to keep you waiting, Doctor," he said. "You're to go right up."

Dr. Prager nodded curtly and the car moved forward.

"I'm new on this job and you got to take precautions, you know," the man called after him, but Dr. Prager wasn't listening. His eyes were fixed on the panorama of the hillside ahead. In spite of himself he was mightily impressed.

There was reason to be—almost half a million dollars' worth of reason. The combined efforts of a dozen architects, topiarists, and landscape gardeners had served to create what was popularly known as "the Garden of Eden." Although the phrase was a complimentary reference to Eve Eden, owner of the estate, there was much to commend it, Dr. Prager decided. That is, if one can picture a Garden of Eden boasting two swimming pools, an eight-car garage, and a corps of resident angels with power mowers.

This was by no means Dr. Prager's first visit, but he never failed to be moved by the spectacle of the palace on the hill. It was a fitting residence for Eve, the First Woman. The First Woman of the Ten Box-Office Leaders, that is.

The front door was already open when he parked in the driveway, and the butler smiled and bowed. He was, Dr. Prager knew, a genuine English butler, complete with accent and sideburns. Eve Eden had insisted on that, and she'd had one devil of a time obtaining an authentic specimen from the employment agencies. Finally she'd managed to locate one—from Central Casting.

"Good afternoon," the butler greeted him. "Mr. Dennis is in the library, sir. He is expecting you."

Dr. Prager followed the manservant through the foyer and down the hall. Everything was furnished with magnificent taste—as Mickey Dennis often observed, "Why not? Didn't we hire the best interior decorator in Beverly Hills?"

The library itself was a remarkable example of calculated decor. Replete with the traditional overstuffed chairs, custom-made by a firm of reliable overstuffers, it boasted paneled walnut walls, polished mahogany floors, and a good quarter mile of bookshelves rising to the vaulted ceiling. Dr. Prager's glance swept the shelves, which were badly in need of dusting anyway. He noted a yard of Thackeray in green, two yards of brown Thomas Hardy, complemented by a delicate blue Dostoevski. Ten feet of Balzac, five feet of Dickens, a section of Shakespeare, a mass of Molière. Complete works, of course. The booksellers would naturally want to give Eve Eden the works. There must have been two thousand volumes on the shelves.

In the midst of it all sat Mickey Dennis, the agent, reading a smudged and dog-eared copy of *Variety*.

As Dr. Prager stood, hesitant, in the doorway, the little man rose and beckoned to him. "Hey, Doc!" he called. "I been waiting for you!"

"Sorry," Dr. Prager murmured. "There were several appointments I couldn't cancel."

"Never mind the appointments. You're on retainer with us, ain'cha? Well, sweetheart, this time you're really gonna earn it."

He shook his head as he approached. "Talk about trouble," he muttered—although Dr. Prager had not even mentioned the subject. "Talk about trouble, we got it. I ain't dared call the studio yet. If I did there'd be wigs floating all over Beverly Hills. Had to see you first. And you got to see *her*."

Dr. Prager waited. A good fifty percent of his professional duties consisted of waiting. Meanwhile he indulged in a little private speculation. What would it be this time? Another overdose of sleeping pills—a return to narcotics—an attempt to prove the old maxim that absinthe makes the heart grow fonder? He'd handled Eve Eden before in all these situations and topped it off with more routine assignments, such as the time she'd wanted to run off with the Japanese chauffeur. Come to think of it, that hadn't been exactly routine. Handling Eve was bad; handling the chauffeur was worse, but handling the chauffeur's wife and seven children was a nightmare. Still, he'd smoothed things over. He always smoothed things over, and that's why he was on a fat yearly retainer.

Dr. Prager, as a physician, generally disapproved of obesity, but when it came to yearly retainers he liked them plump. And this was one of the plumpest. Because of it he was ready for any announcement Mickey Dennis wanted to make.

The agent clutched his arm now. "Doc, you gotta put the freeze on her, fast! This time it's murder!"

Despite himself, Dr. Prager blanched. He reached up and tugged reassuringly at his goatee. It was still there, the symbol of his authority. He had mastered the constriction in his vocal chords before he started to speak. "You mean she's killed someone?"

"No!" Mickey Dennis shook his head in disgust. "*That* would be bad enough, but we could handle it. I was just using a figger of speech, like. She wants to murder herself, Doc. Murder her career, to throw away a brand-new seven-year non-cancelable no-option contract with a percentage of the gross. She wants to quit the industry."

"Leave pictures?"

"Now you got it, Doc. She's gonna walk out on four hundred grand a year."

There was real anguish in the agent's voice—the anguish of a man who is well aware that ten percent of four hundred thousand can buy a lot of convertibles.

"You gotta see her," Dennis moaned. "You gotta talk her out of it, fast."

Dr. Prager nodded. "Why does she want to quit?" he asked.

Mickey Dennis raised his hands. "I don't know," he wailed. "She won't give any reasons. Last night she just up and told me. Said she was through. And when I asked her politely just what the hell's the big idea, she dummied up. Said I wouldn't understand." The little man made a sound like trousers ripping in a tragic spot. "Damned right I wouldn't understand! But I want to find out."

Dr. Prager consulted his beard again with careful fingers. "I haven't seen her for over two months," he said. "How has she been behaving lately? I mean, otherwise?"

"Like a doll," the agent declared. "Just a living doll. To look at her you wouldn't of thought there was anything in her head but sawdust. Wrapped up the last picture clean, brought it in three days ahead of schedule. No blowups, no goofs, no nothing. She hasn't been hitting the sauce or anything else. Stays home mostly and goes to bed early. Alone, yet." Mickey Dennis made the pants-ripping sound again. "I might of figgered it was too good to be true."

"No financial worries?" Dr. Prager probed.

Dennis swept his arm forward to indicate the library and the expanse beyond. "With *this*? All clear and paid for. Plus a hunk of real estate in Long Beach and two oil wells gushing like Lolly Parsons over a hot scoop. She's got more loot than Fort Knox and almost as much as Crosby."

"Er—how old is Eve, might I ask?"

"You might ask, and you might get some funny answers. But I happen to know. She's thirty-three. I can guess what you're thinking, Doc, and it don't figger. She's good for another seven years, maybe more. Hell, all you got to do is look at her."

"That's just what I intend to do," Dr. Prager replied. "Where is she?"

"Upstairs, in her room. Been there all day. Won't see me." Mickey Dennis hesitated. "She doesn't know you're here either. I said I was gonna call you and she got kinda upset."

"Didn't want to see me, eh?"

"She said if that long-eared nanny goat got within six miles of this joint she'd—" The agent paused and shifted uncomfortably. "Like I mentioned, she was upset."

"I think I can handle the situation," Dr. Prager decided.

"Want me to come along and maybe try and soften her up a little?"

"That won't be necessary." Dr. Prager left the room, walking softly.

Mickey Dennis went back to his chair and picked up the magazine once more. He didn't read, because he was waiting for the sound of the explosion.

When it came he shuddered and almost gritted his teeth until he remembered how much it would cost to buy a new upper plate. Surprisingly enough, the sound of oaths and shrieks subsided after a time, and Dennis breathed a deep sigh of relief.

The doc was a good headshrinker. He'd handle her. He was handling her. So there was nothing to do now but relax.

2

"Relax," Dr. Prager said. "You've discharged all your aggression. Now you can stretch out. That's better."

The spectacle of Eve Eden stretched out in relaxation on a chaise longue was indeed better. In the words of many eminent lupine Hollywood authorities, it was the best.

Eve Eden's legs were long and white and her hair was long and blonde; both were now displayed to perfection, together with a whole series of coming attractions screened through her semitransparent lounging pajamas. The face that launched a thousand close-ups was that of a petulant child, well-versed in the more statutory phases of juvenile delinquency.

Dr. Prager could cling to his professional objectivity only by clinging to his goatee. As it was, he dislodged several loose hairs and an equal number of loose impulses before he spoke again.

"Now," he said, "tell me all about it."

"Why should I?" Eve Eden's eyes and voice were equally candid. "I didn't ask you to come here. I'm not in any jam."

"Mr. Dennis said you're thinking of leaving pictures."

"Mr. Dennis is a cockeyed liar. I'm not thinking of leaving. I've left, period. Didn't he call the lawyers? Hasn't he phoned the studio? I told him to."

"I wouldn't know," Dr. Prager soothed.

"Then he's the one who's in a jam," Eve Eden announced happily. "Sure, I know why he called you. You're supposed to talk me out of it, right? Well, it's no dice, Doc. I made up my mind."

"Why?"

"None of your business."

Dr. Prager leaned forward. "But it is my business, Wilma."

"Wilma?"

Dr. Prager nodded, his voice softening. "Wilma Kozmowski. Little Wilma Kozmowski. Have you forgotten that I know all about her? The little girl whose mother deserted her. Who ran away from home when she was twelve and lived around. I know about the waitress jobs in Pittsburgh, and the burlesque show, and the B-girl years in Calumet City. And I know about Frank, and Eddie, and Nino, and Six, and—all the others." Dr. Prager smiled. "You told me all this yourself, Wilma. And you told me all about what happened after you became Eve Eden. When you met me you weren't Eve Eden yet, not entirely. Wilma kept interfering, didn't she? It was Wilma who drank, took the drugs, got mixed up with the men, tried to kill herself. I helped you fight Wilma, didn't I, Eve? I helped you *become* Eve Eden, the movie star. That's why it's my business now to see that you stay that way. Beautiful, admired, successful, happy—"

"You're wrong, Doc. I found that out. If you want me to be happy, forget about Eve Eden. Forget about Wilma, too. From now on I'm going to be somebody else. So please, just go away."

"Somebody else?" Dr. Prager leaped at the phrase. An instant later he leaped literally.

"What's that?" he gasped.

He stared down at the floor, the hairs in his goatee bristling as he caught sight of the small white furry object that scuttled across the carpet.

Eve Eden reached down and scooped up the creature, smiling.

"Just a white rabbit," she explained. "Cute, isn't he? I bought him the other day."

"But—but—"

Dr. Prager goggled. It was indeed a white rabbit which Eve Eden cradled in her arms, but not *just* a white rabbit. For this rabbit happened to be wearing a vest and a checkered waistcoat, and Dr. Prager could almost swear that the silver chain across the vest terminated in a concealed pocket watch.

"I bought it after the dream," Eve Eden told him.

"Dream?"

"Oh, what's the use?" She sighed. "I might as well let you hear it. All you headshrinkers are queer for dreams anyway."

"You had a dream about rabbits?" Dr. Prager began.

"Please, Doc, let's do it my way," she answered. "This time *you* relax and I'll do the talking. It all started when I fell down this rabbit hole. . . ."

3

In her dream Eve Eden said, she was a little girl with long golden curls. She was sitting on a riverbank when she saw this white rabbit running close by. It was wearing the waistcoat and a high collar, and then it took a watch out of his pocket, muttering, "Oh dear, I shall be too late." She ran across the field after it, and when it popped down a large rabbit hole under a hedge, she followed.

"Oh no!" Dr. Prager muttered. "Not *Alice!*"

"Alice who?" Even Eden inquired.

"*Alice in Wonderland.*"

"You mean that movie Disney made, the cartoon thing?"

Dr. Prager nodded. "You saw it?"

"No. I never waste time on cartoons."

"But you know what I'm talking about, don't you?"

"Well—" Eve Eden hesitated. Then from the depths of her professional background an answer came. "Wasn't there another movie, way back around the beginning of the Thirties? Sure, Paramount made it, with Oakie and Gallagher and Horton and Ruggles and Ned Sparks and Fields and Gary Cooper. And let's see now, who played the dame—Charlotte Henry?"

Dr. Prager smiled. *Now* he was getting somewhere. "So that's the one you saw, eh?"

Eve Eden shook her head. "Never saw that one either. Couldn't afford movies when I was a brat, remember?"

"Then how do you know the cast and—"

"Easy. Gal who used to work with Alison Skipworth told me. She was in it too. And Edna May Oliver. I got a good memory, Doc. You know that."

"Yes." Dr. Prager breathed softly. "And so you must remember reading the original book, isn't that it?"

"Was it a book?"

"Now look here, don't tell me you've never read *Alice in Wonderland,* by Lewis Carroll. It's a classic."

"I'm no reader, Doc. You know that too."

"But surely as child you must have come across it. Or had somebody tell you the story."

The blonde curls tossed. "Nope. I'd remember if I had. I remember everything I read. That's why I'm always up on my lines. Best sight reader in the business. I not only haven't read *Alice in Wonderland,* I didn't even know there was such a story, except in a screenplay."

Dr. Prager gave an irritable tug at his goatee. "All right. You *do* have a remarkable memory, I know. So let's think back now. Let's think back very carefully to your earliest childhood. Somebody must have taken you on their lap, told you stories."

The star's eyes brightened. "Why, sure!" she exclaimed. "That's right! Aunt Emma was always telling me stories."

"Excellent." Dr. Prager smiled. "And can you recall now the first story she ever told you? The very first?"

Eve Eden closed her eyes, concentrating with effort. When her voice came it was from far away. "Yes," she whispered. "I remember now. I was only four. Aunt Emma took me on her lap and she told me my first story. It was the one about the drunk who goes in this bar, and he can't find the john, see, so the bartender tells him to go upstairs and—"

"No," said Dr. Prager. "No, no! Didn't she ever tell you any fairy tales?"

"Aunt Emma?" Eve Eden laughed. "I'll say she didn't. But stories—she had a million of 'em! Did you ever hear the one about the young married couple who wanted to—"

"Never mind." The psychiatrist leaned back. "You are quite positive you have never read or heard or seen *Alice in Wonderland?*"

"I told you so in the first place, didn't I? Now, do you want to hear my dream or not?"

"I want to very much," Dr. Prager answered, and he did. He took out his notebook and uncapped his fountain pen. In his own mind he was quite certain that she had heard or read *Alice,* and he was interested in the reasons for the mental block which prevented her from recalling the fact. He was also interested in the possible symbolism behind her account. This promised to be quite an enjoyable session. "You went down the rabbit hole," he prompted.

"Into a tunnel," Eve continued. "I was falling, falling very slowly."

Dr. Prager wrote down *tunnel—womb fixation?* And he wrote down *falling dream.*

"I fell into a well," Eve said. "Lined with cupboards and bookshelves. There were maps and pictures on pegs."

Forbidden sex knowledge, Dr. Prager wrote.

"I reached out while I was still falling and took a jar from a shelf. The jar was labeled 'Orange Marmalade.'"

Marmalade—Mama? Dr. Prager wrote.

Eve said something about "Do cats eat bats?" and "Do bats eat cats?" but Dr. Prager missed it. He was too busy writing. It was amazing, now that he thought of it, just how much Freudian symbolism was packed into *Alice in Wonderland.* Amazing, too, how well her subconscious recalled it.

Eve was now telling how she had landed in the long hall with the doors all around and how the rabbit disappeared, muttering, "Oh, my ears and whiskers, how late it's getting." She told about approaching the three-legged solid-glass table with the tiny golden key on it, and Dr. Prager quickly scribbled *phallic symbol.* Then she described looking through a fifteen-inch door into a garden beyond and wishing she could get through it by shutting up like a telescope. So Dr. Prager wrote *phallic envy.*

"Then," Eve continued, "I saw this little bottle on the table, labeled 'Drink Me.' And so I drank, and do you know something? I did shut up like a telescope. I got smaller and smaller, and if I hadn't stopped drinking I'd have disappeared! So of course I couldn't reach the key, but then I saw this glass box under the table labeled 'Eat Me,' and I ate and got bigger right away."

She paused. "I know it sounds silly, Doc, but it was real interesting."

"Yes indeed," Dr. Prager said. "Go on. Tell everything you remember."

"Then the rabbit came back, mumbling something about a Duchess. And it dropped a pair of white gloves and a fan."

Fetishism, the psychiatrist noted.

"After that it got real crazy." Eve giggled. Then she told about the crying and forming a pool on the floor composed of her own tears. And how she held the fan and shrank again, then swam in the pool.

Grief fantasy, Dr. Prager decided.

She went on to describe her meeting with the mouse and with the other animals, the caucus race, and the recital of the curious poem about the cur, Fury, which ended, "I'll prosecute you, I'll be judge, I'll be jury—I'll try the whole cause and condemn you to death."

Superego, wrote Dr. Prager and asked, "What are you afraid of, Eve?"

"Nothing," she answered. "And I wasn't afraid in the dream either. I liked it. But I haven't told you anything yet."

"Go on."

She went on, describing her trip to the rabbit's house to fetch his gloves and fan and finding the bottle labeled "Drink Me" in the bedroom. Then followed the episode of growth, and being stuck inside the house (*Claustrophobia,* the notebook dutifully recorded), and her escape from the animals who pelted her with pebbles as she ran into the forest.

It was *Alice* all right, word for word, image for image. *Father image* for the caterpillar, who might (Dr. Prager reasoned wisely) stand for himself as the psychiatrist, with his stern approach and enigmatic answers. The *Father William* poem which followed seemed to validate this conclusion.

Then came the episode of eating the side of the mushroom, growing and shrinking. Did this disguise her drug addiction? Perhaps. And there was a moment when she had a long serpentine neck and a pigeon mistook her for a serpent. A viper was a serpent. And weren't drug addicts called "vipers"? Of course. Dr. Prager was beginning to understand now. It was all symbolic. She was telling about her own life. Running away and finding the key to success—alternating between being very "small" and insignificant and trying every method of becoming "big" and important. Until she entered the garden—her Garden of Eden here—and became a star and consulted him and took drugs. It all made sense now.

He could understand as she told of the visit to the house of the Duchess (*mother image*) with her cruel "Chop off her head." He anticipated the baby who turned into a pig and wrote down *rejection fantasy* quickly.

Then he listened to the interview with the Cheshire cat, inwardly marveling at Eve Eden's perfect memory for dialogue.

"'But I don't want to go among mad people,' I said. And the crazy cat came back with, 'Oh, you can't help that. We're all mad here. I'm mad. You're mad.' And I said, 'How do you know I'm mad?' and the cat said, 'You must be—or you wouldn't have come here.' Well, I felt plenty crazy when the cat started to vanish. Believe it or not, Doc, there was nothing left but a big grin."

"I believe it," Dr. Prager assured her.

He was hot on the trail of another scent now. The talk of madness had set him off. And sure enough, now came the tea party. With the March Hare and the Mad Hatter, of course—the *Mad* Hatter. Sitting in front of their house (*asylum,* no doubt) with the sleeping dormouse between them. Dormouse—*dormant* sanity. She was afraid of going insane, Dr. Prager decided. So much so did he believe it that when she quoted the line, "Why is a raven like a writing desk?" he found himself writing down, *Why is a raving like a Rorschach test?* and had to cross it out.

Then came the sadistic treatment of the poor dormouse and another drug fantasy with mushrooms for the symbol, leading her again into a beautiful garden. Dr. Prager heard it all: the story of the playing-card people (*club* soldiers and *diamond* courtiers and *heart* children were perfectly fascinating symbols too!).

And when Eve said, "Why, they're only a pack of cards after all—I needn't be afraid of them," Dr. Prager triumphantly wrote *paranoid fantasies: people are unreal.*

"Now I must tell you about the croquet game," Eve went on, and so she told him about the croquet game and Dr. Prager filled two whole pages with notes.

He was particularly delighted with Alice-Eve's account of the conversation with the ugly Duchess, who said among other things, "Take care of the sense and the sounds will take care of themselves," and "Be what you seem to be—or more simply, never imagine yourself not to be otherwise than what it might appear to others that what you were or might have been was not otherwise than what you had been who have appeared to them to be otherwise."

Eve Eden rattled it off, apparently verbatim. "It didn't seem to make sense at the time," she admitted. "But it does now, don't you think?"

Dr. Prager refused to commit himself. It made sense all right. A dreadful sort of sense. This poor child was struggling to retain her identity. Everything pointed to that. She was adrift in a sea of illusion, peopled with Mock Turtles—*Mock* Turtle, very significant, that—and distorted imagery.

Now the story of the Turtle and the Gryphon and the Lobster Quadrille began to take on a dreadful meaning. All the twisted words and phrases symbolized growing mental disturbance. Schools taught "reeling and writhing" and arithmetic consisted of "ambition, distraction, uglification, and derision." Obviously fantasies of inferiority. And Alice-Eve growing more and more confused with twisted, inverted logic in which "blacking" became "whiting"—it was merely an inner cry signifying she could no longer tell the difference between black and white. In other words, she was losing all contact with reality. She was going through an ordeal—a trial.

Of course it was a trial! Now Eve was telling about the trial of the Knave of Hearts, who stole the tarts (*Hadn't Eve once been a "tart" herself?*) and Alice-Eve noted all the animals on the jury (*another paranoid delusion: people are animals*) and she kept growing (*delusions of grandeur*) and then came the white rabbit reading the anonymous letter.

Dr. Prager pricked up his own ears, rabbit fashion, when he heard the contents of the letter.

> "My notion was that you had been
> (before she had this fit)
> An obstacle that came between
> Him, and ourselves, and it.
> Don't let him know she liked them best
> For this must ever be
> A secret kept from all the rest
> Between yourself and me."

Of course. A *secret,* Dr. Prager decided. Eve Eden had been afraid of madness for a long time. That was the root of all her perverse behavior patterns, and he'd never probed sufficiently to uncover it. But the dream, welling up from the subconscious, provided the answer.

"I said I didn't believe there was an atom of meaning in it." Eve told him. "And the Queen cried, 'Off with her head,' but I said, 'Who cares for *you?* You're nothing but a pack of cards.' And they all rose up and flew at me, but I beat them off, and then I woke up fighting the covers."

She sat up. "You're been taking an awful lot of notes," she said. "Mind telling me what you think?"

Dr. Prager hesitated. It was a delicate question. Still, the dream content indicated that she was perfectly well aware of her problem on the subliminal level. A plain exposition of the facts might come as a shock but not a dangerous one. Actually a shock could be just the thing now to lead her back and resolve the initial trauma, whatever it was.

"All right," Dr. Prager said. "Here's what I think it means." And in plain language he explained his interpretation of her dream, pulling no punches but, occasionally, his goatee.

"So there you have it," he concluded. "The symbolic story of your life—and the dramatized and disguised conflict over your mental status which you've always tried to hide. But the subconscious is wise, my dear. It always knows and tries to warn. No wonder you had this dream at this particular time. There's nothing accidental about it. Freud says—"

But Eve was laughing. "Freud says? What does he know about it? Come to think of it, Doc, what do you know about it either? You see, I forgot to tell you something when I started. I didn't just *have* this dream." She stared at him, and her laughter ceased. "I bought it," Eve Eden said. "I bought it for ten thousand dollars."

4

Dr. Prager wasn't getting anywhere. His fountain pen ceased to function and his goatee wouldn't respond properly to even the most severe tugging. He heard Eve Eden out and waved his arms helplessly, like a bird about to take off. He felt like taking off, but on the other hand he couldn't leave this chick in her nest. Not with a big nest egg involved. But why did it have to be so involved?

"Go over that again," he begged finally. "Just the highlights. I can't seem to get it."

"But it's really so simple," Eve answered. "Like I already told you. I was getting all restless and keyed up, you know, like I've been before. Dying for a ball, some new kind of kick. And then I ran into Wally Redmond and he told me about this Professor Laroc."

"The charlatan," Dr. Prager murmured.

"I don't know what nationality he is," Eve answered. "He's just a little old guy who goes around selling these dreams."

"Now wait a minute—"

"Sure, it sounds screwy. I thought so, too, when Wally told me. He'd met him at a party somewhere and got to talking. And pretty soon he was spilling his— you'll pardon the expression—guts about the sad story of his life and how fed up he was with everything, including his sixth wife. And how he wanted to get away from it all and find a new caper.

"So this Professor Laroc asked him if he'd ever been on the stuff, and Wally said no, he had a weak heart. And he asked him if he'd tried psychiatry, and Wally said sure, but it didn't help him any."

"Your friend went to the wrong analyst," Dr. Prager snapped in some heat. "He should have come to a Freudian. How could he expect to get results from a Jungian—"

"Like you say, Doc, relax. It doesn't matter. What matters is that Professor Laroc sold him this dream. It was a real scary one, to hear him tell it, all about being a burglar over in England someplace and getting into a big estate run by a little dwarf with a head like a baboon. But he liked it; liked it fine. Said he was really relaxed after he had it: made him feel like a different person. And so he bought another, about a guy who was a pawnbroker, only a long time ago in some real gone country. And this pawnbroker ran around having himself all kinds of women who—"

"*Jurgen*," Dr. Prager muttered. "And if I'm not mistaken, the other one was from *Lukundoo*. I think it was called 'The Snout.'"

"Let's stick to the point, Doc," Eve Eden said. "Anyway, Wally was crazy about these dreams. He said the professor had a lot more to peddle, and even though the price was high, it was worth it. Because in the dream you felt like somebody else. You felt like the character you were dreaming about. And, of course, no hangover, no trouble with the law. Wally said if he ever tried some of the stuff he dreamed about on real women they'd clap him into pokey, even here in Hollywood. He planned to get out of pictures and buy more. Wanted to dream all the time. I guess the professor told him if he paid enough he could even *stay* in a dream without coming back."

"Nonsense!"

"That's what I told the man. I know how you feel, Doc. I felt that way myself before I met Professor Laroc. But after that it was different."

"You met this person?"

"He isn't a person, Doc. He's a real nice guy, a sweet character. You'd like him. I did when Wally brought him around. We had a long talk together. I opened up to him, even more than I have to you, I guess. Told him all my troubles. And he said what was wrong with me was I never had any childhood. That somewhere underneath there was a little girl trying to live her life with a full imagination. So he'd sell me a dream for that. And even though it sounded batty it made sense to me. He really seemed to understand things I didn't understand about myself.

"So I thought here goes, nothing to lose if I try it once, and I bought the dream." She smiled. "And now that I know what it's like I'm going to buy more. All he can sell me. Because he was right, you know. I don't want the movies. I don't want liquor or sex or H or gambling or anything. I don't want Eve Eden. I want to be a little girl, a little girl like the one in the dream, having adventures and never getting hurt. That's why I made up my mind. I'm quitting, getting out while the getting is good. From now on, me for dreamland."

Dr. Prager was silent for a long time. He kept staring at Eve Eden's smile. It wasn't *her* smile—he got the strangest notion that it belonged to somebody else. It was too relaxed, too innocent, too utterly seraphic for Eve. It was, he told himself, the smile of a ten-year-old girl on the face of a thirty-three-year-old woman of the world.

And he thought *hebephrenia* and he thought *schizophrenia* and he thought *incipient catatonia* and he said, "You say you met this Professor Laroc through Wally Redmond. Do you know how to reach him?"

"No, he reaches me." Eve Eden giggled. "He sends me, too, Doc."

She was really pretty far gone, Dr. Prager decided. But he had to persist. "When you bought this dream, as you say, what happened?"

"Why, nothing. Wally brought the professor here to the house. Right up to this bedroom actually. Then he went away and the professor talked to me and I wrote out the check and he gave me the dream."

"You keep saying he 'gave' you this dream. What does that mean?" Dr. Prager leaned forward. He had a sudden hunch. "Did he ask you to lie down, the way I do?"

"Yes. That's right."

"And did he talk to you?"

"Sure. How'd you guess?"

"And did he keep talking until you went to sleep?"

"I—I think so. Anyway, I did go to sleep, and when I woke up he was gone."

"Aha."

"What does that mean?"

"It means you were hypnotized, my dear. Hypnotized by a clever charlatan, who sold you a few moments of prepared patter in return for ten thousand dollars."

"But—but that's not true!" Eve Eden's childish smile became a childish pout. "It was *real*. The dream, I mean. It *happened*."

"Happened?"

"Of course. Haven't I made that clear yet? The dream *happened*. It wasn't like other dreams. I mean, I could feel and hear and see and even taste. Only it wasn't *me*. It was this little girl. Alice. I was Alice. That's what makes it worthwhile, can't you understand? That's what Wally said, too. The dream place is real. You *go* there, and you *are* somebody else."

"Hypnotism," Dr. Prager murmured.

Eve Eden put down the rabbit. "All right," she said. "I can prove it." She marched over to the big bed—the bed large enough to hold six people, according to some very catty but authenticated reports. "I didn't mean to show you this," she said, "but maybe I'd better."

She reached under her pillow and pulled out a small object which glittered beneath the light. "I found this in my hand when I woke up," she declared. "Look at it."

Dr. Prager looked at it. It was a small bottle bearing a white label. He shook it and discovered that the bottle was half-filled with a colorless transparent liquid. He studied the label and deciphered the hand-lettered inscription which read simply, "Drink Me."

"Proof, eh?" he mused. "Found in your hand when you woke up?"

"Of course. I brought it from the dream."

Dr. Prager smiled. "You were hypnotized. And before Professor Laroc stole away—and *stole* is singularly appropriate, considering that he had your check for ten thousand dollars—he simply planted this bottle in your hand as you slept. That's my interpretation of your proof." He slipped the little glass container into his pocket. "With your permission, I'd like to take this along," he said. "I'm going to ask you now to bear with me for the next twenty-four hours. Don't make any announcements about leaving the studio until I return. I think I can clear everything up to your satisfaction."

"But I am satisfied," Eve told him. "There's nothing to clear up. I don't want to—"

"Please." Dr. Prager brushed his brush with authority. "All I ask is that you be patient for twenty-four hours. I shall return tomorrow at this same time. And meanwhile, try to forget about all this. Say nothing to anyone."

"Now wait a minute, Doc—"

But Dr. Prager was gone. Eve Eden frowned for a moment, then sank back on the chaise longue. The rabbit scampered out from behind a chair and she picked it up again. She stroked its long ears gently until the creature fell asleep. Presently Eve's eyes closed and she drifted off to slumber herself. And the child's smile returned to her face.

5

There was no smile, childish or adult, on Dr. Prager's face when he presented himself again to the gatekeeper on the following day.

His face was stern and set as he drove up to the front door, accepted the butler's greeting, and went down the hall to where Mickey Dennis waited.

"What's up?" the little agent demanded, tossing his copy of *Hollywood Reporter* to the floor.

"I've been doing a bit of investigating," Dr. Prager told him. "And I'm afraid I have bad news for you."

"What is it, Doc? I tried to get something out of her after you left yesterday, but she wasn't talking. And today—"

"I know," Dr. Prager sighed. "She wouldn't be likely to tell you, under the circumstances. Apparently she realizes the truth herself but won't admit it. I have good reason to believe Miss Eden is disturbed. Seriously disturbed."

Mickey Dennis twirled his forefinger next to his ear. "You mean she's flipping?"

"I disapprove of that term on general principles," Dr. Prager replied primly. "And in this particular case the tense is wrong. *Flipped* would be much more correct."

"But I figgered she was all right lately. Outside of this business about quitting, she's been extra happy—happier'n I ever seen her."

"Euphoria," Dr. Prager answered. "Cycloid manifestation."

"You don't say so."

"I just did," the psychiatrist reminded him.

"Level with me," Dennis pleaded. "What's this all about?"

"I can't until after I've talked to her," Dr. Prager told him. "I need more facts. I was hoping to get some essential information from this Wally Redmond, but I can't locate him. Neither his studio nor his home seems to have information as to his whereabouts for the past several days."

"Off on a binge," the agent suggested. "It figgers. Only just what did you want from him?"

"Information concerning Professor Laroc," Dr. Prager answered. "He's a pretty elusive character. His name isn't listed on any academic roster I've consulted, and I couldn't find it in the City Directory of this or other local communities. Nor could the police department aid me with their files. I'm almost afraid my initial theory was wrong and that Professor Laroc himself is only another figment of Eve Eden's imagination."

"Maybe I can help you out there, Doc."

"You mean you met this man, saw him when he came here with Wally Redmond that evening?"

Mickey Dennis shook his head. "No. I wasn't around then. But I been around all afternoon. And just about a half hour ago a character named Professor Laroc showed up at the door. He's with Eve in her room right now."

Dr. Prager opened his mouth and expelled a gulp. Then he turned and ran for the stairs.

The agent sought out his overstuffed chair and riffled the pages of his magazine.

More waiting. Well, he just hoped there wouldn't be any explosions this afternoon.

6

There was no explosion when Dr. Prager opened the bedroom door. Eve Eden was sitting quietly on the chaise longue, and the elderly gentleman occupied an armchair.

As Dr. Prager entered, the older man rose with a smile and extended his hand. Dr. Prager felt it wise to ignore the gesture. "Professor Laroc?" he murmured.

"That is correct." The smile was a bland blend of twinkling blue eyes behind old-fashioned steel-rimmed spectacles, wrinkled creases in white cheeks, and a rictus of a prim, thin-lipped mouth. Whatever else he might be, Professor Laroc aptly fitted Mickey Dennis's description of a "character." He appeared to be about sixty-five, and his clothing seemed of the same vintage, as though fashioned in anticipation at the time of his birth.

Eve Eden stood up now. "I'm glad you two are getting together," she said. "I asked the professor to come this afternoon so we could straighten everything out."

Dr. Prager preened his goatee. "I'm very happy that you did so," he answered. "And I'm sure that matters can be set straight in very short order now that I'm here."

"The professor has just been telling me a couple of things," Eve informed him. "I gave him your pitch about me losing my buttons and he says you're all wet."

"A slight misquotation," Professor Laroc interposed. "I merely observed that an undertaking of the true facts might dampen your enthusiasm."

"I think I have the facts," Dr. Prager snapped. "And they're dry enough. Dry, but fascinating."

"Do go on."

"I intend to." Dr. Prager wheeled to confront Eve Eden and spoke directly to the girl. "First of all," he said, "I must tell you that your friend here is masquerading under a pseudonym. I have been unable to discover a single bit of evidence substantiating the identity of anyone named Professor Laroc."

"Granted," the elderly man murmured.

"Secondly," Dr. Prager continued, "I must warn you that I have been unable to ascertain the whereabouts of your friend Wally Redmond. His wife doesn't know where he is, or his producer. Mickey Dennis thinks he's off on an alcoholic fugue. I have my own theory. But one fact is certain—he seems to have completely disappeared."

"Granted," said Professor Laroc.

"Third and last," Dr. Prager went on. "It is my considered belief that the man calling himself Professor Laroc did indeed subject you to hypnosis and that, once he had managed to place you in a deep trance, he deliberately read to you from a copy of *Alice in Wonderland* and suggested to you that you were experiencing the adventures of the principal character. Whereupon he placed the vial of liquid labeled 'Drink Me' in your hand and departed."

"Granted in part." Professor Laroc nodded. "It is true that I placed Miss Eden in a receptive state with the aid of what you choose to call hypnosis. And it is true that I suggested to her that she enter into the world of *Alice,* as Alice. But that is all. It was not necessary to read anything to her, nor did I stoop to deception by supplying a vial of liquid, as you call it. Believe me, I was as astonished as you were to learn that she had brought back such an interesting souvenir of her little experience."

"Prepare to be astonished again then," Dr. Prager said grimly. He pulled the small bottle from his pocket and with it a piece of paper.

"What's that, Doc?" Eve Eden asked.

"A certificate from Haddon and Haddon, industrial chemists," the psychiatrist told her. "I took this interesting souvenir, as your friend calls it, down to their laboratories for analysis." He handed her the report. "Here, read for yourself. If your knowledge of chemistry is insufficient, I can tell you that H_2O means water." He smiled. "Yes, that's right. This bottle contains nothing but half an ounce of water."

Dr. Prager turned and stared at Professor Laroc. "What have you to say now?" he demanded.

"Very little." The old man smiled. "It does not surprise me that you were unable to find my name listed in any registry or directory of activities, legal or illegal. As Miss Eden already knows, I chose to cross over many years ago. Nor was 'Laroc' my actual surname. A moment's reflection will enable you to realize that 'Laroc' is an obvious enough anagram for 'Carroll,' give or take a few letters."

"You don't mean to tell me—"

"That I am Lewis Carroll, or rather, Charles Lutwidge Dodgson? Certainly not. I hold the honor of being a fellow alumnus of his at Oxford, and we did indeed share an acquaintance—"

"But Lewis Carroll died in 1898," Dr. Prager objected.

"Ah, you *were* interested enough to look up the date." The old man smiled. "I see you're not as skeptical as you pretend to be."

Dr. Prager felt that he was giving ground and remembered that attack is the best defense. "Where is Wally Redmond?" he countered.

"With the Duchess of Towers, I would presume," Professor Laroc answered. "He chose to cross over permanently, and I selected *Peter Ibbetson* for him. You see, I'm restricted to literature which was directly inspired by the author's dream, and there's a rather small field available. I still have Cabell's *Smirt* to sell, and *The Brushwood Boy* of Kipling, but I don't imagine I shall ever manage to dispose of any Lovecraft—too gruesome, you know." He glanced at Eve Eden. "Fortunately, as I told you, I've reserved something very special for you. And I'm glad you decided to take the step. The moment I saw you my heart went out to you. I sensed the little girl buried away beneath all the veneer, just as I sensed the small boy in Mr. Redmond. So many of you Hollywood people are frustrated children. You make dreams for others but have none of your own. I am glad to offer my modest philanthropy—"

"At ten thousand dollars a session!" Dr. Prager exploded.

"Now, now," Professor Laroc chided. "That sounds like professional jealousy, sir! And I may as well remind you that a permanent crossover requires a fee of fifty thousand. Not that I need the money, you understand. It's merely that such a fee helps to establish me as an authority. It brings about the necessary transference relationship between my clients and myself, to borrow from your own terminology. The effect is purely psychological."

Dr. Prager had heard enough. This, he decided, was definitely the time to call a halt. Even Eve Eden in her present disturbed state should be able to comprehend the utter idiocy of this man's preposterous claims.

He faced the elderly charlatan with a disarming smile. "Let me get this straight," he began quietly. "Am I to understand that you are actually selling dreams?"

"Let us say, rather, that I sell experiences. And the experiences are every bit as real as anything you know."

"Don't quibble over words." Dr. Prager was annoyed. "You come in and hypnotize patients. During their sleep you suggest they enter a dream world. And then—"

"If you don't mind, let us quibble a bit over words, please," Professor Laroc said. "You're a psychiatrist. Very well, as a psychiatrist, please tell me one thing. Just what *is* a dream?"

"Why, that's very simple," Dr. Prager answered. "According to Freud, the dream phenomenon can be described as—"

"I didn't ask for a description, Doctor. Nor for Freud's opinion. I asked for an exact definition of the dream state, as you call it. I want to know the etiology and epistemology of dreams. And while you're at it, how about a definition of 'the hypnotic state' and of 'sleep'? And what is 'suggestion'? After you've given me precise scientific definitions of these phenomena, as you love to call them, perhaps you can go on and explain to me the nature of 'reality' and the exact meaning of the term 'imagination.'"

"But these are only figures of speech," Dr. Prager objected. "I'll be honest with you. Perhaps we can't accurately describe a dream. But we can observe it. It's like electricity: nobody knows what it *is*, but it's a measurable force which can be directed and controlled, subject to certain natural laws."

"Exactly," Professor Laroc said. "That's just what I would have said myself. And dreams are indeed like electrical force. Indeed, the human brain gives off electrical charges, and all life—matter—energy—enters into an electrical relationship. But this relationship has never been studied. Only the physical manifestations of electricity have been studied and harnessed, not the psychic. At least, not until Dodgson stumbled on certain basic mathematical principles, which he imparted to me. I developed them, found a practical use. The dream, my dear doctor, is merely an electrically charged dimension given a reality of its own beyond our own space-time continuum. The individual dream is weak. Set it down on paper, as some dreams have been set down, share it with others, and watch the charge build up. the combined electrical properties tend to create a *permanent* plane—a dream dimension, if you please."

"I don't please," answered Dr. Prager.

"That's because you're not receptive," Professor Laroc observed smugly. "Yours is a negative charge rather than a positive one. Dodgson—Lewis Carroll—was positive. So was Lovecraft and Poe and Edward Lucas White and a handful of others. Their dreams live. Other positive charges can live in them, granted the proper method of entry. It's not magic. There's nothing supernatural about it at all, unless you consider mathematics as magic. Dodgson did. He was a professor of mathematics, remember. And so was I. I took his principles and extended them, created a practical methodology. Now I can enter dream worlds at will, cause others to enter. It's not hypnosis as you understand it. A few words of non-Euclidean formula will be sufficient—"

"I've heard enough," Dr. Prager broke in. "Much as I hate to employ the phrase, this is sheer lunacy."

The professor shrugged. "Call it what you wish," he said. "You psychiatrists are good at pinning labels on things. But Miss Eden here has had sufficient proof through her own experience. Isn't that so?"

Eve Eden nodded, then broke her silence. "I believe you," she said. "Even if Doc here thinks we're both batty. And I'm willing to give you the fifty grand for a permanent trip."

Dr. Prager grabbed for his goatee. He was clutching at straws now. "But you can't," he cried. "This doesn't make sense."

"Maybe not your kind of sense," Eve answered. "But that's just the trouble. You don't seem to understand there's more than *one* kind. That crazy dream I had, the one you say Lewis Carroll had first and wrote up into a book—it makes sense to you if you really *live* it. More sense than Hollywood, than this. More sense than a little kid named Wilma Kozmowski growing up to live in a half-million-dollar palace and trying to kill herself because she can't be a little kid any more and never had a chance to be one when she was small. The professor here, he understands. He knows everybody had a right to dream. For the first time in my life I know what it is to be happy."

"That's right," Professor Laroc added. "I recognized her as a kindred spirit. I saw the child beneath, the child of the pure unclouded brow, as Lewis Carroll put it. She deserved this dream."

"Don't try and stop me," Eve cut in. "You can't, you know. You'll never drag me back to your world, and you've got no reason to try—except that you like the idea of making a steady living off me. And so does Dennis, with his lousy ten per-cent, and so does the studio with its big profits. I never met anyone who really liked me as a person except Professor Laroc here. He's the only one who ever gave me anything worth having. The dream. So quit trying to argue me into it, Doc. I'm not going to be Eve any more or Wilma either. I'm going to be Alice."

Dr. Prager scowled, then smiled. What was the matter with him? Why was he bothering to argue like this? After all, it was so unnecessary. Let the poor child write out a check for fifty thousand dollars—payment could always be stopped. Just as this charlatan could be stopped if he actually attempted hypnosis. There were laws and regulations. Really, Dr. Prager reminded himself, he was behaving like a child himself: taking part in this silly argument just as if there actually was something to it besides nonsense words.

What was really at stake, he realized, was professional pride. To think that this old mountebank could actually carry more authority with Eve Eden than he did himself!

And what was the imposter saying now, with that sickening, condescending smile on his face?

"I'm sorry you cannot subscribe to my theories, Doctor. But at least I am grateful for one thing, and that is that you didn't see fit to put them to the test."

"Test? What do you mean?"

Professor Laroc pointed his finger at the little bottle labeled "Drink Me" which now rested on the table before him. "I'm happy you merely analyzed the contents of that vial without attempting to drink them."

"But it's nothing but water."

"Perhaps. What you forget is that water may have very different properties in other worlds. And this water came from the world of Alice."

"You planted that," Dr. Prager snapped. "Don't deny it."

"I do deny it. Miss Eden knows the truth."

"Oh, does she?" Dr. Prager suddenly found his solution. He raised the bottle, turning to Eve with a commanding gesture. "Listen to me now. Professor Laroc claims, and you believe, that this liquid was somehow transported from the dream world of *Alice in Wonderland*. If that is the case, then a drink out of this bottle would cause me to either grow or to shrink. Correct?"

"Yes," Eve murmured.

"Now wait—" the professor began, but Dr. Prager shook his head impatiently.

"Let me finish," he insisted. "All right. By the same token, if I took a drink from this bottle and nothing happened, wouldn't it prove that the dream-world story is a fake?"

"Yes, but—"

"No 'buts.' I'm asking you a direct question. Would it or wouldn't it?"

"Y-yes. I guess so. Yes."

"Very well, then." Dramatically, Dr. Prager uncorked the little bottle and raised it to his lips. "Watch me," he said.

Professor Laroc stepped forward. "Please!" he shouted. "I implore you—don't—"

He made a grab for the bottle, but he was too late.

Dr. Prager downed the half ounce of colorless fluid.

7

Mickey Dennis waited and waited until he couldn't stand it any longer. There hadn't been any loud sounds from upstairs at all, and this only made it worse.

Finally he got the old urge so bad he just had to go on up there and see for himself what was going on.

As he walked down the hall he could hear them talking inside the bedroom. At least he recognized Professor Laroc's voice. He was saying something about, "There, there, I know it's quite a shock. Perhaps you'd feel better if you didn't wait—do you want to go now?"

That didn't make too much sense to Mickey, and neither did Eve's reply. She said. "Yes, but don't I have to go to sleep first?"

And then the professor answered, "No, as I explained to him, it's just a question of the proper formulae. If I recite them we can go together. Er—you might bring your checkbook along."

Eve seemed to be giggling. "You too?" she asked.

"Yes. I've always loved this dream, my dear. It's a sequel to the first one, as you'll discover. Now if you'll just face the mirror with me—"

And then the professor mumbled something in a very low voice, and Mickey bent down with his head close to the door but he couldn't quite catch it. Instead his shoulder pushed the door open.

The bedroom was empty.

That's right, empty.

BRIAN LUMLEY

As I write this, Robert Bloch is alive. To a great many people who know him far better than I do, I think he always will be. I make that statement from observation. Just to see Bob Bloch at a convention—his effect on the people around him, their reaction to him—is to know that he's much loved. Not just by his fans but also by his contemporaries, his friends.

His contributions to the weird field will live, certainly, and no matter how frequently the title PSYCHO flashes up on the big or small screens of today or the multimedia displays of the future, Bob's name will light up right alongside on the screens of our minds. Bob Bloch might or might not appreciate that fact (in one way he would—in another he wouldn't), but it remains a fact nevertheless.

I remember, most recently, Dragoncon, Atlanta, July 1993. Robert Bloch, Forrest J Ackerman, myself, one or two others—we sat down and ate a meal together. Forry had been, well, sort of caretakering Bob, who seemed pretty slow on his feet—but not slow on the uptake. His conversation sparkled, as always. He told his clever stories with expressions, pregnant pauses, gestures, and remarkably few words. In answer to some other's witty (or half-witty) remark, there would always be a counter; to every thrust a riposte. The mind was quicksilver. The body . . . was a little slower.

Another time (some convention or other), I had occasion to remark that a certain story of his had sparked my interest in the Cthulhu Mythos, contributary to my becoming a writer myself. Bob sighed and said yes, he had a lot to answer for, but he had no doubt the day would dawn when he'd be called upon to atone for his sins. He was so straight-faced, I didn't know to laugh or cry. Seeing my indecision, he said, "Smile, for God's

at I thought
quote he'd
book Press.
g a psychic
f the Worms.
verest, and,
d ever said
!" Who else

you believe,
Found in a
off searching

for other Mythos tales, and this is hardly the place to go into it again. But briefly: "Notebook" is the classic Mythos tale, a story of unrelenting horror closely akin to the nightmare we have all known, of running from a monstrous *something* as if our feet were stuck in glue, or running in ever-decreasing circles that take us back, exhausted, to our original starting point—and so face to face with the inescapable horror!

Now, especially in the present circumstances, it strikes me that despite the fantasy of the story, there are also parallels with real life. And in this respect, and with regard to the Lovecraft connection, there's something else that deserves mention. I'll keep it till last.

Back to Atlanta, 1993:

I was serving punch at one of my infamous (but less than lethal) parties. Bob and Forry showed up out of nowhere. And so did a bunch of the girls from the Betty Page lookalike competition, still clad in their lingerie! Bob refilled his glass and asked me, "Who are these girls?" The look of astonishment on his face was quite wonderful to see. And I saw my chance to outsmart him, probably the only chance I'd ever get.

"Fans," I said, and shrugged. "Boring, isn't it? All my fans look pretty much the same . . . flimsily clad young girls."

He looked at his drink, then at Forry—who was looking similarly bemused—then at his drink again, and finally back to me, and said, "Brian, you've *got* to give me the recipe some time. This beats rose-colored spectacles all to hell!"

You just couldn't go one up on Robert Bloch.

Knowing my penchant for Bloch, Tom Doherty had brought me a copy of Bob's *Once Around the Bloch* from New York. This was just out; I think Bob had only just received his own first copy. I gave it to him to sign, and he said, "Did Tom make you pay for it?"

I went along with the joke and answered, "Of course!"

"Yeah, well I *told* him to!" he said. And he signed it: "To Brian Lumley, whose work packs as much punch as his parties!"

I remember reading something by or about Bob Bloch, in connection

RAMSEY CAMPBELL

Bob Bloch has meant a great deal to me for pretty well as long as I can remember. He's had my heart since I was a boy; when I read his tale "Notebook Found in a Deserted House." Not many years later, his "Terror in Cut-Throat Cove" was quite possibly the last piece of prose to give me nightmares. He was becoming a legend to me, and when I first appeared in professional print in August Derleth's *Dark Mind, Dark Heart,* it was a very special extra pleasure for me to be in the same book as Bob.

Came the 1975 World Fantasy Convention, and when I was chosen as the least worthy of the judges of the first World Fantasy Awards, I was able to repay at least a little of the pleasure and encouragement and example he'd given me over the years, by adding my voice to the votes for him to receive the Life Achievement Award. Better still, after years of exchanging friendly letters, I met him, and found him even more charming and funny and wise than he was in his handwriting. All that remained was for my family to have the pleasure, and so they did in Huntsville eleven years later, where he was guest of honor and we swapped genial insults on the podium.

What else can I say? I feel as though he has been my friend ever since I first read him. He's the kind of man whose only enemies are knaves and fools. As long as books are read he will make friends. I wish I had as many myself.

He is such fun to be with that in his company one tends to forget his way with terror, the wicked gleam in his eye notwithstanding. But it was as a purveyor of nightmares that he first presented himself to me with the following tale, in *Screen Chills and Macabre Stories,* a long-forgotten magazine with all the lifespan of a mayfly. Since it doesn't appear in Randall Larson's bibliography of his work, I wonder if Bob even knew it existed. His title had been changed to "Them Ones," but whatever title it bears, I think it's among his scariest tales, and my favorite. It's a privilege for me to help bring it to a new audience.

NOTEBOOK FOUND IN A DESERTED
HOUSE

First off, I want to write that I never did anything wrong. Not to nobody. They got no call to shut me up here, whoever they are. They got no reason to do what I'm afraid they're going to do, either.

I think they're coming pretty soon, because they've been gone outside a long time. Digging, I guess, in that old well. Looking for a gate, I heard. Not a regular gate, of course, but something else.

Got a notion what they mean, and I'm scared.

I'd look out the windows but of course they are boarded up so I can't see.

But I turned on the lamp, and I found this here notebook so I want to put it all down. Then if I get a chance maybe I can send it to somebody who can help me. Or maybe somebody will find it. Anyway, it's better to write it out as best I can instead of just sitting here and waiting. Waiting for *them* to come and get me.

I better start by telling my name, which is Willie Osborne, and that I am 12 years old last July. I don't know where I was born.

First thing I can remember is living out Roodsford way, out in what folks call the back hill country. It's real lonesome out there, with deep woods all around and lots of mountains and hills that nobody ever climbs.

Grandma use to tell me about it when I was just a little shaver. That's who I lived with, just Grandma on account of my real folks being dead. Grandma was the one who taught me how to read and write. I never been to a regular school.

Grandma knew all kinds of things about the hills and the woods and she told me some mighty queer stories. That's what I thought they was, anyway, when I was little and living all alone with her. Just stories, like the ones in books.

Like stories about *them ones* hiding in the swamps, that was here before the settlers and the Indians both and how there was circles in swamps and big stones called alters where *them ones* use to make sacrifices to what they worshiped.

Grandma got some of the stories from her Grandma she said—about how *them ones* hid in the woods and swamps because they couldn't stand sunshine, and how the Indians kept out of their way. She said sometimes the Indians would leave some of their young people tied to trees in the forest as a sacrifice, so as to keep *them ones* contented and peaceful.

Indians knew all about *them* and they tried to keep white folks from noticing too much or settling too close to the hills. *Them ones* didn't cause much trouble, but they might if they was crowded. So the Indians give excuses for not settling, saying there weren't enough hunting and no trails and it was too far off from the coast.

Grandma told me that was why not many places was settled even today. Nothing but a few farmhouses here and there. She told me *them ones* was still alive and sometimes on certain nights in the Spring and Fall you could see lights and hear noises far off on the tops of the hills.

Grandma said I had an Aunt Lucy and a Uncle Fred who lived out there right smack in the middle of the hills. Said my Pa used to visit them before he got married and once he heard *them* beating on a tree drum one night along about Halloween time. That was before he met Ma and they got married and she died when I come and he went away.

I heard all kinds of stories. About witches and devils and bat men that sucked your blood and haunts. About Salem and Arkham because I never been to a city and I wanted to hear tell how they were. About a place called Innsmouth with old rotten houses where people hid awful things away in the cellars and the attics. She told me bout the way graves was dug deep under Arkham. Made it sound like the whole country was full of haunts.

She use to scare me, telling about how some of these things looked and all but she never would tell me how *them ones* looked no matter how much I asked. Said she didn't want me to have any truck with such things—bad enough she and her kin knew as much as they did—almost too much for decent God fearing people. It was lucky for me I didn't have to bother with such ideas, like my own ancestor on my father's side, Mehitabel Osborne, who got hanged for a witch back in the Salem days.

So they was just stories to me until last year when Grandma died and Judge Crubinthorp put me on the train and I went out to live with Aunt Lucy and Uncle Fred in the very same hills that Grandma use to tell about so often.

You can bet I was pretty excited, and the conductor let me ride with him all the way and told me about the towns and everything.

Uncle Fred met me at the station. He was a tall thin man with a long beard. We drove off in a buggy from the little deepo—no houses around there or nothing—right into the woods.

Funny thing about those woods. They was so still and quiet. Gave me the creeps they was so dark and lonesome. Seemed like nobody had ever shouted or laughed or even smiled in them. Couldn't imagine anyone saying anything there excep in whispers.

Trees and all was so old, too. No animals around or birds. Path kind of overgrown like nobody used it much ever. Uncle Fred drove along right fast, he didn't hardly talk to me at all but just made that old horse hump it.

Pretty soon we struck into some hills, they was awfully high ones. They was woods on them, too, and sometimes a brook come running down, but I didn't see no houses and it was always dark like a twilight, wherever you looked.

Lastly we got to the farmhouse—a little place, old frame house and barn in a clear space with trees all around kind of gloomy-like. Aunt Lucy come out to meet us, she was a nice sort of little middle-aged lady who hugged me and took my stuff in back.

But all this don't hold with what I'm supposed to write down here. It don't matter that all this last year I was living in the house here with them, eating off the stuff Uncle Fred farmed without ever going into town. No other farms around here for almost four mile and no school—so evenings Aunt Lucy would help me with my reading. I never played much.

At first I was scared of going into the woods on account of what Grandma had told me. Besides, I could tell as Aunt Lucy and Uncle Fred was scared of something from the way they locked the doors at night and never went into the woods after dark, even in summer.

But after a while, I got used to the idea of living in the woods and they didn't seem so scarey. I did chores for Uncle Fred, of course, but sometimes in afternoons when he was busy, I'd go off by myself. Particular by the time it was fall.

And that's how I heard one of the things. It was early October, I was in the glen right by the big boulder. Then the noise started. I got behind that rock fast.

You see, like I say, there isn't any animals in the woods. Nor people. Excep perhaps old Cap Pritchett the mailman who only comes through on Thursday afternoons.

So when I heard a sound that wasn't Uncle Fred or Aunt Lucy calling to me, I knew I better hide.

About that sound. It was far-away at first, kind of a dropping noise. Sounded like the blood falling in little spurts on the bottom of the bucket when Uncle Fred hung up a butchered hog.

I looked around but I couldn't make out nothing, and I couldn't figure out the direction the noise was from either. The noise sort of stopped for a minute and they was only twilight and trees, still as death. Then the noise started again, nearer and louder.

Sounded like a lot of people running, or walking all at once, moving this way. Twigs busting under feet and scrabbling in the bushes all mixed up in the noise. I scrunched down behind that boulder and kep real quiet.

I can tell that whatever makes the noise, it's real close now, right in the glen. I want to look up but dassn't because the sound is so loud and *mean*. And also there is an awful smell like something that was dead and buried being uncovered again in the sun.

All at once the noise stops again and I can tell that whatever makes it is real close by. For a minute the woods are creepy-still. Then comes the sound.

It's a voice and it's not a voice. That is, it doesn't *sound* like a voice but more like a buzzing or croaking, deep and droning. But it *has* to be a voice because it is saying words.

Not words I could understand, but words. Words that made me keep my head down, half afraid I might be seen and half afraid I might see something. I stayed there sweating and shaking. The smell was making me pretty sick, but that awful, deep droning voice was worse. Saying over and over something like

"E uh shub nigger ath ngaa ryla neb shoggoth."

I can't hope to spell it out the way it sounded, but I heard it enough times to remember. I was still listening when the smell got awful thick and I guess I must have fainted because when I woke up the voice was gone and it was getting quite dark.

I ran all the way home that night, but not before I saw where the thing had stood when it talked—and it *was* a thing.

No human being can leave tracks in the mud like goat's hoofs all green with slime that smell awful—not four or eight, but a couple *hundred!*

I didn't tell Aunt Lucy or Uncle Fred. But that night when I went to bed I had terrible dreams. I thought I was back in the glen, only this time I could see the thing. It was real tall and all inky-black, without any particular shape except a lot of black ropes with ends like hoofs on it. I mean, it had a shape but it kep changing—all bulgy and squirming into different sizes. They was a lot of mouths all over the thing like puckered up leaves on branches.

That's as close as I can come. The mouths was like leaves and the whole thing was like a tree in the wind, a black tree with lots of branches trailing the ground, and a whole lot of roots ending in hoofs. And the green slime dribbling out of the mouths and down the legs was like sap!

Next day I remembered to look in a book Aunt Lucy had downstairs. It was called a mythology. This book told about some people who lived over in England and France in the old days and was called Druids. They worshiped trees and thought they was alive. Maybe this thing was like what they worshiped—called a nature-spirit.

But these Druids lived across the ocean, so how could it be? I did a lot of thinking about it the next couple days, and you can bet I didn't go out to play in those woods again.

At last I figgered it out something like this.

Maybe those Druids got chased out of the forests over in England and France and some of them was smart enough to build boats and come across the ocean like old Leaf Erikson is supposed to have. Then they could maybe settle in the woods back here and frighten away the Indians with their magic spells.

They would know how to hide themselves away in the swamps and go right on with their heathen worshiping and call up these spirits out of the ground or wherever they come from.

Indians use to believe that white gods come from out of the sea a long time ago. What if that was just another way of telling how the Druids got here? Some real civilized Indians down in Mexico or South America—Aztecs or Inkas, I guess—said a white god come over in a boat and taught them all kinds of magic. Couldn't he of been a Druid?

That would explain Grandma's stories about *them ones,* too.

Those Druids hiding in the swamps would be the ones who did the drumming and pounding and lit the fires on the hills. And they would be calling up *them ones,* the tree spirits or whatever, out of the earth. Then they would make sacrefices. Those Druids always made sacrefices with blood, just like the old witches. And didn't Grandma tell about people who lived too near the hills disappearing and never being found again?

We lived in a spot just exactly like that.

And it was getting close to Halloween. That was the big time, Grandma always said.

I began to wonder—how soon now?

Got so scared I didn't go out of the house. Aunt Lucy made me take a tonic, said I looked peaked. Guess I did. All I know is one afternoon when I heard a buggy coming through the woods I ran and hid under the bed.

But it was only Cap Pritchett with the mail. Uncle Fred got it and come in all excited with a letter.

Cousin Osborne was coming to stay with us. He was kin to Aunt Lucy and he had a vacation and he wanted to stay a week. He'd get here on the same train I did—the only train they was passing through these parts—on noon, October 25th.

For the next few days we was all so excited that I forgot all my crazy notions for a spell. Uncle Fred fixed up the back room for Cousin Osborne to sleep in and I helped him with the carpenter parts of the job.

Days got shorter right along, and the nights was all cold with big winds. It was pretty brisk the morning of the 25th and Uncle Fred bundled up warm to drive through the woods. He meant to fetch Cousin Osborne at noon, and it was seven mile to the station. He wouldn't take me, and I didn't beg. Them woods was too full of creaking and rustling sounds from the wind—sounds that might be something else, too.

Well, he left, and Aunt Lucy and I stayed in the house. She was putting up preserves now—plums—for over the winter season. I washed out jars from the well.

Seems like I should have told about them having two wells. A new one with a big shiny pump, close to the house. Then an old stone one out by the barn, with the pump gone. It never had been any good, Uncle Fred said, it was there when they bought the place. Water was all slimy. Something funny about it, because without a pump, sometimes it seemed to back up. Uncle Fred couldn't figure it out, but some mornings water would be running out over the sides—green, slimy water that smelled terrible.

We kep away from it and I was by the new well, till along about noon when it started in to cloud up. Aunt Lucy fixed lunch, and it started to rain hard with thunder rolling in off the big hills in the west.

Seemed to me Uncle Fred and Cousin Osborne was going to have troubles getting home in the storm, but Aunt Lucy didn't fret about it—just made me help her put up the stock.

Come five o'clock, getting dark, and still no Uncle Fred. Then we begun to worry. Maybe the train was late, or something happened to the horse or buggy.

Six o'clock and still no Uncle Fred. The rain stopped, but you could still hear the thunder sort of growling off in the hills, and the wet branches kep dripping down in the woods, making a sound like women laughing.

Maybe the road was too bad for them to get through. Buggy might bog down in the mud. Perhaps they decided to stay in the deepo over night.

Seven o'clock and it was pitch dark outside. No rain sounds any more. Aunt Lucy was awful worried. She said for us to go out and post a lantern on the fence rail by the road.

We went down the path to the fence. It was dark and the wind had died down. Everything was still, like in the deep part of the woods. I felt kind of scared just walking down the path with Aunt Lucy—like something was out there in the quiet dark, someplace, waiting to grab me.

We lit the lantern and stood there looking down the dark road and, "What's that?" said Aunt Lucy, real sharp. I listened and heard a drumming sound far away.

"Horse and buggy," I said. Aunt Lucy perked up.

"You're right," she says, all at once. And it is, because we see it. The horse is running fast and the buggy lurches behind it, crazy-like. It don't even take a second look to see something has happened, because the buggy don't stop by the gate but keeps going up to the barn with Aunt Lucy and me running through the mud after the horse. The horse is all full of lather and foam, and when it stops it can't stand still. Aunt Lucy and I wait for Uncle Fred and Cousin Osborne to step out, but nothing happens. We look inside.

There isn't anybody in the buggy at all.

Aunt Lucy says, "Oh!" in a real loud voice and then faints. I had to carry her back to the house and get her into bed.

I waited almost all night by the window, but Uncle Fred and Cousin Osborne never showed up. Never.

The next few days was awful. They was nothing in the buggy for a clue like to what happened, and Aunt Lucy wouldn't let me go along the road into town or even to the station through the woods.

The next morning the horse was dead in the barn, and of course we would of had to walk to the deepo or all those miles to Warren's farm. Aunt Lucy was scared to go and scared to stay and she allowed as how when Cap Pritchett comes by we had best go with him over to town and make a report and then stay there until we found out what happened.

Me, I had my own ideas what happened. Halloween was only a few days away now, and maybe *them ones* had snatched Uncle Fred and Cousin Osborne for sacrefice. *Them ones* or the Druids. The mythology book said Druids could even raise storms if they wanted to with their spells.

No sense talking to Aunt Lucy, though. She was like out of her head with worry, anyway, just rocking back and forth and mumbling over and over, "They're gone" and "Fred always warned me" and "No use, no use." I had to get the meals and tend the stock myself. And nights it was hard to sleep, because I kep listening for drums. I never heard any, though, but still it was better than sleeping and having those dreams.

Dreams about the black thing like a tree, walking through the woods and sort of rooting itself to one particular spot so it could pray with all those mouths—pray down to that old god in the ground below.

I don't know where I got the idea that was how it prayed—by sort of attaching its mouths to the ground. Maybe it was on account of seeing the green slime. Or had I really seen it? I'd never gone back to look. Maybe it was all in my head—the Druid story and about *them ones* and the voice that said "shoggoth" and all the rest.

But then, where was Cousin Osborne and Uncle Fred? And what scared the horse so it up and died the next day?

Thoughts kep going round and round in my head, chasing each other, but all I knew was we'd be out of here by Halloween night.

Because Halloween was on a Thursday, and Cap Pritchett would come and we could ride to town with him.

Night before I made Aunt Lucy pack and we got all ready, and then I settled down to sleep. There was no noises, and for the first time I felt a little better.

Only the dreams come again. I dreamed a bunch of men come in the night and crawled through the parlor bedroom window where Aunt Lucy slept and got her. They tied her up and took her away, all quiet, in the dark, because they had cat-eyes and didn't need light to see.

The dream scared me so I woke up while it was just breaking into dawn. I went down the hall to Aunt Lucy right away.

She was gone.

The window was wide open like in my dream, and some of the blankets was torn.

Ground was hard outside the window and I didn't see footprints or anything. But she was gone.

I guess I cried then.

It's hard to remember what I did next. Didn't want breakfast. Went out hollering "Aunt Lucy" and not expecting any answer. I walked to the barn and the door was open and the cows were gone. Saw one or two prints going out the yard and up the road, but I didn't think it was safe to follow them.

Some time later I went over to the well and then I cried again because the water was all slimy green in the new one, just like the old.

When I saw that I knew I was right. *Them ones* must of come in the night and they wasn't even trying to hide their doings any more. Like they was sure of things.

Tonight was Halloween. I had to get out of here. If *them ones* was watching and waiting, I couldn't depend on Cap Pritchett showing up this afternoon. I'd have to chance it down the road and I'd better start walking now, in the morning, while it was still light enough to make town.

So I rummaged around and found a little money in Uncle Fred's drawer of the bureau and Cousin Osborne's letter with the address in Kingsport he wrote it from. That's where I'd have to go after I told folks in town what happened. I'd have some kin there.

I wondered if they'd believe me in town when I told them about the way Uncle Fred had disappeared and Aunt Lucy, and about *them* stealing the cattle for a sacrefice and about the green slime in the well where something had stopped to drink. I wondered if they would know about the drums and the lights on the hills tonight and if they was going to get up a party and come back this evening to try and catch *them ones* and what they meant to call up rumbling out of the earth. I wondered if they knew what a "shoggoth" was.

Well, whether they did or not, I couldn't stay and find out for myself. So I packed up my satchel and got ready to leave. Must of been around noon and everything was still.

I went to the door and stepped outside, not bothering to lock it behind me. Why should I with nobody around for miles?

Then I heard the noise down the road.

Footsteps.

Somebody walking along the road, just around the bend.

I stood still for a minute, waiting to see, waiting to run.

Then he came along.

He was tall and thin, and looked something like Uncle Fred only a lot younger and without a beard, and he was wearing a nice city kind of suit and a crush hat. He smiled when he saw me and come marching up like he knowed who I was.

"Hello, Willie," he said.

I didn't say nothing, I was so confuzed.

"Don't you know me?" he said. "I'm Cousin Osborne. Your Cousin Frank." He held out his hand to shake. "But then I guess you wouldn't remember, would you? Last time I saw you, you were only a baby."

"But I thought you were suppose to come last week," I said. "We expected you on the 25th."

"Didn't you get my telegram?" he asked. "I had business."

I shook my head. "We never get nothing here unless the mail delivers it on Thursdays. Maybe it's at the station."

Cousin Osborne grinned. "You are pretty well off the beaten track at that. Nobody at the station this noon. I was hoping Fred would come along with the buggy so I wouldn't have to walk, but no luck."

"You walked all the way?" I asked.

"That's right."

"And you come on the train?"

Cousin Osborne nodded.

"Then where's your suitcase?"

"I left it at the deepo," he told me. "Too far to fetch it along. I thought Fred would drive me back there in the buggy to pick it up." He noticed my luggage for the first time. "But wait a minute—where are you going with a suitcase, son?"

Well, there was nothing else for me to do but tell him everything that happened.

So I said for him to come into the house and set down and I'd explain.

We went back in and he fixed some coffee and I made a couple sandwiches and we ate, and then I told him about Uncle Fred going to the deepo and not coming back, and about the horse and then what happened to Aunt Lucy. I left out the part about me in the woods, of course, and I didn't even hint at *them ones*. But I told him I was scared and figgered on walking to town today before dark.

Cousin Osborne he listened to me, nodding and not saying much or interrupting.

"Now you can see why we got to go, right away," I said. "Whatever come after them will be coming after us, and I don't want to spend another night here."

Cousin Osborne stood up. "You may be right, Willie," he said. "But don't let your imagination run away with you, son. Try to separate fact from fancy. Your Aunt and Uncle have disappeared. That's fact. But this other nonsense about things in the woods coming after you—that's fancy. Reminds me of all that silly talk I heard back home, in Arkham. And for some reason there seems to be more of it around this time of year, at Halloween. Why, when I left—"

"Excuse me, Cousin Osborne," I said. "But don't you live in Kingsport?"

"Why to be sure," he told me. "But I did live in Arkham once, and I know the people around here. It's no wonder you were so frightened in the woods and got to imagining things. As it is, I admire your bravery. For a 12 year old, you've acted very sensibly."

"Then let's start walking," I said. "Here it is almost 2 and we better get moving if we want to make town before sundown."

"Not just yet, son," Cousin Osborne said. "I wouldn't feel right about leaving without looking around and seeing what we can discover about this mystery. After all, you must understand that we can't just march into town and tell the sheriff some wild nonsense about strange creatures in the woods making off with your Aunt and Uncle. Sensible folks just won't believe such things. They might think I was lying and laugh at me. Why they might even think you had something to do with your Aunt and Uncle's—well, leaving."

"Please," I said. "We got to go, right now."

He shook his head.

I didn't say any more. I might of told him a lot, about what I dreamed and heard and saw and knew—but I figgered it was no use.

Besides, these was some things I didn't want to say to him now that I had talked to him. I was feeling scared again.

First he said he was from Arkham and then when I asked him he said he was from Kingsport but it sounded like a lie to me.

Then he said something about me being scared in the woods and how could he know that? I never told him *that* part at all.

If you want to know what I really thought, I thought maybe he wasn't really Cousin Osborne at all.

And if he wasn't, then—who was he?

I stood up and walked back into the hall.

"Where you going, son?" he asked.

"Outside."

"I'll come with you."

Sure enough, he was watching me. He wasn't going to let me out of his sight. He came over and took my arm, real friendly—but I couldn't break loose. No, he hung on to me. He knew I meant to run for it.

What could I do? All alone in the house in the woods with this man, with night coming on, Halloween night, and *them ones* out there waiting.

We went outside and I noticed it was getting darker already, even in afternoon. Clouds had covered up the sun, and the wind was moving the trees so they stretched out their branches, like they was trying to hold me back. They made a rustling noise, just as if they were whispering things about me, and he sort of looked up at them and listened. Maybe he understood what they were saying. Maybe they were giving him orders.

Then I almost laughed, because he *was* listening to something and now I heard it too.

It was a drumming sound, on the road.

"Cap Pritchett," I said. "He's the mailman. Now we can ride to town with him in the buggy."

"Let me talk to him," he says. "About your Aunt and Uncle. No sense in alarming him, and we don't want any scandal, do we? You just run along inside."

"But Cousin Osborne," I said. "We got to tell the truth."

"Of course, son. But this is a matter for adults. Now run along. I'll call you."

He was real polite about it and even smiled, but all the same he dragged me back up the porch and into the house and slammed the door. I stood there in the dark hall and I could hear Cap Pritchett slow down and call out to him, and him going up to the buggy and talking, and then all I heard was a lot of mumbling, real low. I peeked out through a crack in the door and saw them. Cap Pritchett was talking to him friendly, all right, and nothing was wrong.

Except that in a minute or so, Cap Pritchett waved and then he grabbed the reins and the buggy started off again!

Then I knew I'd have to do it, no matter what happened. I opened the door and ran out, suitcase and all, down the path and up the road after the buggy. Cousin Osborne he tried to grab me when I went by, but I ducked around him and yelled, "Wait for me, Cap—I'm coming—take me to town!"

Cap slowed down and stared back, real puzzled. "Willie!" he says. "Why I thought you was gone. He said you went away with Fred and Lucy—"

"Pay no attention," I said. "He didn't want me to go. Take me to town. I'll tell you what really happened. Please, Cap, you got to take me."

"Sure I'll take you, Willie. Hop right up here."

I hopped.

Cousin Osborne come right up to the buggy. "Here, now," he said, real sharp. "You can't leave like this. I forbid it. You're in my custody."

"Don't listen to him," I yelled. "Take me, Cap. Please!"

"Very well," said Cousin Osborne. "If you insist on being unreasonable. We'll all go. I cannot permit you to leave alone."

He smiled at Cap. "You can see the boy is unstrung," he said. "And I trust you will not be disturbed by his imaginings. Living out here like this—well, you understand—he's not quite himself. I'll explain everything on the way to town."

He sort of shrugged at Cap and made signs of tapping his head. Then he smiled again and made to climb up next to us in the buggy seat.

But Cap didn't smile back. "No, you don't," he said. "This boy Willie is a good boy. I know him. I don't know you. Looks as if you done enough explaining already, Mister, when you said Willie had gone away."

"But I merely wanted to avoid talk—you see, I've been called in to doctor the boy—he's mentally unstable—"

"Stables be damned!" Cap spit out some tobacco juice right at Cousin Osborne's feet. "We're going."

Cousin Osborne stopped smiling. "Then I insist you take me with you," he said. And he tried to climb into the buggy.

Cap reached into his jacket and when he pulled his hand out again he had a big pistol in it.

"Git down!" he yelled. "Mister, you're talking to the United States Mail and you don't tell the Government nothing, understand? Now git down before I mess your brains all over this road."

Cousin Osborne scowled, but he got away from the buggy, fast.

He looked at me and shrugged. "You're making a big mistake, Willie," he said.

I didn't even look at him. Cap said, "Gee up," and we went off down the road. The buggy wheels turned faster and faster and pretty soon the farmhouse was out of sight and Cap put his pistol away, and patted me on the shoulder.

"Stop that trembling, Willie," he said. "You're safe now. Nothing to worry about. Be in town little over an hour or so. Now you just set back and tell old Cap all about it."

So I told him. It took a long time. We kep going through the woods, and before I knew it, it was almost dark. The sun sneaked down and hid behind the hills. The dark began to creep out of the woods on each side of the road, and the trees started to rustle, whispering to the big shadows that followed us.

The horse was clipping and clopping along, and pretty soon they were other noises from far away. Might have been thunder and might have been something else. But it was getting night-time for sure, and it was the night of Halloween.

The road cut off through the hills now, and you could hardly see where the next turn would take you. Besides, it was getting dark awful fast.

"Guess we're in for a spell of rain," Cap said, looking up. "That's thunder, I reckon."

"Drums," I said.

"Drums?"

"At night in the hills you can hear them," I told him. "I heard them all this month. It's *them ones*, getting ready for the Sabbath."

"Sabbath?" Cap looked at me. "Where you hear tell about a Sabbath?"

Then I told him more about what had happened. I told him all the rest. He didn't say anything, and before long he couldn't of answered me anyway, because the thunder was all around us, and the rain was lashing down on the buggy, on the road, everywhere. It was pitch-black outside now, and the only time we could see was when lightning flashed. I had to yell to make him hear me—yell about the things that caught Uncle Fred and come for Aunt Lucy, the things that took our cattle and then sent Cousin Osborne back to fetch me. I hollered out about what I heard in the wood, too.

In the lightning flashes I could see Cap's face. He wasn't smiling or scowling—he just looked like he believed me. And I noticed he had his pistol out again and was holding the reins with one hand even though we were racing along. The horse was so scared he didn't need the whip to keep him running.

The old buggy was lurching and bouncing, and the rain was whistling down in the wind and it was all like an awful dream but it was real. It was real when I hollered out to Cap Pritchett about that time in the woods.

"Shoggoth," I yelled. "What's a shoggoth?"

Cap grabbed my arm, and then the lightning come and I could see his face, with his mouth open. But he wasn't looking at me. He was looking at the road and what was ahead of us.

The trees sort of come together, hanging over the next turn, and in the black it looked as if they were alive—moving and bending and twisting to block our way. Lightning flickered up again and I could see them plain, and also something else.

Something black in the road, something that wasn't a tree. Something big and black, just squatting there, waiting, with ropy arms squirming and reaching.

"Shoggoth!" Cap yelled. But I could scarcely hear him because the thunder was roaring and now the horse let out a scream and I felt the buggy jerk to one side and the horse reared up and we was almost into the black stuff. I could smell an awful smell, and Cap was pointing his pistol and it went off with a bang that was almost as loud as the thunder and almost as loud as the sound we made when we hit the black thing.

Then everything happened at once. The thunder, the horse falling, the shot, and us hitting as the buggy went over. Cap must of had the reins wrapped around his arm, because when the horse fell and the buggy turned over, he went right over the dashboard head first and down into the squirming mess that was the horse—and the black thing that grabbed it. I felt myself falling in the dark, then landing in the mud and gravel of the road.

There was thunder and screaming and another sound which I had heard once before in the woods—a droning sound like a voice.

That's why I never looked back. That's why I didn't even think about being hurt when I landed—just got up and started to run down the road, fast as I could, run down the road in the storm and the dark with the trees squirming and twisting and shaking their heads while they pointed at me with their branches and laughed.

Over the thunder I heard the horse scream and I heard Cap scream, too, but I still didn't look back. The lightning winked on and off, and I ran through the trees now because the road was nothing but mud that dragged me down and sucked at my legs. After a while I began to scream, too, but I couldn't even hear myself for thunder. And more than thunder. I heard drums.

All at once I busted clear of the woods and got to the hills. I ran up, and the drumming got louder, and pretty soon I could see regular, not just when they was lightning. Because they was fires burning on the hill, and the booming of the drums come from there.

I got lost in the noise; the wind shrieking and the trees laughing and the drums pounding. But I stopped in time. I stopped when I saw the fires plain; red and green fires burning in all that rain.

I saw a big white stone in the center of a cleared-off space on top of the hill. The red and green fires was around and behind it, so everything stood out clear against the flames.

They was men around the alter, men with long gray beards and wrinkled-up faces, men throwing awful-smelling stuff on the fires to make them blaze red and green. And they had knives in their hands and I could hear them howling over the storm. In back, squatting on the ground, more men pounded on drums.

Pretty soon something else come up the hill—two men driving cattle. I could tell it was our cows they drove, drove them right up to the alter and then the men with the knives cut their throats for a sacrefice.

All this I could see in lightning flashes and in the fire lights, and I sort of scooched down so I couldn't get spotted by anyone.

But pretty soon I couldn't see very good any more, on account of the way they threw stuff on the fire. It set up a real thick black smoke. When this smoke come up, the men began to chant and pray louder.

I couldn't hear words, but the sounds was like what I heard back in the woods. I couldn't see too good, but I knew what was going to happen. Two men who had led the cattle went back down the other side of the hill and when they come up again they had new sacrefices. The smoke kep me from seeing plain, but these was two-legged sacrefices, not four. I might of seen better at that, only now I hid my face when they dragged them up to the white alter and used the knives, and the fire and smoke flared up and the drums boomed and they all chanted and called in a loud voice to something waiting over on the other side of the hill.

The ground began to shake. It was storming, they was thunder and lightning and fire and smoke and chanting and I was scared half out of my wits, but one thing I'll swear to—the ground began to shake. It shook and shivered and they called out to something, and in a minute something came.

It came crawling up the hillside to the alter and the sacrefice, and it was the black thing of my dreams—that black, ropy, slimy jelly tree-thing out of the woods. It crawled up and it flowed up on its hoofs and mouths and snaky arms. And the men bowed and stood back and then it got to the alter where they was something squirming on top, squirming and screaming.

The black thing sort of bent over the alter and then I heard droning sounds over the screaming as it came down. I only watched a minute, but while I watched the black thing began to swell and *grow*.

That finished me. I didn't care any more. I had to run. I got up and I run and run and run, screaming at the top of my lungs no matter who heard.

I kep running and I kep screaming forever, through the woods and the storm, away from that hill and that alter, and then all at once I knew where I was and I was back here at the farmhouse.

Yes, that's what I'd done—run in a circle and come back. But I couldn't go any further, I couldn't stand the night and the storm. So I run inside here. At first after I locked the door I just lay right down on the floor, all tuckered out from running and crying.

But in a little while I got up and hunted me some nails and a hammer and some of Uncle Fred's boards that wasn't split up into kindling.

I nailed up the door first then boarded up all the windows. Every last one of them. Guess I worked for hours, tired as I was. When it was all done, the storm died down and it got quiet. Quiet enough for me to lie down on the couch and go to sleep.

Woke up a couple hours ago. It was daylight. I could see it shining through the cracks. From the way the sun come in, I knew it was afternoon already. I'd slept through the whole morning, and nothing had come.

I figured now maybe I could let myself out and make town on foot, like I'd planned yesterday.

But I figgered wrong.

Before I got started taking out the nails, I heard him. It was Cousin Osborne, of course. The man who said he was Cousin Osborne, I mean.

He come into the yard, calling "Willie!" but I didn't answer. Then he tried the door and then the windows. I could hear him pounding and cussing. That was bad.

But then he began mumbling, and that was worse. Because it meant he wasn't out there alone.

I sneaked a look through the crack, but he already went around to the back of the house so I didn't see him or who was with him.

Guess that's just as well, because if I'm right, I wouldn't want to see. Hearing's bad enough.

Hearing that deep croaking, and then him talking, and then that croaking again.

Smelling that awful smell, like the green slime from the woods and around the well.

The well—they went over to the well in back. And I heard Cousin Osborne say something about, "Wait until dark. We can use the well if you find the gate. Look for the gate."

I know what that means now. The well must be a sort of entrance to the underground place—that's where those Druid men live. And the black thing.

They're out in back now, looking.

I been writing for quite a spell and already the afternoon is going. Peeking through the cracks I can see it's getting dark again.

That's when they'll come for me—when it's dark.

They'll break down the doors or the windows and come and take me. They'll take me down into the well, into the black places where the shoggoths are. There must be a whole world down under the hills, a world where they hide and wait to come out for more sacrefices, more blood. They don't want any humans around, except for sacrefices.

I saw what the black thing did on the alter. I know what's going to happen to me.

Maybe they'll miss the real Cousin Osborne back home and send somebody to find out what become of him. Maybe folks in town will miss Cap Pritchett and go on a search. Maybe they'll come here and find me. But if they don't come soon it will be too late.

That's why I wrote this. It's true, cross my heart, every word of it. And if anyone finds this notebook where I hide it, come and look down the well. The old well, out in back.

Remember what I told about *them ones.* Block up the well and clean out them swamps. No sense looking for me—if I'm not here.

I wish I wasn't so scared. I'm not even scared so much for myself, but for other folks. The ones who might come after and live around here and have the same thing happen—or worse.

You just got to believe me. Go to the woods if you don't. Go to the hill. The hill where they had the sacrefice. Maybe the stains are gone and the rain washed the footprints away. Maybe they got rid of the traces of the fire. But the alter stone must be there. And if it is, you'll know the truth. There should be some big round spots on that stone. Round spots about two feet wide.

I didn't tell about that. At the last, I did look back. I looked back at the big black thing that was a shoggoth. I looked back as it kep swelling and growing. I guess I told about how it could change shape, and how big it got. But you can't hardly imagine how big or what shape and I still dassn't tell.

All I say is look. Look and you'll see what's hiding under the earth in these hills, waiting to creep out and feast and kill some more.

Wait. They're coming now. Getting twilight and I can hear footsteps. And other sounds. Voices. And other sounds. They're banging on the door. And sure enough—they must have a tree or a plank to use for battering it down. The whole place is shaking. I can hear Cousin Osborne yelling, and that droning. The smell is awful, I'm getting sick, and in a minute—

Look at the alter. Then you'll understand what I'm trying to tell. Look at the big round marks, two feet wide, on each side. That's where the big black thing grabbed hold.

Look for the marks and you'll know what I saw, what I'm afraid of, what's waiting to grab you unless you shut it up forever under the earth.

Black marks two feet wide, but they aren't just marks.

What they really are is *fingerprints!*

The door is busting o———

BILL WARREN

The first thing by Robert Bloch that I recall reading was, as it happens, *Psycho.* I was very curious about Alfred Hitchcock's new movie, having flipped over *North by Northwest,* and when I saw a paperback with Janet Leigh's screaming face on the cover, I bought it immediately.

What really struck me about the novel was the dark sense of humor that popped up every now and then, including in the shower murder that Hitchcock filmed so brilliantly. In Bob's book, it was far more terse, just two lines, about how the knife cut off her scream. "And her head," the chapter concluded. Yow! I was about sixteen when I read that, and didn't know you were "allowed" to make sardonic wisecracks about death and dismemberment. The novel was a real education.

Years later, I told Bob truthfully that I had figured out the ending of the novel while reading it, but I was very uncomfortable about it, since the description of Norman Bates in the novel certainly didn't match Anthony Perkins—but it did match *me.* Bob told me that he had based Bates on two people, Ed Gein, "The Wisconsin Ghoul," and—well, he asked me never to reveal publicly who the other person was, but though that man is now gone too, I'll honor Bob's request.

Because I honor Bob.

When I moved to Los Angeles in 1966, I was intensely shy, but also deeply curious, and when Forrest J Ackerman invited my wife and me to a screening of *WereWolf of London* in the screening room at the home of Magic Castle founder Milt Larsen, I was very excited about going—not only for the movie, but because actor Christopher Lee was going to be there. I was impressed when Robert Bloch turned up at the screening, too, impressed and dazzled. And surprised.

By that time, having adored *Psycho,* I had been reading everything by Bloch I could find. Even though the same thread of humor wove through much of his writing, I still assumed the man himself would look like one of the lurkers in the darkness in a Charles Addams cartoon. Instead, I met a tall, funny man with a big grin and a cigarette in a long, long holder, friendly and highly knowledgeable about horror movies. It seemed entirely appropriate that Lee, who was also very witty, had come to the screening *with* Bloch.

I don't know the point at which he changed from "Mr. Bloch" to "Bob" for me, but it wasn't long thereafter. At one of the huge parties he used to have, Forry Ackerman thrilled me by asking me to get Bob to inscribe a copy of the *The Opener of the Way*—and then giving *me* the book, as a gift (in front of Bob, so Bloch could autograph it for me).

It was at those parties that Bob Bloch often sought me out, talking to me about things I was interested in, drawing me out and seeking my opinions. He was so gracious about this, but also so casual and relaxed, without any sense of being patronizing, that it didn't occur to me for years that he was doing this because he recognized in me the shyness I'm sure he once felt at such gatherings.

When he was a young man, even a boy, his favorite writer, H. P. Lovecraft, had taken him under his wing (via letters; to Bob's regret, they never met in person), helped him with his fiction, treated him with respect, generosity, and sympathy—and that's how Bloch himself treated budding writers from then on. And not just writers, either. Science fiction fandom had been deeply important to Bob in his adolescence, and he realized its value to others all his life. As he grew in fame, he realized that his name meant something to the publishers of fanzines; I know that he made a point of writing a letter of comment to the editor of every fanzine he was sent. He also contributed to fanzines so often that two books of his fannish writings have been published.

He continued this effort of drawing people into the spotlight all along, in many venues. If he gave a speech at a convention, he would mention by name many people in the audience, because it gave them a thrill, and because it pleased Bob to be able to provide that thrill. He wanted people to feel good about themselves, and he liked being in a position to bring that about. While my wife Beverly and I were having lunch with him at a *Dark Shadows* convention, he suddenly remarked on how he had known her for years, but she had never seemed to age. Since that very morning she had been dismayed to discover her hair had a lot of gray in it, his comment couldn't have come at a better time, and she rushed over to embrace a surprised, pleased Bob. And I was very proud to find myself mentioned in his autobiography.

As a writer, Bloch was a giant in his fields, but I always felt there was something holding him back, something he learned in writing for the pulps that he could not quite rid himself of. He's a very good mystery and suspense writer, and an even better writer of horror—but I always had the impression that an *even better* writer lurked there, that if he had felt wealthy enough to give up that kind of moneymaking writing for a year, he could have turned out an authentic masterpiece—not of genre fiction, but of American fiction in general. His screenplays are much the same way: clever, witty thrillers for William Castle (Bob's best film overall is probably *Strait-Jacket*), amusing anthology films for Amicus a few years later. But they all play just a little like Bob had even more to offer. I've seen very few of his teleplays; I'm intensely curious about them.

As a person, Bob Bloch was honest, direct, and kind; he had a temper—I occasionally saw him angry at duplicity and vulgarity—and there were people he strongly disliked. But there weren't many of them, and there were hundreds who loved *him*. I know that I was always not just pleased but delighted to see him. And he always seemed pleased to encounter Beverly and me; he seemed to enjoy chatting with me about old movies, about which he had an engraved-in-steel memory, particularly for the character actors of long ago. Once, I overheard him and comic book artist Don Rico talk about vaudeville, and discovered that Bob was an expert on that subject, too. Every time I talked to him, every time I heard him give a speech or appear on a panel at a convention, I learned something. He was a great teacher—and had he been an actual teacher at actual schools, he would have been one of the best.

He was always so accessible to everyone, even when he'd rather not have been. At a banquet years ago, a well-known Los Angeles character—and I use the term advisedly—had Bob backed into a corner, going on and on about this and that. Bob was too good-hearted to simply walk away, but when Beverly realized what was going on, and ran up, crying, "Mr. Bloch, Mr. Bloch! Can I have your autograph?", he went off with her gratefully. He even put up with being introduced as (and I swear this happened), "Robert Pssitcho Bloch." He didn't revel in his fame, but he enjoyed it in an offhand, unstressed manner.

I have never heard anyone say an unkind word about Robert Bloch, and I've been around people who had nothing kind to say about *anyone*. But he wasn't adored or beloved, either; he was far too much one of us to be placed on that kind of pedestal. He was a *friend,* not an idol. He was a good a man as I have ever known.

"The Clown at Midnight," my selection for this book, is an essay Bob wrote for *Rogue* in 1960; I first saw it when Forry Ackerman reprinted it in a shorter version in *Famous Monsters of Filmland*. Thanks to Harlan Ellison, the version here is the original, *Rogue* version.

Bloch wrote this out of annoyance with the new trends in horror movies that were turning up at the time. Hammer Films in England had opened a new door, in Technicolor, with heaving bosoms and lots of blood, and some people—including Bob Bloch—at first had a hard time accepting this as a new, but legitimate, approach to horror on screen.

These people had grown up with the Gothic style of the classic Universal chillers, and saw the new type of movie as a kind of degeneration.

In time, Bloch did come to appreciate the Hammer films as movies, but he was never comfortable with the degree of gore on screen. "The Clown at Midnight" marks his initial thoughts on the subject.

For me personally, "The Clown" was one of the most influential articles I have ever read—even though I don't agree with very much of what he says about the movies that were new in 1960. He talks about the shudder films of "our youth," since he was, as far as he knew when he wrote the piece, addressing only adults. I was seventeen when I read the piece, and madly in love with science fiction and horror movies, the new ones— I hadn't had much opportunity yet to see the old ones—so Bloch's article outraged me at the same time that it amused me.

But what the article ultimately, and most importantly, did for me was to stun me into realizing for the first time that this kind of film could be discussed seriously, but not pompously.

For years, film criticism fell into three camps only: the academic, intellectual approach; the breezy, popular culture approach of magazines like *Time* and the daily newspaper; and the ingrown, insular approach of the "trades," *Variety, Hollywood Reporter,* and so on. Only the popular culture approach regularly expressed much humor, but it was rare to find anyone there who admitted that horror (or science fiction) movies could actually be *good movies.*

With "The Clown at Midnight," Robert Bloch took that as a given. And he was both serious in his discussion, and funny in his approach. I was blown away. This was before Pauline Kael did this same thing with all movies: that it is not only possible, but necessary, to treat even standard Hollywood output with both seriousness and a humorous lack of pretension. Bloch was there first, even if confined pretty much to discussing what have come to be called "genre movies." And he changed me forever.

Incidentally, even Jove nods: In the article, Bob refers to "a technicolor *Blood of Dracula*" when he's really referring to *Horror of Dracula.* And while he accurately describes one of the great shock scenes of all time, he ascribes it to *Cat People,* when it actually occurred in another Val Lewton film, *The Leopard Man.* But whether he was precisely accurate in all details, what he had to say was of value—and it still is.

THE CLOWN AT MIDNIGHT

𝕵 *Horror is my business.*
The insurance agent peddles protection and security—I sell terror and dread. The doctor guards your heart; I devote my professional skill to inducing failure in same. Some people live by their wits; I live by scaring you out of yours.

For the past twenty-five years I've been a professional writer of horror fiction for magazines, books, radio and TV shows. And when I'm not creating nightmares of my own, I spend my spare time investigating the nightmares of other people—namely the so-called "horror" movies being foisted off on the public via TV and theater screens.

It used to be, back in the bad old days when apples were sold on street corners and cars had rumble seats, that the horror film was practically an art-form as well as being almost as hot at the box-office as Bank Night. The terror tale was filmed with more Tender Loving Care than Eisenhower gets at Walter Reed, and imaginative producers never forgot for a moment that the viewer had an imagination of his own.

Unfortunately, for better or for worse, the folklore of the land is changing. Just as Halloween, with its ghosts and goblins, has been transformed into a sub-teen Thanksgiving with Tricks-or-Treats replacing the turkey, so has the horror movie suffered a sea-change into something strictly for laughs, with genuine grue and imagination being replaced by a vat of ketchup and a false face that wouldn't frighten a timid two-year-old.

The shudder salesmen have sold out and the average horror flick nowadays evokes more gaiety than goose-pimples.

But it boots no good to shed melancholy tears over the fright films of our youth that populated our dark and lonely bedrooms with images of Frankenstein's Monster and the Mummy gibbering just beyond the counterpane. It's more instructive, perhaps, to look into the reasons why the morbid has been changed into the unintentionally mirthful.

Much as we dislike to consider it, one answer keeps cropping up: Hollywood no longer knows what horror is.

We *could* get philosophical at this point and wonder if it's really that simple or if it's just that people can't be horrified anymore. A casual glance at any paper will prove that the monsters currently roaming a city's streets after dark are far more horrible, in one sense, than anything Hollywood has yet dreamed up. And it was not too long ago that human beings were eliminated by the carload lots in the gas chambers of Belsen and Dachau—certainly the pinnacle of horror as far as human history goes. In addition, everybody reading this is probably painfully aware (though none of us like to think about it) that all somebody has to do is push the wrong button and half of humanity will go up in smoke and radioactive ashes.

But all of this—while certainly horrible to contemplate—is not true *horror* as such. Horror is something peculiar to the individual.

It's a small child's (and quite frequently an adult's!) fear of the dark—and most particularly the phantoms of the imagination that populate the dark.

It's the fear of a human being who doesn't act, think, or look like a human being—the fear of deformity, the fear of insanity, and even (far more pathetically) the fear of a cerebral palsy victim. (There, but for the grace of God . . .)

It's the fear of spiders and snakes and the pale horrors you find under rocks in the woods.

It's the fear of the unknown, the unexpected, the not-quite-seen.

When *I* was an eight-year-old I saw Lon Chaney in *The Phantom of the Opera*—and gazed upon the face of naked fear. Within the past year I attended a revival of the same film. And despite the flickering flaws of this dated melodrama, the scene where Chaney is unmasked exerted the same monstrous magic upon a modern audience.

Since the 1925 version of *The Phantom,* Hollywood has arrayed itself in noseputty and fright-wig hundreds of times. And yet only a score of genuinely shivery efforts have actually emerged from the studios (and practically none since World War II).

During the '30s, the movie moguls outdid themselves and gave us a *Dracula,* a *Frankenstein,* a *Mummy,* and a *Wolf Man,* and even a few fairly respectable sequels. And then some pillow-head decided that since it was such a thin line between horror and hilarity, why not erase the line altogether? The integrity of the horror film was quickly corrupted and the honest seeker after shudders was lured into a back alley inhabited by Abbott and Costello and the Bowery Boys. Just about the time Frankenstein was due to meet Pa and Ma Kettle, some giddy genius discovered liquid latex and the "monster film" was born. (Frankenstein's Monster, we'll admit, may have been the first of these, but the horror depended on far more than just a fright face with high forehead, dank hair, scars, and two collar studs projecting from the neck.)

Things began emerging from Outer Space—or the equally empty regions between a producer's ears. The screens of the nation were invaded by a horde of Giant Cockroaches, Giant Bedbugs, and Giant Spirochetes (all of which warmed the hearts of the pest-exterminators at the same time they cooled the ardor of the true horror fan).

That these not-so-Grand Guignol efforts make money is undeniable. Vast audiences still watch the tired old travesties on television and turn out for each new double feature. But if producers believe these films show a profit because this is what the public really wants, then they must also believe that most bums drink canned heat because they prefer it to bonded whiskey or vintage champagne. Let's face it—audiences lap up their pictures only because nothing better is available.

While today's films prove that Hollywood has progressed in the use of camera tricks, animation, miniature photography and make-up, they also prove a total ignorance of what inspires the release of fear. One of the best examples is a produced-in-Japan flick (an American outfit later picked it up and dubbed in some English dialogue and narrator in the person of Raymond Burr, currently popular as TV's Perry Mason) called *Godzilla*. The *pièce de résistance* of the film is a ten-story monster that cheerfully tears apart the city of Tokyo, evoking all kinds of admiration for the experts who built the miniature sets but no true feeling of horror on the part of the audience. (As von Clausewitz is reputed to have said, "One death is a tragedy; a million are statistics.")

On the other hand, an excellent example of true horror in a film is the sight of one dwarfed, armless and legless torso crawling through the mud in an old movie called *Freaks*. This scene was enough to raise the hackles of the most sophisticated audience.

Of course, film producers are not entirely to blame—they have been influenced by the censors, who have curiously limited the size of the canvas upon which the horror film producers can paint. The censors who were not happy with the "morbidity" of *Freaks* were singularly undisturbed when walls of fire toppled upon helpless thousand in *War of the Worlds*. One lone ripper-murderer tempts the censorial blue-pencil far more than a *Beast From 20,000 Fathoms* whose poisonous presence perils an entire city. A ripper, you see, may suddenly drop his knife and produce another type of weapon. A *Beast* is entirely moral in his relationships with women and is content—if you'll pardon the allusion—to merely eat them or trample them to death.

Let's look at a few of the better examples of horror films and see what the censors have done—or undone.

After thirty years of repetition and burlesque, it is hardly probable that an audience can view the original *Frankenstein* and recapture its initial impact. It's even less likely if they catch bits and pieces of it sandwiched in between the bra and deodorant commercials on a 21-inch tube. But in its day, *Frankenstein* qualified as a true tale of terror. Its theme, "The Monster is loose!" is still the basis of most so-called "science-fiction" movies today. The first few scenes of the shambling monstrosity walking backwards or stumbling around the castle convey a genuine sense of the unearthly.

There are, or were originally, *two* versions of *Frankenstein*. In the one generally shown and currently revived on TV, the Monster befriends a little girl on a river bank and watches her toss flowers into the water, petal by petal. There is an abrupt cutaway from the scene, and when next we see the girl she is dead, being carried into town by her stunned father.

In the banned version, the flower-tossing episode is continued and the Monster, not out of cruelty but merely through confusion, picks up the child and tosses her into the water. He is too ignorant to understand; if the pretty petals looked even prettier when they floated, why not a pretty girl?

The censors thought otherwise, apparently. They would rather cut the scene and leave the unmistakable—and to me, far more ghastly—inference that the Monster had probably ravished the child and then disposed of her body. The true horror is thus discarded in favor of a sordid situation immediately identifiable by the newspaper-reading public.

In *King Kong,* another genuine all-out horror fantasy, there is a scene where the giant ape, loose in New York, holds the squirming body of a man between his huge teeth. The censors left this alone, but they removed a scene where the same ape picks away at the heroine's garments out of mere curiosity.

They also eliminated the scene where Kong, searching for the heroine, plucks a girl from her hotel room and then, realizing he has made a mistake, drops her to the street below. Gruesome? Yes, but it *is*, after all, a horror movie. (In this case, of course, the horror lies in the utter casualness with which Kong drops her.) And I can't quite comprehend why a censor would scissor this out and retain the graphic close-up of a man screaming between the clenched teeth of a 60-foot gorilla.

The same film contained a sequence where members of the exploring party are eaten by a sea-monster and dashed to death in a chasm. The chasm scene conclusion, where some of them are devoured by giant spiders, was excised. (It would seem that the capricious censors are also dieticians; sea-monsters can eat men, but spiders cannot.)

If censors have a distorted idea of what constitutes real horror, audiences seem to retain more than their share of misconceptions. In film after film, the great Lon Chaney played a succession of cripples and deformed men; he earned a deserved reputation as "The Man of a Thousand Faces." But aside from his role as the Phantom in *Phantom of the Opera,* Chaney seldom played outright "monster" roles. Usually he sacrificed his life for the heroine. Yet to the public, Chaney was a maker of "horror movies."

The same is true of Karloff. After his *Frankenstein* series and *The Mummy,* he appeared in dozens of films and a great many of them featured him for what he is—a mild-mannered man with a lisp. The theme song for these allegedly blood-curdling shockers might well have been "That Silver-Haired Daddy of Mine." Time after time Karloff was a kindly, elderly physician or scientist with the inevitable nubile daughter. Upon completing a discovery or invention which he idealistically hopes will aid humanity, he inadvertently causes the death of some innocent bystander or bit-player, whereupon he is persecuted by the police or by the real villain who wants to misuse the apparatus. Karloff thereupon goes off his rocker faster than Whistler's Mother if she'd landed on a pin-cushion and tries to get rid of his tormentors. In the end, to save his daughter, he sacrifices his own life. Despite the laboratory scenes and the inevitable threats and grimaces of the "mad scientist" role, these films will hardly horrify anyone except lovers of good drama.

Karloff played the Monster in two sequels to his *Frankenstein* but each subsequent version managed to dilute the blood-letting (though we do have fond memories of the Monster shrieking in agony as the old mill goes up in flames, and another in which he drowns in what looks like a vat of bubbling oatmeal). At times Karloff has appeared as a loutish criminal or the innocent victim of some other "mad scientist" and his experiments. Quite understandably, he seeks revenge until exterminated by bumping into a rheostat. Again, the shock of these sequences is purely electrical.

Lon Chaney, Jr., has consistently been cast, or rather miscast—for he is considered, with some cause, an excellent actor—in routine villain roles. He has moved in and out of various series chronicling the resurrections of various monsters, mummies, vampires, and victims of Five O'Clock Shadow. Most conspicuous among the latter is *The Wolf Man*. Chaney, an innocent young man brought up in the U.S., returns to his ancestral home in England and falls prey to a werewolf. He is quite unhappy in his role as a hairy heir, but this doesn't save him. In the end, his father beats him to death with a silver-headed cane. (Apparently the censors saw no symbolism in the plight of a son who becomes obsessed with bestial instincts and pursues females by night.)

Neither, incidentally, have the censors read the true meaning of the Lust Legend into the various versions of *Dr. Jekyll and Mr. Hyde*. Dr. Jekyll, who becomes transformed into a sexual sadist at the sight of an "easy" girl after drinking a potion which acts suspiciously like an aphrodisiac, has been played with properly terrifying effect by John Barrymore, Frederic March, and Spencer Tracy. The "metamorphosis" scenes are worthy of inclusion in any listing of cinematic horrors. But aside from these brief moments, the films are pure—or impure—sex-dramas. The censors eliminated some of the "morbid" close-ups of bestial Mr. Hyde beating the beejezus out of his girl friend—in Tracy's case a truly beautiful Ingrid Bergman—but never bothered to eliminate his other bestial activities.

True horror was also lacking, oddly enough, in the antics of such esteemed "monsters" as Bela Lugosi and Peter Lorre. Both achieved success in thinly disguised sex-operas. *Dracula* ostensibly portrayed a vampire in full denture but actually celebrated the career of the nocturnal prowler. Lugosi symbolized the Continental Seducer, sleek-haired and irresistible; he was merely another version of the Filthy Foreigner originally portrayed by Erich von Stroheim. Von Stroheim kissed hands and Lugosi bit necks but both were primarily sex-menaces, not true monsters. Lugosi, like other specialists in the *genre,* later drifted into routine villain roles, along with Claude Rains, Lionel Atwill, and John Carradine.

Peter Lorre first won fame in the German film *M* but his monster was quite frankly a sex-fiend. In most of his American movies, Lorre has played droll crooks or nasty informers, unpleasant enough at times but hardly frightening. Brief moments in the British version of *The Man Who Knew Too Much* and the American *Stranger on the Third Floor* are almost the only exceptions. In *The Face Behind the Mask* he seeks revenge because of a face scarred by fire (shades of *Mystery of the Wax Museum* and *House of Wax!*) but his motivation is understandable enough.

Just once did Lorre escape being mired in commonplace menace roles. This was in his first American film, *Mad Love.* This was a true shocker—and a flat failure. Karl Freund, who served as cameraman on *The Last Laugh,* directed the picture and created some chilling sequences. The scene where the madman poses as a guillotine victim whose head has been sewed back onto his body is far more terrifying than a dozen glimpses of rubber-suited "Things" emerging from Black Lagoons or descending from Outer Space. Given similar roles, Lorre might still triumph in real horror films. But the last time *I* saw him, he was playing an overweight clown.

So far we've considered what a horror film is *not.* It is *not* a picture where a character, supernatural or human, pursues a woman to bed her in the brush; even a Wolf Man is merely a "wolf" at heart. Nor is it a movie in which a wronged man turns on society in revenge, be it ever so gruesome. It is not a movie that stresses torture or sadism. Even though the Christians are served up to the lions in *Quo Vadis,* this hardly makes it a "horror" epic.

The mere use of supernatural devices is no guarantee in itself: *The Invisible Man* was in some sequences as funny as *Topper.* The modern "science-fiction" movies which pack the passion pits today are palpable spectacles in which miniature sets and the make-up department have the starring roles. "Mysteries" seldom shock us any longer; hands may clutch and bodies fall from closets in the time-honored tradition of Paul Leni's *The Cat and the Canary,* but the Cat was only a man, after all, and so was the *Bat* and the *Gorilla* and the various cinematic incarnations of Jerry Lewis, for that matter.

Stripped of sexual symbolism and sadistic sequences and supernatural or super-scientific skullduggery, most of the supposed "horror movies"—particularly the monster monstrosities being produced lately—just don't fill the double bill. The censors have hacked the heart out of fright flicks and the producers themselves have sold their collective imaginations for a mess of *papier-mâché.*

The few films left, which set out to terrify by any manner or method available, succeed because writer, producer, director, and actors stick steadfastly to their sinister purpose. They know what fear and horror are and they play upon the human emotions with all the skill of a professional musician caressing the strings of a harp.

Scenes in horror movies made by these dedicated souls are usually brilliantly brought off. I do not speak now of the liberal splattering of tomato ketchup in a technicolor *Blood of Dracula.* I have in mind the faint trickle of blood under the door in a scene in *The Cat People* (directed by Val Lewton and starring Simone Simone) where the little girl is locked out of her house by her mother, who thinks that the big cat pursuing her daughter is only a child's fantasy. You don't see the cat, you don't see the girl. You're in the kitchen, listening to the terrified child pleading to be let in. Then the scream . . . and the horrible silence . . . and the blood.

There is horror in madness, and when Michael Redgrave, as the crazed ventriloquist, speaks in the dummy's voice in *Dead of Night,* the audience knows the sheer shock of schizophrenia. The world of the pinheaded idiots, midgets, and the armless-legless torso in *Freaks* was enough to inspire nightmares for a solid year of Sundays.

The "It was all a diabolical plot" movie is almost as much of a cheat as the "It was all a dream" picture, but we can forgive it, amidst our shudders, when we see the supposed corpse rising from the tub in *Diabolique* . . . and we feel relief in our screams as it thumbs out its eyeballs.

Fantasy alone is no guarantee of grisliness, unless played as straight and as superbly as the first sequence of the British film *Three Cases of Murder.* The episode titled *In the Picture* is indeed the stuff bad dreams are made of. In it, a visitor to an art gallery is carefully inspecting a landscape painting of an old deserted house when suddenly a light goes on in one of the windows of the house.

Monsters and ghosts are not necessarily frightful in themselves; one laughs at the staring extras of the various "zombie" movies, but one shudders at the totally unseen horror of *The Uninvited.* Even a movie like *The Thing* had its moments of true horror as the blanket left on the cake of ice in which the monster is frozen helps to defrost it. We see only the slow drip-drip-drip of water from under the blanket and then hear the sudden-stifled scream from the soldier left to guard it. And who can forget the scene where the monstrous half-vegetable arm erupts from the greenhouse?

I hold no brief for the monster movies and the science-fiction (so called) films made today in which a skeleton dances over the ceiling of the theater or the seats are wired for shocks—surely the final convincing proof, if any were needed, of the paucity of imagination of today's movie makers. Such films may entertain the kiddies and presumably they serve a purpose for dating couples who need a reason to cuddle in the dark—but they're not true horror pictures. For that matter, the horrors of dope addiction in a *Man with the Golden Arm* serve far better to induce throat-clogging terror.

The sophisticates will probably continue to sneer at *all* horror films, the censors will snip out the perils and, in an unusual switch, save the pruriency, and we who cherish the creeps will continue to haunt the local cinema for shocks and shudders and the wholesome release of fears as old as all mankind.

Where our search will lead, I don't know. It may be that we'll discover the ultimate cinematic horror in a clown. Years ago, Lon Chaney said:

"A clown is funny in the circus ring, but what would be the normal reaction to opening a door at midnight and finding the same clown standing there in the moonlight?"

That, to me, is the essence of true horror—the clown, at midnight.

FOUR IN THE BACK

MICK GARRIS

It was sometime in 1961, at the Reseda Drive-In Theater in the San Fernando Valley. Later, the now–long-defunct theater would achieve fame as the location for Peter Bogdanovich's Boris Karloff film, *Targets,* but that night, it was just a family outing, one that would grow increasingly rare in the waning years of my parents' seventeen-year marriage. But for now, it was still a family of six, conjoined spiritually in the sea green 1957 Chevy station wagon, in the middle of the middle row at the movies.

We almost never went to indoor movies—aside from the expense, there was the unruliness of the Garris tribe to consider. If we took in a movie, it was at the drive-in, and we brought our own snacks. The adults in the front seat and the four kids in back passed around a six-pack of Bubble Up ("You like it; it likes you!"), and a huge, grease-stained grocery bag of homemade popcorn.

I didn't realize it then, but that night's family film would literally change my life, and not merely in subtle ways. It must seem strange in retrospect that this young family's choice for an evening's entertainment would be *Psycho,* but it seemed the most natural thing in the world at the time. Mom and Dad were in their early thirties. My older brother, George, was all of eleven years old; I—number two—was nine, my brother Craig was seven, leaving little Dee Dee only six.

I shall be forever grateful that modern concerns about the effects of scary movies were less popular in the early sixties. Had I been kept from the monsters of my youth, who knows where my career path might have led? Oh, sure, my old Nana always said that I should forget about "that gruesome stuff," but Nana—unbelievably—was wrong.

Robert Bloch's most famous creation was not the first horrific primal pool into which I'd dipped a toe . . . merely the most explosive. Though my siblings were not drawn to the dark *genre,* it held me deeply in its thrall. Though Hitchcock's film proved to be "fun for the entire family" that night at the drive-in, and we brothers mercilessly taunted poor Dee Dee with our repeated spontaneous recreations of the "Mrs. Bates! Mrs. Bates!" scene, imitating the creak of the old chair in the cellar and the reveal of Mother's desiccated face, it left no scars, no fears of showers, no dark dreams.

Except, perhaps, in me.

But those were welcome, waking dreams; they never haunted my sleep.

Though *Psycho* the movie was an introduction to new worlds of imagination to me, *Psycho* the novel introduced me to the written words of Robert Bloch. I was gleefully astonished by the playfulness of his dark fantasies, and devoured everything I could find with his name on it. Bloch, Bradbury, and Matheson were the literary lights of my life, and it all began with that night at the drive-in.

Perhaps it was a silent need I had to vacation from the gradual deterioration of my parents' marriage, or a need to make a sensate connection to the most primal fears imaginable—without the pain—that made horror and fantasy such a welcome visitor to my own imagination. But I loved it, needed it, devoured it. Bloch's literary voice, in particular, lent such joy to his world of Rippers and madmen, such a *joie de morte* that I felt I was getting letters from a twisted friend.

Later, I was delighted by interviews with him in *Famous Monsters,* where he would trade god-awful puns with Forrest J Ackerman. I loved to see mugging shots of this gnomelike bloodletter leering up from the cheap newsprint.

Bloch and his brethren felt like very special friends to me; mine was not a very social childhood, and absolutely *no one* I knew cared a whit for the monsters and madmen that littered my festering young mind. The intelligence of his writing was an inspiration.

Who knew that—some decades later—I would have the opportunity to play with Bloch's own football, that fate would toss me the opportunity to direct a film based on those very characters that incited my dark dreams to begin with?

The film *Psycho IV: The Beginning* was an inexpensive prequel/sequel to the Hitchcock classic, written by Joseph Stefano, who, in addition to creating and producing *The Outer Limits* for television, had written the adaptation of Bloch's novel for Hitchcock. I don't know what Bloch thought of our film, but suspect that he didn't like it—if he ever even *saw* it. He was not involved in its creation, probably resented that it came from Stefano; word is that there was some mutual resentment between the two men.

But one hopes he knew how much respect there was for the original novel. Our executive producer, Hilton Green, was Hitchcock's assistant director on the original film; Perkins returned as the adult Norman Bates

(Henry Thomas played him in his youth); many of the original film's sets and props were used. Throughout the planning and making of the film, the byword was respect for the original. And that went beyond the original film. In the beginning, there was the word, and that word was by Bloch.

Though I met him once—briefly—I never knew Robert Bloch. But we had a rich, one-sided relationship that started with a date at the drive-in.

WILLIAM PETER BLATTY

W hen I was a high school freshman in Brooklyn, one of the happiest and most inspiring hours I ever spent found me reading a Robert Bloch short story aloud to a classmate over the phone. This gem had appeared in *Fear,* a pulp magazine to which I was addicted, along with *The Shadow* and *Doc Savage,* and was wryly entitled "A Good Knight's Work." But what was it doing in the pages of *Fear?* Breezily written and Runyonesque, it wasn't meant to be scary at all, it was *funny,* and the moment I finished it I felt I had to share it. And that's what started my career as a writer: I wanted to do *that*—to make people laugh by telling a story. Many years and comic novels and screenplays later, I read *Psycho,* the lord and inspiration of modern fright novels, and I instantly decided that I wanted to do *that.*

God knows, I tried.

And so for the laughter and the goose bumps and for the inspiration for both, I am forever indebted to Robert Bloch. For the first time in fifty years I have just reread "A Good Knight's Work." I still love it.

Thanks again, Bob. Thanks.

A GOOD KNIGHT'S WORK

I am stepping on the gas, air is pouring into the truck and curses are pouring out, because I feel like I get up on the wrong side of the gutter this morning.

Back in the old days I am always informing the mob how I am going to get away from it all and buy a little farm in the country and raise chickens. So now I raise chickens and wish I am back in the old days raising hell.

It is one of those things, and today it is maybe two or three of them, in spades. Perhaps you are lucky and do not live in the Corn Belt, so I will mention a few items to show that the guy naming it knows what he's talking about.

This morning I wake up at four A.M. because fifty thousand sparrows are holding a Communist rally under the window. I knock my shins over a wheelbarrow in the back yard because the plumbing is remote. When I get dressed I have to play tag with fifty chickens I am taking to market, and by the time that's over I am covered with more feathers than a senator who gets adopted by Indians in a newsreel. After which all I do is load the cacklers on the truck, drive fifty miles to town, sell biddies at a loss, and drive back—strictly without breakfast.

Breakfast I must catch down the road at the tavern, where I got to pay ten bucks to Thin Tommy Malloon for protection.

That is my set-up and explains why I am not exactly bubbling over with good spirits. There is nothing to do about it but keep a stiff upper lip—mostly around the bottle I carry with me on the trip back.

Well, I am almost feeling better after a few quick ones, and am just about ready to stop my moans and groans when I spot this sign on the road.

I don't know how it is with you. But this is how it is with me. I do not like signs on the road a bit, and of all the signs I do not like, the SIAMESE SHAVE signs I hate in spades.

They stand along the highway in series, and each of them has a line of poetry on it so when you pass them all you read a little poem about SIAMESE SHAVE. They are like the Old Lady Goose rhymes they feed the juveniles, and I do not have any love for Ma Goose and her poetry.

Anyhow, when I see this first sign I let out some steam and take another nip. But I cannot resist reading the sign because I always do. It says:

DON'T WEAR A LONG BEARD

And a little further on the second one reads:

LIKE A GOAT

Pretty soon I come to the third one, saying:

JUST TAKE A RAZOR

And all at once I'm happy, hoping maybe somebody made a mistake and the fourth sign will say:

AND CUT YOUR THROAT!

So I can hardly wait to see the last one, and I'm looking ahead on the road, squinting hard. Then I slam on the brakes.

No, I don't see a sign. There is a *thing* blocking the road, instead. *Two* things.

One of these things is a horse. At least, it looks more like a horse than anything else I can see on four drinks. It is a horse covered with a kind of awning, or tent, that hangs down over its legs and out on its neck. In fact, I notice that this horse is wearing a mask over its head with eyeholes, like it belongs to the Ku Klux Klan.

The other *thing* is riding the horse. It is all silver, from head to foot, and there is a long plume growing out of its head. It looks like a man, and it has a long sharp pole in one hand and the top off a garbage can in the other.

Now when I look at this party I am certain of only one thing. This is not the Lone Ranger.

When I drive a little closer my baby-blue eyes tell me that what I am staring at is a man dressed up in a suit of armor, and that the long, sharp pole is a little thing like a twelve-foot spear with a razor on the end.

Who he is and why he is dressed up this way may be very interesting to certain parties like the State police, but I am very far away from being one. Also I am very far away from Thin Tommy Malloon who is waiting for my ten bucks protection money.

So when I see Old Ironsides blocking the road, I place my head outside the window and request, "Get the hell out of the way, buddy!" in a loud but polite voice.

Which turns out to be a mistake, in spades and no trump.

The party in the tin tuxedo just looks at the truck coming his way, and cocks his iron head when he sees steam coming from the radiator. The exhaust is beginning to make trombone noises, because I am stepping hard on the gas, and this seems to make up the heavy dresser's mind for him.

"Yoiks!" howls his voice behind his helmet. "A dragon!"

And all at once he levels that lance of his, knocks his tootsies against the horse's ribs, and starts coming head-on for the truck.

"For Pendragon and England!" he bawls, over the clanking. And charges ahead like a baby tank.

That twelve-foot razor of his is pointed straight for my radiator, and I do not wish him to cut my motor, so naturally I swing the old truck out of the way.

This merely blows the radiator cap higher than the national dept, and out shoots enough steam and hot air to supply a dozen congressmen.

The horse rears up, and the tintype lets out a yap, letting his lance loose. Instead of hitting my radiator, it smashes my windshield.

Also my temper. I stop the truck and get out, fast. "Now, listen, buddy," I reason with him.

"Aha!" comes the voice from under the helmet. "A wizard!" He uses a brand of double-talk I do not soon forget. "Halt ye, for it is Pallagyn who speaks."

I am in no mood for orations, so I walk up to him, waving a pipe wrench.

"Bust my windows, eh, buddy? Monkey business on a public highway, is it? I'm going to—Yow!"

I am a personality that seldom hollers "Yow!" even at a burlesque show, but when this armor-plated jockey slides off his horse and comes for me, he is juggling a sharp six feet of sword. And six feet of sword sailing for your neck is worth a "Yow!" any day, I figure.

I also figure I had better duck unless I want a shave and a haircut, and it is lucky for me that Iron-lung has to move slow when he whams his sword down at me.

I come up under his guard and give him a rap on the old orange with my pipe wrench.

There is no result.

The steel king drops his sword and lets out another roar, and I caress his helmet again with the wrench. Still no result. I get my result on the third try. The wrench breaks.

And then his iron arms grab me, and I am in for it.

The first thing I know, everything is turning black as solitary, and my sparring partner is reaching for a shiv at his belt. I get my foot there, fast.

All I can do is push forward, but it works. About a hundred and fifty pounds of armor loses balance, and there is nothing for the guy inside to do except to go down with it. Which he does, on his back. Then I am on his chest, and I roll up the Venetian blind on the front of his helmet.

"Hold, enough!" comes the double-talk from inside. "Prithee, hold!"

"Okay, buddy. But open up that mail box of yours. I want to see the face of the jerk that tries to get me into a traffic accident with a load of tin."

He pulls up the shutters, and I get a peek at a purple face decorated with red whiskers. There are blue eyes, too, and they look down, ashamed.

"Ye are the first, O Wizard, to gaze upon the vanquished face of Sir Pallagyn of the Black Keep," he mumbles.

I get off his chest like it was the hot seat. Because, although I am very fond of nuts, I like them only in fruit cakes.

"I've got to be going," I mention. "I don't know who you are or why you are running around like this, and I maybe ought to have you run in, but I got business up the road, see? So long."

I start walking away and turn around. "Besides, my name is not O. Wizard."

"Verily," says the guy who calls himself Sir Pallagyn, getting up slow, with a lot of rattling. "Ye are a wizard, for ye ride a dragon breathing fire and steam."

I am thinking of the fire and steam Thin Tommy Malloon is breathing right now, so I pay little or no attention, but get in the truck. Then this Pallagyn comes running up and yells, "Wait!"

"What for?"

"My steed and arms are yours by right of joust."

Something clicks inside my head, and even if it is an eight ball, I get interested. "Wait a minute," I suggest. "Just who are you and where do you hang out?"

"Why," says he, "as I bespoke, O Wizard—I am Sir Pallagyn of the Black Keep, sent here ensorcelled by Merlin, from Arthur's court at Camelot. And I hang out at the greves in my armor," he adds, tucking in some cloth sticking out of the chinks and joints in his heavy suit.

"Huh?" is about the best I can do.

"And besting me in fair combat, ye gain my steed and weapons, by custom of the joust." He shakes his head, making a noise like a Tommy-gun. "Merlin will be very angry when he hears of this, I wot."

"Merlin?"

"Merlin, the Gray Wizard, who sent me upon the quest," he explains. "He it was who sped me forward in Time, to quest for the Cappadocian Tabouret."

Now I am not altogether a lug—as you can tell by the way I look up some of the spelling on these items—and when something clicks inside my noggin it means I am thinking, but difficult.

I know I am dealing with the worst kind of screwball—the kind that bounces—but still there is some sense in what he is saying. I see this King Arthur and this Merlin in a picture once, and I see also some personalities in armor that are called knights, which means they are King Arthur's trigger men. They hang out around a big table in a stone hideout and are always spoiling for trouble and going off on quests—which means putting the goniff on stuff which doesn't belong to them, or copping dames from other knights.

But I figures all this happens maybe a hundred years ago, or so, over in Europe, before they throw away their armor and change into colored shirts to put the rackets on an organized paying basis.

And this line about going forward in Time to find something is practically impossible, unless you go for Einstein's theory, which I don't, preferring Jane Fonda.

Still, it is you might say unusual, so I answer this squirrel. "What you're trying to tell me is that you come here from King Arthur's court and some magician sends you to find something?"

"Verily, O Wizard. Merlin counseled me that I might not be believed," says Pallagyn, sadlike. He chews on his mustache, without butter. He almost looks like he is promoting a weeper.

"I believe you, buddy," I say, wanting to cheer him up and also get out of here.

"Then take my mount and weapons—it is required by law of the joust," he insists.

Right then I figure I would rather take a drink. I do. It makes me feel better. I get out and walk over to the oat burner. "I don't know what to do with this four-legged glue barrel," I tell him, "or your manicure set, either. But if it makes you happy, I will take them with me."

So I grab the nag and take him around back of the truck, let down the ramp and put him in. When I get back, Sir Pallagyn is piling his steel polo set into the front seat.

"I place these on the dragon for thee," he says.

"This isn't a dragon," I explain. "It's a Ford."

"Ford? Merlin did not speak of that creature." He climbs into the seat after his cutlery, looking afraid the steering wheel will bite him.

"Hey, where you going?"

"With thee, O Wizard. The steed and weapons are thine, but I must follow them, even into captivity. It is the law of the quest."

"You got laws on the brain, that's your trouble. Now listen, I don't like hitch-hikers—"

Then I gander at my ticker and see it is almost ten and remember I am to meet Thin Tommy at eight. So I figure, why not? I will give this number a short lift down the pike and dump him where it is quiet and forget him. Maybe I can also find out whether or not there is somebody missing from Baycrest, which is the local laughing academy, and turn him in. Anyway, I have my date to keep, so I start the truck rolling.

This Pallagyn lets out a sort of whistle through his whiskers when I hit it up, so I say, "What's the matter, buddy, are you thirsty?"

"No," he gasps. "But we are flying!"

"Only doing fifty," I tell him. "Look at the speedometer."

"Fifty what? Speedometer?"

My noggin is clicking like a slot machine in a church bazaar. This baby isn't faking! I get another look at his armor and see it is solid stuff—not like fancy-dress costumes, but real heavy, with little designs in gold and silver running through it. And he doesn't know what a car is, or a speedometer!

"You need a drink," I say, taking it for him, and then passing him the bottle.

"Mead?" he says.

"No, Haig & Haig. Try a slug."

He tilts the bottle and takes a terrific triple-tongue. He lets out a roar and turns redder than his whiskers.

"I am bewitched!" he yells. "Ye black wizard!"

"Hold it. You'll cool off in a minute. Besides, I'm not a wizard. I'm a truck farmer, believe it or not, and don't let them kid you down at the Bastille. I'm through with the rackets."

He gets quieter in a minute and begins to ask me questions. Before I know it,

I am explaining who I am and what I am doing, and after another drink it doesn't seem so screwy to me any more.

Even when he tells me about this Merlin cat putting a spell on him and sending him through Time to go on a quest, I swallow it like my last shot. I break down and tell him to call me Butch. In a few minutes we're practically cell mates.

"Ye may call me Pallagyn," he says.

"O.K., Pal. How about another slug?"

This time he is more cautious, and it must go down fairly well, because he smacks his lips and doesn't even turn pink.

"Might I inquire as to your destination, O Butch?" he lets out after a minute or so.

"You might," I say. "There it is, straight ahead."

I point out the building we are just coming to. It is a roadhouse and tavern called "The Blunder Inn," and it is in this rat hole that Thin Tommy Malloon hangs his hat and holster. This I explain to Pal.

"It doth not resemble a rat hole," he comments.

"Any place where Thin Tommy gets in must be a rat hole," I tell him, "because Thin Tommy is a rat. He is a wrongo but strongo. Nevertheless, I must now go in and pay him his ten dollars for protection or he will sprinkle lye on my alfalfa."

"What do you mean?" asks Pallagyn.

"Yes, Pal. I have a little farm, and I must pay Thin Tommy ten a week or else I will have trouble, such as finding ground glass in my hen mash, or a pineapple in my silo."

"Ye pay to keep vandals from despoiling the crops?" asks the knight. "Would it not be expedient to discover the miscreants and punish them?"

"I *know* who would wreck the farm if I didn't pay," I reply. "Thin Tommy."

"Ah, now methinks I comprehend thy plight. Thou art a serf, and this Thin Thomas is thy overlord."

Somehow this remark, and the way Pallagyn says it, seems to show me up for a sucker. And I have just enough drink in me to resent it.

"I am no serf," I shout. "As a matter of fact, I am waiting a long time to fix the clock of this Thin Tommy. So today I pay him no ten dollars, and I am going in to tell him so to what he calls his face."

Pallagyn listens to me kind of close, because he seems pretty ignorant on English and grammar, but he catches on and smiles.

"Spoken like a right true knight," he says. "I shall accompany ye on this mission, for I find in my heart a liking for thy steadfast purpose, and a hatred of Thin Thomas."

"Sit where you are," I says, fast. "I will handle this myself. Because Thin Thomas does not like strangers coming into his joint in the daytime without an invitation, and you are dressed kind of loud and conspicuous. So you stay here," I tell him, "and have a drink."

And I pull up and climb out of the car and march into the tavern fast.

My heart is going fast also, because what I am about to do is enough to make any heart go fast in case Thin Tommy gets an idea to stop it from beating altogether. Which he sometimes does when he is irked, particularly over money.

Even so I walk up to the bar and sure enough, there is Thin Tommy standing there polishing the glasses with boxing gloves on. Only when I look again I realize these are not boxing gloves at all, but merely Thin Tommy's hands.

Thin Tommy is not really thin, you understand, but is called that because he weighs about three hundred fifty pounds—stripped—such as once a month, when he takes a bath.

"So, it's you!" he says, in a voice like a warden.

"Hello, Thin Tommy," I greet him. "How are tricks."

"I will show you how tricks are if you do not cough up those ten berries fast and furious," grunts Thin Tommy. "All of the others have been here two or three hours ago, and I am waiting to go to the bank."

"Go right ahead," I tell him. "I wouldn't stop you."

Thin Tommy drops the glass he is polishing and leans over the bar. "Hand it over," he says through his teeth. They are big yellow teeth, all put together in not such a pleasant grin.

I grin right back at him because how can he see my knees shaking?

"I have nothing for you, Tommy," I get out. "In fact, that is why I am here, to tell you that from now on I do not require protection any longer."

"Ha!" yells Thin Tommy, pounding on the bar and then jumping around it with great speed for a man of his weight. "Bertram!" he calls. "Roscoe!"

Bertram and Roscoe are Tommy's two waiters, but I know Tommy is not calling them in to serve me.

They come running out of the back, and I see they have experience in such matters before, because Bertram is carrying a blackjack, and Roscoe has a little knife in his hand. The knife worries me most, because I am practically certain that Roscoe is never a Boy Scout.

By the time I see all this, Thin Tommy is almost on top of me, and he lets go with one arm for my jaw. I bend my head down just in time, but Thin Tommy's other hand catches me from the side and slaps me across the room. I fall over a chair, and by this time Bertram and Roscoe are ready to wait on me. In fact, one of them pulls out the chair I fell over, and tries to hit me on the head with it.

I let out a yell and grab up a salt cellar from the table. This I push down Bertram's mouth, and I am just ready to throw a little pepper in Roscoe's eyes when Thin Tommy crashes over, grabs the knife from Roscoe's hand, and backs me into the corner.

All at once I hear a crash outside the door, and somebody hollers, "Yoiks! Pendragon and Pallagyn!"

Into the room gallops Sir Pallagyn. He has got his sword in one hand, and the empty bottle in the other, and he is full to the eyeballs with courage.

He lets the bottle go first and it catches Bertram in the side of the head, just when he is getting the salt cellar out of his mouth. Bertram slides down with a sort of moan, and Roscoe and Tommy turn around.

"It's one of them there rowboats, like in science fiction!" remarks Thin Tommy.

"Yeah," says Roscoe, who is all at once very busy when Pallagyn comes for him with his sword. In fact Roscoe is so busy he falls over the chair and lands on his face, which gets caught in a cuspidor. Pallagyn is ready to whack him one when Thin Tommy drops hold of me and lets out a grunt.

He grabs up the blackjack and the dagger both in the same hand and lets fly. They bounce off Pallagyn's helmet, of course, so Thin Tommy tries a chair. This doesn't work, either, so he picks up the table.

Pallagyn just turns kind of surprised and starts coming for him. And Thin Tommy backs away.

"No . . . no—" he says. All at once he reaches into his hip pocket and pulls out the old lead poisoner.

"Watch out!" I yell, trying to get to Tommy before he can shoot. "Duck, Pal—duck!"

Pallagyn ducks, but he is still running forward and his armor is so heavy he can't stop if he wants to keep from falling over.

The gun goes off over his head, but then Sir Pallagyn is going on, and he runs right into Thin Tommy, butting his head into his stomach. Thin Tommy just gives one "Ooooof!" and sits down backward, holding his belly where the helmet hits it, and he turns very green indeed.

Pallagyn sticks out sword, but I say, "Never mind. This ought to teach him a lesson."

Going out, Thin Tommy just manages to whisper to me, "Who's that guy?"

"That," I tell him, "is my new hired man. So if I was you, I wouldn't plant any pineapples on my farm, because he is allergic to fruit."

So we leave and climb back into the truck.

"Thanks, Pal," I say. "You not only throw a scare into that monkey but you also save my life. I am in debt to you, whoever you are, and if Thin Tommy doesn't serve such rotgut, I would take you back in and buy you a drink."

"Verily, 'tis a trifle," says Pallagyn.

"I'll do you the same some day, Pal," I tell him. "You are my buddy."

"Ye could help me now, methinks."

"How?"

"Why, in pursuit of my quest. I was sent here by Merlin to seek the Cappadocian Tabouret."

"I do not know anything about the new night clubs," I tell him. "I am not an uptown boy any longer."

"The Cappadocian Tabouret," says Pallagyn, ignoring me, "is the table on which the Holy Grail will rest, once we find it."

"Holy Grail?"

So Pallagyn begins to tell me a long yarn about how he is living in a castle with this King Arthur and a hundred other triggers who are all knights like he is. As near as I get it, all they do is sit around and drink and fight each other, which makes it look like this King Arthur is not so good in controlling his mob.

The brain in this outfit is this guy Merlin, who is a very prominent old fuddy in the Magician's Union. He is always sending the lads out to rescue some dames that have been snatched, or to knock off the hoods of other mobs, but what he is really interested in is this Holy Grail.

I cannot exactly catch what the Holy Grail is, except it's kind of a loving cup or trophy that has disappeared from some hock shop back there in the Middle Ages. But everybody is hot to find it, including the big boys in the mob like Sir Galahad and Sir Lancelot.

When Pallagyn mentions these two I know I hear of them some place, so naturally I ask questions and find out quite a bit about ancient times and knights and how they live and about the tournaments—which are pretty much the same as the Rose Bowl games, without a take—and many other items which are of great interest to an amateur scholar like myself.

But to slice a long story thin, Merlin cannot put the finger on this Holy Grail yet, although he is sending out parties every day to go on these quests for it. But he is a smart cookie in many another way, and one of his little tricks is to get himself high and then look into the future. For example, he tells King Arthur that he is going to have trouble some time ahead, and Pallagyn says he may be right, because he personally notices that this Sir Lancelot is making pigeon noises at Arthur's bird. But gossip aside, one of the things Merlin sees in the future is this Cappadocian Tabouret, which is a sacred relic on which the Holy Grail is supposed to sit.

So the old hophead calls in Sir Pallagyn and says he is sending him on a quest for the glory of Britain, to get this table for the Holy Grail and bring it back.

All Merlin can do to help him is put a spell on him and send him into the future to the time where he sees the Tabouret.

And he tells him a little about these times and this country, sprinkles a little powder on him, and all at once Pallagyn is sitting on his horse in the middle of County Truck AA, where I find him.

"That is not exactly the easiest story in the world to believe," I remark, when Pallagyn finishes.

"Here I am," says the knight, which is about as good an answer as any.

For a minute I think I can understand how he must feel, being shipped off through Time into a new territory, without even a road map to help him. And since he is a good guy and saves my life, I figure the least I can do is try.

"Doesn't this old junkie give you a hint where it might be?" I ask.

"Merlin? Forsooth, he spoke of seeing it in a House of the Past."

"What kind of house?"

"House of the Past, methinks he named it."

"Never hear of it," I says, "unless he means a funeral parlor. And you don't catch me going into any stiff hotel."

I say this as we are driving into my yard, and I stop the truck.

"Let's grab a plate of lunch," I suggest. "Maybe we can think of something."

"Lunch?"

"Scoff. Bread."

"Here?"

"Yeah. This is my pad—house."

I salvage Pallagyn out of the car and take him inside. Then, while I fix the food, he sits there in the kitchen and asks me a thousand screwy questions. He is very ignorant about everything.

It turns out that back in his times, there is not enough civilization to put in your ear. He doesn't know what a stove is, or gas, and I can see why they call them the Dark Ages when he tells me he never sees an electric light.

So I tell him everything, about cars and trains and airplanes and tractors and steamships, and then I break down and give him a few tips on how citizens live.

I hand it to him about the mobs and the rackets and the fuzz, and politics and elections. Then I give him a few tips about science—machine guns and armored cars and tear gas and pineapples and fingerprints—all the latest stuff.

It is very hard to explain these matters to such an ignorant guy as this Pallagyn, but he is so grateful that I want to give it to him straight.

I even show him how to eat with a knife and fork, as it turns out at lunch that King Arthur's court doesn't go in for fancy table manners.

But I am not a schoolteacher, and after all, we are not getting any closer to Sir Pallagyn's problem, which is snatching this Tabouret in his quest.

So I begin asking him all over again about what it is and what it looks like and where this fink Merlin said to find it.

And all he manages to come clean with is that it's in the House of the Past, and that Merlin sees it in a jag.

"Big place," he says. "And the Tabouret is guarded by men in blue."

"Police station?" I wonder.

"It is in a transparent coffin," he says.

I never see any of these, though I hear Stinky Raffelano is in one after he catches his slugs last year.

"Ye can see but cannot touch it," he remembers.

All at once I get it.

"It's under glass," I tell him. "In a museum."

"Glass?"

"Never mind what that is," I say. "Sure—guards. House of the Past. It's in a museum in town."

I tell him what a museum is, and then start thinking.

"First thing to do is get a line on where it is. Then we can figure out how to pull the snatch."

"Snatch?"

"Steal it, Pal. Say—do you know what it looks like?"

"Verily. Merlin described it in utmost detail, lest I err and procure a spurious Tabouret."

"Good. Give me a line on it, will you?"

"Why, it is but a wooden tray of rough boards, with four short legs set at the corners. Brown it is in hue, and it spans scarce four hands in height. Plain it is, without decoration or adornment, for it was but crudely fashioned by the good Cappadocian Fathers."

"So," I say. "I think maybe I have a notion. Wait here," I tell him, "and improve your education."

And I hand him a copy of a girlie magazine. I go down to the cellar, and when I come up after a while, Sir Pallagyn comes clanking up to me, all excited.

"Pray, and who is this fair damsel?" he asks, pointing out a shot of a broad in a bikini. "She has verily the appearance of the Lady of the Lake," he remarks. "Albeit with more . . . more—"

"You said it, Pal," I agree. "Much more, in spades. But here—does this look like the table you're after?"

"Od's blood, it is the very thing! From whence didst thou procure it?"

"Why, it's nothing but a piece of old furniture I find laying down in the basement. A footstool, but I knock the stuffing out of it and scrape off some varnish. Now, all you got to do is get this Merlin to wave his wand and call you back, and you hand him over the goods. He will never catch wise," I say, "and it will save us a lot of trouble."

Pallagyn's puss falls in a little and he starts chewing his red mustache again.

"I fear, Sir Butch, thy ethics are not of the highest. I am aquest, nor could I present a spurious Tabouret in sight of mine own conscience."

So I see I am in for it. Of course it will be easy for me to tell this tin can to go chase his quest, but somehow I feel I owe him a good turn.

"I will work things out in a jiffy, Pal. You just go out and put your nag in the stable, and when you come back, I will have things set."

"On thy honor?" he says, smiling all of a sudden.

"Sure. Shake."

He shakes until his armor rattles.

"Never mind," I say. "Take care of the nag and leave it to me."

He clunks out and I get busy on the phone.

When he comes back I am ready.

"Come on out and hop in the truck," I invite. "We are on our way to pick up that furniture for you."

"Indeed? Then we really quest together, Sir Butch?"

"Don't ask any questions," I remark. "On your way."

I notice he fumbles with that magazine a minute, and when he sees me looking he blushes.

"I wouldst carry the image of this fair lady, as is the custom of the quest," he admits, tucking the picture of the broad in his helmet, so only her legs stick out over his forehead.

"Okay by me, Pal. But come on, we got a drive ahead of us."

I grab up a pint, the fake Tabouret, and a glass cutter, head for the truck, and we're off.

It is a long drive, and I have plenty of time to explain the lay of the land to Sir Pallagyn. I tell him how I call the museum and find out if they have this table in hock. Then I hang up and call back in a different voice, telling them that I am an express man with a suit of armor on hand for them which I will send over.

"Pretty neat, hey, Pal?" I ask.

"But I do not comprehend. How did you talk to the museum if it is in the city and—"

"I am a wizard myself," I let it go.

"Still, I fail to perceive the plan. What place has armor in a House of the Past?"

"Why, it's a relic. Don't you know nobody wears armor no more? It's all bulletproof vests."

"Still, how doth that contrive for us to—snatch—the Tabouret?"

"Don't you get it? I'll carry you into the museum like an empty suit of armor. Then we will spot this Tabouret. I will set you down in a corner, and when the joint closes up you can snatch it very quick indeed. You can use this glass cutter to get it out, substitute this fake furniture in the case, and nobody will be hep to it the next morning. Simple."

"By're Lady, 'tis a marvel of cunning!"

I admit it sounds groovy myself. But I notice we are now coming into some traffic, so I stop the truck and say, "From now on you are just a suit of armor with nothing inside. You climb into the back of the truck so citizens will not give you the queer eye, and lie quiet. When we get to the museum I will drag you out, and you just hold still. Remember?"

"Verily."

So Pallagyn hops into the back of the truck and lies down and I head into the city. Before I get too far I take myself a couple of quick ones because I am a little nervous, being so long since I pull a job.

I am not exactly floating but my feet do not touch bottom when we get downtown. Which is why I accidentally touch a fender of the car ahead of me when we stop in traffic. In fact I touch it so it drops off.

It is a big black Rolls, and an old Whitey with a mean-looking puss opens the door and leans out and says:

"Here now, you ruffian!"

"Who are you calling a ruffian, you bottle-nosed old baboon?" I answer, hoping to pass it off quiet.

"Aaaaargh!" says Whitey, climbing out of his buggy. "Come along, Jefferson, and help me deal with this hoodlum."

It is funny he should call me such when I feel sure he never sets peepers on me before in his life, but then it is a small world. And the chauffeur that hauls out after him is much too big to be running around in a small world. He is not only big but mean-looking, and he comes marching right at me along with old Whitey.

"Why don't you go away and soak your feet?" I suggest, still wanting to be diplomatic and avoid trouble. But Whitey does not go for my good advice.

"Let me have your license," he growls. "I am going to do something about reckless drivers that smash into cars."

"Yeah," says the big chauffeur, sticking his red face into the window. "Maybe this fellow would slow down a little if he was driving with a couple of black eyes."

"Now wait a minute," I suggest. "I am very sorry if I bump into you and lose my temper, but I am on my way to the museum in a hurry with a rush order. If you look in the back of the truck, you will see a suit of armor I am delivering there."

As it turns out this is not such a hot suggestion at that. Because when I see Whitey and the chauffeur marching at me I have the presence of mind to toss the whiskey bottle in the back of the truck. And now Sir Pallagyn has got a gander at it, so when Whitey hangs his nose over the side, there is Pal, taking a snifter.

When he sees the old guy coming he stops still with his arm in the air, snapping his visor shut with the bottle in his mouth.

"Here, what's this?" snaps Whitey.

"Huh?"

"What's that bottle doing stuck in the visor of this helmet? And what's making the arm hold on to it?"

"I don't know, mister. That's how I find it when I unpack it this morning."

"Something wrong," insists old Whitey. "They didn't drink whiskey way back then."

"It's pretty old whiskey," I tell him.

"I'll vouch for that," he says, real nasty, "if your breath is an indication. I think you ought to be run in for drunken driving."

"Say," pipes up Jefferson, the big chauffeur. "Maybe this guy doesn't even own the truck like he says. He might have stole this armor."

Whitey smiles like a desk sergeant. "I never thought of that. Now, sir"—and he wheels on me fast—"if you know so much about this particular bit of armor, perhaps you can tell me the name of its original wearer."

"Why . . . why . . . Sir Pallagyn of the Round Table," I stammer.

"Pallagyn? Pallagyn? Never heard of him," snaps Whitey. "He never sat at the Round Table."

"He is always under it," I say. "Quite a lush."

"Preposterous! This is all a fraud of some sort."

"Look!" Jefferson yells. "The whiskey!"

We all look around, and sure enough the whiskey is disappearing from the bottle because Pallagyn is gargling it down very quiet.

"Fraud!" says Whitey, again, and taps the helmet with his cane.

"Come on, where did you steal this from?" growls Jefferson, grabbing me by the collar. And Whitey keeps hitting the helmet.

"Desist, by blessed St. George!" roars Pallagyn, sitting up. "Desist, ere I let air through thy weasand, thou aged conskiter!"

Whitey stands there with the cane in the air and his mouth is open wide enough to hang a canary in. Pal sees the cane and grabs for his sword.

"A joust, is it?" he yells.

And all around us the citizens are honking their horns and staring out, but when they see Pallagyn standing up and waving his pocketknife they drive away very fast.

"Robot!" mumbles Whitey.

"Rodent, am I?" and Pallagyn begins to slice away at Whitey's breadbasket.

"Hey!" yells the chauffeur, dropping me. "Cut that!" He makes a dive for the knight, but he sees him climbing up into the truck and bobs him with the whiskey bottle. The big guy falls down and sits still. Whitey dances around for a minute and then runs for his car.

"I am a trustee of the museum," he bawls. "And whatever that thing is, it isn't going on display. Witchcraft—that's what it is!"

Now this is a fine time for the fuzz to show up, but when he does I quick-motion to Pal to hold still and grab the copper by the collar.

"This guy and his chauffeur back into me," I say. "And if you smell the chauffeur you see he is drunk; as a matter of fact he is out. That old bird is also a lush, but me," and I step on the gas, "I am in a hurry to deliver this armor to a museum, and I do not wish to press charges."

"Hey—" says the beat daddy, but I pull away fast. I am around the corner before he has time to cry "Wolf!" and I take it up several alleys.

Meanwhile I bawl out Pallagyn in all suits.

"From now on," I tell him, "you don't make a move, no matter what happens. Understand?"

"Hic," says Pallagyn.

"The only way I can get you into the museum is for you to be quiet and lay limp," I say.

"Hic."

"Here we are," I tell him, pulling up in back of the big gray building, into the loading zone.

"Hic."

"Shut your trap," I snarl.

Pallagyn pulls down his visor.

"No, wait." He is still hiccuping, so I yank his plume off and stuff it into his mouth.

"Now, be quiet and leave it to me," I say. I get the table under one arm and slip the glass cutter into one pocket. Then I open the back of the truck and slide Pallagyn down the ramp to the ground.

"Ugh! Oooof!" he groans, under his helmet.

"Sh! Here we go!"

It is not so easy to drag Pallagyn along by the arms, but I manage to hoist him up the platform and get him past the door. There is a guard standing there.

"New armor," I tell him. "Where is your hardware department?"

"Funny. Nobody told me to expect a delivery. Oh, well, I'll let you set it up. Dr. Peabody will probably arrange to place it tomorrow."

He looks at me, all red in the puss, trying to drag Pallagyn along.

"Funny it should be so weighty. I thought armor was light."

"This baby is wearing heavy underwear," I tell him. "How about giving me a hand?"

He helps lift Pallagyn and we carry him through a lot of halls into a big room.

There are a lot of suits of armor standing around the walls, and several are hanging on wires from the ceiling, but I see something else and let out a snort.

Sure enough, in the center of the room is a glass case, and inside it is standing a little table just like the one I have under my arm.

I set the thing down and the guard notices it for the first time.

"What you got here?" he asks.

"The armor is supposed to stand on it," I explain. "It comes with the set."

"Oh. Well, just stand it up against the wall. I got to get back to the door."

And he goes away. I take a quick gander up and down and see the place is empty. It is getting dark and I figure it is closing time already.

"Here we are," I whisper.

"*Hic*," says Pallagyn.

He opens his visor and takes a look at the Tabouret.

"Verily, it is that for which I seek," he whispers. "My thanks, a thousandfold."

"Forget it. Now all you got to do is wait till it gets a little darker, then make the snatch."

I go up to the case and tap it.

"Why," I say, "this is real luck. It opens from the back and you don't even have to use the glass cutter."

But Pallagyn is not paying any attention. He is looking around at the armor on the walls.

"Gawain!" he snorts.

"What?"

" 'Tis the veritable armor of Sir Gawain!" he yaps. "One of the Brotherhood of the Round Table."

"You don't say!"

"Aye—and yonder stands the coat of mail of Sir Sagramore! Indeed! I recognize the main of Elderford, he that is cousin to Sir Kay. And Maligaint—"

He is rattling off the names of old friends, clanking around and tapping the tin, but it all looks like a bunch of spare parts in a hot car hide-out to me.

"I am among friends," he chuckles.

"Yeah? Don't be too sure. If these museum babies ever find out what you're up to, it's good-bye quest. Now get to work, quick. I got to be going back." I push him over to the case. "I'll watch the door for you in case anyone is coming," I whisper. "You switch the Tabourets. Snap to it."

So I stand there, and Pallagyn makes for the case, trying not to clank too loud. It is dark and quiet, and creepy.

Pallagyn gets the case open in no time, but he has trouble in hauling out the Tabouret, because it has nails holding it down.

He is grunting and yanking on it and I am shaking because he is maybe going to rouse a guard.

"I cannot say much for this guy Merlin," I comment. "He is supposed to help you knights over the hard spots, but I do not notice he has done you a good turn yet."

"Nay, I have thee to thank for my success," Pallagyn says. "For, lo, my quest is ended!"

And he rips the Tabouret loose and slides the other one in. Then he closes the glass again and marches over across the room.

Only right in the middle of it he lets out a squawk and falls down on the stone floor when his foot slips.

There is a loud crash like all hell is breaking loose.

It does.

Guys are yelling down the hall and I hear feet running this way. I get over to Pallagyn and help him up, but just as I am easing him onto his feet a squad of guards charges into the room and the heat is very much on.

"Stop, thief!" yells the guy in the lead, and the whole gang charges down on us. Pallagyn is trying to stand still again and I am yanking open a window, but when he sees them coming, Pal lets out a whoop and drops the Tabouret, waving his sword around.

"Stand back ere I skewer thy livers!" he howls. Then he turns to me. "Make haste, Sir Butch, and effect thy escape whilst I hold off yon varlets."

"Give me that," I say, grabbing at the sword. "I'll hold them off and you get out of her and gallop back to your Merlin with the Bingo prize."

"There he is, men!" yells a new voice. Coming through the door is none other than Old Whitey in person, and behind him are about eight cops. Then the cops are ahead of him, because they are coming for us, fast. A fat sergeant has his gun extremely out.

"Pendragon and England!" yells Pallagyn, patting the first cop on his bald spot with the flat side of his sword.

"Hell and Damnation!" bawls the sergeant. He lets go of a slug, which bounces off Pallagyn's helmet.

"Superman!" hollers another cop.

"Get him, boys!" screams Whitey.

It is a picnic without ants. I plant one on the sergeant's neck, and Pal wades in with his sword. But the other six push us back into a corner, and the guards come up behind them. As fast as we knock them down, the others close in. They swarm over us like a gang of Airedales on a garbage heap.

"Here we go," I gasp out, punching away.

"Be of good . . . uh . . . heart!" roars Pallagyn. He slices away. All at once he slips and the sword falls. And two coppers jump him before he can get up. The sergeant gets his gun out again and points it at me.

"Now then—" he says. The boys grab us and push us forward.

All at once Pallagyn closes his eyes. "Merlin!" he whispers. "Aid!"

Something very unusual happens here. The first thing I notice is a lot of clanking and scraping coming from the dark corners of the room.

And then there is more noise, like Pallagyn's armor makes, only louder.

"For Arthur and England!" Pallagyn yells. "Gawain, Sagramore, Eldevord, Maligaint!—"

"Aye, we come!"

Out of the dark crashes a half dozen suits of armor; but there are men in them now. It is the armor from the walls, and I see Pallagyn's gang is here.

"Merlin sends help!" he grunts. And then he grabs his sword and wades in.

The others are whacking up the cops already, and there is a smashing of tinware. Some of the fuzz are running and the guards make for the door. As fast as they get there, the suits of armor hanging on the walls drop down on their necks and throw them.

In a minute it is all through.

Pallagyn stands in the center of the room holding the Tabouret and all the guys in armor huddle around him.

"The quest is over," he says. "Thanks to Merlin, and Sir Butch, here—"

But I am not here any more. I am sneaking out of the window, fast, because I have enough trouble and do not like to get mixed up in hocus-pocus or magician's unions. So I do not stay, but drop over the ledge.

Before I do so I think I see a flash of lightning or something, but cannot be sure. Anyway, I look around once more and see the museum room is empty. There are a lot of cops lying on the floor and a lot of empty suits of armor are standing around, but there is nothing in them. I look for Pallagyn's suit and it is gone. So I blink my eyes and head for the truck, which I drive the hell away from there.

That is how it is, and I do a lot of thinking on my way home. Also the air helps to sober me up and I remember that I am practically drunk all the time since morning.

In fact, I am drunk since before I meet this Pallagyn if I ever do meet him and it is not imagination.

Because when I look back in the museum I do not see him any more and I wonder if it is all something I dream up out of air and alcohol. It bothers me, and I know that whatever happens at the museum will not leak out in print, because cops are touchy about such matters and as far as they know nothing is missing.

Then I figure maybe Thin Tommy Malloon can tell me if I drop in, so on the way home I park the truck at his tavern and step inside.

Nobody is behind the bar but Bertram, and when he sees me he is very polite.

"I would like to speak with Thin Tommy," I say.

Bertram gulps. "He is upstairs lying down," he says. "In fact, he does not feel so well since you bop him in the belly this morning."

"What do you mean I bop him?" I ask. "My buddy does that."

"You come in alone," Bertram tells me. He gives me a long look, but there are customers in the joint so I just shrug and walk out.

So the rest of the way home I am up tight, because I figure either Bertram is lying to me or I am nuts. And right now I would just as soon be a little nuts as admit anything so screwy could happen.

Which is how it stands with me. I am sober, and I am done with chasing around for the day. If I lay off drinking shellac, I will not see any more knights in armor with dopey stories about magicians and quests. I will let bygones be bygones and be a good boy.

That suits me, so I back the truck into the garage.

And then I get out and start cursing all over again.

All at once I know for sure whether or not it all happens.

Because standing there in the garage is that dizzy nag with the mask over the head that I have Sir Pallagyn put into the stable.

Do you know anybody who wants to buy a horse, cheap? It's only twelve hundred years old.

A CHIP OFF THE OLD BLOCH

SHELDON JAFFERY

My fondness for Bob Bloch dates back to 1982 when Bob generously shared with me, a total unknown in the field of horror, information about his Arkham House books, *The Opener of the Way* and *Pleasant Dreams,* for inclusion in my first book, *Horrors and Unpleasantries.* Therefore, when Ricia Mainhardt graciously asked me to contribute a memorial to Bob and introduce a favorite story, the job was easy.

In selecting a favorite Bob Bloch story, one is tempted to safely state the obvious. No one could fault a tribute to the classic, everybody's favorite, "Yours Truly, Jack the Ripper," beyond which there is no peer in Ripperology (a coined word if ever I saw one), or "The Skull of the Marquis de Sade," or Bob's germinal venture into the psychological horror area, "One Way to Mars," a hastily written, last-minute addition to Bob's first hardcover collection, Arkham House's *The Opener of the Way.* The 1959 Hugo winner, "That Hell-Bound Train," could also be in the running. But, for my money, I favor a story which reflects Bob's innate humanity, and, by humanity, I include not only the marvelous, benevolent side of Bob Bloch, but the dark side which is present in all of us. Bob, for all his sweetness and humor, could display a temper when provoked. That temper sometimes manifested itself in a story. And that's my story.

The incident happened following DeepSouthCon in Huntsville, Alabama, in June 1987, where Bob was one of the guests of honor. The convention, that year, was sort of a mini–World Fantasy Convention, with such writers in attendance as Hugh Cave, Ramsey Campbell, Charlie Grant, Dennis Etchison, and Karl Edward Wagner. I had decided to go at the last minute, as I wanted to see Hugh and Peggy Cave and publicize the Cave collection which I had compiled and edited, *The Corpse-Maker.* The collection was scheduled to appear soon, as was Audrey Parente's biography of Cave, *Pulpman's Odyssey* (both published by Starmont House, 1988), for which Bob had written an introduction, a kindness not uncommon to him.

On Sunday, following the convention, I took a shuttle to the Huntsville airport to catch my flight to Memphis and eventually return to Cleveland on a connecting flight. Bob, as guest of honor, got VIP treatment. Lucky Bob. He was driven to the airport by two of the convention gofers in an expensive sports car as a testament to his celebrity status. In fact, he was taken by a route that would enable him to see some of the local highlights, which, in Huntsville, Alabama, was probably a burning barn. The problem was, Bob couldn't see very well, having recently suffered from severe eye problems which had incapacitated him most of the weekend. Another problem was that Bob didn't want to see the sights, even if he could see. He wanted to get home to his wife, Eleanor, who would be waiting for him at LAX when his plane arrived. Add to that the problem that the sightseeing tour got the driver somewhat lost, so they didn't arrive at the airport until after Bob's seat to Los Angeles via Atlanta had been given away to a stand-by traveler. Fortunately, an alternate flight plan was arranged which rerouted Bob through Memphis at a cost roughly approximating the national debt. Bob was somewhat upset. One might even say that he was enraged, and it took a lot to bring that emotion out in him.

The gofers left him fuming at the gate and hightailed it away from the vicinity where Bob's colorful pejoratives had draped themselves around their shoulders and were polluting the atmosphere at a record clip. Then they saw me coming, told me what had happened, and begged me to try to ameliorate the situation, a task that would certainly be no more difficult than parting the Red Sea. What the hell, I figured, one of our boys had done it before—I'd give it my best shot.

Well, I accompanied Bob onto the plane, which was the same flight that I was taking, made sure the stewardesses gave him plenty of attention, deboarded with him in Memphis, and stayed and chatted with him until his flight boarded for Los Angeles, about a half-hour before mine left for Cleveland. There was actually no harm done, as the flight on which Bob was rerouted arrived at about the same time as the original flight, and Eleanor, who was meeting his plane at LAX, had been alerted to the change.

I wondered then if the perpetrators of that real-life fiasco would be treated rather sadistically in one of Bob's future yarns, if his mood at the airport was any indication. While in the Memphis airport, Bob told me about an incident in Paris in which he had been a victim of a pickpocket gang of gamins while attending a science fiction convention. This provided the basis for a story which had appeared in *Night Cry* in 1986 called "The Yougoslaves," in which a Faginlike character suffered irreversible damage at the hands of the protagonist, who had cause to avenge a wrong that had been done him by some street urchins. Like Bob, the victim of the outrage was not a man to fool with. That story, then, is my recommended entry as a tribute to Bob's baser instincts and, ultimately, his humanity.

THE YOUGOSLAVES

❦ *I didn't come to Paris for adventure.*

Long experience has taught me there are no Phantoms in the Opera, no bearded artists hobbling through Monmartre on stunted legs, no straw-hatted *boulevardiers* singing the praises of a funny little honey of a Mimi.

The Paris of story and song, if it ever existed, is no more. Times have changed, and even the term "Gay Paree" now evokes what in theatrical parlance is called a bad laugh.

A visitor learns to change habits accordingly, and my hotel choice was a case in point. On previous trips I'd stayed at the Crillon or the Ritz; now, after a lengthy absence, I put up at the George V.

Let me repeat, I wasn't seeking adventure. That first evening I left the hotel for a short stroll merely to satisfy my curiosity about the city.

I had already discovered that some aspects of Paris remain immutable; the French still don't seem to understand how to communicate by telephone, and they can't make a good cup of coffee. But I had no need to use the phone and no craving for coffee, so these matters didn't concern me.

Nor was I greatly surprised to discover that April in Paris—*Paris in the spring, tra-la-la-la*—is apt to be cold and damp. Warmly dressed for my little outing, I directed my footsteps to the archways of the Rue de Rivoli.

At first glance Paris by night upheld its traditions. All of the tourist attractions remained in place; the steel skeleton of the Eiffel Tower, the gaping maw of the Arch of Triumph, the spurting fountains achieving their miraculous transubstantiation of water into blood with the aid of crimson light.

But there were changes in the air—quite literally—the acrid odor of traffic fumes emanating from the exhausts of snarling sports-cars and growling motor bikes racing along to the counterpoint of police and ambulance sirens. Gershwin's tinny taxi-horns would be lost in such din; I doubt if he'd approve, and I most certainly did not.

My disapproval extended to the clothing of local pedestrians. Young Parisian males now mimicked the youths of other cities; bare-headed, leather-jacketed and blue-jeaned, they would look equally at home in Times Square or on Hollywood Boulevard. As for their female companions, this seemed to be the year when every girl in France decided to don atrociously wrinkled patent leather boots which turned shapely lower limbs into the legs of elephantiasis victims. The *chic* Parisienne had vanished, and above the traffic's tumult I fancied I could detect a sound of rumbling dismay as Napoleon turned over in his tomb.

I moved along under the arches, eyeing the lighted window-displays of expensive jewelry mingled with cheap gimcracks. At least the Paris of tourism hadn't altered; there would still be sex-shops in the Pigalle, and somewhere in the deep darkness of the Louvre the Mona Lisa smiled enigmatically at the antics of those who came to the city searching for adventure.

Again I say this was not my intention. Nonetheless, adventure sought me.

Adventure came on the run, darting out of a dark and deserted portion of the arcade just ahead, charging straight at me on a dozen legs.

It happened quickly. One moment I was alone; then suddenly and without warning, the children came. There were six of them, surrounding me like a small army—six dark-haired swarthy-skinned urchins in dirty, dishevelled garments, screeching and jabbering at me in a foreign tongue. Some of them clutched at my clothing, others jabbed me in the ribs. Encircling me they clamored for a beggar's bounty, and as I fumbled for loose change one of them thrust a folded newspaper against my chest, another grabbed and kissed my free hand, yet another grasped my shoulder and whirled me around. Deafened by the din, dazed by their instant attack, I broke free.

In seconds they scattered swiftly and silently, scampering into the shadows. As they disappeared I stood alone again, stunned and shaken. Then, as my hand rose instinctively to press against my inner breast-pocket, I realized that my wallet had disappeared too.

My first reaction was shock. To think that I, a grown man, had been robbed on the public street by a band of little ragamuffins, less than ten years old!

It was an outrage, and now I met it with rage of my own. The sheer audacity of their attack provoked anger, and the thought of the consequences fueled my fury. Losing the money in my wallet wasn't important; he who steals my purse steals trash.

But there was something else I cherished; something secret and irreplaceable. I carried it in a billfold compartment for a purpose; after completing my sightseeing jaunt I'd intended to seek another destination and make use of the other item my wallet contained.

Now it was gone, and hope vanished with it.

But not entirely. The sound of distant sirens in the night served as a strident reminder that I still had a chance. There was, I remembered, a police station near the Place de la Vendôme. The inconspicuous office was not easy to locate on the darkened street beyond an open courtyard, but I managed.

Once inside, I anticipated a conversation with an *inspecteur,* a return to the

scene of the affair in the company of sympathetic *gendarmes* who were knowledgeable concerning such offenses and alert in ferreting out the hiding-place of
my assailants.

The young lady seated behind the window in the dingy outer office listened
to my story without comment or a change of expression. Inserting forms and carbons in her typewriter, she took down a few vital statistics—my name, date of
birth, place of origin, hotel address, and a short inventory of the stolen wallet's
contents.

For reasons of my own I neglected to mention the one item which really mattered to me. I could be excused for omitting it in my excited state, and hoped to
avoid the necessity of doing so unless the *inspecteur* questioned me more closely.

But there was no interview with an *inspecteur.* And no uniformed officer appeared. Instead I was merely handed a carbon copy of the *Récépissé de Déclara-
tion;* if anything could be learned about the fate of my wallet I would be notified
at my hotel.

Scarcely ten minutes after entering the station I found myself back on the
street with nothing to show for my trouble but a buff-colored copy of the report.
Down at the very bottom, on a line identified in print as *Mode Opératoire—Préci-
sions Complémentaires,* was a typed sentence reading *"Vol commis dans la Rue par
de jeunes enfant yougoslaves."*

"Yougoslaves?"

Back at the hotel I addressed the question to an elderly night-clerk. Sleepy
eyes blinking into awareness, he nodded knowingly.

"Ah!" he said. "The gypsies!"

"Gypsies? But these were only children—"

He nodded again. "Exactly so." And then he told me the story.

Pickpockets and purse-snatchers had always been a common nuisance here,
but within the past few years their presence had escalated.

They came out of Eastern Europe, their exact origin unknown, but
"yougoslaves" or "gypsies" served as a convenient label.

Apparently they were smuggled in by skillful and enterprising adult crimi-
nals who specialized in educating children in the art of thievery, very much as
Fagin trained his youngsters in the London of Dickens' *Oliver Twist.*

But Fagin was an amateur compared to today's professors of pilfering. Their
pupils—orphans, products of broken homes, or no homes at all—were recruited
in foreign city streets, or even purchased outright from greedy, uncaring parents.
These little ones could be quite valuable; an innocent at the age of four or five became a seasoned veteran after a few years of experience, capable of bring in as
much as a hundred thousand American dollars over the course of a single year.

When I described the circumstances of my own encounter the clerk
shrugged.

"Of course. That is how they work, my friend—in gangs." Gangs, expertly
adept in spotting potential victims, artfully instructed how to operate. Their
seemingly spontaneous outcries were actually the product of long and exacting
rehearsal, their apparently impromptu movements perfected in advance. They

danced around me because they had been choreographed to do so. It was a bandits' ballet in which each one played an assigned role—to nudge, to gesture, to jab and jabber and create confusion. Even the hand-kissing was part of a master plan, and when one ragged waif thrust his folded newspaper against my chest it concealed another who ducked below and lifted my wallet. The entire performance was programmed down to the last detail.

I listened and shook my head. "Why didn't the police tell me these things? Surely they must know."

"*Oui, m'sieur.*" The clerk permitted himself a confidential wink. "But perhaps they do not care." He leaned across the desk, his voice sinking to a murmur. "Some say an arrangement has been made. The yougoslaves are skilled in identifying tourists by their dress and manner. They can recognize a foreign visitor merely by the kind of shoes he wears. One supposes a bargain has been struck because it is only the tourists who are attacked, while ordinary citizens are spared."

I frowned. "Surely others like myself must lodge complaints. One would think the police would be forced to take action."

The clerk's gesture was as eloquent as his words. "But what can they do? These yougoslaves strike quickly, without warning. They vanish before you realize what has happened, and no one knows where they go. And even if you managed to lay hands on one of them, what then? You bring this youngster to the police and tell your story, but the little ruffian has no wallet—you can be sure it was passed along immediately to another who ran off with the evidence. Also, your prisoner cannot speak or understand French, or at least pretends not to.

"So the *gendarmes* have nothing to go by but your word, and what can they do with the kid if they did have proof, when the law prohibits the arrest and jailing of children under thirteen?

"It's all part of the scheme. And if you permit me, it is a beautiful scheme, this one."

My frown told him I lacked appreciation of beauty, and he quickly leaned back to a position of safety behind the desk, his voice and manner sobering. "Missing credit cards can be reported in the morning, though I think it unlikely anyone would be foolish enough to attempt using them with a forged signature. It's the money they were after."

"I have other funds in your safe," I said.

"*Très bien.* In that case I advise you to make the best of things. Now that you know what to expect, I doubt if you will be victimized again. Just keep away from the tourist-traps and avoid using the Métro." He offered me the solace of a smile which all desk clerks reserve for complaints about stalled elevators, lost luggage, faulty electrical fixtures, or clogged plumbing.

Then, when my frown remained fixed, his smile vanished. "Please, my friend! I understand this has been a most distressing occurrence, but I trust you will chalk it up to experience. Believe me, there is no point in pursuing the matter further."

I shook my head. "If the police won't go after these children—"

"Children?" Again his voice descended to a murmur. "Perhaps I did not make myself clear. The yougoslaves are not ordinary kids. As I say, they have been trained by masters. The kind of man who is capable of buying or stealing a child and corrupting it for a life of crime is not likely to stop there. I have heard certain rumors, *m'sieur,* rumors which make a dreadful sort of sense. These kids, they are hooked on drugs. They know every manner of vice but nothing of morals, and many carry knives, even guns. Some have been taught to break and enter into homes, and if discovered, to kill. Their masters, of course, are even more dangerous when crossed. I implore you, for your own safety—forget what has happened tonight and go on your way."

"Thank you for your advice." I managed a smile and went on my way. But I did not forget.

I did not forget what had happened, nor did I forget I'd been robbed of what was most precious to me.

Retiring to my room, I placed the DO NOT DISTURB tag on the outer doorknob and after certain makeshift arrangements I sank eventually into fitful slumber.

By the following evening I was ready; ready and waiting. Paris by night is the City of Light, but it is also the city of shadows. And it was in the shadows that I waited, the shadows under the archways of the Rue de Rivoli. My dark clothing was deliberately donned to blend inconspicuously with the background; I would be unnoticed if the predators returned to seek fresh prey.

Somehow I felt convinced that they would do so. As I stood against a pillar, scanning the occasional passer-by, I challenged myself to see the hunted through the eyes of the hunters.

Who would be the next victim? That party of Japanese deserved no more than a glance of dismissal; it wasn't wise to confront a group. By the same token, those who traveled in pairs or couples would be spared. And even the lone pedestrians were safe if they were able-bodied or dressed in garments which identified them as local citizens.

What the hunters sought was someone like myself, someone wearing clothing of foreign cut, preferably elderly and obviously alone. Someone like the grey-bearded old gentleman who was approaching now, shuffling past a cluster of shops already closed for the night. He was short, slight of build, and his uncertain gait hinted at either a physical impairment or mild intoxication. A lone traveller on an otherwise-deserted stretch of street—here was the perfect target for attack.

And the attack came.

Out of the deep dark doorway to an arcade the yougoslaves danced forth, squealing and gesticulating, to suddenly surround their startled victim.

They ringed him, hands outstretched, their cries confusing, their fingers darting forth to prod and pry in rhythm with the outbursts.

I saw the pattern now, recognized the roles they played. Here was the hand-kisser, begging for bounty, here the duo tugging at each arm from the rear, here the biggest of the boys, brandishing the folded paper to thrust it against the oldster's chest while an accomplice burrowed into the gaping front of the jacket below. Just behind him the sixth and smallest of the band stood poised. The instant the wallet was snatched it would be passed to him, and while the others continued their distraction for a few moments more before scattering, he'd run off in safety.

The whole charade was brilliant in its sheer simplicity, cleverly contrived so that the poor old gentleman would never notice his loss until too late.

But I noticed—and I acted.

As the thieves closed in I stepped forward, quickly and quietly. Intent on their quarry, they were unaware of my approach. Moving up behind the youngster who waited to receive the wallet, I grasped his upraised arm in a tight grip, bending it back against his shoulderblade as I yanked him away into the shadows. He looked up and my free hand clamped across his oval mouth before he could cry out.

He tried to bite, but my fingers pressed his lips together. He tried to kick, but I twisted his bent arm and tugged him along offbalance, his feet dragging over the pavement as we moved past the shadowy archway to the curb beyond.

My rental-car was waiting there. Opening the door, I hurled him down onto the seat face-forward. Before he could turn I pulled the handcuffs from my pocket and snapped them shut over his wrists.

Locking the passenger door, I hastened around to the other side of the car and entered, sliding behind the wheel. Seconds later we were moving out into the traffic.

Hands confined behind him, my captive threshed helplessly beside me. He could scream now, and he did.

"Stop that!" I commanded. "No one can hear you with the windows closed."

After a moment he obeyed. As we turned off onto a side-street he glared up at me, panting.

"*Merde!*" he gasped.

I smiled. "So you speak French, do you?"

There was no reply. But when the car turned again, entering one of the narrow alleyways off the Rue St.-Roch, his eyes grew wary.

"Where are we going?"

"That is a question for you to answer."

"What do you mean?"

"You will be good enough to direct me to the place where I can find your friends."

"Go to hell!"

"*Au contraire.*" I smiled again. "If you do not cooperate, and quickly, I'll knock you over the head and dump your body in the Seine."

"You old bastard—you can't scare me!"

Releasing my right hand from the steering wheel I gave him a clout across the mouth, knocking him back against the seat.

"That's a sample," I told him. "Next time I won't be so gentle." Clenching my fist, I raised my arm again, and he cringed.

"Tell me!" I said.

And he did.

The blow across the mouth seemed to have loosened his tongue, for he began to answer my questions as I reversed our course and crossed over a bridge which brought us to the Left Bank.

When he told me our destination and described it, I must confess my surprise. The distance was much greater than I anticipated, and finding the place would not be easy, but I followed his directions on a mental map. Meanwhile I encouraged Bobo to speak.

That was his name—Bobo. If he had another, he claimed he did not know it, and I believed him. He was nine years old but he'd been with the gang for three of them, ever since their leader spirited him off the streets of Dubrovnik and brought him here to Paris on a long and illegal route while hidden in the back of a truck.

"Dubrovnik?" I nodded. "Then you really are a yougoslave. What about the others?"

"I don't know. They come from everywhere. Wherever he finds them."

"Your leader? What's his name?"

"We call him Le Boss."

"He taught you how to steal like this?"

"He taught us many things." Bobo gave me a sidelong glance. "Listen to me, old man—if you find him there will be big trouble. Better to let me go."

"Not until I have my wallet."

"Wallet?" His eyes widened, then narrowed, and I realized that for the first time he recognized me as last night's victim. "If you think Le Boss will give you back your money then you really are a fool."

"I'm not a fool. And I don't care about the money."

"Credit cards? Don't worry, Le Boss won't try to use them. Too risky."

"It's not the cards. There was something else. Didn't you see it?"

"I never touched your wallet. It was Pepe who took it to the van last night."

The van, I learned, was always parked just around the corner from the spot where the gang set up operations. And it was there that they fled after a robbery. Le Boss waited behind the wheel with the motor running; the stolen property was turned over to him immediately as they drove off to safer surroundings.

"So Le Boss has the wallet now," I said.

"Perhaps. Sometimes he takes the money out and throws the billfold away. But if there was more than money and cards inside as you say—" Bobo hesitated, peering up at me. "What is this thing you're looking for?"

"That is a matter I will discuss with Le Boss when I see him."

"Diamonds, maybe? You a smuggler?"

"No."

His eyes brightened and he nodded quickly. "Cocaine? Don't worry, I get some for you, no problem—good stuff, not the junk they cut for street trade. All you want, and cheap, too."

I shook my head. "Stop guessing. I talk only to Le Boss."

But Bobo continued to eye me as I guided the car out of the suburban residential and industrial areas, through a stretch of barren countryside, and into an unpaved side road bordering the empty lower reaches of the river. There were no lights here, no dwellings, no signs of life—only shadows, silence, and swaying trees.

Bobo was getting nervous, but now he forced a smile.

"Hey, old man—you like girls? Le Boss got one the other day."

"Not interested."

"I mean *little* girls. Fresh meat, only five, six maybe—"

I shook my head again and he sidled closer on the seat. "What about boys? I'm good, you'll see. Even Le Boss says so—"

He rubbed against me; his clothes were filthy and he smelled of sweat and garlic. "Never mind," I said quickly, pushing him away.

"Okay," he murmured. "I figured if we did a deal you'd give up trying to see Le Boss. It's just going to make things bad for you, and there's no sense getting yourself hurt."

"I appreciate your concern." I smiled. "But it's not me you're really worried about. You'll be the one who gets hurt for bringing me, is that not so?"

He stared at me without replying but I read the answer in his fear-filled eyes.

"What will he do to you?" I said.

The fear spilled over into his voice. "Please *m'sieu*—don't tell him how you got here! I will do anything you want, anything—"

"You'll do exactly what I say," I told him.

He glanced ahead, and again I read his eyes.

"Are we here?" I asked. "Is this the place?"

"*Oui.* But—"

"Be silent." I shut off the motor and headlights, but not before the beam betrayed a glimpse of the river bank beyond the rutted side road. Through the tangle of trees and rampant underbrush I could see the parked van hidden from sight amidst the sheltering shadows ahead. Beyond it, spanning the expanse of the river, was a crude and ancient wooden foot-bridge, the narrow and rotting relic of a bygone era.

I slipped out of the car, circling to the other side, then opened the passenger door and collared my captive.

"Where are they?" I whispered.

"On the other side." Bobo's voice was faint but the apprehension it held was strong. "Please, don't make me take you there!"

"Shut up and come with me." I jerked him forward toward the trees, then halted as I stared across the rickety old makeshift bridge. The purpose it served in the past was long forgotten, and so was the huge oval on the far bank which opened close to the water's edge.

But Le Boss had not forgotten. Once this great circular conduit was part of the earliest Paris sewer-system. Deep within its depths, dozens of connecting branches converged into a gigantic single outlet and spewed their waste into the water below. Now the interior channels had been sealed off, leaving the main tunnel dry but not deserted. For it was here, within a circle of metal perhaps twenty feet in diameter, that Le Boss found shelter from prying eyes, past the unused dirt road and the abandoned bridge.

The huge opening gaped like the mouth of Hell, and from within, the fires of Hell blazed forth.

Actually the fires were merely the product of candlelight flickering from tapers set in niches around the base of the tunnel beyond. I sensed that their value was not only practical but precautionary, for they could be quickly extinguished in the event of an alarm.

Alarm?

I tugged at Bobo's soiled collar. "The lookout," I murmured. "Where is he?"

Reluctantly the boy stabbed a finger in the direction of tall and tangled weeds bordering the side of the bridge ahead. In the shadows I made out a small shape huddled amidst surrounding clumps of vegetation.

"Sandor." My captive nodded. "He's asleep."

I glanced up. "What about Le Boss and the others?"

"Inside the sewer. Further back, where nobody can see them."

"Good. You will go in now."

"Alone?"

"Yes, alone." As I spoke I took out my key and unlocked the handcuffs, but my grip on Bobo's neck did not loosen.

He rubbed his chafed wrists. "What am I supposed to do?"

"Tell Le Boss that I grabbed you on the street, but you broke free and ran."

"How do I say I got here?"

"Perhaps you hitched a ride."

"And then—"

"You didn't know I was following you, not until I caught you here again. Tell him I'm waiting on this side of the river until you bring me my key. Once I get it I will go away—no questions asked, no harm done."

Bobo frowned. "Suppose he doesn't have the key?"

"He will," I said. "You see, it's just an old brass gate-key, but the handle is shaped into my family crest. Mounted in the crest is a large ruby."

Bobo's frown persisted. "What if he just pried it loose and threw the key away?"

"That's possible." I shrugged. "But you had better pray he didn't." My fingers dug into his neck. "I want that key, understand? And I want it now."

"He's not going to give it to you, not Le Boss! Why should he?"

For answer I dragged him forward toward the sleeping sentry in the weeds. Reaching into my jacket I produced a knife. As Bobo gaped in surprise, I aimed a kick at the slumbering lookout. He blinked and sat up quickly, then froze as I pressed the tip of the broad blade against his neck.

"Tell him that if you don't bring me back the key in five minutes I'll cut Sandor's throat."

Sandor believed me, I know, because he started to whimper. And Bobo believed me too, for when I released my grip on his collar he started running toward the bridge.

Now there was only one question. Would Le Boss believe me?

I sincerely hoped so. But for the moment all I could do was be patient. Yanking the snivelling Sandor to his feet, I tugged him along to position myself at the edge of the bridge, staring across it as Bobo reached the mouth of the sewer on the other side. The mouth swallowed him, and I stood waiting.

Except for the rasp of Sandor's hoarse breathing, the night was still. No sound emanated from the great oval of the sewer across the river, and my vision could not penetrate the flashing of flame from within.

But the reflection of the light served me as I studied my prisoner. Like Bobo he had the body of a child, but the face peering up at me was incongruously aged—not by wrinkles but by the grim set of his cracked lips, the gaunt hollows beneath protruding cheekbones, and the sunken circles outlining the eyes above. The eyes were old, those deep dark eyes that had witnessed far more than any child should see. In them I read a present submissiveness, but that was merely a surface reaction. Beyond it lay a cold cunning, a cruel craftiness governed not by intelligence but by animal instinct, fully developed, ready for release. And he was an animal, I told myself; a predator, dwelling in a cave, issuing forth to satisfy ageless atavistic hungers.

He hadn't been born that way, of course. It was Le Boss who transformed the innocence of childhood into amoral impulse, who eradicated humanity and brought forth the beast beneath.

Le Boss. What was he doing now? Surely Bobo had reached him by this time, told his tale. What was happening? I held Sandor close at knife-point, my eyes searching the swirl of firelight and shadow deep in the tunnel's iron maw.

Then, suddenly and shockingly, the metal mouth screamed.

The high, piercing echo rose only for an instant before fading into silence, but I knew its source.

Tightening my grip on Sandor's ragged collar and pressing the knife-blade close to this throat, I started toward the foot-bridge.

"No!" he quavered. "Don't—"

I ignored his panting plea, his futile efforts to free himself. Thrusting him forward, I crossed the swaying structure, averting my gaze from the dank depths beneath and focusing vision and purpose on the opening ahead.

Passing between the flame-tipped teeth of the candles on either side, I dragged Sandor down into the yawning throat beyond. I was conscious of the odor now, the odor of carrion corruption which welled from the dank inner recesses, conscious of the clang of our footsteps against the rounded metal surface, but my attention was directed elsewhere.

A dark bundle of rags lay across the curved base of the tunnel ahead. Skirting it as we approached, I saw I'd been mistaken. The rags were merely a covering, outlining the twisted form beneath.

Bobo had made a mistake too, for it was his body which sprawled motionless there. The grotesque angle of his neck and the splinter of bone protruding from an outflung arm indicated that he had fallen from above. Fallen, or perhaps hurled.

My eyes sought the rounded ceiling of the sewer. It was, as I'd estimated, eas-ily twenty feet high, but I didn't have to scan the top to confirm my guess as to Bobo's fate.

Just ahead, at the left of the rounded iron wall, was a wooden ladder, propped against the side of a long, broad shelf mounted on makeshift scaffolding which rose perhaps a dozen feet from the sewer's base. Here the candles were af-fixed to poles at regular intervals, illuminating a vast jumbled heap of hand-lug-gage, rucksacks, attaché-cases, boxes, packages, purses and mouldy, mildewed articles of clothing, piled into a thieves' mountain of stolen goods.

And here, hunching before them on a soiled and aging mattress, amidst a lit-ter of emptied and discarded bottles, squatted Le Boss.

There was no doubt as to his identity; I recognized him by his mocking smile, the cool casualness with which he rose to confront me after I'd forced San-dor up the ladder and onto the platform.

The man who stood swaying before us was a monster. Forgive the term, but there is no other single word to describe him. Le Boss was well over six feet tall, and the legs enclosed in the dirt-smudged trousers of his soiled suit were bowed and bent by the sheer immensity of the burden they bore. He must have weighed over three hundred pounds, and the fat bulging from his bloated belly and torso was almost obscene in its abundance. His huge hands terminated in fingers as thick as sausages.

There was no shirt beneath the tightly stretched suit jacket and from a cord around his thick neck a whistle dangled against the naked chest. His head was bullet-shaped and bald. Indeed, he was completely hairless—no hint of eye-brows surmounted the hyperthyroid pupils, no lashes guarded the red-rimmed sockets. The porcine cheeks and sagging jowls were beardless, their fleshy folds worm-white even in the candlelight which glittered against the tiny, tawny eyes.

I needed no second glance to confirm my suspicions of what had occurred before my arrival here; the scene I pictured in my mind was perfectly clear. The coming of Bobo, the breathless, stammered story, his master's reaction of mingled disbelief and anger, the fit of drunken fury in which the terrified bringer of bad tidings had been flung over the side of the platform to smash like an empty bot-tle on the floor of the sewer below—I saw it all too vividly.

Le Boss grinned at me, his fleshy lips parting to reveal yellowed stumps of rotting teeth.

"Well, old man?" He spoke French, but his voice was oddly accented; he could indeed be a yougoslave.

I forced myself to meet his gaze. "You know why I'm here," I said.

He nodded. "Something about a key, I take it."

"Your pack of thieves took it. But it's my property."

His grin broadened. "My property now." The deep voice rumbled with mock-ing relish. "Suppose I'm not inclined to return it?"

For answer I shoved Sandor before me and raised the knife, poising it against his neck. My captive trembled and made mewing sounds as the blade pressed closer.

Le Boss shrugged. "You'll have to do better than that, old man. A child's life isn't important to me."

I peered down at Bobo's body lying below. "So I see." Striving to conceal my reaction, I faced him again. "But where are the others?"

"Playing, I imagine."

"Playing?"

"You find that strange, old man? In spite of what you may think, I'm not without compassion. After all, they are only children. They work hard, and they deserve the reward of play."

Le Boss turned, gesturing down toward the far recesses of the sewer. My eyes followed his gaze through the shifting candle-glow, and for the first time I became aware of movement in the dim depths. Faint noises echoed upward, identifiable now as the sound of childish laughter. Tiny shapes moved below and beyond, shapes which gleamed white amid the shadows.

The yougoslaves were naked, and at play. I counted four of them scuttling and in quatting the far reaches of the tunnel.

But wait! There was a fifth figure, slightly smaller than the others who loomed over it and laughed as they pawed the squirming shape or tugged at the golden hair. Over their mirth rose the sound of sobbing, and over that, the echo of Bobo's voice.

Hey, old man—you like girls? Fresh meat, only five, six maybe—

Now I could see only too clearly. Two of the boys held their victim down, spread-eagled and helpless, while the other two—but I shall not describe what they were doing.

Glancing away, I again met Le Boss's smile. Somehow it seemed more hideous to me than the sight below.

He groped for a bottle propped against the pile of loot beside him and drank before speaking. "You are distressed, eh?"

I shook my head. "Not as much as you'll be unless you give me back my key."

He smiled. "Empty threats will get you nothing but empty hands."

"My hands aren't empty." I jabbed the knife at Sandor's neck, grazing the flesh, and he squealed in terror.

Le Boss shrugged. "Go ahead. I told you it doesn't matter to me."

For a moment I stood irresolute. Then, with a sigh I drew the knife back from Sandor's throat and released my hold on his sweat-soaked collar. He turned and raced off to the ladder behind me, and I could hear his feet scraping against the rungs as he descended. Mercifully, the sound muffled the laughter from below.

Le Boss nodded. "That's better. Now we can discuss the situation like gentlemen."

I lifted my knife. "Not as long as I have this, and you have the key."

"More empty threats?"

"My hands are not empty." I took a step forward as I spoke.

He chuckled. "I swear I don't know what to make of you, old man. Either you are very stupid or very brave."

"Both, perhaps." I raised the knife higher, but he halted my advance with a quick gesture.

"Enough," he wheezed. Turning, he stooped and thrust his pudgy hand into a tangle of scarves, kerchiefs and handbags behind him. When he straightened again he was holding the key.

"Is this what you're after?"

"Yes. I knew you wouldn't discard it."

He stared at the red stone gleaming dully from the crested handle. "I never toss away valuables."

"Just human lives," I said.

"Don't preach to me, old man. I'm not interested in your philosophy."

"Nor I in yours." I stretched out my hand, palm upward. "All I want is my key."

His own hand drew back. "Not so fast. Suppose you tell me why."

"It's not the ruby," I answered. "Go ahead, pry it loose if you like."

Le Boss chuckled again. "A poor specimen—big enough, but flawed. It's the key itself that interests you, eh?"

"Naturally. As I told Bobo, it opens the gate to my estate."

"And just where is this estate of yours?"

"Near Bourg-la-Reine."

"That's not too far away." The little eyes narrowed. "The van could take us there within the hour."

"It would serve no purpose," I said. "Perhaps 'estate' is a misnomer. The place is small and holds nothing you'd be interested in. The furnishings are old, but hardly the quality of antiques. The house itself has been boarded-up for years since my last visit. I have other properties elsewhere on the Continent where I spend much of my time. But since I'll be here for several weeks on business, I prefer familiar surroundings."

"Other properties, eh?" Le Boss fingered the key. "You must be quite rich, old man."

"That's none of your affair."

"Perhaps not, but I was just thinking. If you have money, why not conduct your business in comfort from a good hotel in Paris?"

I shrugged. "It is a matter of sentiment—"

"Really?" He eyed me sharply, and in the interval before speaking, I noted that the sounds below had ceased.

My voice broke the sudden silence. "I assure you—"

"*Au contraire.* You do not assure me in the least." Le Boss scowled. "If you do own an estate, then it's the key to the house that's important, not the one for the gate. Any locksmith could open it for you without need of this particular key."

He squinted at the burnished brass, the dulled brilliance of the ruby imbedded in the ornate crest. "Unless, of course, it isn't a gate-key after all. Looks to me more like the key to a strong-box, or even a room in the house holding hidden valuables."

"It's just a gate-key." Again I held one hand as the other gripped the knife. "But I want it—now."

"Enough to kill?" he challenged.

"If necessary."

"I'll spare you that." Grinning, Le Boss reached down again into a bundle of discarded clothing.

When he turned to face me he held a revolver in his hand.

"Drop that toothpick," he said, raising the weapon to reinforce his command.

Sighing, I released my grasp and the knife fell, clattering over the side of the open platform to the surface of the sewer below.

Impelled by blind impulse, I turned hastily. If I could get to the ladder—

"Stand where you are!"

It wasn't his words but the sharp clicking sound which halted me. Slowly I pivoted to face the muzzle of his cocked revolver.

"That's better," he said.

"You wouldn't murder me—not in cold blood."

"Let's leave it up to the kids." As Le Boss spoke his free hand fumbled for the whistle looped around his neck. Enfolding it in blubbery lips, he blew.

The piercing blast echoed, reverberating from the rounded iron walls beside me and below. Then came the answering murmurs, the sudden thud of footsteps. Out of the corner of my eye I glanced down and saw the four naked figures—no, there were five now, including the fully-clothed Sandor—moving toward the platform on which we stood.

Again I conjured up a vision of hell, of demons dancing in the flames. But the flames were merely candlelight and the bodies hurrying beneath were those of children. It was only their laughter which was demonic; their laughter, and their gleefully contorted faces.

As they approached I caught a glimpse of what they held in their hands. Sandor had scooped up the knife from where it had fallen and the others held weapons of their own—a mallet, a wooden club, a length of steel pipe, the serrated stump of a broken wine-bottle.

Le Boss chuckled once more. "Playtime," he said.

"Call them off!" I shouted. "I warn you—"

He shook his head. "No way, old man."

Old man. That, I swear, is what did it. Not the menace of the gun, not the sight of the loathsome little creatures below. It was just the phrase, the contempt with which it had been repeated over and over again.

I knew what he was thinking—an unarmed, helpless elderly victim had been trapped for torment. And for the most part he was right; I was weaponless, old, trapped.

But not helpless.

Closing my eyes, I concentrated. There are subsonic whistles which make no audible sound, and there are ways of summoning which require no whistles at all. And there's more than human vermin infesting abandoned sewers, lurking in the far recesses of tangled tunnels, but responsive to certain commands.

Almost instantly that response came.

It came in the form of a purposeful padding, of faint noises magnified by sheer numbers. It came in the sound of squeaks and chittering, first as distant echoes, then in closer cacophony as my summons was answered.

Now the yougoslaves had reached the ladder at the far side of the platform. I saw Sandor mount the lower rungs, knife held between clenched teeth—saw him halt as he too heard the sudden, telltale tumult. Behind Sandor his companions turned to seek its source.

They cried out then, first in surprise, then in alarm, as the grey wave surged toward them along the sewer's length; the grey wave, flecked with hundreds of red and glaring eyes, a thousand tiny teeth.

The wave raced forward, curling around the feet and ankles of the yougoslaves before the ladder, climbing and clinging to legs and knees. Screaming, they lashed out with their weapons, trying to beat back the attack, but the wave poured on, forward and upward. Furry forms leaped higher, claws digging into waists, teeth biting into bellies. Sandor pulled himself up the ladder with both hands, but below him the red eyes rose and the grey shapes launched up from behind to cover his unprotected back with a blanket of wriggling bodies.

Now the screams from below were drowned out by the volume of shrill screeching. The knife dropped from between Sandor's lips as he shrieked and toppled down into the writhing mass that had already engulfed his companions. Flailing helplessly, their faces sank from sight in the rising waves of the grey sea.

It happened so quickly that Le Boss, caught by surprise, could only stare in stunned silence at the shambles below.

It was I whose voice rose above the bedlam. "The key," I cried. "Give me the key."

For answer he raised his hand—not the one holding the key, but the one grasping the gun.

His fingers were trembling, and the muzzle wavered as I started toward him. Even so, at such close range I realized he couldn't miss. And he didn't.

As he squeezed the trigger the shots came in rapid succession. They were barely audible in the uproar from the tunnel, but I felt their impact as they struck my chest and torso.

I kept on, moving closer, hearing the final, futile click as he continued to press the trigger of his emptied revolver. Looking up, eyes red with rage, he hurled the weapon at my head. It whizzed past me, and now he had nothing left to clutch but the key. His hands started to shake.

My hand went out.

Snatching the key from his pudgy paw, I stared at his frantic face. Perhaps I should have told him he'd guessed correctly; the key was not meant to open a gate. I could have explained the ruby in the crest—the symbol of a lineage so ancient that it still adhered to the olden custom of maintaining a tomb on the estate. The key gave me access to that tomb, not that it was really needed; my branch of the line had other resting-places, and during my travels I always carried with me what was necessary to afford temporary rest of my own. But during my stay here the tomb was both practical and private. Calling a locksmith would be unwise and inconvenient, and I do not relish inconvenience.

All this I could have told him, and much more. Instead I pocketed the key bearing the great flawed ruby that was like a single drop of blood.

As I did so, I realized that the squeals and chittering below had faded into other sounds compounded of claws ripping through cloth, teeth grating against bone.

Unable to speak, unable to move, Le Boss awaited my approach. When I gripped his shoulders he must have fainted, for there was only a dead weight now to ease down onto the platform floor.

Below me my brothers sated their hunger, feasting on the bodies of the yougoslaves.

Bending forward to the fat neck beneath me, in my own way I feasted too.

What fools they were, these creatures who thought themselves so clever! Perhaps they could outwit others, but their little tricks could not prevail against me. After all, they were only yougoslaves.

And I am a Transylvanian.

ROBERT BLOCH: AN APPRECIATION

STEPHEN KING

The part of imagination which would become, in the course of time, my "writer's mind" inclined toward horror fiction from the very beginning. It was fired first by the vulgar horror of the E. C. comic books, then by the classical horror of H. P. Lovecraft—he of the cyclopean horrors and great galumphing sentences—and then by the short stories of Robert Bloch, stories which provided a perfect bridge between the two. Although influenced by HPL, Bob was too puckish and too lively to become one of the "Lovecraft Circle elders," like Frank Belknap Long or Zelia Bishop or Clark Ashton Smith. Yet horror tales, supernatural tales, and the literature of the imagination were clearly much more than play to Bloch; he loved to explore the darker depths of the human soul—he was, like so many writers in this genre, a scuba diver armed with a pen instead of a speargun—and took his gift for the fantastic seriously.

As a poor kid growing up in a single-parent family in the fifties and sixties, I could never have afforded the Arkham House collections of his work (although I lusted after them), but I *was* able to afford the Belmont paperback editions containing those stories. Even when *Yours Truly, Jack the Rippers* and *Horror-7* upped the ante from 35¢ to a ball-busting 50¢ (*60¢* by the time the paperback version of *Psycho* with Janet Leigh screaming her head off on the cover appeared), I found a way to afford them. I *had* to afford them. I had become a horror junkie by the time I was fifteen or so, and in the quiet years before I went off to college, Robert Bloch was the pusher with the best stuff. He didn't teach me everything I know, but he taught me at least one invaluable lesson: to enjoy it. To have fun with it.

He was a fine writer and an even finer human being. I remember how pleased I was—aw, tell the truth, how *star-struck* I was—when I first met him in California, and how quickly he set me at ease, telling stories about movie stars (we were in L.A. at the time), and cracking me up by referring to Forest Lawn Cemetery as "the Disneyland of the Dead." Some years later, at the World Fantasy Convention in Maryland, Bob showed up beside me at a raucous room-party and said, "Kirby McCauley says I'm supposed to tell you some stories about how it was in the old days. Do you want to hear?"

I told him I did, and Bob led me over to one corner of the room, where we sat on the floor, cross-legged like kids. For the next two hours, Bob told me stories about how it was in the old days, when the Elder Gods—not Cthulhu and Nyarlahotep and Yogsothoth, but Robert Howard and Seabury Quinn and, yes, Robert Bloch—walked the earth. He told me stories about the movies and movie-stars, too—people like Alfred Hitchcock and Joan Crawford, with whom he worked on *Strait-Jacket*—but it was the *writing* stories I was most hungry to hear, stories about how it was to see your byline on the cover of *Weird Tales* or to eat lunch at the automat with John Campbell, and these were the stories Bob told the best.

He was a man of wit and gentleness and great, great talent. He was also a man who knew how to be kind to younger writers. He seemed to understand that most of us—the "young Turks" of the late seventies and early eighties who are now the middle-aged scribblers of the nineties—really idolized him, and how much we envied him the people he had known and talked to in his life. He knew those things . . . but he never took advantage of them.

"I actually have the heart of a young boy," Bob liked to say. "I keep it in a jar on my desk." It was a line I used often, always attributing it to Bob (who also owns the greatest story title of the twentieth century, in my opinion—a Lefty Feep opus titled "Time Wounds All Heels"), because it had a sly sort of charm. When some well-meaning idiot asks, "Where do you get your ideas?" or "Why do you write such horrible things?" Bob's answer turns the responsibility for the question back to where it belongs . . . upon the questioner. There's a comic subtlety in the line that Bob could almost have trademarked. But he *didn't* have the heart of a small boy; he had the heart of a kind, imaginative man whose vision was keenly attuned to the shadows that nest in the dark places. He'll be missed in the fantasy community, and he'll be missed by yours truly, Steve the Ripper, in a much more personal sense. Even now, I can't believe that his spooky, sarcastic voice has been silenced. There is no voice on the contemporary scene which can replace it, and that is a great loss.

STEPHEN JONES

I can no longer recall the first book by Robert Bloch I read; it might have been *The Living Demons* (a British reprint collection of the early 1970s) or, more likely, *Horror-7*—a compilation of tales from *The Opener of the Way* and *Pleasant Dreams*—which boasted a striking green cover with a still from the movie *Torture Garden* (1967), which Bob scripted.

Whichever paperback volume was my introduction to his macabre fiction, it certainly made enough of an impression on my teenage imagination that I scoured the bookstores for more. I came to *Psycho* and his other novels sometime later, but by then I had amassed a sizable number of collections and anthologies that featured his often blackly humorous tales.

Then in 1979 I was asked to program a season of movies at London's prestigious National Film Theatre under the banner title "Fantasy Authors on Film." A celebration of the (not always successful) marriage between fiction and film, I decided it would be a fun idea to get the authors themselves to write the accompanying notes. The picture I chose as representative of Bob's work was *Asylum* (1972), which he scripted from his classic stories "Mannikins of Horror," "Frozen Fear," "The Weird Tailor," and "Lucy Comes to Stay."

Suffice to say that Bob graciously replied to my tentative solicitation letter and supplied his own, unique insights into the film-making process from the writer's point of view. As a bonus, I began in intermittent correspondence with one of my favorite writers from the "*Weird Tales* circle."

It wasn't long before I was pestering him again. Firstly, it was for an interview-by-mail about his experiences with Amicus Films, published in the premier issue of *Halls of Horror* magazine. As usual, Bob patiently and eloquently answered my questions. Not long afterwards, he allowed me to reprint two of his more obscure stories (which originally appeared under the pseudonym "Tarleton Fiske") in *Fantasy Tales*, the small press magazine I co-edited with David Sutton.

When Dave and I published our first anthology together, *The Best Horror from Fantasy Tales* inevitably included one of those stories, "The Sorcerer's Jewel," as well as a glowing quote from Bob on the jacket flap. Since then, I have been fortunate to include his fiction in many of the anthologies I have edited, notably the *Mammoth Books of Terror, Vampires, Zombies,* and *Frankenstein.*

Bob was also kind enough to contribute original material to a number of other projects I was involved with, including a fascinating essay on Alexander Laing's 1934 novel *The Cadaver of Gideon Wyck* for *Horror 100 Best Books*; a ghoulishly funny poem to *Now We Are Sick*; and, more recently, an introduction to *The Illustrated Psycho Movie Guide*.

Not only was he a delight to work with from an editor's point of view, but he was one of the very few authors who would always spare the time to send a brief letter of thanks whenever he received his contributor's copies. Even when I was sometimes less than satisfied with the finished product, these handwritten notes from Bob (usually scrawled in blue marker on an airletter) would always lift my spirits and encourage me to continue.

Although we had been corresponding for some years, I remained reticent about introducing myself to him at conventions. He was always surrounded by fans and fellow writers, and I simply didn't think he would remember me. When I finally summoned up the courage to ask him to sign my copy of *Pleasant Dreams,* he not only knew exactly who I was, but inscribed the book: "With great admiration!" I couldn't have been more thrilled.

We met infrequently on other occasions and found time to talk at some length at the Horror Writers of America meeting in Providence (where he received the Life Achievement Award), the first World Horror Convention in Nashville (where he was presented with the Grand Master Award), and for a final time at the *Famous Monsters of Filmland* thirty-fifth anniversary weekend in Virginia. When he announced his illness, I wrote him a heart-felt letter of good-bye, which I hope he read.

Bob's gone now, but he has left behind a legacy of stories, novels, and movies that will doubtless influence generations to come in the same way that his work has inspired and delighted me (as well as numerous others) over the decades.

With such a wealth of riches to choose from, I found it all the more difficult to select a story for this collection. It would perhaps have been too easy to pick such favorite tales as "The Opener of the Way," "The Cloak," "Yours Truly, Jack the Ripper," "The Plot Is the Thing," or "Enoch," amongst numerous others.

Instead, I've chosen a somewhat guilty pleasure. In the early 1970s,

Bob scripted two made-for-TV movies for director Curtis Harrington. Both films featured casts of veteran performers; but whereas *The Cat Creature* (1973) was ostensibly the writer's tribute to Val Lewton's stylish horror-noir films of the 1940s, the much more bizarre *The Dead Don't Die,* made the following year, was based on Bob's own story (sans the exclamation mark in the original title).

I saw the movie first, and was delighted by its impressive lineup of B-movie stars, which included George Hamilton, Linda Cristal, Joan Blondell, Ralph Meeker, James McEachin, Reggie Nalder, Milton Parsons, Yvette Vickers, and Ray Milland as the mysterious zombie master. When I finally found a copy of the original tale, it turned out to be even more enjoyable.

"The Dead Don't Die!" was first published as the cover story in the July 1951 edition of the pulp magazine *Fantastic Adventures*. Bob admitted that the story was written around the title, foistered on him by the editor. Always the consummate professional, he turned in a 25,000-word novelette that is probably a great deal more interesting than the assignment deserved. Famed artist Virgil Finlay contributed two superb illustrations for the story, and he obviously had fun, at the author's expense, by utilizing Bob's features on an unfortunate victim of the walking dead.

To be honest, this is perhaps not one of Robert Bloch's greatest works—I'm sure there will be plenty of those included elsewhere in this volume. But what "The Dead Don't Die!" ably illustrates is Bob's lifelong commitment to his craft as a working writer. As his fascinating autobiography *Once Around the Bloch* reveals, he could (and often would) turn his skill to writing almost anything. I have always believed that this is the mark of the true professional.

He also knew that the first rule of all good fiction is to entertain the reader. The following tale does that superbly, with a style and skill that is unmistakably a chip off the old Bloch. . . .

THE DEAD DON'T DIE!

🎵 *This is a story that never ends.*

This is a story that never ends, but I know when it started. Thursday, May 24th, was the date. That night was the beginning of everything for me.

For Cono Colluri it was the end.

Cono and I were sitting there, playing two-handed stud poker. It was quiet in his cell, and we played slowly, meditatively. Everything would have been all right except for one thing. We had a kibitzer.

No matter how calmly we played, no matter how unemotional we appeared to be, we both were aware of another presence. The other, the kibitzer, stayed with us all night long.

His name was Death.

He grinned over Cono's shoulder, tapped him on the arm with a bony finger, selected the cards for every shuffle. He tugged at my hands, poked me in the back when I dealt.

We couldn't see him, of course. But we knew he was there, all right. Watching, watching and waiting; those big blind holes in the skull sneaking a look at the clock and counting the minutes, those skeleton fingers tapping away the seconds until dawn.

Because in the morning, no matter what cards turned up and no matter how much money changed hands, Death would win the game. The game, and Cono Colluri.

It's funny, looking back on it now, to figure out how the three of us happened to get together that particular evening—Cono, myself, and Death.

My story's straight enough. About six months beforehand I'd taken a Civil Service exam and ended up for a probationary period as a guard at State Pen. I wasn't too excited about the job when I got it, but I felt it might give me routine, a small but steady income, and a chance to turn out a book on the side. By the time a few months had passed, I knew I was wrong. The idea of turning out a novel in a background of security sounded fine when I started, but there was no security in a guard's life. I found I couldn't write. The bars and the concrete penned me in just as much as any of my charges. And I began to develop my own sense of guilt.

I guess my trouble was too much empathy. That's a big word—meaning the ability to put yourself in the other fellow's place. "There but for the grace of God go I"—you know that feeling. I had it, but double. Instead of writing at night, I tossed around on my bunk and suffered the torments of the thousand men under my charge.

That's how I got friendly with Cono, I guess—through empathy.

Cono came to the death cell in an awful hurry. His had been a short trial and a merry one—the kind of thing the newspapers like to play up as an example of "quick justice." He'd been a professional strong man with a carnival—the James T. Armstrong Shows. The story was that he got too jealous of his wife and one of the other performers. At any rate, one morning they found Cono lying dead drunk in his trailer. His wife was with him, but she wasn't drunk—merely dead. Somebody had pressed two thumbs against the base of her neck, and something had snapped.

It was an ideal setup for "quick justice" and that's just what Cono Colluri got. Within three weeks he was on his way to the death-house, and for the past two weeks he'd been a guest of the state. A temporary guest. And he was moving out tomorrow morning—for good.

That, of course, explains why Death showed up at our little card party. He belonged there.

Oh, perhaps not for the entire night. He undoubtedly had rattled down the short—oh so terribly short!—corridor to the little room with the big chair. He'd probably peered and eaves-dropped on the electricians who tested the switches. He'd certainly have stopped in at the warden's office to make sure that the mythical pardon from the Governor wasn't on its way.

Yes, Death must have checked all those things to make certain that this was really a farewell card party. And now the uninvited guest was kibitzing as Cono and I dealt our hands.

I knew he was there, and Cono knew it too, but I have to hand it to the big man. He was cool. He'd always been cool; on the stand, swearing his innocence, he'd never lost his temper. Here in the cell, talking to the warden, to the other guards, to me, he'd never broken down. Just told his story over and over again. Somebody had slipped a Mickey in his drink and when he woke up, Flo was dead. He'd never harmed her.

Of course, nobody believed him at the trial. Nobody believed him in the prison, either; the warden, the guards, even the other convicts knew that he was guilty and ready to fry.

That's why I had the honor of spending the last night with him—he'd made a special request for my presence. Because, believe it or not, I believed him.

Blame it on empathy again, or on the very fact that I noticed he never lost his temper. The way he talked about the case, the way he talked about his wife, the way he talked about the execution—everything was out of character for a "crime of passion" murderer. Oh, he was a big brute, and a rough-looking one, but he never acted on impulse.

I guess he took to me right away. We used to talk, nights, after I drew guard assignment on his bloc. He was the only prisoner awaiting execution, and it was natural that we'd get to talking.

"You know I didn't do it, Bob," he'd tell me—over and over again, but there was nothing else to talk about, for him—"It must have been Louie. He lied at the trial, you know. He had been drinking with me, no matter what he says, and he offered me a slug out of the bottle behind the cookhouse, after the last show. That's the last thing I remember. So I figure he must have done it. He was always hanging around Flo anyway, the little crumb. The Great Ahmed warned me, said he saw it in the crystal. But of course, he came into court with this alibi and—oh what's the use?"

There was no use at all, and he knew it. But he told me over and over again. And I believed him.

Now, this last night, he wasn't talking. Maybe it was because Death was there, listening to every word. Maybe it was because they'd shaved his head and slit his trouser legs and left him to wait out these last few hours.

Cono wasn't talking, but he could still grin. He could and he did—smiling at me and looking like a great big overgrown college boy with a crew haircut. Come to think of it, he wasn't much more than just that; only Cono had never gone to college. He went with his first carney at fifteen; married Flo when he was twenty-three, and now he was going to the chair two days before his twenty-fifth birthday. But he smiled. Smiled, and played poker.

"My king is high," he said. "Bet a quarter."

"See you," I answered. "Let's have another card."

"King still high. Check. Funny thing, aces aren't coming up much tonight."

I didn't answer him. I didn't have the heart to tell him that I was cheating. I'd taken the Ace of Spades out of the pack and put it in my pocket before the game started. I didn't want him to get that particular card on the table tonight of all nights.

"Fifty cents on the king," said Cono.

"See you," I said. "I've got a pair of nines."

"Pair of kings." He turned up his cards. "I win."

"You're just naturally lucky," I told him—and wished I hadn't.

But he smiled. I couldn't face that smile, so I looked at my watch. That was another mistake, and I realized it as soon as I made the gesture.

His smile didn't alter. "Not much time left, is there?" he said. "Seems to be getting light."

"Another hand?" I suggested.

"No." Cono stood up. Shaved head, slit trousers and all, he was still an impressive sight. Six feet four, two hundred and ten pounds, in the prime of life. And in just an hour or so they would strap him into the chair, turn on the juice, twist that smile into a grimace of agony. I couldn't look at him, thinking those thoughts. But I could feel Death looking; gazing and gloating.

"Bob, I want to talk to you."

"Shall we order breakfast? You know what the warden said—anything you want, the works."

"No breakfast." Cono put his hand on my shoulder. The fingers that were supposed to have broken a woman's neck barely pressed my skin. "Let's fool 'em and skip the meal. That'll give the nosey reporters something to talk about."

"What's up?"

"Nothing much. But I got things to tell you."

"Why me in particular?"

"Who else is there left? I got no friends. Got no family I know of. And Flo's gone . . ."

For the first time I saw a look of anger flicker across the big man's face. I knew then what whoever had killed Flo was lucky when Cono got the chair.

"So it has to be you. Besides, you believe me."

"Go on," I said.

"It's about the dough, see? Flo and me, we were saving for a house. Got better'n eight grand stashed away. Somebody's gonna, get it, so why not you? I wrote this here letter, and I want you to have it."

He pulled the envelope out from under his bunk. It was sealed, and scrawled across its face in the sprawling handwriting of a schoolboy was the name, "The Great Ahmed."

"Who's he?"

"I told you, he's the mitt reader with the carney. A nice guy, Bob. You'll like him. He stuck up for me at the trial, remember? Told about Louie hanging around Flo. Didn't do any good because he couldn't prove nothing, but he was—what did the lawyer say?—a character witness. Yeah. Anyhow, he banks for all us carneys with the show.

"Take the letter. It says to give you the money. He'll do it, too. All you got to do is look him up."

I hesitated. "Wait a minute, Cono. You'd better think this over. Eight thousand dollars is a lot of money to pass out to a virtual stranger—"

"Take it, pal." Again he smiled. "There's a string tied to the bundle, of course."

"What do you want?"

"I want you to use some of that dough to try and clear me. Oh, I know you haven't got much of a chance, and nothing to work on. But maybe, with the dough, you'll get an angle, turn something up. You're leaving this joint anyway."

I jerked my head at that. "How did you know?" I asked. "Why, I only told the warden yesterday afternoon—"

"Word goes around." Cono smiled. "They give me the office that you're springing yourself out of here this Saturday. That you aren't satisfied to be a screw the rest of your life. So I says to myself, why not give him the eight grand as a kind of going-away present? Seeing as how we're both going away."

I balanced the envelope on my palm. "The Great Ahmed, eh? And you say he's with the show?"

"Sure. You'll find their route in *Billboard*." Cono smiled. "They must be somewhere around Louisville right now. Heading north as it gets warmer. I'd sort of like to see the old outfit again, but . . ."

The smile faded. "One more favor, Bob."

"Name it."

"Scram out of here."

"But—"

"You heard me. Scram. I expect visitors pretty soon, and I don't want you to stick around."

I nodded, nodded gratefully. Cono was sparing me that final ordeal—the warden, the priest, the mumbling farewell, the shuffling down the corridor.

"Goodbye, Bob. Remember, I'm depending on you."

"I'll do what I can. Goodbye, Cono."

The big hand enveloped mine. "I'll be seeing you around," he said.

"Sure."

"I mean it, Bob. You don't believe this is the end, do you?"

"Maybe you're right. I hope so." I had no intention of getting into a discussion about the after-life with Cono, in his situation. Personally, I had a pretty good idea that once the juice was turned on, Cono would be turned off—forever. But I couldn't tell him that. So I just shook hands, put the letter in my pocket, unlocked the cell, and walked out.

At the end of the corridor I turned around and looked back. Cono stood against the bars, his body outlined against the yellow light but blending into the shadows that come with dawn. There was another shadow behind him—a big, black shadow outlining a ghost of a figure.

I recognized the shadow. Old Man Death.

That was the last I saw—just the two of them, waiting together. Cono and Old Man Death.

I went downstairs, then, to my bunk. The night shift came off and the day shift went on. They were all talking about the execution. They tried to pump me, but I didn't say anything. I sat there on the edge of the bunk, looking at my watch and waiting.

Upstairs they must have gone through the whole routine, just the way you always see it in the B movies. Opening the door. Handcuffing him to a guard on either side. Marching down the corridor. Yes, just about now it would be happening. The night shift went outside to get the news, leaving me alone on my bunk. I looked at my watch again. Now was the time.

They'd be strapping him down now, putting that damned black cloth over his eyes. I could see him sitting there; a big, gentle hulk of a man with a tired smile on his face.

Maybe he was guilty, maybe he was innocent—I didn't know. But the whole stupid business of execution, of "justice" and "punishment" and "the full penalty of the law" hit me in the pit of the stomach. It was cruel, it was senseless, it was wrong.

The seconds ticked away. I watched the little hand crawl around the face of the watch and tried to figure it out. One minute Cono would be alive. A jolt of electric current and he'd be dead. Trite idea. But it's the eternal mystery all of us live with. And die with.

What was the answer? I didn't know. Nobody knew. Nobody except the kibitzer. Old Man Death knew the answer. I wondered if he had a watch. No, why should he? What's Time to Death?

Thirty seconds.

Sure, I'd quit my job. I'd try to clear Cono. But what good would it do him? He'd never know. He'd be dead.

Twenty seconds.

The hand crawled around, and the thoughts crawled around. What's it like to be dead? Is it a sleep? Is it a sleep with dreams? Is it just dreams but no rest, no peace?

Ten seconds.

One moment you're alive, you can feel and hear and smell and see and move. And the next—nothing. Or—something. What's the change like? Like suddenly turning out the lights?

Now.

The lights went out.

First they dimmed, then they flickered, then they went out. Only for a second, mind you. But that was long enough.

Long enough for Cono to die.

Long enough for me to shudder.

Long enough for Death to reach out, grinning, and claim his prey in the dark . . .

I was still in a daze when I hit the railroad station on Saturday morning. So much had happened in the last two days I still couldn't figure it out.

First of all, there was that business about Cono's body. I'd gone to the warden, of course, with the story about the money, and I more or less expected to handle funeral expenses from Cono's funds when I got them.

"His cousin will bury him," the warden told me. "Got a call this morning."

"But I thought he had no relatives."

"Turns out he has, all right. Fellow named Varek. Oh, it's legitimate, we always check. The Doc insists—makes him mad every time somebody shows up and cheats him out of an autopsy."

The warden had chuckled, but I didn't laugh.

And the warden hadn't chuckled long. Because the next day, Louie had confessed.

Louie the contortionist, that is—the man Cono claimed had given him the knockout drops in his drink. The warden got a wire, of course, but the whole story hit the papers that afternoon. It seems he'd just walked into the stationhouse in Louisville and confessed. Came out with the entire statement without a sign of emotion. Said he just wanted to clear his conscience once he knew Cono was dead. He'd hated Cono, wanted Flo, and when she repulsed him he rigged up the murder to get revenge on both of them.

The story was lurid enough, but it had gaps in it. The report I read claimed Louie was a hophead. He was too calm, too unemotional. "Glassy-eyed" was the way they put it. They were going to give him a psychiatric test.

Well, I wished them luck, the whole lot of them—psychiatrists and district attorneys and smart coppers and penologists. All I knew was that Cono was innocent. And he was dead.

By this time I'd already checked on the Armstrong Shows through *Billboard*. They were playing Louisville this week, all right. I sent through my wire Friday afternoon. Saturday morning I got a telegram signed by the advance agent in Paducah.

GREAT AHMED LEFT SHOW THREE WEEKS AGO STOP OPENING OWN MITT CAMP IN
CHICAGO STOP WILL CHECK FORWARDING ADDRESS AND NOTIFY LATER

So I was on my way to Chicago and eight thousand dollars. I'd hole up in some hotel and wait for news on the Great Ahmed. And after that—well, with the money, my writing problems would be solved.

Actually, I should have been happy enough at the way it had all turned out. Cono's name was cleared, I was out of the whole sordid grind forever, and I had eight grand coming, in cash.

But something bothered me. It wasn't just the irony of Cono Colluri's innocence. It was the inexplicable feeling that things weren't settled, that they were only beginning. That I had somehow been caught up in something that would sweep me along to—

"Chicago!" bawled the conductor.

And there I was, in the Windy City at 5 p.m. on Saturday, May 25th. It wasn't windy today. As I lugged my grip out of the LaSalle Street Station I walked straight into a pouring rain.

There's something about a storm in Chicago. It seems to melt all the taxicabs away. I stood there, contemplating the downpour, watching the cars inch along under the El tracks. The sky was dark and dirty. The water dribbled inkstains along the sides of the buildings. I couldn't stand watching it in my present mood.

So I walked. I turned corners several times. Pretty soon there was a hotel. It wasn't a good hotel. It was located too far south to be even a decent hotel. But that didn't matter. I needed a place to stay in for a couple of days until the money was located. And right now, I had to get out of the rain. My suit was soaked, and the cardboard in the luggage had taken a beating.

I went in, registered. A bellboy took me up to my room on the third floor. Apparently he hadn't expected me. At least, he didn't know about my coming in time to shave. But he opened my door, deposited my luggage and asked if there'd be anything else now. Then he held out his hand. It would have taken me all day to give him a decent manicure, so I put a quarter in his palm instead. He was just as happy with that.

Then he left, I opened my grip, changed clothes, and went out to eat. The rain had moderated to a drizzle. I stopped in the lobby long enough to get eyed by the night clerk, the house dick, and a woman with improbable red hair.

During the pause I managed to send off a telegram to the advance man of the carney, giving him my new address and requesting action on locating the Great Ahmed. That concluded my business for the day.

At least, I thought it did at the time.

Nothing happened to change my mind during supper. I ate at a fish joint and contemplated the delightful prospect of returning to my crummy room and holing up for the weekend.

I don't know if you've ever spent a Sunday alone in downtown Chicago, but if you haven't, I offer you one word of advice.

Don't.

There's something about the deserted canyons on a Sunday that tears the heart out of a man. Something about the grey sunlight reflected from grimy roofs. Something about the crumpled bits of soiled paper flopping listlessly along empty streets. Something about the mournful rattle of the half-empty elevated trains. Something about the barred shop-windows and chained doors. It gets to you, does things to your insides. You start wondering whether or not, in the midst of all this death and decay, you're really alive.

The prospect didn't please me at all. I finished my meal, put another quarter in another palm, and wandered out down the street.

After all, it was still Saturday night. And Saturday night was different. The rain had definitely stopped now, and the street was black and gleaming. Neon light reflections wriggled like crimson and gold serpents across my path.

You know what serpents do, of course. They tempt you. These particular neon serpents were saying, "Come in. Have a drink. You've got nothing to do tonight anyway, and nobody to do it with. Sit down. Place your order. Relax. You're due for a little relaxation after six months in prison. It's a long sentence. You know what a con does after he's sprung. You're entitled to a little fun."

There were serpents all around me. Serpents spelling out the names of taverns, night-clubs, come-on joints, clips, dives. All I had to do was take my choice.

Instead, I walked back to the hotel, went in the lobby, and checked with the night clerk to make sure my telegram was really on the way to the carney. Then I went up to my room and rid myself of all money except for a ten-dollar bill. I wasn't taking any chances on getting rolled.

The night was still young. I'd probably feel young myself with a few drinks in me. I went back down to the lobby and toyed with the notion of the hotel bar.

The improbable redhead had disappeared, and so had the house dick. The place was almost deserted now. Almost, but not quite. There was a blonde sitting in a chair near the elevator. I'd looked at her once when I'd come downstairs and now I looked at her again.

She was worth a second look.

Genuine. That's the only word to describe her. Genuine. To begin with, she was a real blonde. No peroxide glint, no unnatural accent in makeup. The fur she wore was real, and so were the diamonds.

Those diamonds really stopped me. The ring was too big to be phoney. Even if the stone were flawed, it must have set her (or somebody) back a pretty penny. And the same went for the big choker that clung to her neck in a glittering caress.

Her smile seemed genuine, too.

And that was the phoney part.

Why should she smile at me? Me, with my forty-dollar suit and my ten-dollar bill tucked away in its watch pocket?

I didn't get it. And I didn't want it. I walked towards the lobby entrance to the hotel bar. She stood up and followed.

I walked into the dimly-lit bar, around it, and out the front door to the street. I'd do my drinking somewhere else, thank you.

There was a little place across the street down the block. I ran into it, crossing in mid-traffic. Before I opened the door I glanced back to make sure that she wasn't following. Then I went in.

The joint was small—an oval bar and five or six booths grouped on either side of a juke-box. The bartender on duty was lonesome.

"What'll it be, Mac?"

"Rye. Top shelf."

He poured. I drank. Just like that. Fast. The stuff was bonded, like a bank messenger.

"Refill, please."

He poured. I watched his black bowtie. It was beginning to wobble in anticipation of the conversation forming in his larynx. Abruptly it stopped wobbling.

Because the door opened and she came in. Big as life, and even blonder. The neon on the juke-box did things to her diamond choker.

There was no place to hide. No real reason for me to hide, for that matter. She came right over, sat down, motioned to the bartender. "The same," she said. Nice, rich, husky voice.

She watched the man pour, then transferred her gaze to me. Her eyes matched the diamonds she was wearing.

"Let's sit in a booth," she suggested.

"Why?"

"We can talk there."

"What's wrong with right here?"

"If you prefer."

"What's the proposition?"

"I want you to come with me, to meet somebody."

"You'll have to talk plainer than that, lady."

"I said we should take a booth."

"Nothing wrong with mentioning names right here in the open."

"No." She shook her head. Those diamonds shed enough light to blind a pedestrian walking across the street. "I am not permitted to mention names yet. But it will be to your advantage to come with me."

"Sorry, lady. I'd have to know more about it." I looked down at my glass. "For example, who sent you to me. How you found me. Little details like that. Maybe they're nothing to you. Me, I find them fascinating."

"This is no time to make jokes."

"I'm serious. And I say I'm not playing unless you tell me the name of the team."

"All right, Bob. But—"

That did it. The name. Of course, she could have picked it up off the hotel register easily enough. But it jarred me more than anything else up to that point. It jarred me right on down to my feet.

"Good-night," I said.

She didn't answer. As I walked out, she was still staring at me. Blue diamond eyes winked me out of the tavern.

I walked out. I didn't go back to my room and I didn't go to another tavern. I headed north, crossed under the El tracks into the Loop. There was a burlesque show. I bought a ticket and sat through a dreary performance of which I remember nothing except the old blackout skit about the photographer in the park who complained that the squirrels were nibbling his equipment.

I spent my time trying to fit the pieces together. Who was this girl? A friend of Cono's? A friend of Flo's? A friend of the Great Ahmed's? A friend of the carney advance man? Or just a friend?

Cono was dead and Flo was dead. They couldn't tell her where to find me. Ahmed didn't know I existed, let alone where I was. The carney advance man wouldn't know my address until the telegram arrived.

Could it be that she had a line into the prison and had learned I was about to receive eight thousand dollars?

Was she simply working the hotel, picking my name from the register at random?

But if so, what was this story about a proposition, and meeting somebody?

It didn't make sense. I sat there a while and tried to figure the deal out, then I left.

Eleven o'clock. I headed back to the hotel. This time I peeked into the lobby before entering. She wasn't around. I slid unobtrusively past the entrance so the night clerk wouldn't pay attention. He was reading a science-fiction magazine and didn't look up.

The elevator operator took me to the fifth floor without removing his eyes from the Racing Form. Quite a bunch of students in this hotel. Probably working their way through mortician's school.

I walked down to the door of my room very quietly. I listened at the keyhole before I unlocked the door. Then I opened it fast and switched on the light.

No blonde.

I examined the closet, the washroom. Still no blonde. Then and only then I went to the phone, called room service, and ordered a pint of rye and some ice.

It was still Saturday night and I was still entitled to a drink, without strange blondes butting in.

But when the drinks came, I found the blonde was still with me. Prancing around inside my skull, making propositions, winking her diamonds at me.

It didn't take me long to finish the bottle and it didn't take the bottle long to finish me.

Somewhere along the line I managed to undress, don pyjamas, and slump across the bed. Somewhere along the line I drifted off to sleep.

And that's when it started.

I was back in the burlesque house, sitting in the crummy seat, watching the stage. This time the performance was more interesting. There was a new comic in the cast—a tall fellow with a shaved head. He looked something like Cono. In fact, he was Cono. Big as life. A chorus line danced out behind him; eight, count 'em, eight nifty little numbers. They danced, kicked, whirled. Cono noticed them. He did a little shuffling dance of his own, gyrating to the end of the line. Then he reached out—in the old familiar gesture used by the late Ted Healy in chastising his stooges—and flicked them across the neck. One by one. As his fingers touched each girl in turn, she changed.

Heads dangled limply from broken necks. The eight dancing girls became eight dancing cadavers. Eight, count 'em, eight. The dancing dead. The dancing dead, with skulls for heads. Skulls with diamond eyes.

Dead arms reached out and scrabbled in dead skull-sockets. They picked out the diamonds and threw them at me. I twisted and turned, sweated and squirmed, but I couldn't dodge. The diamonds hit me, seared me with icy fire.

Cono laughed. The girls danced off stage and he was all alone. All alone except for the chair. It stood there in the center of the stage and the lights went down. As the spotlight narrowed, Cono moved towards its center, closer to the chair. He had to stay within the circle of light or die.

Then the circle narrowed still further and he was sitting in the chair. As if by magic, squirrels danced out on the stage. They each carried a tiny thong, and each bound the thong around Cono's arm or leg or neck until he sat there criss-crossed with thongs that lashed him to the chair.

I don't have to tell you what kind of a chair it was. What else would it be?

And I don't have to tell you what was going to happen next. Even in my dream I knew it, and I struggled frantically to wake up.

But I couldn't. I couldn't even leave my seat in the theatre. Because while I had been watching Cono getting bound into the chair, somebody had bound me!

Now I was sitting in an electric chair, hands tied, feet tied, electrodes clamped and ready. I tugged and tore, but I couldn't move. They had me, all right. It had all been a trick, a dirty trick to get my attention away from myself.

I knew that now. Because suddenly Cono burst his bonds with a flick of his fingers, the same fingers that had killed the dancing girls. He stood up and laughed because it was a joke. A joke on me.

He wasn't going to die. I was. He'd live. He'd get the eight thousand dollars and the blonde, and I'd fry. Just as soon as they turned on the juice. The bonded juice. The neon lights were winking now and the bartender was ready to pull the switch as soon as the conductor called out "Chicago!" and now they were getting ready to give the signal. While waiting, Cono stood on the stage and amused me with card tricks. He pulled the Ace of Spades out of his mouth and held it up for me to see.

Then it was time. Somebody came onstage and handed him a telegram from the carney and that was the signal for them to yell "Chicago!"

The switch was ready. I felt the cold sweat running down my spine, felt the electrodes bite into the side of my leg, the side of my head. And then, they pulled the switch—

I woke up.

I woke up, sat up in bed and stared out the window.

Through the windowpane, the blonde stared back at me.

I could only see her face, and that was funny, because it was a full window. Then I realized it was because she wasn't vertical, but horizontal. And only her face was pointed towards me.

Shall I make it plainer?

I mean she was floating in empty air outside my window.

Floating in empty air and smiling at me with her icy eyes aglitter.

Then I really woke up.

The second dream, or the second part of the dream, was so real I had to stagger over to the window and convince myself that there was no one outside. It took me a minute before my trembling legs would support me and carry me that distance, so if she really had been at the window there'd have been enough time for her to get back down the fire escape and disappear.

Of course she wasn't there.

And she couldn't have been, because there was no fire-escape. I gazed down at a sheer drop of five floors to the closed and empty courtyard below. It was black down there, black as the Ace of Spades.

I don't know what I should have done under the circumstances; all I know is what I did do.

I shoved my head under the cold water faucet, towelled my face dry, dressed, and rushed out of my room in search of a drink.

And that's when the next nightmare started.

There was this little joint three blocks south of the hotel. I ran all the way, couldn't stop running until I'd covered that much distance. The street was deserted and it was dark, and only this little joint had a rose light burning in the window. It was the light that drew me, because I was afraid of the dark.

I opened the door and a blast of smoke and sound hit me in the face but I ploughed through it blindly to the bar.

"Shot of whiskey!" I said, and meant it.

The bartender was a tall, thin man and he had a glass eye that almost fell out as he bent his head while pouring my drink. I didn't pay very much attention to it at the time; I was too busy getting the drink down.

Then it fascinated me. I didn't want to stare at it, so I looked away—looked down the bar, into the seething center of smoke and sound.

That was a mistake.

Sitting on the stool next to me was a little man who was sipping a glass of beer. He had to sip, because he had no arms. He lapped at the glass the way a cat laps at a saucer of cream. Watching him was a blind man. Don't ask me how I knew he could see, but I got the impression of watching from the tilt of the head, the focus of the dark glasses.

I whirled around and nearly collided with the man on crutches. He was standing there arguing with the man on the floor—the one without legs. Down the bar a way; somebody was banging with a steel hook affixed to his elbow. I could scarcely hear the thumping because the juke box was playing so loudly. Sure enough, there were dancers present; the inevitable two women, both of them engrossed in their movements. They had to watch carefully, because both of them were on crutches.

There were others present, too—others in the booths. The man with the bandaged head. The man with the hole where his nose should be. The man with the great purple growth bulging over his collar. The lame, the halt, the blind.

They didn't pay any attention to me. They were having fun. And in a moment I realized what I'd stumbled into. It was a street beggar's tavern. I saw the tin cup set alongside the shotglass, the placard resting against the beer bottle. What was the name of the dump in Victor Hugo's *Notre Dame de Paris?* "The Court of Miracles" he called it. And this was it.

They were happy enough, drinking. They forgot their physical ills. Maybe liquor would cure me of my mental ills. It was worth a try. So I had another drink.

Along about the third drink somebody must have slipped out. Along about the fourth drink somebody must have come back. And in a minute or two, she walked in.

I didn't see her, at first. The reason I sensed her presence was because the noise cut down. The juke box stopped and didn't start again. The conversation dropped to a hush.

That's when I looked around and noticed her. She was sitting in a booth, all alone, just watching me.

She made a little gesture of invitation and I shook my head. That was all. Then she raised her glass and offered me a silent toast.

I turned, noted my re-filled glass, and toasted her. Then I downed my drink. The bartender with the glass eye had another waiting for me.

"On the lady," he said.

"No thanks, chum."

He looked at me. "Whatsa matter? She's a nice lady."

"Sure she is. Nobody's questioning that."

"So whyn'cha drink it?"

"I've had enough, that's why." I had, enough and to spare, I suddenly realized. The room was beginning to spin a little.

"Come on, drink up. We're all friends here."

The bartender didn't look friendly. Neither did anyone else. For the first time I grew aware of the fact that everyone was looking at me. Not at her—at me. The legless, the armless, the blind. In fact, the blind man took off his dark glasses in order to see me better, and one of the crowd slapped his crutch on the bar and walked a little closer.

The Court of Miracles! Where the blind see and the lame walk! Of course it was; and half of these beggers were fakes. They were as sound as I was—sounder, perhaps.

And there was a whole roomful of them, all looking at me. None of them seemed happy any longer. They were quiet; so quiet I could hear the click of the key in the lock as the armless man locked the door.

Oh, he had arms now; they'd emerged from beneath a bulky vest. But I wasn't interested in that. I was interested in the fact that the door was locked. And I was here, inside.

She stared and they stared.

The bartender said, "How about it, chum?"

"Not today." I stood up. That is, I tried to stand up. My legs were wobbly. Something was wrong with them. Something was wrong with my eyes, too.

"What's the trouble?" drawled the bartender. "Afraid of being slipped a Mickey?"

"No!" It was hard to talk. Only gasps came out. "You already slipped me one the drink before this. When she came in, and gave you the signal."

"Wise guy, huh?"

"Yes!" I managed to spin around, fast. Fast enough to grab the whiskey-bottle off the bar and hold it cocked. My other hand supported me.

"Now—open that door or I'll let you have it," I panted. "Come on, move fast."

The bartender shrugged. There was neither fear nor malice in his glass eye.

My own eyes were turning to glass. I tried to focus them on the bartender, tried not to look at the creeping, crawling cripples that slithered closer all around me, brandishing canes and crutches and uttering little grunts and whimpers and moans.

"Open that door!" I wheezed, while they crept closer and closer, stretching out their arms and tensing to spring.

"All right, chum!"

That was the signal for them to rush me. Somebody swung a crutch, somebody clawed at my legs. I began to spin and go down.

I swung the bottle, clearing an arc, and they fell back, but only for a moment. The bartender aimed a punch, so I swung the bottle again.

Then they came back. It was like fighting underwater, like fighting in a dream. And this was a dream, a nightmare of crawlers, of slithering shapes tearing at me, dragging me down.

The bartender hit me again, so I raised the bottle and brought it down. It landed on his head with a dull crunch.

For a moment he stood there, and the glass eye popped out of its socket and rolled along the bar. It stared up at him and watched as he sagged slowly and fell.

Then it stared at me as the man with the artificial arm hit me across the neck with the hook.

I felt the blow land and melt my spine.

The glass eye watched as I collapsed into roaring darkness and when I went down, it winked.

When I woke up, she was stroking my forehead.

Not bad. Lots of men would have traded places with me at the moment— lying there in the cool dusk, on a comfortable bed, with a beautiful blonde stroking my forehead.

Too bad some other guy didn't show up, because I would have traded him in a flash.

I'd have thrown in a splitting headache, free of charge, and a taste in the mouth like the bottom of the Chicago Drainage Canal.

But nobody showed up to take my place, so I just stayed there. When she said, "Drink this," I drank. When she said, "Close your eyes and wait for the pain to go away," I closed my eyes and waited.

Miraculously, the pain went away.

The headache and the taste vanished. I opened my eyes again, wiggled my fingers and toes.

I was lying on this bed in a darkened room. The shades were drawn, but enough light filtered through to bring life to the diamond choker, and the diamond ring and the diamond eyes. The diamond eyes regarded me candidly.

"Feel better now?"

"Yes."

"That's good. Then there's nothing to worry about."

How right she was. Nothing to worry about except where I was, and why. I suppose a little of my bitterness crept over into my reply.

"Thanks," I said. "Thanks for everything you've done for me. Including getting me knocked out."

"That's no way to look at it," answered the blonde. "After all, I saved your life."

"You mean those beggars would have killed me?"

"No. But the police might."

"Police?"

"Yes." She drew a long breath. "After all, you did murder that bartender."

"What?"

"You hit him with the bottle. He's dead."

I sat up, faster than I would have believed possible. "Come on, let me out of here," I snapped.

"They'll be on the lookout for you," she told me. "It's not safe for you to go just now. You're among friends here."

"Friends!"

"Don't misunderstand. If you'd only listened to me in the first place and come along sensibly, all this would never have happened."

I had no answer for that one. All I knew was that if she spoke the truth, I was a murderer. And I knew what they did to murderers. They sat them down in a chair and turned on the juice and fried them. A faint odor of singed flesh tainted my nostrils.

"How do I know you're not lying?" I asked.

"I can furnish proof if you like, later. Right now, I want you to meet a friend." She put her hand on my shoulder and even through the shirt I could feel the icy coldness of her flesh. She was cold and hard, like a diamond.

"As long as I'm meeting friends, we might as well establish a few facts," I suggested. "You know my name. Now, what's yours? And where am I?"

She smiled and stood up. "My name is Vera. Vera LaValle. We are in a home on the South Side. And, although you didn't think to ask me, it's Monday evening. You've been unconscious for almost forty-eight hours."

I stood up, then. It wasn't a spectacular performance. I glanced down at myself in the dim light and what I saw wasn't pretty.

"Why don't you go in and bathe, clean up a bit?" Vera suggested. "I'll go out and bring back some food. You can eat it before our meeting."

Without waiting for my reply, she went out. Went out and locked the door.

It was getting to be a habit. Everybody that I met locked me in. Of course, that's what you do with murderers. Dangerous people to have around. Always killing bartenders, for instance. And if I was a murderer . . .

I doubted it. The whole thing was phoney from start to finish. Things like that just didn't happen to me. I was the original timid soul. Couldn't lick my weight in wild flowers.

Then, again . . .

There was blood on my suit. Blood on my shirt. Blood on the back of my neck, crusted blood from where the steel hook had landed.

I went into the bathroom, filled the tub, undressed, bathed. There was a nice array of soap and towels, all laid out and waiting for me. I even found an electric shaver to plug in. I felt a lot better once I was cleaned up.

When I dressed, I was surprised to discover a fresh white shirt conveniently placed on top of a clothes hamper. My genial host or hostess thought of everything.

By the time I stepped out of the bathroom she had returned. She had four sandwiches wrapped in cellophane, a double cardboard cup of coffee, and a wedge of pie. She didn't say anything while I ate. It only took me about six minutes to dispose of the meal and latch onto a cigarette from my pocket. I offered her one.

"No, thanks. I do not smoke."

"Funny. I thought all women did nowadays."

"I tried it once. Many years ago. Of course, it wasn't a cigarette."

This didn't seem to be getting me anywhere. "About that friend I was going to meet. Where is he?"

"Waiting outside the door," she said. "Shall I ask him in?"

"By all means. Don't keep the gentleman waiting." My tone was facetious, but I didn't feel very gay. I don't know what I really expected. Years of reading—and writing—horror fiction had conditioned me to almost everything. A Mad Doctor, perhaps, coming to recommend a certain brand of cigarettes. A Mad Scientist with a beaker-full of monkey glands. A Mad Professor with a driver's license for a flying saucer.

The last person I expected to see when the door opened was a friend. But it was a friend who walked in. It was Cono.

Cono Colluri. The man who died in the electric chair.

He stood there in the twilight and looked at me. He wore a battered trench-coat with the collar turned up, and he had a hat pulled down over his eyes like a movie gangster, but I recognized him. It wasn't a double, or a stooge, or somebody made up to resemble him. It was Cono. Cono in the flesh. The dead flesh—reanimate and alive!

Changed? Of course he had changed. There was a dreadful facial tic, where the muscles had been pulled and torn by the convulsive spasm of the shock. And he was pale. Pale as death. But he lived. He walked. He talked . . .

"Hello, Bob. I've been waiting for you."

"She—she told me."

"Too bad you wouldn't come at once. I should have used more sense, let her tell you who wanted to see you. But I figgered you wouldn't of believed her."

"Yes. I guess that's right." I fumbled for words while he stood there, stood there looking at me. "How— how are you?"

That was a fine thing to ask. But he didn't seem to mind.

In fact, he smiled. The smile creased the side of his face and got tangled up in the tic, but he made it. "Oh, I'll live," he said. "I'll live forever."

"What?"

"That's the pitch, Bob. That's why I had to see you. I'm going to live forever. Varek fixed that."

Varek? Where had I heard that name before?

"He's the one who claimed my body. You remember."

Yes, I remembered. The mysterious cousin. "But how did he know you weren't dead, and how did he revive you?"

"I was dead, Bob. Deader'n a doornail. And he fixed me up. He can fix anybody up, Bob. Bring them back. Make it so's they never die. And that's where you come in."

"Me?"

"I been telling him about you. About how smart you are, all that stuff you write. He needs somebody like you for the outside—to front. Somebody with brains. Young. And alive."

Alive. I was alive, all right, but I wondered if I was awake and sane. Talking to a dead man . . .

"Come here, Bob. I can see you don't believe me."

I moved closer to Cono.

"Feel my skin. Go ahead."

I put my hand on his wrist. It was cold. Cold, but solid. Up close I could see the waxen pallor of Cono's face. Cono's death-mask. The tic rippled across it and he smiled again.

"Don't be scared. I'm real. It's real. He can do it. He can bring back the dead. Don't you see what it means? What a big thing it is, if it's handled right?"

"I see. But I still can't understand where I fit in."

"Varek will tell you all about it. Come on, I want you to talk to him."

I followed Cono Colluri out of the room. Vera smiled and nodded as we left, but she didn't accompany us as we walked down the long corridor to a stairway. Descending the stairs into the soft, subdued light of the parlors below, I became conscious of a peculiar odor. It smelled like stale air, steam heat and the scent of mingled flowers.

"Say, just where are we, anyway?" I asked.

"Funeral home," Cono answered. "Didn't you know?"

I hadn't known. But I might have guessed. Living quarters upstairs and down here the parlors. The parlors, the soft lights and the scent of flowers.

We walked across a carpeted hallway, and I glanced around me. It was the way Cono had said; this was a funeral home, and a rather shabby one. Perhaps that's why there were no bodies lying in state, no mourners. Varek had set this up for a front, and I rather suspected that if I made a dash for it and tried the front door I would find it locked.

But I didn't make a dash for it. I followed Cono into the darkened parlor to the left, to meet Mr Varek.

I walked in and Cono lumbered over to the corner. He walked stiffly, awk-
wardly. The muscles in his body were taut with shock. But he did pretty well for
a dead man.

He was turning on a lamp in the corner, he was closing the door behind us.
I paid no attention. I was staring down at the coffin on the trestle. Staring down
at the body in the coffin. The body of the man with the glass eye.

It was the bartender I'd killed.

He lay there on the cheap satin, dressed in a worn black suit. Somebody had put
the glass eye back in place and it stared up at me sardonically. The other eye was
closed, and the general effect was that of a wink.

There we were—me and the man I'd killed. I looked at him, and he looked
at me.

He looked at me!

Yes. It happened. The eyelid rolled back. The eye opened. It focussed on me.
And the mouth, the bound mouth, relaxed its smirk. The lips parted.

And from the corpse came the voice: "Hello, Bob. I'm Nicolo Varek."

"You—"

"Oh, I'm not the bartender you killed. He's dead enough, as you can see for
yourself. His body isn't breathing."

It wasn't either. The corpse was still a corpse, but something was alive, something lived inside it. Lived and looked and talked.

"I'm just taking temporary residence. So that I can talk to you, without having to travel a great distance. You can appreciate the convenience."

I couldn't, at that moment. I could only stand and gape and feel the sweat
trickling down under my armpits.

"You've been a long time coming, Bob. But it was inevitable that we should
meet. Cono has told me all about you, and of course I have other ways of gaining information. Many ways."

"I'm sure." It came out before I could stop it, but the corpse chuckled. The
sound was a death-rattle.

"How typical of you to say that. How characteristic! Ah, yes, I've studied your
background, your work. You interest me greatly. That is why I have gone to all
this trouble to arrange our meeting."

I nodded, but said nothing. I was waiting.

"I'm inclined to give Cono credit for finding you. It's quite true, I can use you."

"Dead or alive?" That remark came out before I could stop it, too.

"Alive, of course. But don't think I'm not appreciative of the distinction.
You're a man of keen wit, sir. And I admire you for it. One seldom finds acerbity
in these decadent days."

"Look," I said, beginning to recover a little composure. "I'm not used to in-
dulging in character analysis with a corpse. Just what do you want of me?"

"Your services, sir. Your professional services. For which, needless to say, you
will be generously rewarded. In perpetuity, I might add."

"Cut the double-talk. I've had enough from Vera, and from poor Cono—"

"*Poor* Cono? I would hardly endorse the adjective. Were it nor for me, my dear sir, Cono would be languishing in an unmarked grave. Whereas, thanks to my efforts, he is among the quick rather than the dead. And if you wish plain talk, sir, you shall have it.

"I am Nicolo Varek, man of science. I have perfected a means, a methodology, a therapy if you like, which defeats what men call death. Defeats death? It goes beyond that, far beyond. For those whom I revive also possess the boon of eternal life. Eternal life!"

Crazy talk. But it was coming from the mouth of a corpse, and I believed it. There was no hint of fakery or collusion—no ventriloquist could open the cadaver's eye, manipulate his dead lips. I saw, and I heard. And I believed.

"Yes, I can give life to the dead. As to the how and the why of it, well, that's my secret. My priceless, precious, perfect secret.

"And what do you think the use of that secret is worth, sir? What is the proper fee for the boon of eternal life? A million dollars, perhaps?

"There are many men with a million dollars in this world, my friend. Do you think any of them would hesitate to part with that sum if I could assure them of continued existence?

"But there's the rub. They must be assured. And at the same time the secret must remain a secret. For this reason I must continue to operate anonymously. There is nothing men would stop at in order to extract my secret from me—if I were known to them as its possessor. How often I've faced torture and death myself at the hands of those who suspected I might save them!

"You say I have helpers aplenty? That I can summon up an army of the dead, if need be, to assist me in my aims? That is true—but only within certain limits. The dead must be controlled. And I cannot carry out my plans completely without the aid of living humanity. I need a man of prescience, a man of integrity. Such as yourself, sir."

"I don't see what you're driving at."

"A business arrangement. You might even go so far as to call it a partnership. With myself as the silent partner. You as the go-between. Our product: Eternal life. Our goal: Unlimited wealth, unlimited power."

"Sounds a bit too easy."

"Do not mistake it, my friend. There are innumerable obstacles to overcome, many problems to face and to solve. I can provide for them all, however. This had been a cherished dream of mine for centuries. Yes, centuries."

"Who are you, anyway?"

The corpse chuckled. "So many men have asked that question of me, so many times! Yet I find it best not to answer. My handiwork is proof that I speak truth, and that is all you need. Trust me, and we shall rule.

"Yes, rule! Surely you can see what power lies in my secret. The hold it will give us both over the great ones of this world, now and forever! We'll seek our fortunes first, and the rest shall come.

"I have the plans well laid. You will be able to go forth and proclaim the gift of eternal life to the world. Nor shall you lack for assistance. I can summon a host to your command, to do your bidding and mine. We shall broadcast the tidings: There is no more death, for those who can pay the price! Eternal life, and more; special powers, new powers.

"But you'll learn all this and more in time to come. You'll learn the methods I've devised for bringing the news to the world. Of course, it would never do to make a really public announcement or statement; it must all be cloaked in mysticism and the proper formulae. We'll start a cult, attract the wealthy, and reveal the truth only to the select few.

"Now, sir, how does my proposal strike you? Eternal life, eternal riches, eternal power?"

I didn't say anything for a long moment. I stared at the corpse that told me men could live forever.

"Silence means consent," said the voice.

"Not necessarily. I was just wondering—what if I refuse?"

"I'm sorry you even mention the possibility. For it forces me to remind you that you really have no choice in the matter."

"You mean you'll kill me if I don't? Kill me and animate my corpse, I suppose?"

"Come now, surely you give me credit for more subtlety than that? I've already gone to a great deal of trouble and risk to bring you here, as you know. I cannot jeopardize my plans to any further extent. And you would be of no use to me as a corpse. Besides, there is no need for me to kill you. If you walk out of here, you're as good as dead anyway."

"Meaning?"

"Meaning that you are wanted for murder. For killing this poor one-eyed citizen of a free republic. The bartender."

"But he's alive, you've revived him—"

"Not like the others. It's purely temporary, you understand. I can keep him animated as long as I choose, and I will do so if you consent. I'll even put him back to work in the bar." Again the chuckle. "It won't be the first time a dead man has walked abroad with none the wiser. If only you knew or even suspected how many of the dead presently mingle with the living, thanks to the Varek method!"

I shuddered. The single eye of the corpse was omniscient. The voice purred on: "If you refuse, he becomes a corpse again. With a dozen witnesses to swear you killed him. I'll not wreak vengeance—the full majesty of the law will attend to that. And your story of mysterious women and corpses that talk and a walking dead man will not help you or save you. I believe you realize that.

"But you won't refuse. Because you can see what I'm offering you. Wealth and power. The goals, the dreams of every man. A chance for eternal life yourself, such as I enjoy. Think it over, sir, think well upon it. Life or death?"

I thought. I thought well upon it. And everything within me clamored for assent. Oh, it's easy enough to be a hero when there's no temptation. But the cynic who said every man has his price knew human nature. There aren't many who wouldn't settle for eternal life, eternal wealth and eternal power even at the price of their souls—and the souls of everyone else, for that matter.

The souls of everyone else . . .

I looked at Cono. My friend, Cono Colluri. The late Cono Colluri who went to his death looking like an overgrown college boy. Cono, who left me eight thousand bucks and a promise to clear his name.

Where was Cono now?

He wasn't here in this room. His body was here, and it moved and it talked, but the soul . . .

There was a tic, there was torment, there was twisting torture. Not real life. This was a stranger, a bulking walking corpse. No emotions, no warmth, no humanity.

Sure, I could sell myself out. But I couldn't sell out the world.

So I stared down at the corpse and I said, "No. I'm sorry, Varek. I've got to refuse, and take my chances."

"The decision is final?"

"Final."

"Very well. You've had your chance."

The mouth shut. The eye closed. The dead bartender was truly dead again. I saw the light fade away from the countenance, then I moved back. Back, into Cono Colluri's arms.

I might have known Varek would lie. That he'd never let me out of that room alive. If I hadn't realized it before, I knew it now. Because the cold arms wrapped around me. And the great thumbs rose up to my neck, ready to press and squeeze.

"Cono!" I gasped. "It's me—your friend—don't—"

You can't argue with a corpse.

You can only fight. Fight and pant, and try to keep the strangling hands away from your throat. I hit him with everything I had. Nothing happened. Nothing happened, except that he bent me back, back . . .

I sagged then. Sagged so suddenly that he went down with me. As I fell, I twisted. His grip broke. I rolled under the trestle. He groped after me. I dumped coffin and all on his head. He went down. Blind corpse-eyes sought me. I ran. I made it down the hall with no one to stop me. He lumbered to his feet, came groping after me.

I knew the front door would be locked. But there was a glass panel, and next to it in the hall somebody had placed a large urn.

I grabbed it up, smashed the glass, and stepped through.

Then I was out on the street, running. It was night. The air was cool.

It was good to be free.

Free, and wanted for murder.

Have you ever wondered what it feels like to be a murderer?

I can tell you.

It feels like rabbits who hear the baying of a hunting dog. It feels like lying in bed with the covers pulled over your head and Pa coming up the stairs to give you a spanking. It feels like waiting for the Doctor to sterilize the instruments.

You don't walk down the street when you're a murderer. You skulk through the alleys. You don't take the streetcar and you don't pass any cops. And when you finally get down-town to your hotel, you walk a long time before you go inside the lobby. You look around very carefully to make sure it's deserted.

And when you do go in, you don't ask for the key to your room. The police might be waiting up there. Or somebody else. Somebody that's dead, but alive. Waiting to grab you and—

I had the feeling, but I kept it out of my face and voice long enough to ask the clerk and the desk whether or not there had been any message for me.

You see, I had to play one hunch; that the hotel hadn't been tipped off. Varek wouldn't, as long as he thought I was coming in with him. And now, there was still that chance. If I could only get the message . . .

It was waiting for me, the precious little yellow envelope stuck in the pigeonhole. The telegram from the carney. I ripped it open and read:

GREAT AHMED AT FORTY THREE EAST BRENT STREET UNDER NAME RICHARDS.

That was all, and it was enough. Brent was a street on the near North side. Walking distance. I could take an El and bypass the Loop, if I was willing to risk it.

I was. Ahmed, or Richards, had the money.

I had to. Ahmed, or Richards, could save me.

I did. Ahmed, or Richards, was the answer.

Brent Street was about a mile across the bridge after I left the El. It was a long, hard mile. I kept to the shadows, kept my face averted from passersby. But nothing happened. I stopped in front of the dingy old brownstone frost that was graced with the numerals 43, lit my last cigarette, and went up the steps to press the buzzer.

Then I waited.

It was a good two minutes before the door opened. During that time I speculated quite a bit about the man I was going to meet.

Would it be the Great Ahmed in a turban? A swarthy man with a pointed beard, deepset burning eyes and a singsong voice?

Would it be the suave, cultivated, cosmopolitan Mr Richards, a con man from the carney, dressed a little too garishly, with a voice too soft and smooth?

It was important for me to know. Because I'd have to throw myself on the man's mercy.

The door opened to answer my question.

"The Great Ahmed?" I asked.

"Yes. Please come in."

I came in. Into the light of the hall-way, where I could see my host.

He wasn't Ahmed and he wasn't Richards, either.

He was nobody.

A small man of about fifty, with thin, greying hair. Wrinkled face, watery blue eyes, almost grey. Come to think about it, his skin was grey, too. And he wore a grey suit. Quiet and inconspicuous. About as far away from a carney type as I could have possibly imagined.

How to describe him? In Hollywood, he'd be what they'd call a Barry Fitzgerald type without the smile and the brogue. Somebody's uncle. The kindly bachelor uncle.

I hoped he'd be mine.

"You are the Great Ahmed?" I asked, still not sure, still not sold.

"Yes. You want a reading?"

"Uh . . . yes."

I might as well stall for a while until I was sure. The way things had been happening, I wouldn't have trusted my own brother.

It was a big house, an old house, one of those places built for people to live in at a time when most families had eight or nine children instead of a television set.

The Great Ahmed led me down a long hallway, past two or three doors leading, inevitably, to a sunporch, a parlor, a library. The room he ushered me into was a sort of secondary parlor, towards the rear of the house. It had plenty of solid mahogany in it; old pieces, but durable. There was a massive center table and the inevitable grouping of chairs as if for a seance. But there was nothing of the medium's workshop or the clairvoyant's clip-joint about this place.

I took advantage of the light in the room to study my host a little more closely, but I can't say I learned much. He was just a tired, middle-aged man, and I wondered how he managed the grift with a tough carney outfit. He didn't look the part of an Oriental mystic at all.

Even when he told me to sit down and produced a crystal ball from a cupboard, I wasn't impressed. The ball itself was small, and a trifle dusty. As a matter of fact, he brushed it off with his sleeve, smiling sheepishly as he did so.

Then he sat down, stared into the ball, and smiled again.

"The reading is three dollars," he said. "An offering, you understand, not a fee. Fee's against the law here."

"Shoot the three bucks," I said.

"Very well." His eyes left my face. They focussed on the ball. Grey eyes, a trifle bloodshot.

I sat very quietly while he stared. He cleared his throat. He fidgeted. Then he spoke.

He told me my name.

He told me where I'd been working.

"You are a friend of the late Cono Colluri," he said, his eyes downcast. "And you are here to collect his money. A sum amounting to eight thousand, two hundred and thirty-one dollars."

He paused. I felt the perspiration running along the collar of my nice white shirt—the one from the funeral parlor, probably stolen off a stiff.

He paused, and I stared at him. Nice little man in grey, but he knew too much. I'd never believed in "occult powers," and yet here he was, telling me these things.

After what I'd gone through in the past three days, I felt that I couldn't take much more. My whole concept of the universe was shattering, and along with it, my sanity. Dead men walking, me a murderer, and now a man who actually reads minds. It was too much . . .

"Take it easy, friend." The Great Ahmed stood up, slowly. "I didn't mean to upset you so. It was a cheap trick, I guess."

His hands moved upwards from under the table. They held an envelope and a sheet of paper.

With a start, I recognized Cono's letter.

"Picked it out of your pocket when I brushed against you in the hall," smiled the little man. "Then held it under the table and read it while you thought I was reading the crystal. Old bit of business, but effective."

I nodded, and tried to smile in a way that conveyed my relief.

"So you're Cono's friend," said the Great Ahmed. "He wrote me about you, you know. A couple of weeks ago. Didn't mention the money, though. It was a tragedy, wasn't it?"

"Then you know about the confession?"

"Yes. Louie was a rat." The smile left his face. "Too bad, a messy business. I'm glad I left the show."

He walked around to the cabinet, stooped, and opened the lower drawer with a small key. He took out a big black tin box. Another key opened it. He began to pile bills on the table—big bills, hundreds and thousands.

"Here's your money," he said, sorting a pile and pushing it across to me.

"But . . . don't you want some kind of paper, some kind of identification or signature?"

"You're Cono's friend. I trust you."

He smiled shyly, and his hands made a gesture of dismissal.

"You trust me, eh?"

"Why not?"

I took a deep breath and came out with it. I had to come out with it to somebody, or go crazy. "Because I'm wanted for murder, that's why!"

The Great Ahmed sat down again, still smiling. "And you want to tell me all about it, is that it? Well, go ahead. I'm listening."

I went ahead, and he listened. It took up a long time, but I told him the whole story—from the time I hit town until the time Cono hit me.

He sat there, a little grey idol, quietly gazing off into the gloom.

"And so now you want to clear your name, eh? And rescue Cono, I suppose? And put the finger on this man Varek, whoever he may be?"

I nodded.

"That's a big order. A mighty big order, friend. You know, of course, that your whole story sounds a bit implausible?"

"It sounds screwier than blazes," I told him. "But it's true. Every word of it."

"Granted. So the problem arises, where do we go from here?"

I glanced at the eight grand plus, lying before me on the table. Suddenly I shoved it back across to him.

"Will this help you to figure things out for me?" I asked. "Because if it will, take it. Part of it or all of it. Whatever it may cost to clear me, to save Cono. To pin a rap on that rat, Varek."

"You trust me to come in with you?" he asked.

"I've trusted you with my story. With my life. The money isn't important. If you're Cono's friend, you'll help."

"Good enough." The Great Ahmed sorted the bills and stacked them up next to the tin box. "From now on, I'm your man. Full time. Now to our problem." He pushed the crystal ball aside. "This won't help us any, I'm afraid. We have to face facts."

"Fact number one," I said, "is that the heat is on me."

"Which means you'll have to lay low. That makes me the outside man," he said.

"Correct. So it's your move."

"My move is to the hotel," Ahmed answered. "To your room. Sooner or later somebody is going to show up there, looking for you. The law will be around. But so will your blonde charmer, and some of the rest of Varek's friends. Perhaps even Cono himself. At any rate, chances are I'll find someone to tail; someone who will lead me to the funeral home or wherever else Varek hides out. He probably has a dozen or more places to hang his hat. If he wears a hat."

"I keep wondering," I mused. "What kind of a creature is this man? And his secret of eternal life—"

"He may have it," Ahmed retorted, "but you don't. And from the looks of you, a little sleep is in order. I'll take you upstairs to a bedroom. You might as well get a good night's rest while I go to work."

I didn't argue with him. The weariness pulled at my knees as I followed him up the stairs.

"You'll have to trust to me and to luck," said the little grey man. "Right now all I can tell you is I'm playing a hunch. That I can go back to the hotel, pick up the trail, and somehow have it lead me to Cono. He's the weak spot in the whole setup, for us. If I can handle him, he'll tell me what we have to know about Varek. Then we'll figure out how to deal with him."

"Sounds logical," I said, as we entered a small bedroom at the end of the corridor.

"Sounds mighty weak and flimsy, to tell the truth," replied my host. "But it's all we have to work on right now. I hope that by the time I return there'll be a little more to work on. Now—here we are. You don't fit into my pyjamas, but I think you'll find the bed is comfortable enough. I'll be on my way. Go to sleep, and pleasant dreams to you."

He waved and went out. I sank back on the bed, scarcely mindful of the click of the key in the lock. Then I sat up. "Here we go again!" I muttered.

My voice must have carried, because he called from beyond the door. "Locking you in. Got a cleaning woman who gets here in about an hour, and I don't want to take any chances. If your description has been braodcast, that is."

"Good enough," I answered. "But you'd better come back."

"I'll be back: And with good news. Don't you worry about a thing. When the Great Ahmed takes over, he takes over."

I lay back, kicked off my shoes, loosened my tie and belt, and then crawled under the covers. His footsteps receded into silence.

Here I was, in a strange house, in a strange bed, my future dependent on the integrity and the ability of a man I hadn't known a half hour.

Somehow, though, I trusted him. I had to trust him, of course, because there was nobody else. I wondered about the Great Ahmed, or Richards—if that was his real name. What he'd been doing hanging around a carney. Why he'd set up a three-dollar-a-throw crystal reading parlor here. Little colorless middle-aged nobody, without even a good line of patter to hand out. But the son-of-a-gun knew how to pick pockets!

That reassured me. He wasn't the schmoe he appeared to be. But was he good enough to handle a man who raised the dead?

I couldn't answer that one now. There was nothing to do but wait. Wait and rest. Rest and sleep.

The room was dark. The night came in at me through the window. I got up and pulled the shade. I didn't want the night. It contained too much that could hurt me. Police, detectives, Varek and the walking dead. Better the special darkness of the room, the special darkness behind my closed eyes. The darkness of sleep.

The darkness of dreams . . .

Funny, the people you run into when you're asleep. Like this negro, for instance. He was just a common citizen, like hundreds of thousands of others on Chicago's South Side. He was riding on the El and I was riding on the El, hanging on the strap next to him.

I wouldn't have even given him a second glance, except for one little thing.

He was dead.

Yes, he was dead. When the El lurched, and he toppled against me, and I saw the rolling whites of his empty eyes, felt the cold, the ebon coldness of his black skin, I knew he was dead. A black corpse, hanging to a strap in the El.

I knew he was dead, and he knew I knew it. Because he smiled. And the deep bass voice rumbled up from the depths—from the depths of his empty grave, his plundered and cheated grave—and he said, "Don't look at me. 'Cause I ain't the only one. They's a lot of 'em dead around heah. A lot of 'em. Look!"

I looked. I gazed down the aisle of the lurching El and I saw them, recognized them. Some of the passengers were alive, of course, and I could tell that at a glance. But there were others. Many others. The quiet ones. The ones with the fixed, cold stares. The ones who didn't talk. Who sat alone. Who carefully avoided touching other bodies. They were pale, they were stiff, they were dead.

Most of the men wore their good suits, because that's the way they were dressed in the undertaking parlors. Most of the women wore too much powder and rouge, because the morticians fixed them that way. Oh, I recognized them. And the Negro nudged me with his icy finger and grinned a grin that held neither mirth nor malice nor any human emotion.

"Zombies," he said. "Tha's what they calls us. Zombies. Walkin' dead. Walkin', talkin' dead. Walkin' and talkin' because the Man say so. The Man. The Big Voodoo Man."

"Varek!" I said.

The El lurched again. The lights went out. Something was happening to the power. Maybe because I'd spoken the name.

The black corpse thought so. In the darkness all I saw was eye-white and tooth-white, flashing at me. "You went and done it," the voice rumbled. "Sayin' the name!"

And all the corpses in all the cars groaned and murmured, "He said the name!"

Suddenly the car gave a sickening lurch and I knew we were going off the track, going over. The corpses rolled against me in waves, and we were twisting and turning, falling, falling . . .

I landed. You're supposed to wake up before you land, but I didn't. Because I went too deep. The car crashed down into the sewers. I wasn't hurt. I was flung free. And I crawled along in the darkness, without eye-white and tooth-white flashing. Just red, this time. Little red lights.

"Rats," I told myself. "Rat eyes."

"We take the form of rats, yes. And of bats. And of other things. But we are not animals. We are not men either." The voice at my ear was soft but imperative. "They call us—vampires!"

I couldn't see him, or the others, but I heard the chittering laughter rise all around me, rise and turn to metallic mockery as it boomed off the sewer walls.

"Vampires. He raised us from the dead, he made us. In the big church up on Division Street, Father Stanislaus makes the Holy Sign against us. But we do not care. He is fat and old, that priest, and he will die. We can never die. We walk the night, we feast, and we own the world below."

Another voice droned in: "It's like this under the whole city, did you know that? And under every city. There's always places to hide, if you're clever. You can tunnel from place to place, come and go as you please, and nobody knows. Nobody sees. Nobody hears. And you can lift the manhole covers, drag down what you want, and dispose of what's left without leaving any evidence. Oh, it's clever and no mistake, and we can thank the Master for it all."

I nodded. "You mean Varek," I said.

They howled at that, and the sound nearly tore my head in two as the echo hammered from the metal walls. They howled, and then they scrabbled towards me in the darkness, but I ran. I ran and waded and crawled and swam through muck and filth, seeking an opening, seeking a light, seeking an escape from the world of death and darkness here below.

I found it, found it at last. The round metal lid above my head which led to safety. Safety and the cool darkness of a cellar. A chink of light guided me to a stairway and the door above. I came out into a kitchen, moved past to the bedroom, and peered through the door.

Edgar Allan Poe sat by the bedside and made strange motions with his slim white hands. Two doctors were in attendance, and all focussed their gaze on the apparition lying on the bed; the gaunt, skeletal countenance peered up from the pillows with glazed and glassy eyes.

The patient had white whiskers and incongruously black hair; outside of the animation in his eyes he might have passed for dead, and none would be the wiser.

But Poe's hands moved, commanding the sleeper to awake, and as I watched, he awakened.

Ejaculations of "Dead! dead!" absolutely burst from the tongue and not the lips of the sufferer, and his whole frame at once—within the space of a single minute or even less, shrunk—crumbled—absolutely rotted away. Upon the bed, before that whole company, there lay a nearly liquid mass of loathsome, of detestable putridity.

Then I fled, screaming, from the house of M. Valdemar.

But wherever I went, there were the dead.

Poe couldn't raise Valdemar. But Varek could. And he had. In my dream, I saw the proof. I tramped the streets of Chicago and recognized the faces. That stiff-lipped, unsmiling doorman in front of the ritzy Gold Coast hotel—he was dead. The black-haired girl on the end of the switch-board at the Merchandise Mart, the one who said, "Number please?" in such a mechanical fashion—she was Varek's puppet, too. There was an elevator operator at Field's and three men who worked the night shift at a big steel plant out near Gary. An old precinct sergeant over in Garfield Park was a walking corpse and even his wife didn't suspect. But what the precinct sergeant didn't know was that his captain was also a cadaver, and neither of them knew the secret of one of the Cook County judges.

The dead—there were hundreds of them. Maybe thousands. Because Chicago isn't the only city in the world, and Varek had been everywhere.

I walked along, and then I ran. Because I couldn't stand it any longer, couldn't stand to see the faces, the empty eyes. I couldn't stand being jostled by a corpse in the crowded Loop. I ran and I ran until I came to the Great Ahmed's house and I came up to the bedroom, battered down the locked door, and crawled in bed here with myself again, knowing that I was safe at last, I was here, I could wake up into a world of reality—*where dead men still walked!*

"And they have other powers, too."

Who had told me that? Varek himself, in the bartender's body. *Other powers.* Powers like levitation—like floating through space, through windows high off the ground . . .

It had happened once before in a dream, and now it was happening again.

I could see her face at the bedroom window. Vera's face. The pale blonde hair. The diamond choker. Floating outside the window, bumping against it. Her hands groped out. She was opening the window from outside.

Funny that I should see it that way, because I'd pulled the shade down, and it was up now. So was the window. She was coming into the room, floating in gently, softly, ever so quietly. And now she landed, without a bump or a thump or a shudder, on the tips of her delicate toes. She was dead, too, of course. I knew it now. Her stare was glassy. She moved by automatic compulsion only. It was like a hypnotic trance, with every motion directed by an outside, an alien force.

Glassy-eyed, like a drugged Assassin. And like an Assassin, she drew the dagger from her waist. It was a long, slim, feminine-looking weapon, but it was deadly. The steel was diamond-bright. Why did she remind me of diamonds? Because of the choker. I gazed at the choker now as she tiptoed over to the bed. I wanted to watch it.

Better than watching the dagger. Because the dagger was a menace. It was coming up over my throat. In a moment it would come down, the point would bury itself in my neck, over the jugular.

All I had to do was watch the diamonds in her choker. And in a minute it would be all over. The knife was coming down, the knife that would end my life, the knife that would make me one with Varek's army—the army of the dead.

It came down, fast.

The glitter of that frantically falling blade broke the spell. Instantaneously, I realized that I was seeing it. There was a knife, and it was coming down at my throat.

I jerked my head to one side on the pillow and slammed my body forward, upward. My hands closed around solid flesh. Cold flesh.

Vera LaValle twisted wildly in my arms.

I sat up, hands moving to her wrist. I pressed it back until the knife dropped to the carpet. She fought me silently, her face a Medusa's mask, blonde curls tumbling like serpents over her cold, bare shoulders.

Suddenly her head dropped. I caught a glimpse of strong white teeth grimacing towards my neck. Vampire teeth, seeking my jugular.

I tore at her throat. My hands ripped the choker, dug beneath it. It came free, and fell. My hands closed around her neck, then came away.

I could not touch the thin red line, the scar that encircled her neck completely.

My hands came away, and I slapped her, hard.

Abruptly, she sank to the bed. The glassiness left her eyes and something like recognition flooded her face.

"Where am I?" whispered Vera LaValle.

"In a bedroom on Brent Street," I answered. "The Great Ahmed's place. You floated through the window and tried to kill me."

"He put me under," she murmured. "Then he sent me here and levitated me. I didn't know."

I nodded, but said nothing.

"You believe me, don't you?" she implored. "I didn't know. He promised me that he'd never make me do that again. But he did. He always does. Even now, I can't trust him. He can do anything he likes with me, because I'm—"

She stopped abruptly, and I filled it in for her.

"Because you're dead," I told her. "I know."

Her eyes widened. "How did you find out?"

For answer, I pointed at her throat. She noticed then that the choker had been torn away. Her hands covered the red scar on her neck and she stared at me for a long moment. Then, with a sigh, she swept her hair back into place.

"Tell me about it," I said. "Maybe I can help."

"Nobody can help. Nobody."

"I can try. And the more you tell me, the more I have to work with. That is, if it's safe to talk."

She thought that one over for a moment. "Yes, it will be, for at least a half hour now. He goes into a sort of coma when he levitates one of us; it requires terrific concentration. But if he comes out of it and discovers I've failed, anything can happen."

The fear was coming back into her eyes, and I sought to capture her attention again, quickly.

"Half an hour," I said. "That's time enough. Tell me about it from the beginning. What happened to you?"

Vera LaValle sighed. Her hands stroked the scar, softly. "All right," she said.

I lighted a cigarette and sat up, offering her the pack. She shook her head and I said. "Oh, that's right, I remember now. You don't smoke, do you?"

"I can't," said Vera LaValle. "I haven't been able to smoke, or drink, or eat. Not since I was beheaded—in 1794."

In 1794, the Terror ruled France. You could run into almost anything under the Terror. You might encounter a Citizen Robespierre or a man called—ironically enough—St Just.

If you did so, the chances were that they would introduce you to still another man with a more apt name—Samson, the executioner.

And Samson, in turn, would direct you to La Guillotine.

Everybody in France knew La Guillotine. Despite the feminine appellation, La Guillotine was not a giddy female—although she turned a lot of heads.

La Guillotine was the Terror incarnate. The head-chopping Terror. The beheading blade that waited until you were ripe for it, then chopped and filled the basket beneath it with rich and rotting fruit.

In 1794, the Terror ruled France, and you might run into almost anything. If you were Vera LaValle, age 20, daughter of Lucien LaValle the wealthy merchant, you walked in constant danger of your life.

Wealthy merchants were not popular these days. Wealthy merchants had to twist and turn, fawn and cringe, resort to almost any strategem in order to try and escape from Paris before the order came—the fatal summons to the Tribunal. Better to ride out of the city in a dung-cart than to the Place de la Concorde in a tumbril.

No wonder Lucien LaValle betook himself to desperate measures and consorted with strange people in an effort to procure a means of deliverance before it was too late. Paris was aswarm with rogues and adventurers, thieves and sharpers who fattened on the misery of the remaining members of the nobility or the well-to-do. Some of them, for a price, could procure passports or arrange an unauthorized passage across the border or the English Channel.

Lucien LaValle, wealthy widower with a handsome, marriageable daughter, thought that he had found a solution.

Somewhere, somehow, in heaven knows what den or dive or stew, he encountered Nicolo Varek. Varek, the friend of the illustrious Comte St Germain. Varek, the *confidant* of the mighty Cagliostro. Varek, the alchemist, the mystic, the seeker of the Philosopher's Stone. Varek who boasted of powers greater than those of the two great charlatans he claimed to have known—and taught. Varek, the unsmiling, the cold, the ageless. But—and this was the crux of the matter—Varek the foreigner. Varek, the holder of the priceless possession, the Russian visa. The passport to freedom for himself and family.

Varek had no family, now. But Vera LaValle was young, she was *chic*, she was eminently well dowered. If she were a wife, and Lucien LaValle an official member of Varek's family—then what would there be to stop the *ménage* from leaving France?

It was a reasonable proposition, and Lucien LaValle presented it to Varek on many occasions.

He shrugged. There was work to be done here in Paris, he said. Great things were afoot. He had never been presented to Mademoiselle LaValle, and no doubt she was all her fond father proclaimed her to be but still . . . A man in Varek's position is above matrimony and the calls of the flesh. And as to money (and here Varek shrugged again), he fortunately was in a position to command a fortune whenever he wished. No, it would not be advisable to leave the country now. As a matter of fact, everything depended upon remaining.

Lucien LaValle was eloquent. When eloquence fell upon deaf ears, he was insistent. When insistence failed, he resorted to tears. He sank to his knees. He wept and implored. And in the end, Nicolo Varek consented to meet the merchant's daughter, to talk to her.

That was enough for LaValle. He returned home elated, and put his case to Vera.

"Consider now how much depends upon your conduct," he told her. "Be charming—sprightly—gay. This Varek, he has a long face. He needs cheering. He needs your youth."

Vera LaValle nodded dutifully. No need to instruct her in coquetry. Long before he revealed his hopes and plans, she was miles ahead of her father. He had found a man who could save them—at a price. What the price was did not matter. Her father would pay his share and she would gladly pay hers.

She bathed, dressed, perfumed and painted for the interview. The meeting took place in the parlor and it was unchaperoned. A carriage drove up in the dusk, and Vera LaValle met Nicolo Varek under candlelight.

And it was thus that Varek, the friend of the nobility, the mentor of magicians, the peer of alchemists—Varek, the man who was above matrimony or the commonplace emotional reactions of ordinary men—fell in love.

Candlelight and coquetry definitely won the day, and the night. The suave, cold middle-aged man became a stammering, intense importuner. As to the matter of age, Varek was quite explicit on that point.

"Do not think of me as old, my dear," he reassured her. "For I am truly ageless. There are secrets I possess, secrets you shall share with me. Oh, we will share a great deal, you and I!"

He began to boast then, like any love-sick youth, and to confide.

Varek was Russian by birth, but the date of that birth and the details of his parentage would (he smirked) astound her. Suffice for him to say that he came of noble blood. He had been educated at the leading universities of Europe, but the bulk of his learning came from extended sojourns in Mongolia and Hindustan where he had studied occultism and the forbidden mysteries. Upon his return to Europe, he had visited Italy and imparted some of his wisdom to Cagliostro— wisdom which Cagliostro misused in his unscrupulous career. Varek, still seeking disciples, later gave instruction to the Comte de St Germain, whose mastery of mass illusion and the principles of levitation enabled him to win fame and fortune.

But he, Varek, was not interested in such trivia. True, as an alchemist he had sought to transmute baser metals to gold. But he soon realized that cultivation of other powers was more important. Once he had developed them, fame and fortune would be his for the asking.

There were two secrets, and two only, which were worth possessing. One of them was the secret of eternal youth, and the other, the secret of eternal life.

To the discovery of these secrets, Varek had dedicated himself for scores of years.

It was a costly study, an expensive search. In order to finance himself he had, at times, resorted to base means. As an alchemist he was acquainted with the group that centered around La Voisin, and he admitted assisting that notorious female in her preparation of poisons. He had also been familiar with the clique surrounding the infamous de Montespan.

"But that was ages ago!" cried Vera, when she heard him. "Over a hundred years!"

Nicolo Varek, the unsmiling one, smiled. "Exactly," he said. "You see, I succeeded in at least part of my quest. I did discover the secret of eternal youth. Discovered it and possessed myself of it."

"You are over a hundred?" Vera murmured.

Varek inclined his head. "I assure you, time is a relative concept. You will not find me less ardent a lover due to my age, no less honorable a man because of my past associations. As you realize, we who seek the mysteries have always been on the fringes of society. We skulk in darkness, we consort with the underworld, we compound with the charlatans simply because we have never been accepted by the scholars and the savants. They are jealous of our achievements, these so-called 'men of science'—although virtually all they know or hope to know has come from our work.

"Yes, it is we alchemists who have given them their chemistry, we sorcerers who have preserved what little is known of medicine and physiology and biology, we mystics who have the only knowledge which can develop into a science of the mind."

"I don't understand," Vera said. "What are you trying to tell me?"

"I'm telling you not to be afraid of me." he answered. "It has been said that I am a cheat, a liar, a fraud, a scoundrel, a magician, a murderer. Very well—I am all these things, but to a purpose. That purpose is power, power greater than you can dream!

"I've played my part behind the scenes these years past, my dear—and you've seen the result! I've had my interview with Mademoiselle Charlotte Corday, and Marat died. I've talked to Citizen Robespierre's brother, and Danton is no more. I've ways and means to pull the strings and make the puppets dance. And the end will be power. Great power. Once France is properly disrupted, there are other lands ripe for revolution.

"Revolution, my dear, always ends in dictatorship. Dictatorship, my dear, always ends in megalomania on the part of those who rule. And what would a megalomaniac do for the secret of eternal youth or the secret of eternal life—or both?

"Ah, yes, it will end only one way: My way. I shall rule the rulers! Think of that, my dear. Within a few years, Nicolo Varek will be the unseen ruler of the world. And you, his empress, his queen."

Varek came closer, and Vera could see the paper thinness of his bloodless lips. He might have been forty, he might have been four hundred. "The secret of eternal youth. How does that please you, my little one? To be always young, always as you are today? To live, to rule, to enjoy the senses to the full forever? I have that gift for you, that dowry.

"And soon—sooner than I dare tell you—I shall have the other, too. The Great Secret. Eternal life! I've a laboratory here—you must see it—where I experiment. In times like these, there is no shortage of subjects. Samson sells me the unclaimed ones every day." The bloodless lips formed a bloody smile. "I'm getting closer and closer to the solution," Varek told her. "And once it's gained, the world is mine. Ours!"

It was mawkish melodrama, but it was also naked nightmare. For the little lisping, whispering, sniggering creature came closer and closer, and then he was no longer braggart or stammerer but merely a lustful automaton. He pawed at Vera LaValle and she endured his carrion breath upon her neck for a moment. But only for a moment. Then she wrenched free, and Varek, losing his balance, tumbled grotesquely to the floor.

Vera LaValle laughed.

She didn't refuse his offer of marriage. She didn't call him an old man, a liar, a murderer, a repulsive fool. She didn't do anything but laugh.

Her laugh said all those things.

Nicolo Varek rose, tugged at his ruffled clothing, and bowed coldly. *"Adieu,"* he said. And left.

Vera LaValle waited. She waited for Lucien to scamper in, rubbing his hands briskly in anticipation. She waited for the effect of her story upon him; his crest-fallen stare, his agitation, his frantic reiteration of, "Why, why, why? He was our only hope, our only chance! Why?"

She waited, then, for the summons. It came soon enough.

Somebody had denounced Citizen LaValle and his daughter. As usurers, as enemies of the People.

She waited for the trial, and it was short. Lucien sobbed when he heard the verdict, but she shrugged.

She waited, then, for the tumbril.

Waited, those last few days, alone. For Lucien LaValle hung himself one gloomy Sunday morning and she was left alone.

She was alone, and waiting, that last night when Varek came.

Citizens were not allowed to visit with prisoners in their cells on the eve of execution. But Varek was not a citizen. He was not a man at all in the ordinary concept of the word. He was a mocking shadow that glided silently to her cell.

One moment nothing, and the next, Varek was there. Whispering in the darkness.

"Vera, Vera LaValle, listen to me! I have news for you. Great news!"

Silence, as he waited for a reply. But she said nothing. After a moment, he continued: "Remember what I told you? About the laboratory, the experiments, the secret of eternal life? I have it at last, Vera—I have it at last! Oh, it's not exactly all I'd hoped, and much remains to be done in refining the method. But it's the goal of sorcery through the ages, the dream of science. And I have it. For you. For us!"

Silence once more. Vera LaValle did not move. He spoke again: "Eternal life, Vera! I swear it's the truth; I can give you eternal life. All you need do is say the word and you're free. I can get you out as easily as I got you in. And now you can be young forever, alive forever! You must believe me, you must!"

Vera turned and faced him through the bars of the cell. She could not see his face in the darkness of the corridor, but he could see her countenance—and the lineaments of loathing.

"I do believe you," she said. "And I tell you that I prefer to die tomorrow morning rather than spend eternity—or a single living moment—with you."

Varek's laugh grated through the gloom. "A plain answer, Mademoiselle LaValle. But I wonder if you have rightly considered what's in store for you. When the tumbril rolls and the sun is gleaming, gleaming on the bright blade of the guillotine? Have you see the heads in the basket, Mademoiselle? Have you seen Samson lift them by the hair and exhibit them to the crowd?"

"You can't frighten me," she whispered.

"Do you know what it's like to be dead? Dead forever and ever? They'll put you in the ground, Mademoiselle, in the cold wet ground. You'll lie there in eternal darkness, lie there and rot and decay into slime and dust. And the lips that you withhold from me will feed kisses to the worms.

"Aren't you afraid of death, Mademoiselle LaValle?"

She shook her head and smiled into the blackness beyond the bars. "Not as much as I fear life with you," she said. "Now, go and leave me in peace."

He broke down, then. The creature cried and begged. "I don't understand, it's never happened before—that a woman, a girl, a mere child should do this to me! I thought I was immune to folly, but since the moment I laid eyes on you I cannot endure the thought of not possessing you. You are a burning in my blood, you must know that and you cannot refuse—you cannot! But you must be mine of your own free will, not by force. I want you willingly, and I must have you." Varek sobbed, and it was the dry and dusty sobbing of a reanimated mummy, rustling in the darkness.

Once again, Vera LaValle shook her head. "No," she said.

Varek's sob held not grief but rage. "Good enough," he cried. "If I'm not fit for you, I commend you to a new lover. To Death! Death shall embrace you, twine his bony fingers in your curls, take your head as a souvenir of his conquest. *Adieu*—I leave you to hold tryst with your beloved. He'll not be long now!"

And he left her.

Then and only then did Vera break down. For she had lied. She did fear death. The thought of dying terrified her past all comprehension, and now in the darkness she could almost see the grinning presence of Death incarnate; the skeleton in the black coat, the grinning skull covered with a cowl.

He was still with her the next morning, when the guards came. He walked with her to the tumbril, and as she and five other weeping and bedraggled women took their places, Death climbed in beside them.

Death grinned at Vera LaValle as she rode through the streets of Paris to the site of execution. Death pointed his finger at the roaring crowd, the prancing Citizen Samson and his grimacing assistants. Death showed her the shrieking silhouette of the knife against the dawn-drenched sky.

Death was with her as she walked to the platform. Death helped her up the stairs, and it seemed to Vera in the delirium of the last few moments that not Samson but Death himself was the executioner—removing her cloak, binding her arms forcing her to kneel and gaze down at the bottom of the basket when all the time she wanted to gaze up; gaze up at the knife, the bright blade of the knife which was the only real thing left in the world.

Then, as the roar of the crowd came up, the blade of the guillotine came down.

Death took Vera LaValle in his arms.

And—released her!

"You want to know what it's like, of course," she told me, sitting there on the bed, thousands of miles and lifetimes later. "But I don't remember. There was no pain, no sensation, and yet I *felt,* I was conscious in a new way. There was no sense of duration, either.

"Then the pain came back, and I was alive.

"I had this pain in the throat, and in the head.

"I opened my eyes. I saw the bandage on my neck. I saw the silver tube coiling to the top of my spine. And I saw Varek.

"You know what happened, of course. Samson had sold me to Varek after the execution. He took me to his laboratory and brought me back to life.

"I realized it, naturally, at once. But I can never convey to you the horror of that moment—when I discovered that he had sewed my head back on my body!

"It was grotesque, it was ludicrous, and it was somehow blasphemous. But despite it all, in the weeks to come, I learned to respect the power, the wisdom, the genius of Nicolo Varek.

"My convalescence, if you can call it that, was slow. It was not easy, with the crude techniques he had painfully evolved, for Varek to keep me alive and nurse me back to a semblance of health and sanity. But he did it. Since that time I've learned a great deal about what he does to reanimate the dead, and still I haven't grasped the true secret."

She paused, and I cut in: "You say he sewed your head back on? But that's . . . incredible."

Vera pointed at the scar and smiled wanly. "Would you find it equally incredible if I told you that there's a metal plate covering half of my skull—that there is metal, some sort of machinery, extending down the neck and into the upper spine? That Varek, in 1794, was using electrical voltage and a sort of miniature dynamo for metabolic regulation? That the control he exercised and still exercises is a combination of hypnotism and an extension of brain-waves transformed into electric current? Yet it's true, all of it. I am an automaton—operating on the power generated from within plus the current fed me by Varek at a distance. I'm alive yet not alive. I do not age or change, I do not eat or sleep. But there's something worse than sleep. Something much worse." She shuddered. "That's when he *turns me off.*"

Either she was crazy or I was. Or both of us. This I knew. But I believed her. I believed the cold-eyed, cold-skinned creature with the livid scar who talked to me across the centuries.

"He's done it to me, many times, temporarily and to suit his convenience or his needs. But I've seen him do it to others—permanently. It's horrible. They die, then; die a second death. A hideous death, forever.

"That's the hold he has over me, over all of us. The ability to turn us off. Because there's something inside that wants to live, fights to live. Oh, how can I tell you the story of what took a hundred and sixty years to live?" Vera glanced around the room, and for a moment her agitation seemed completely human. "There's not time; he'll come out of it now, hear us."

I pressed her. I had to know the rest. "Quickly, then," I urged. "What happened after you recovered?"

"He was still experimenting. I was his first complete success. There were others . . . corpses . . . that he revived temporarily. But they were damaged, warped. Completely insane. At the time, he hadn't perfected his methodology of control. Several escaped. There was an ugly scandal. And Robespierre's dictatorship fell. He went to the guillotine himself. Varek no longer had protection in Paris. So we fled.

"The Embargo was on, and the only ship we could find was bound for the colonies. We ended up in Haiti, just the two of us.

"It was a strange relationship. He no longer desired me, of course—and I think he almost regretted his monstrous act of revival. Gradually he set about to make me his servant. And of course, he succeeded. I was alone, helpless, literally dependent on him for my existence.

"I offer no apologies for serving Varek. I had no choice. And he was master.

"It didn't take long for him to establish himself in Haiti and in San Domingo. He had brought money and jewels. We took a mansion; he posed as a planter. And immediately set about fomenting an insurrection. You know what happened to Haiti a few years later, when Toussaint L'Ouverture, Dessalines and Christophe revolted against the French. Varek played his part. Blood flowed, and there were bodies for Varek's new laboratories. Black bodies to experiment upon. Black bodies to toil on the plantations.

"It was at this time that a new superstition arose. The one about zombies. The walking dead. Can you understand now just why and how this belief was born?"

I nodded, thinking of my dreams. There was a horrid logic and conviction behind her words. Varek had created the concept of the zombie. His creatures walking the world.

"The blacks were primitive, simple. Varek bungled often. He was still groping, evolving methods and techniques. The botched jobs were the zombies.

"And the vampires—that was Hungary, of course."

I raised an eyebrow. "But Varek isn't responsible for the belief in vampires. That's an ancient superstition."

"Correct," answered Vera. "But we went to Hungary from Haiti because of the belief. Because, there, tales of the walking dead would be ascribed to superstition and no one would investigate too closely if some of Varek's experiments moved freely over the countryside. Also, Varek wished to follow the latest developments in European scientific research. Even before the Revolution, he had worked briefly with Anton Mesmer in the development of hypnotism. Now he was interested in the new psychology.

"You see, attaining the power he dreams of is a long and a complicated process. It involves much more than merely the ability to control the reanimated bodies of the dead. At first, Varek could not keep a corpse alive except by constant hypnotic control. He had to focus his own energies every moment. Then he reached a stage were he could fix a behavior pattern for hours, or days, and turn to other matters. But that is not enough.

"Each reanimated corpse must be provided for—given a new identity, a new life, a new *role* to play. Varek moulds the puppets, breathes life into them, and then he must manipulate the strings. Dozens, scores of puppets, on dozens of separate stages; all play their part in one involved drama.

"He had to enter into scientific fields, enter into politics. How much of the intrigue behind the Third Empire in France was due to his work, I'll never know. For in 1847 I rebelled; I tried to get away. And as punishment he *turned me off for seventy years!*"

Vera's white death-mask contorted in remembered agony. "For seventy years I followed Varek across the world as baggage—in an ice-packed coffin. And meanwhile he meddled with science, he pulled strings, and he waited. What's time to Varek?

"I awoke in Russia, during the Revolution. By this time he'd come to realize that he needed living allies; men to work in front of the public. Dupes and spies. He'd made some connection with a monk, Rasputin. There was a plan to kill the young Tsarevitch and then bring him back to life again; the Czar and Czarina would be at his mercy, from that point on. But somebody murdered Rasputin, and we fled Russia for a spell. That's when I was reanimated again.

"Varek believes in Revolution, you know. A time of turmoil and disruption is what he needs; it gives him an opportunity to profit by confusion. New and untried leaders arise, and he comes to them with hints of what he can do. He presents plans and attempts to gain control of those who form governments.

"We returned to Russia, and I aided him. I had no choice. It was that or lying in darkness—refrigerated darkness, now, thanks to modern conveniences." She smiled wryly. "You can guess what he's been up to since then. You can guess who was behind the scenes in some of Pavlov's experiments. Varek reached members of that group. You can guess that sooner or later the Comintern got wind of it. But what you do not know—and what history does not show—is just how perilously close Russia came to developing a truly mechanized army in the 1930's. An army of the dead!"

I lit a cigarette and tried not to look at the clock on the bureau; the clock that was ticking the minutes away.

"We were in Germany, then, and Varek attempted to sell his notion to the New Order. But his spokesmen fell out of power, and in 1939 we fled again. We were in Canada for a few years, in Manitoba and further north. Varek waited out the war. But he has infinite patience, infinite cunning.

"He can afford to wait—wait for centuries, if necessary. He's a strange man, Varek. He has possessed vast wealth, and lost it time and time again fleeing from country to country. He has a chameleon-like ability to alter his personality his appearance. He is—But what's the use of telling you? You're doomed."

I crushed out the cigarette.

"Now let's get down to cases," I suggested. "He sent you to kill me. Why?"

"Because you know about Cono. His offer was genuine, at first. He is still looking for a man, for many men, who will serve him as living allies. But you refused, and because you understand his power, you must die."

"Yet, Cono is such an insignificant cog in his machine," I persisted. "A dumb strong-man from a carnival. I can't see why a man with Varek's gigantic plans would bother with such a trivial matter."

"Then you don't know Varek. He has plans within plans. He's not lived quietly for the past few years for nothing. He's been waiting—waiting for the next war. The big one. The one his plans have indirectly fomented.

"There's a great laboratory set up already, somewhere in Sorora. It is capable of . . . processing . . . the dead almost on a factory assembly line. Its services will be offered to the highest bidder when the time comes. Whichever side runs out of manpower and needs a new army of workers, a new army of fighters. Don't you understand? That's where it all leads to, Varek's dream; to create a world run by slaves—by the dead!"

"He'll never get away with it."

"I'm not so sure. The past few years have brought the scientific developments he needs. There are new methods of controlling bodies *en masse*. Radio, electronics, blood plasma all play a part in his schemes.

"For years now he's been in the background, waiting for the right time. When war comes he will have emissaries ready to approach the new leaders. He knows how to get to the wealthy, the powerful, and intrigue them. That has been my job in the past. He intended to have your help, too—and probably the help of a hundred men like you."

"That's the one point that isn't clear to me yet," I told her. "Just exactly how does he manage to insinuate himself into the confidence of the men on top?"

Vera smiled. The ghost of a smile, the smile of a ghost. "Simple. Have you ever heard of the Fox sisters? Or D. D. Home or Angel Annie or Madame Blavatsky?"

I nodded. "Spiritualist mediums or mystics, weren't they?"

"Yes. During my . . . sleep . . . Varek was able to hit on that gambit. The same one used earlier by St Germain and Cagliostro. Through the ages the wealthy, the powerful have always had one weakness. A belief in superstition. A longing to pierce the veil of the Mysteries. They've always followed the seers, flocked to the occultists, confided in them. No need to explain the phenomenon. It exists."

"True enough." I said. "So Varek allies himself with the mediums. They act as his front men. They attract the rich. And Varek watches, waits, chooses those he wants or can use, and then steps into the picture and reveals his plans."

"Exactly." Vera sighed. "It was that way with Rasputin, if you remember. He was the key to the Czar's influence. And he's ready to start again."

"But the mediums aren't trustworthy, many are frauds," I argued.

"And many are not. Take D. D. Home, for example. No less a scientist than Crookes verified the fact that Home levitated himself out of a third storey window and floated back in through another. It actually happened, time and time again. But what Crookes didn't know is that little, tubercular, wan Mr Home had been dead for a year—and Varek animated him, hypnotized him, and then levitated him by concentration. Just as he levitated me tonight and sent me to kill you."

Vera paused. I stared at her white face in the gloom. And as I stared, something happened. A spasm contorted her countenance, the same dreadful tic that had afflicted Cono. I watched her as her mouth opened and a voice came out. But it was not Vera LaValle's voice. It was the voice of the dead bartender, the voice of Varek.

"Yes," it told her, as much as it told me. "I sent you to kill him. And you failed. Failed and then talked. I cannot afford to have you talk any more, Vera. I'm going to turn you off. *Forever.*"

The voice shut off abruptly. It had to shut off, for there was no longer a means of utterance. The spasm in Vera's face swept down over her body in a single hideous horripilation. For a moment she swayed there, shuddering convulsively. Then—she *melted.*

There was a change, and it wasn't a collapse. It was a running together, as though flesh were falling in on splintering bone. She shrank, dwindled before my eyes—and then she crumbled.

Somebody had taken the wax doll that was Vera LaValle, and held it over a roaring flame. In an instant she ran together, fused.

I stared at the floor, stared at the heap of fine white ash surrounding a charred and twisted cluster of wires linked to a metal plate.

Vera LaValle was gone.

Vera was gone and I was alone in the bedroom. Or was I?

If I'd had any doubts about Varek's power, they were gone now. They'd vanished with Vera, and taken a part of my sanity with them.

Let's face it; I was panicked. Varek knew where I was, and that meant I would no longer be safe here. Not safe from him, not safe from the police. I wondered what had happened to Ahmed. For all I knew, Varek had attended to him, too. And I couldn't stick around and wait.

I went over to the door. It was locked, of course, and I'd have to force it. I gave it the old college try. You see them do it every day in the movies and on television. Brawny, broad-chested hero puts his shoulder to the locked door. The door gives way. Simple.

Try it sometime. Desperate as I was, all I managed to gain was a bruised shoulder. Then I picked up a chair. That was a better deal. The panel splintered. I broke the lock.

Then I was running down the hall in darkness, groping at the head of the stairs, clumping down them, racing through the hall to the front door. If a cleaning-woman had showed up, she didn't show.

I made the door, opened it. The night air hit me. So did a hand.

"What's the rush, friend?"

I gasped with panic, then with relief.

Ahmed bustled in, rubbing his hands. "Hold it," he said. "I've got news for you."

I shook my head. "I've got news for you, too," I said.

"What do you mean?"

I decided to risk it. He had to be shown. I took him by the arm and steered him back up the stairs. If you think it wasn't hard for me to force myself into that room again, you've got another guess. But it had to be done that way.

"Take a look," I said.

His little gray eyes examined the charred ashes on the floor. He stooped and picked up the metal plate, contemplated the dangling wires protruding from it.

"What's this?"

"All that remains of Vera LaValle. She visited me with a knife. I got her to talk and then she was . . . shut off."

"I don't follow you."

"Sit down," I sighed. "I'll have to explain, but I want to make it fast."

I did. The Great Ahmed nodded. He wasn't upset, he wasn't alarmed, he wasn't horrified. Somehow, his very calmness managed to reassure me.

"It ties together," he said, as I concluded. "It fits. Every bit of it."

"How do you know?"

"Because I've seen Cono. You were right about the hotel, friend. He came back. And when he found me hiding in the closet he tried to kill me." Ahmed smiled and held up a skeleton key. "I needn't tell you how I got in the room," he grinned. "But to make a long story short, the same thing happened as must have happened to you and Vera here. I managed to calm him down—he recognized me, of course. To be brutally frank, I resorted to an old Varek trick; a little hypnosis of my own. Varek must have been directing his own energies elsewhere, possibly to levitate Vera LaValle.

"At any rate, Cono talked. Of course, he's newly reborn, as it were, and he doesn't have too many details. Also, he's not the best example of a scientific mind." Ahmed smiled, briefly. "Still, he told more than he thought he was telling.

"Did you know that Varek has hideouts established in almost every principal city in the world? And that each of them contains anywhere from a dozen to several hundred bodies under refrigeration, ready for reanimation at any time? A sort of dead storage.

"Also, there are the walkers. More of them than you'd suspect. Although it's really quite easy to detect them because they all have one thing in common—the red scar on the neck."

I started at that. "You mean, he cuts off their heads before he revives them?"

Ahmed shrugged. "Not completely, now. But an operation is performed. A deep incision is made at the base of the brain. The metal plate is grafted into place and the wires"—here he picked up the charred mass from the floor and waved it—"are put into place. Meanwhile, the hypnotic control is established."

"It's a form of hypnotism, then? But I don't get it."

The Great Ahmed shook his head. "It isn't easy. But then, what do any of us understand about the life process? We don't know what governs our physiological continuity; makes our hearts beat and our lungs take in and expel air without conscious control. You might say we operate our own bodies through autohypnosis and that keeps us alive.

"And what's death? Various organs 'die' at different times after the heart stops. We can understand the process of decay, but we can't define or truly measure death. Why, I defy anyone to tell me exactly what sleep is, let alone death!

"Sleep—that's a form of hypnosis, too.

"And, somehow, Varek has harnessed that portion of the mind which functions automatically in life, in sleep; kept it going in the state we describe as death. The common denominator is electrical energy; brain-waves, which can be measured electrically, you know. Varek has managed to apply hypnotic principles to the electric current of the body; magnetism controlling magnetism. That's why he performs the operation, inserts the metal plates in the brain and the spine. To alter the 'hookup,' you might say."

The little man spoke earnestly, as though he were lecturing a backward pupil. I listened, with equal earnestness now as he waved his finger at me.

"Let me put it simply. You might compare the human body to a radio set, and Varek to a radio station. His operation consists of putting in the proper tubes and condensers to make the set forever receptive to his hypnotic wave-length. It's all electrical. Once control is established, he can broadcast impulses forever. That's a vast oversimplification, but you get the idea."

"Not completely," I said. "What about the bartender?"

"Oh, there are exceptions. The bartender was one. There Varek resorted to a temporary hookup. Probably gave his entire concentration to animating him temporarily, just to talk to you. As he concentrated entirely to levitate Vera. Those special things require special efforts. But with the vast army of dead, Varek—to return to our little analogy of a radio station—merely sends out a host of previously prepared 'transcriptions' in the shape of hypnotic suggestions. The dead 'play' the hypnotic suggestions through four hours. And Varek need pay no more attention to them than an engineer who puts on long-playing records for broadcasting. They operate automatically.

"And that, of course, is the weakness. Sometimes Varek doesn't pay attention; or he watches the wrong body. Then it's possible for someone else, with a stronger hypnotic wavelength to 'jam' reception in a corpse—capture its attention, divert its purpose. As I did with Cono tonight at the hotel. And as you did with Vera."

"Lucky for both of us we did," I said. "But what else happened? What else did you find out? Why is Varek operating in Chicago now? And—this is the jackpot question—what's the secret of his own eternal life?"

The Great Ahmed smiled. "You want a lot for a few hours' work, friend," he answered gently. "Some of those questions you'll have to find out about for yourself. All I can do is give you that opportunity."

"Meaning?"

"Meaning I made a deal with Cono. And I think he can be trusted—as long as Varek doesn't get to him. Cono has promised to lead you direct to Varek himself tonight."

"Now?" I was genuinely startled.

Ahmed glanced at his wristwatch. "In about three quarters of an hour. You're to meet him in the lobby of the Wrigley Building at eleven-thirty. Alone."

I didn't like that at all, and he could see it even before I spoke. "What's the big idea?" I asked. "Why aren't you coming along?"

The little man returned my gaze with unmoved composure. "For a very obvious reason; it might be a trap. Then Varek'd have both of us. As it is, you'll have to take your chances. And if anything does go wrong, I'll still be able to carry on, to follow through. After all, that's why you hired me. And I aim to finish the job."

He was silent for a moment. "Think it over," he said. "You don't have to go, you know. And I don't mind telling you I'd hesitate before taking such a risk."

I nodded. "Somebody's got to do it," I said. "So if you'll call a cab for me . . ."

Ahmed smiled and held out his hand. "Good boy," he said. He turned and led the way downstairs. He phoned for a cab in the hall.

"I don't know where you're going or what you'll get into," he mused. "And of course, under the circumstances, you can't have the cops tagging along. You'll just have to use your head. Try and keep in touch with me, tip me off what's going on and what to do."

"Why don't you follow me in another cab?" I suggested. "Then, no matter where Cono takes me, you'll at least have the address."

"Good idea." Ahmed stepped to the phone and put in another call. The he nudged me. "And here's a little idea of my own," he said.

He held out his hand next to my poocket and dumped something cold and hard. I reached for it and came up with a .38 fully loaded.

"Just in case," he told me. "I'll feel better if you have something along for company."

I grinned my gratitude as we walked out of the door of 43 East Brent and waited for the cabs to arrive. Mine rolled up first, but his turned the corner a moment later.

"Let's go," he said. "Be careful now."

"Same to you," I answered. Then, "Wrigley Building," I told the driver. And we were off.

It was a nice, warm, moonless night. I leaned back in the cab as we jolted downtown and tried to relax. I'll give you three guesses how well I succeeded.

We kept stopping at corners, corners with cops on them. I hid my face and thanked my lucky stars there was no moon.

When we hit Chicago Avenue and a red light, I took a long chance. I leaned out of the cab, yelled at a newsboy, and bought a paper. Just idle curiosity. I wanted to see if they had my picture in today. With some of the latest gossip. Such as the offering of a reward, dead or alive.

I riffled through the pages rapidly, but no success greeted my efforts. Maybe they didn't care. Maybe they were used to killing bartenders in Chicago.

Killing—

The little squib caught my eye. With the Louisville dateline. James T. Armstrong Shows . . . Louis Preusser, 43 . . . Confessed murderer of . . . Psychiatrists declared under influence of hypnosis and drugs . . .

It was the follow-up on the story of Louie's confession. He'd walked in, glassy-eyed, and confessed. I wondered what the whole deal was. The Great Ahmed would know. Maybe I'd better ask him before I went on.

I glanced behind to see if his cab was trailing mine. Nothing was in sight. Maybe his driver had taken Clark Street instead. He'd catch up to me. Nobody seemed to have any trouble at all catching up to me whenever they wanted to.

Take Vera LaValle, for instance. She'd found me at the Great Ahmed's after I'd been there for less than an hour. That was one question I needed an answer for. How did she—and Varek—know I was there?

I'd remember to ask Ahmed that.

But—*would he tell me?*

Maybe you're a scientist, a great scientist. Maybe you're a sorcerer too, a wizard. You can raise the dead, and you stay alive yourself. But it's still quite a trick to pick one person out of four million and send a killer right to his door. Unless somebody tips you off.

The tip off. That was it.

Ahmed goes out. Ahmed sells out. Of course! He went to the hotel, just as he said he would, with the eight grand in his pocket. Maybe he saw Cono there, maybe he saw somebody else. Maybe he even saw Varek himself. And he made a deal. He told Varek where I was. Varek sent Vera to kill me.

When enough time had passed, Ahmed came back to see if the job was accomplished. It must have surprised him to find me alive.

So he came up with the story about meeting Cono. Why? It hadn't, come to think of it, sounded too good at the time. This business about winning Cono over with hypnosis. And Cono leading me to Varnek.

But seeing me alive, he'd told me the story for a purpose. Ahmed was a great guy for purposes, all right. He must even have given me the gun for a purpose.

I tried to figure it out as we roared down Michigan. I could see the gleaming lighted spire that chewing gum built, right ahead. I'd be there in a minute now.

What had Varek said? Something about not bothering to kill me because the law would do it.

And here I came riding up to the Wrigley building, with a gun in my pocket. An armed murderer.

I knew what to look for now. It wouldn't be Ahmed's cab; he wouldn't show up at all, I was sure. I was looking for a black prowl car.

I wouldn't see Cono standing in the lobby with a white carnation in his buttonhole, ready to guide me on a conducted tour of Varek's snug harbor. I was more likely to see a couple of downtown boys with their hands in their topcoat pockets. The reception committee from the downtown station.

We started to edge towards the curb, and I added up my score. Exactly 100 per cent right. There was the squad car, there were the boys. They stood patiently, just waiting for somebody to show up. If I knew Ahmed, I felt sure he'd furnish them with a very good description.

We nosed in, slowing down. "Here we are—" the driver began.

"No, we're not," I cut in. "Back to 43 East Brent. And fast. I have another appointment."

We kept going, over the bridge. Nobody looked up. Nobody followed. I kept my hand on the butt of the .38 all the way back. I didn't want to lose it, you see.

It was the Great Ahmed's, and I intended to make sure that I gave it to him.

The house was dark, but then it was always dark. I had the cab park around the corner because I didn't mind walking. In fact, I preferred it. Preferred it so much I went around to the back of the house—the long way around, mind you. Didn't bother me a bit. Nor did it bother me to climb in through a rear bedroom window on the first floor.

I was quiet. Very quiet. Sort of a slow, seething quiet. Little thoughts kept bubbling up in me about what I'd do to Ahmed when I got my hands on him.

So he wasn't the tyupe for a carney grifter, eh? Well, he'd taken me in soon enough. And sold me out even sooner.

I landed on the bedroom floor and padded out, down the hall. No cleaning-woman was around and I knew now that there never had been. Ahmed had locked me in to keep me on ice for Vera LaValle or whoever Varek might send.

Ahmed and Varek—a good team. Maybe Ahmed was the guy Varek needed for a front man!

Of course, he wouldn't look quite so presentable after I got through with him . . .

I tiptoed down the hall, peeked into the library. It was dark. The whole house was dark. I stopped, listened. After a long moment, I became convinced of the truth. I was alone. Ahmed had gone out in his cab but he hadn't returned.

I reached a stairway going up—that led to the bedroom and the other rooms on the second floor. But behind it was another set of stairs, going down. I decided to have myself a look. Curiosity killed a cat of course—but *this* cat carried a .38.

The basement was big and dusty. Old fashioned furnace, the usual stationary washtubs, a coal-bin, a fruit-cellar. I pushed open the door and stared at the usual assortment of dusty, empty jars in the light thrown by a naked bulb dangling from the center of the small room.

Nothing in the cellar to interest me. My hunch was cold.

I was cold!

Standing in the deserted fruit-cellar a little past midnight of a warm May evening, I was cold. Cold as ice! I felt the cold air all around me. But where was it coming from?

A draft blew against my trouser cuffs. I looked down.

There was a round metal lid set in the floor of the fruit-cellar. I stooped, touched it. The iron was icy. I groped for the ring, lifted the lid. I gazed down into darkness.

Then I walked away, making a circuit of the cellar until I found what I needed and expected to find—the inevitable handy flashlight.

I returned to the fruit-cellar and pointed the beam down. It focused on the iron rungs of a ladder. I took the flashlight in one hand, the gun in the other, and left enough fingers free on both for me to cling to the rungs as I descended.

I lowered myself into icy cold—the coldness of a vast black refrigerator. I went down, down, rung after rung. Finally my feet hit slimy, damp stone. I joggled the flashlight until it bisected a wall with its beams. Eventually I located a light switch.

I flicked it. The light went on, and I saw everything.

I was standing in the center of Varek's laboratory.

Varek—Ahmed. Ahmed—Varek.

It all added up now.

More lights went on.

They went on in the little room with the big filing cabinets. I pried open a lot of drawers that night; the drawers containing the certificates, the visas, the affidavits, the fake credentials, the diplomas, the letters of identity (hadn't Varek convinced the warden he was Cono's cousin?) and all of the mingled memorabilia of hundreds of years of impersonations, imposture, and disguise. Floods, tons of paper. The dust fairly flew.

And more light was shed. I found the long closet with the wardrobe; the Ahmed wardrobe, the sportsman's garments, the shabby workman's garb complete even to the battered tin initialled lunchbox and the union button. The accoutrements of Varek the wealthy man of the world were there, too—and a box containing diamonds and other gems that reminded me of poor Vera LaValle.

Then there was another room, with more files. Letters and newspaper clippings. Ads from the *Personal* columns of ten thousand papers, in a score of languages. *Help Wanted* notices. Lonely Hearts messages. And letters, letters, letters—messages from the millions who later turned up missing. Those who answered Varek's appeal for a wife, a husband, an employee. I got a picture of him sitting there, year after year, sending out his letters, interviewing prospects, recruits for his army of the dead. Recruits who would not be missed, searched for.

There were more lights in other rooms. The big surgery, with the gigantic autoclave; completely modern, completely equipped. I wondered how he'd managed to assemble it here, and then I thought of the dead; the tireless dead who steal, who strain, who slave day and night.

Beyond the modern surgery was medieval horror.

The round, dungeon-like room, dominated by the huge table on which rested the alembics and retorts of an ancient alchemist. The beaker filled with the brownish-red, crusting liquid. The herbs and powders on the shelves; the dried roots in bottles, and the great jars filled with monkeys floating in a nauseous liquid, and other things that looked like monkeys but weren't. The stock of chalk and powders. The great circle drawn upon the floor with the zodiacal signs inscribed in the blue before it. The jar of combustible powder—that was used to make the circle of fire inside a pentagon, according to the thaumaturgists. And on the iron table rested the iron book; the *Grimoire* of the sorcerer.

Sorcery and science! Surgery and Satanism! That was the link, the combination! Sorcery had led to science, as Varek said. His original alchemic experiments had brought him to actual research and enabled him to perfect his method of reanimating the dead.

But that didn't explain his own continued life, his boasts of eternal youth. That was sorcery. That was selling your soul, after lighting the fires and invoking the Author of All Evil.

The rooms, the lighted rooms, seemed to present a panorama of Varek's entire existence across the centuries. Everything was here—and I wondered, now, if he'd told me the truth. If in every great city, unsuspected, beneath a house or a factory or a tenement there existed a duplicate of this place. What had he said? A sort of "dead storage," that was it.

"Dead storage." But where were the dead?

There was another room, beyond the alchemic chamber. I entered it, and the coldness engulfed me. This was *it*. The refrigerator storage space. Where you keep the cold meat.

The cold meat . . .

They lay on slabs, but they weren't sheeted. I could see them all, see their staring faces. Men, women, children, young, old, rich, poor—lavish your categories upon them, they were all here. A host, a hundred or more. Silent but not sleeping, inert but not immovable, rigid without *rigor*. They lay there, waiting, like toys that would soon be wound up by cunning hands and set about to walk in make-belief of life.

It was cold in that room, but cold alone did not make me shiver. I walked through rows of dead, staring into the faces that stared into mine. I don't know what I expected to see. None of them looked familiar—except, perhaps one little blonde who reminded me of someone I'd run into before somewhere.

Then, all at once, I knew what I must do. There was fire outside, and it would serve more purposes than that of conjuring up demons. It could also be used to put them to rest.

I walked back into the other room and picked up the powder box which, when its contents were kindled, traced a pattern of flame on the floor. A circle of fire protected you from demons, it was said, after you evoked them.

I ripped the lid off the box and began to sprinkle the powder about. I worked quickly, but not quickly enough.

Because when I looked up, somebody was standing in the room. He only stood there for a moment, and then he started for me.

It was Cono.

He didn't say anything and I didn't say anything. He came on and I backed away. The cold arms reached out; I'd felt them before. The tic-like grimace leered, and I knew it would keep on leering no matter how many bullets I might waste.

Because the dead don't die.

Because this was the end.

Because he was coming at me like a demon.

But demons can be warded off with fire.

I pulled out the .38 and pressed the trigger. I didn't aim at Cono; I aimed at the powder on the floor.

A circle of flame shot up, almost in Cono's face. He stopped. Dead or alive; fire destroys flesh. And he couldn't get through. Not as long as the fire flared.

I wondered how long that would be. When would the powder's potency be exhausted? Ten minutes, five, two? Whatever the time, I had that long to live and no longer—unless I could convince him.

I talked then. Told him what I thought he'd understand. About Varek being the Great Ahmed, hiding out with the carney for a while and perfecting plans. About seeing Cono and deciding to make him a recruit, then rigging up the murder charge by hypnotizing Louie, getting him to drug Cono and kill Flo.

I told him something about what Varek was, what he planned, what he'd do to Cono, to me, to the whole world if he wasn't stopped and stopped soon. I told him about the sorcery and the science and the bodies that walked everywhere in every city.

The fire began to flicker, to fade, to die down. I talked louder, faster.

And it didn't do any good.

It was like talking to a stone wall.

It was like talking to a dead man.

With a sickening feeling, I realized I'd been in this spot once before. I'd tried then, tried to tell Cono I was his friend, tried to reach his heart, his soul. But dead men have no hearts. Varek was his heart. And I knew of nothing that could touch his soul. Nothing he cared for, nothing he loved. Except Flo!

Then I remembered, remembered the next room and the blonde on the slab. The little blonde with the familiar face—Flo!

"Cono," I said. "Listen to me. You've got to listen. She's in there, too. You didn't know that, did you? He didn't tell you. But he's greedy, he wants them all. He not only took your body, he took Flo's too. She's in the next room, Cono. He cut off her head, put in his damned wires and plates, and now she'll walk for him forever!"

He was blind. Blind and deaf. The flames died, he moved towards me, he caught me up in his arms. I waited for the squeezing strength of his fingers to wrench my life away. But he merely held me, held me and lumbered across the ashes into the next room.

"Show me where," he said, and the tic rippled horribly across his face.

I pointed. Pointed at the face I remembered from a photograph he'd shown me.

Cono saw her. He released me, and his hands went to his head. He kept staring at her, staring and staring, even after Varek came into the room.

That's how it happened. One second we were alone and the next moment he was there—little grey shadow, silent and suave.

No emotion, no surprise, no tension.

Just his soft, quiet voice saying, "Kill him, Cono."

He might have been asking the big man for a match.

But as I stared at Varek—stared at the quiet little middle-aged man with the paper-thin lips—I saw many things.

I saw a vulgar charlatan in a carnival who was in turn a gypsy in Spain who was in turn a Polish count who was in turn a Haitian planter who was a London barrister who was a Polynesian trader who was a Tulsa wildcatter who was a physician in Cairo who was a trapper with Jim Bridger who was a diplomat of Austria who was—it went on and on that way, a hundred incarnations and a hundred lives and all of them were evil.

He faced us with all of that evil, the evil of a hundred and a thousand men, concentrated but quietly so, and he said to Cono again in the voice that could not be denied because it was the voice of mastery, the voice of life over death—"Kill him, Cono."

Cono set me down and I felt his arms close about my body, his hands grasp my throat. He was a robot, an automaton, he could not refuse; he was a zombie, vampire, all the evil legends, all the fear of the dead that return, the dead that never die.

Cono bent me back. And Varek, with a look in his eyes that was a grey ecstasy, came closer and waited for Cono to finish.

That's what Cono wanted, too.

For when Varek came close, Cono moved. One instant he held me—the next, I was free and those huge arms had reached out to engulf Varek.

The little grey man rose, shrieking, in the air. Cono squeezed—there was a sound like somebody stepping on a thin board—and the body of Varek writhed and twisted on the floor like a snake with a broken back.

Cono helped me with the powder, then. There were chemicals, too; enough to start a good-sized blaze.

"Come on," I said. "Time to get out of here."

"I'm staying," he said. "I belong here."

I had no answer to that one. I turned away.

"You got to go now," Cono told me. "Leave me the gun to start the fire. I give you five minutes to get out."

The thing on the floor was mewing. Neither of us looked at it.

"One thing," Cono said. "I want you should know it so you'll maybe feel better. About that bartender. You didn't knock him off. You hit him with a bottle, but that didn't kill him. Varek killed him, later, when they dragged him in back to see how bad he was hurt. But he was going to pin the rap on you. I found out at the funeral home."

"Thanks," I said.

"Now go away," said Cono.

And I went. I walked through the rooms and didn't look back. I climbed the ladder back to the basement. When I reached the top I heard the muffled sound of a shot from below me, far away.

Long before the flames spread, I was out of the house and on my way to the Loop.

Next morning I read about the place burning to the ground, and that was the end.

But this is a story that never ends.

I keep thinking of those "dead storage" places in other cities. I keep wondering if Varek had turned everybody off that night—or if others walked in other places. The way he and Cono and Vera had all told me. "If you only knew how many . . ."

That's what frightens me.

That's why, wherever I go now, I'm afraid of women wearing high collars and chokers. Men in turtleneck sweaters or even a clergyman's collar. I think of the red scar under the scarf. And I wonder.

I wonder when someone or something will float through my window again. I wonder what walks abroad at night and waits to drag me down.

I wonder how I, or you, or anyone can tell, as we go about our daily rounds, which are the living and which are the dead. For all we know, they may be all around us. Because:

The dead don't die!

NEIL GAIMAN

I met Bob Bloch once, and once only, and that I owe to Julius Schwartz. We were in a hallway in Chicago, at the 1990 World Fantasy Convention. Julie zoomed over toward me. When I'm Julie's age, I hope I can still zoom.

"Hey, Gaiman. You ever met Robert Bloch?"

"No."

"You know who he is? Bob Bloch. Wrote *Psycho,* the book, not the movie . . ."

"I know who he is. I'm a fan."

"You know," Julie confided in me, "I used to be his agent." This came as no surprise. Before he was a living legend in the comics world Julie was H. P. Lovecraft's agent, and Ray Bradbury's agent, and was probably H. G. Wells's and Mary Shelley's agent, and, I have no doubt, sold the more speculative books of the Old Testament to the original editors of the Bible.

And with that I was being introduced to Bob Bloch, who was taller and more dapper than I expected (writers being, in the main, a slovenly lot). "Bob, this is Neil Gaiman. He's going to be the Robert Bloch of the 1990s," said Julie Schwartz. And Bob laughed, and I was extremely embarrassed (because, after all, he was *Robert Bloch,* and I certainly am not, nor will I be), and I tried to tell him how much I'd admired him, and for how long, and he was very nice about it. And that was that: my meeting with Bob Bloch. I don't remember what we said—all I remember is how nice he was, how friendly, how kind; and how much he looked like Bob Bloch . . . that surprised me too. I thanked him for the poem he wrote for *Now We Are Sick,* an anthology of grisly verse I had edited with Steve Jones.

We were in a corridor, at a convention, so I didn't get to tell him how long he'd been part of my life. But, when asked to contribute to this volume, I had a chance to reflect.

"If you have a favorite Bloch story, introduce it for the book."

There are a handful of authors who are too much a part of your life to look at objectively: authors who wrote the stories that matter. I couldn't pick my single favorite Harlan Ellison short story (to pick a living author) any more than I could pick my favorite single Fritz Leiber short story (to pick an author who is, also, sadly, no longer with us). Authors who wrote too many good ones—the stories that I read when I was young enough for them to go and live in my soul.

For Bob Bloch, I was able to get it down to three favorite stories.

"Enoch" was the first of his stories I ever read. I was, what? Seven years old? Eight? It was in an anthology of horror stories (the cloth binding was red, although the title of the book is long forgotten), in the library of Mister Harris down the road. He was my friend Christopher's father, and didn't mind if I borrowed his books. I read his battered old copies of *Dracula,* and *The Compleat Werewolf,* and *The World of Null-A.*

I still remember poor Seth, who wasn't mad after all, and Enoch, who made him kill. I spent the rest of my childhood scared of Enoch. Maybe I still am, deep inside. Childhood fears don't die that easily.

The second story on my list of Bloch-busters was "That Hell-Bound Train."

Normally I hate stories with morals. Hate them utterly. Despise them. Loathe them with a loathing that is almost legendary. Also I abominate, abhor, detest, and scorn them. Except for "That Hell-Bound Train," where the moral is, in the final analysis, life itself, and the living of it. It's a story that transcends deal-with-the-Devil stories, and talks instead about what makes us tick, and why none of us are ever quite ready for the ticking to stop. It's perfectly pitched, beautifully crafted, and I've carried it through my adolescence and my adult life. Is this the moment when I'd stop the watch? Well, is it? And the answer I always seem to come up with is Martin's. (But then, he got to press the button, in the end.)

And the last was a story called "Sweets to the Sweet." Again, I was young when I read it. But it stayed with me. And each time I've read it, I've marveled at it. It's a marvel of brevity and technique—every word is there for a reason. It easily bears comparison with the best of John Collier, and of Saki, and it does everything that the twist-ending stories of the Tales from the Crypt variety aspire to do, but so seldom manage—

Half of the story is a conversation, the other half the aftermath of that conversation: a bereaved father is forcing a daughter into a role she is only too willing to accept—that of witch. It's about the powerlessness of children. It's about the power of belief. And it's about cruelty, and it's about magic. It ends with a gross-out: but it's a gross-out in our heads. We hear "a single piercing scream," but all we see is little Irma, gravely munching her candy, skipping "out of the front door, and into the night beyond."

Robert Bloch was one of the masters. I'm honored to be able to acknowledge that publicly. We work in his shadow, and in his debt.

NEIL GAIMAN AND STEPHEN JONES

Being aware of Bob's occasional forays into rhyme, we invited him to submit something to *Now We Are Sick,* our anthology of nasty verse for grown-up children. His contribution arrived in March 1986, typed on the bottom of his usual airletter. "After scanning the names of the contributors you have lined up," he quipped, "I can see where you'll need a touch of class." The poem was so quintessentially Bloch that we decided to give it its own section in the book near the closeout.

WARNING: DEATH MAY BE INJURIOUS TO YOUR HEALTH

When I am dead and buried
It will not matter much
I'll lay there in my coffin
And worms will gnaw my gutch

My face will melt and vanish
To leave a grinning skull
Though what it has to grin at
I'm sure I cannot tull.

I'll have no mailing address
But postmen soon will learn
To bring me anything that's marked:
"Tomb it may concern."

REMEMBERING BOB BLOCH

RAY BRADBURY

There is a double sadness, the fact of Bob being gone and the fact of my being thirty miles away today and not able to speak these words myself. And as we all feel, Bob should be delivering these words himself. His relationship to Death was, like my own, constant and amusing. In the vast candy shop that Life is to all of us, Bob found Death to be a jawbreaker, which he constantly tested, with us as witnesses, again and again, not losing any teeth until now. We were all hoping his fight with the Adversary would be won again, but you can't win forever, and he left a record of more than four hundred encounters and dark victories for us to savor the rest of our lives.

You've heard it all before from me, but let me repeat it again: In the summer of 1946 when I hardly knew my own name and hardly anyone else ever said it aloud, Bob Bloch came into a science fiction convention hall in Los Angeles and called out so every one could hear it, "Where's this guy named Bradbury? I want to meet him!" With tears in my eyes, I went to shake his hand. He invited me to Milwaukee a few weeks later, to stay overnight and drink more strange drinks than I had ever had before and never had again. Knowing him then, I had secret hopes for his future life. They were fulfilled when he met and married Elly. I celebrated for him when I finally met her, and knew that his future would be secure.

Now, to the rough part. In a story of mine many years ago, I wrote about my closest friend John Huft leaving town forever, which was fifty miles away, but it might as well have been a thousand. When he ran off in the sunset I ran after him, yelling: "Okay for you, John. Go on, go off. Leave me, John, and don't come back. I hate you, you hear? I hate you for leaving me." And then I broke down and wept and said, "Oh, no, John, don't listen to me. I didn't mean it. I just hated you going away. Forgive me, John. I take it back. Forgive me, oh please, forgive. I just didn't want you to leave, you hear? Don't leave. Stay here with me." To which I add today, oh Robert, oh Bob, why did you have to go? We'll miss you, Bob. We'll miss you forever, Bob. I know, I know. You simply had to go. There was no way to stay. Lord, Bob, I hope we'll see you again some day. We pray for that. God Bless you, Bob. God rest your dear soul. Good-bye, Bob. Good-bye.

RICHARD MATHESON
AND RICIA MAINHARDT

Finally, we decided to add this story as a special treat, since Bob would have wanted to leave you laughing . . .

THE PIED PIPER FIGHTS THE GESTAPO

𝕵 **When I walked into Jack's Shack I saw Lefty Feep sit-**
ting at his usual booth. With the suit he was wearing, it was impossible not to see him. Even a blind man would have found Feep at once—if he
couldn't see the suit, its color was so loud he'd hear it.

Feep was waving his arms at Jack as I approached. He turned and gave me a
nod of recognition, then continued to place his order.

"Make please with the cheese," he demanded. "But snappy."

"You want some snappy cheese?" Jack inquired.

"I do not care what kind of teeth the cheese is using," Feep asserted. "Just so
there is plenty of it. Let it be long and strong. Let it be mean and green. Let it be
old with mould. But bring me lots of plenty in a fast hurry."

Jack scribbled his order and shuffled away. Lefty Feep turned and I saw his
beady eyes were unstrung.

"Cheese," he whispered reverently. "Limburger with real limbs! Thick brick!
I love it. Swiss is bliss. Cheddar is better. Camembert is the nerts!"

I stared.

"What's the matter?" I asked. "You sound like a cross between Ogden Nash
and Micky Mouse. Since when did you develop such a passion for cheese?"

"It is not all for me," Feep explained. "I take some of it to a friend of mine."

"Are you hanging around with a bunch of rats?"

Feep shook his head. "I do not see Gorilla Gabface for weeks," he declared.

"Then what in the world—" I began, but didn't finish. For Jack returned,
bearing an enormous platter loaded with concentrated nose-torture.

"Ah!" sniffed my companion. "The breeze of cheese! What a stiff whiff!"

The whiff was almost too sniff for me. But Feep inhaled ecstatically.

"It brings memories," he exclaimed.

"It brings suffocation," I corrected.

"Feep picked up a hunk of Roquefort and began to nibble eagerly. All over the cafe, patrons were hastily retreating to tables near the open door. Feep smiled as he saw them go.

"We are alone," he grinned. "Maybe now I can tell you the reason I am so partial to this cow-candy."

"Go ahead," I urged. "But your reason must smell better than your cheese. And if there are as many holes in your story as there are in your limburger—"

Feep waved his Parmesan at me indignantly. Then he bent forward.

"Hold your nose," he muttered. "And I will give you a blow-by-blow description which I guarantee is not to be sneezed at."

It all starts (said Feep) two months ago when I suffer an accident one night. It seems I get my fingers stuck around the handle of a slot machine at a very embarrassing moment—in fact, it is the moment when a couple of bloodhounds break down the door of the joint. They invite everybody to play cops and robbers with them and take a little ride in the city taxi downstairs.

Which we do. Of course, when the patrol wagon arrives down at night court, I am bailed out at once. I think nothing of it and am just getting ready to go, when a little guy rushes up to me and grabs my hand. I recognize him at once for a personality named Boogie Mann.

"I am so grateful to you," he shouts. "How can I ever thank you?"

"What did I do?" I asked, lightly, but politely.

"I hear you give your seat in the patrol wagon to an old tomato who is standing there," he says.

"That's right. So what?"

"She is my mother," says Boogie Mann, and tears of gratitude come into his eyes.

"You are a gentleman and a scholar," he tells me. "Giving a seat in the paddy wagon to my dear old mother."

"It is nothing," I assure him. "She looks like she is too high to stand up anyway."

We walk out of the court together, and all the time this Boogie Mann is thanking me, I am looking him up and down. You see, I never have much to do with such a personality before, because this article happens to be a swing-band fan—what they call a "hep-cat." And I personally have nothing at all to do with swing, not being a hangman. So here and to fore, I steer clear of Boogie Mann and his unusual brand of swing-talk and his dizzy enthusiasm for juke symphonies.

When we get outside, Boogie grabs my shoulder by the padding and hangs on.

"Feep," he says, "I must reward you for what you do tonight. I am going to let you in on a big deal."

"The last time I am let in on a big deal," I answer, "I am holding a full house and the other guy turns up four kings."

"This is terrific," Boogie insists. "I will give you the chance to make a fortune. A fortune. Do you like money?"

Well, this question is easy to answer. I do, and then ask him one.

"What's the angle?" I inquire.

"How would you like to be the agent for the hottest swing musician in the world?" he asks.

"Who is it—Nero and his fiddle?" I crack. But he doesn't bend.

"No, this is the genuine jive," he tells me. "A hep Joe from Buffalo. A walkie-talkie from Milwaukee. Strictly a mutt from Connecticut."

"Who is he, where is he, and how come I get a chance to be ten per center for such a wonder man?"

"That is easy," Boogie tells me. "He is a refugee and nobody discovers him yet. He is playing in a little joint called the Barrel House way down the street, and nobody suspects that he plays the warmest licorice-stick in the business."

"Licorice-stick?"

"Clarinet, of course."

"A refugee, huh?"

"That is right," says Boogie. "The whole band is made up of refugees. Hot Mickey is the leader."

"Hot Mickey?"

"Sure. The outfit bills as *Hot Mickey and His Five Finns.*"

"Do tell."

"They are not Finns, though—most of them are German refugees. But they ride with a solid slide. They groove. They send."

"But can they play?"

"Play?" yells Boogie. "Wait until you hear the way they dig it out of the dugout! The fella on the slush pump is terrific, the guy who handles the gut-bucket can really slap doghouse, and they've got an alligator who really can keep the plumbing humming."

I ask for an explanation, and I find out that Boogie refers to a trombone player, a jerk with a bass viol, and a saxophone snorter.

By this time Boogie is so excited he is dragging me down the street.

"No contract," he yells. "He can get this guy for next to nothing. Take him up-town. I guarantee once you get him in for an audition, any band in the country will offer him half a G a week to start. He's playing for peanuts here—it's the chance of a lifetime! Wait until you see what he does to a crowd. Here we are—just step into the silo."

"What silo?"

"The place where they keep the corn. The dance-hall."

"Sure enough. We are standing in front of a little rat-race track called the Barrel House. Before I can make up my mind, he drags me inside.

It is nothing but a made-over barn, with a bar and a lot of tables instead of stables. A gang of jitterbugs are shagging all over the floor, and up on the platform sits this Hot Mickey and his refugees. They look like refugees from a bathtub to me.

In fact, I never see such a mangy collection of human beings outside of a

Turkish Bath on the day after New Year's Eve. They look like they are dying, and they sound like it, too.

Because they are playing a brand of noise I never hear in all my life, and I once work in a steel foundry for a year. But these cookies are hammering and yammering on horns and trumpets and drums, and they are blasting so loud you would think somebody was building a subway.

But the crowd loves it. The place is packed, and everybody is prancing around with their fingers in the air, and sometimes their skirts. I do not need to take a second squint to see that there really are a lot of finks who go for this kind of bazoo.

Boogie drags me over to a table and leers.

"Listen," he chirps, beaming all over. "Come on and listen," he urges, making me take my fingers out of my ears. "Hear that baby pounding the tusks."

"What?"

"Punching ivory," say Boogie.

"Huh?"

"Playing the piano."

"Oh."

"Scar me, Daddy, eight to the mar," he yells, or something like it. "Feep, I want you should pipe that clarinet."

Me, I do not know a clarinet from a ocarina; in fact, where music is concerned I cannot tell a bass from a hole in a piccolo. But I look for the guy who is playing most loud and proud, and I spot who he refers to.

He is a tall, thin drip tooting on a tall, thin horn. He stands up when he plays, and the rest of the band follows. When I try hard I can hear his clarinet honking way up above the other noise, and it has plenty of rhythm.

In fact, the whole crowd hears it, because they do not wish to stop dancing at all. Whenever a number finishes, they clap their pinkies together so hard and long that the band must keep right on playing.

"See?" whispers Boogie. "What do I tell you? He's a natural. He's hep to the step." Boogie jerks his finger at the mob. "Look—even the bartenders have to dance."

This is a fact. I notice them myself. Also I find my own feet jumping up and down a little. It is really rhythm.

"Pipe that!" grunts Boogie, all of a sudden. He points to the floor. I see a little mouse run out of its hole in the woodwork and scamper up and down in time with the music.

"It takes a real hep-cat to catch mice," Boogie tells me. "Now come on up to the stand and tell this guy you want to be his agent. Tell him you'll line up an audition with a big-time band for him. Take it easy, because he is plenty timid and he doesn't know the score yet, being new in this country."

So when the number is over and the crowd finally finishes clapping and sits down, we slide over to the stand. First Boogie introduces me to the leader.

"Come on, ick, meet the stick," he says. "This is Hot Mickey. Mickey, my pal here would like to talk to your clarinet player."

"Huh," grunts the fat leader. "Is he safe?"

"Strictly a square from Delaware," Boogie tells him. He drags me over to the skinny clarinet man. "They're all nervous about meeting strangers," he whispers. "Afraid of spies on their trail, or something. These refugees have a pretty tough time getting out of Europe. So take it easy."

Then he pushes me up on the platform and grabs the skinny man by the arm.

"Herr Pfeiffer," he says, "I want you should meet your new agent, Lefty Feep."

The skinny guy looks up. He has big, deep eyes, with a light in them like burning reefers. It is a very powerful stare, and when we shake hands I find out he has a very powerful grip.

"Agent?" he says. "I do not need an agent. I have here a good job, I am in this fine orchestra playing, so why in the world should I an agent want?"

This double-talk turns out to be a kind of German accent, but I just pass it off and do what Boogie tells me.

"How would you like to earn big money in a real band?" I brace him. "I can get you a job where you'll be famous overnight."

Pfeiffer shakes his head very fast.

"I do not wish to famous become," he says. "I have on my trail enemies, and I do not wish publoosity." He shakes his long curly hair again.

Then Boogie and I really go to work on him. It takes an hour between dances, but to make a long story, he finally agrees to show up tomorrow, on his night off, for an audition.

So Boogie and I leave, very happy, while he is playing the last number for the evening. When we go out the door, the crowd is making like crazy all over the floor.

"He's a sensation," Boogie yells. "Broadway will love him! Think of the radio—movies—ouch!"

The last word comes from him when he nearly trips going out the door. He stumbles over a gang of mice that are waltzing around in the hall.

"We can at least sell him to Walt Disney," I decide.

But it is not Walt Disney I sell Pfeiffer to the next day. Boogie and I go down and arrange an audition with none other than *Lou Martini and His Cocktail Cavaliers*. They are playing in a big hotel, in what they call the Tiger Room.

Boogie handles all the details. I learn that the way a player auditions is to show up for a regular dance performance and sit in with the rest of the orchestra, to see if his noise fits in with the blasting. And Boogie gives this Lou Martini a terrific buildup about how good Pfeiffer is. From the way he describes his tooting you'd think Pfeiffer is the angel Gabriel instead of a broken-down refugee. But Martini says all right, he'll give him a chance, let him come around tonight with his clarinet for the dinner dance hour. Only Martini warns us that Pfeiffer better be good, because the Tiger Room only caters to the cream of society, and bad music will make them curdle.

So out we go, very steamed up, and I take Pfeiffer up to my place and tell him the good news. Pfeiffer doesn't seem any too pleased—in fact, you would think he has a date to be hung in the Tiger Room. Those big eyes of his get misty and he runs his skinny fingers through the mop on his head.

"*Ach,* this playing I do not like the idea of, Mr. Feep," he grunts. "My music is safer to play a stable in, but on a dance floor not."

"You're terrific," Boogie tells him. "You know all the numbers Martini uses anyway. Besides, you have your own style, and all you do is hot licks, not score-work."

"Perhaps the licks too hot will be for this band," Pfeiffer mourns.

"The crowd will go wild over you," Boogie promises.

"That is what I am afraid of," says Pfeiffer. "Besides, there are on my trail now certain men I do not wish to find me."

"What's the matter, you owe money on that clarinet?" Boogie asks him.

"*Nein.* The instrument, I make it myself a long time ago," Pfeiffer says, "and it is not a clarinet."

"I wonder about that," Boogie tells him. "It does not resemble an American instrument at all, but it sounds like one."

Pfeiffer smiles.

"I can make it sound like many things," he answers. "But I do not make it sound tonight. Positive!"

Well, I see a great opportunity slipping away, so I stick in my oar.

"You have to play, Pfeiffer," I argue. "It's the chance of a lifetime. A young punk like you ought to have a big future."

"You are wrong," he says. "I am not so young and not so punk, and I have a great past. But if the men on my trail up to me catch, I will have no future left at all."

"How will they know?" I tell him. "All you do is sit in on a few numbers with a big band. Nobody will even notice you."

I'm wrong. I find it out that night.

We finally argue Pfeiffer into keeping his date, and at eight in the evening we breeze into the Tiger Room and take him up to Lou Martini, who gives him a seat with the band.

Then Boogie and I sit down at a table and order a couple hamburgers while we wait for the dancing to start. I gander around and I am impressed. The Tiger Room is strictly uptown—some of the customers have as many as six chins, and most of the guys are wearing tuxedos nearly as good as the waiters have. There are a lot of old society tomatoes and a whole gang of debutramps. I begin to worry a little about whether this Pfeiffer is as good as we think he is—because from the looks of this mob they don't go for anything but the best. If they dance, they got to have at least St. Vitus leading the orchestra.

And there is skinny Pfeiffer up on the platform with his old clarinet, wearing the kind of suit they put on window dummies when they want to burn them. His big round eyes are rolling, and he looks frightened and nervous. He keeps staring out at the tables like he was afraid of seeing a ghost, or his mother-in-law.

Then I see they are ready to start. Just before Martini goes out to lead the band, he stops over at our table and throws down a sheaf of papers.

"This is our stock contract," he tells me. "If your man is any good tonight, we'll sign it."

Then Pfeiffer blows, and Boogie and I sit there, biting our nails without ketchup when we see Martini raise his stick.

The music begins. Couples get up from all the tables and begin to break down their arches. They jiggle along, and I look at Pfeiffer and see he is playing kind of soft behind the band. So far, so good.

There is another number, and this one is a little on the torrid side, so I know pretty soon Pfeiffer will have a chance to let out some blasts on his kazoo. Sure enough, comes the second chorus and Pfeiffer begins to let go with those high notes. They shriek out plenty loud, and the rest of the band lets him carry the tune. He has to carry it, the way he is mangling same, but everybody seems to like it. The dancers wiggle a little harder, and when it is over they all push their paws together. Pfeiffer is plenty red in the face, but Martini calls for another number and off they go.

This time he must pick out a special, because it is almost all clarinet. There are some drums, but what you hear is that awful squeaking. It runs up and down my spine like I have frogs down my neck. But these hep-cats are crazy for it. They begin to truck all over the place, and Pfeiffer stands up and blows away.

"Look at that man send!" Boogie shouts.

But I am not looking at that man. I am looking at something else.

We are sitting at a table near the wall, and I happen to glance down when I see it. There is something crawling out of the woodwork, and I recognize it right away. It is a mouse. A big, black mouse. And behind it is another mouse. And another.

I turn away, not believing my peepers, and then I see something else running between two tables. Grey mice. Three or four of them, scampering out onto the dance floor. I turn to the bandstand and I see a couple more, jitterbugging out from underneath.

"Jumping jive!" yells Boogie. "Look twice at the mice!"

And all at once the floor seems to be full of them. They are running and squeaking between the dancers. Some of the society tomatoes notice them for the first time and begin to let out little squeaks themselves, pointing down at their feet.

Martini turns around to see what the matter is and he is so astonished he nearly drops his stick. Then he waves at Pfeiffer. But Pfeiffer doesn't pay any attention. He is blowing his clarinet, and like Boogie says, he is out of this world. His eyes are shut, his face is red, and all he can do is squeal out that high note of his.

And the mice run out, dozens of them, from all over the place. Some of the men are trying to kick them, and a couple of the jitter girls climb up on chairs and go right on dancing while they scream to take them away. A waiter is crossing the floor, running very fast, and he trips over a brown rat.

Everybody is squawking and running at once. By this time mice are climbing up on the tables and grabbing at food, and I see one fat bozo going crazy with the giggles because a mouse crawls into his tuxedo and tickles him.

Boogie runs up to the bandstand and helps Martini grab the clarinet away from Pfeiffer. Meanwhile, I am very interested watching a young tomato at the next table who seems to get a mouse caught in her bustle. She is doing a very torrid rumba even after the music stops.

So the next thing I know is when Martini grabs me by the collar and pushes me out of my chair. He has Pfeiffer's neck in his other hand, and he is sort of kicking Boogie along with his feet in a mild sort of way. Also he is saying things that I do not wish to repeat.

"But what about our contract?" I ask, as he moves us along to the door. "What about our contract?"

"Take a look," Martini gurgles, between curses.

I look back at the table and all I see is a pile of mice scampering around a few strips of paper. They eat our contract for us! And something tells me Martini is not going to make out another one. In fact, he confirms this suspicion when he throws us down the stairs of the Tiger Room.

"Get out and stay out," he shouts. "You rats will bring a bunch of mice into my place!"

"Aw, shut your trap!" yells Boogie, which is not the right thing to say, because Martini turns very red and throws a small chair after us.

It happens to hit me on the head, so the last words I hear come from Martini when he yells after us:

"I'll teach you—trying to put the Pied Piper in my orchestra!"

When I come to, I am sitting in the alley, and somebody is pouring water over my noggin like I am some kind of potted plant. I look up and see Pfeiffer.

"Where is Boogie?" I ask, strictly from confusion.

"I do not know, Herr Feep. He says he wants to make a grab far."

"Grab far? You mean, a get-away?"

"Yes. *Ach,* he runs very fast, that Herr Boogie."

I stand up, and when I do I remember everything. I stare a long stare at this skinny guy with the wild mop of hair, the big bulging eyes, and the funny clarinet.

"What is this Martini yells about you being the Pied Piper?" I get out, finally.

Pfeiffer's eyes turn down and he does a slow shrug. Then he sighs.

"I might as well confess," he whispers. "It is true. That is why tonight I do not wish the music to make. Because when I play, little mice and rats come out. In the stable where it is dark, the customers do not notice take, but when I play upstairs right away they smell a mouse. It is just what I am afraid of."

I listen, but all the while I am wrecking my brains to remember what I hear about this Pied Piper. I catch the gossip when I am a brat in school, I guess. Some burg over in Germany gets filled with rats—even before the Nazis arrive. And instead of calling the exterminator, they hire this guy with the pipe to swing out a few tunes. He plays and the rodents follow him and get drowned. Then he comes back and turns in a bill, but the rats are gone and they try to stall him off on a cash settlement. So he plays again and all their moppets run after his music like jitterbugs and dance away forever.

I ask him about this story, and Pfeiffer shakes his head.

"It is a lie," he hollers, waving his arms. "It is a dirty black lie; propaganda. It is true I go to Brunswick, to Hamelin where the rat-plague is. It is bad, that plague. Across the Volga the rats swim, from Asia they come, brown rats. To Prussia they march, like an army on its stomach traveling. Because they eat everything. Food, merchandise, poultry, flowers, seeds. At buildings they gnaw, at the pipes and walls and the foundations even. Fires they start by gnawing matches. Floods they commence by gnawing dams. In Hamelin there are more rats than people.

"And in Hamelin they hire me the rats to kill. I have my pipe and my music which I learn from traveling in India where they charm serpents. So for the rats a concert I arrange and they follow me to the river and drown dead. This is true.

"But it is a lie that I take away children! It is a lie made up to spoil my business. Now they only mouse-traps use and I am—how you call it?—a bum. It gets so bad I must a job in an orchestra take, playing my pipe like a clarinet. Still, the music I make enchants the rats, so I get from many theatres and cafes on my behind thrown out.

"Then come the Nazis, and because of what I do must from Germany run like a rat myself. What happens after that you know."

Pfeiffer shakes his head. I pat him on the shoulder.

"Why don't you spill this before?" I tell him. "You got a fortune in that pipe of yours and you don't know it! Why, you could set yourself up as a rat-remover and put the exterminator companies out of business!"

"*Nein.* You forget—they are still on my trail, those Nazis, because of what I try to do before I leave. That is why to Pfeiffer I change my name—it is German for Piper. Publoosity would be deadly fatal. The Gestapo wants to take me back. Up to now I sleep in the basement under the Barrel House because I am afraid. Down there the rats and mice protect me. But now I will be caught and they will—how you say so?—bake for me my goose."

"Nuts to that," I console him. "We got no Gestapo over here. The government cleans out fifth columnists. You got nothing to worry about. Just put that in your pipe and play it."

Pfeiffer smiles a little.

"You are kind, Herr Feep."

"Come home with me," I tell him. "I'll figure an angle for you. A guy with your talent—a regular rat Stokowski—you won't have any trouble."

We start off down the side street. I am still talking to Pfeiffer and I pay no attention to the car that pulls up alongside the curb ahead. I just give Pfeiffer the old juice.

"I got a million ideas for you," I am saying. "Maybe not playing in a swing band, but other places. Hold it—I've got it—I see the light!"

But it is not the light I see.

It is the dark. Because when I say this I suddenly feel something hard smack me across the back of the head. A big hand reaches out and grabs me, and just as

I turn around, I get it in the hat-rack again, and everything goes blankety-blank. For the second time that night I am down and out.

And when I wake up I am higher than ever in my life. Twenty thousand feet, to be exact.

I am in a plane, and so is Pfeiffer. We are lying on the seat of the rear compartment, and in the seat ahead a pilot is giving out with the old push and pull.

I sit up, and that is all I can do. Because Pfeiffer and I have our hands and legs tied together in Boy Scout knots.

Only one look at our pilot tells me he is very far from being a Boy Scout. He is a big side of meat with shoulders like a wrestler, and his head is shaved, even though his face isn't. He is wearing a pilot's outfit, but there is a little round badge on his sleeve. Pfeiffer looks at it and shudders.

"*Ach!*" he whispers. "Gestapo!"

Sure enough, I spot the swastika. I give Pfeiffer a nudge.

"What gives?" I ask.

"Just what I am afraid of. They catch up to me, as I know they will. They drag us into the car and take us to some place where this plane in a secret hangar is kept. Now they fly us back to Germany."

I raise my head.

"But feel how cold it is. We're heading north. And look down there—we're over land, not water."

Pfeiffer shakes his head.

"We are probably to Canada going first. To another secret hangar. We make the trip in installments, and I am worried only about the last payment."

The pilot never looks around. It is getting very frigid in the plane, and steam comes out of our yaps when Pfeiffer and I whisper. I squirm closer to him.

"I don't get this," I remark. "Just what is it you do in Germany that makes the Gestapo so hot to catch you?"

"I may as well tell you now," Pfeiffer decides. "I play for the rats."

"So what?"

"You don't understand. I play for the rats over the underground—the secret radio broadcasts against the Nazis. Music I make for them to come out, music I make for them to appear in every city. So they will jaundice bring, and typhus, and the plague. There is a rat for every man, you know—a population of millions. And I play oh so sweetly for the rats, to make them happy, to make them hungry. I play music that is with appetite filled, so they will eat. They will eat under buildings and bite away the foundations. They will destroy docks and warehouses and railroad bridges. They will make sabotage and the machinery up-ge-shcrew."

"I get it."

"So does the Gestapo. Every night I play, hidden away, over the wireless. And every night they hunt for me and my broadcasting set. Because the rats and mice come out and eat. Finally—how you say it?—the heat is upon me. I must smuggle myself from the country out. And now, even here, they have orders to find me and bring me back. So now they do. *Achoo!*"

This last remark is a loud sneeze. It is very cold, and Pfeiffer is shivering. So am I, but not from cold. I merely have to look at the bullet-headed pilot to start shivering.

"You really can get the rats to go on a rampage with your music?" I whisper.

"That is so. Music has charms—*Achoo!*"

I sit there thinking about the screwy pickle I am in, but not for long. Because the pickle develops warts very soon. We start going down. The plane noses over and I look out and see us rushing into blackness. No lights, no nothing.

At first I think we are cracking up, but the pilot is still sitting very calm. Then all at once I see a flare shoot out, and it hangs in the air while we land.

We taxi along some dirt almost into a clump of trees, and some patches of snow.

"Canada, all right," I whisper to Pfeiffer, while the pilot gets out. "Must be another hideout."

This turns out to be a good guess. Because the pilot comes around to the rear door, opens it up, and cuts our feet loose. For the first time I get a full look at his bearded puss, and it is a face that only Karloff's mother could love.

"*Raus!*" he says, kindly dragging Pfeiffer and me out by the neck. "To the cabin—march!"

And he pulls us along the ground toward a little cabin standing there all alone in the wilderness. The door is open and we go inside, Pfeiffer sneezing his way ahead of me.

And he pulls us along the ground toward a small cabin standing there all alone in the wilderness. The door is open and we go inside, Pfeiffer sneezing his way ahead of me.

Now I do not like the buzzard with the beard, but I will take him for a cell-mate any time instead of the personality waiting for us inside the cabin.

He is sitting at a little table, and when we come marching in, he waves us to a seat with a smile and a big black Luger.

He is an old character, but his age does not make him any more harmless than a lot of other old things, such as tigers. He has a big beak of a nose which he points at us like he does the Luger, and behind the schnozz are two red eyes that go through me and come out of the back of my head.

"So," he says to the beard. "You bring guests, *hein?*"

"*Ja,*" snaps the beard, lifting a hand like he wanted to leave the room. "*Heil Hitler.*" And he stands at attention.

"Good, good. This is Pfeiffer. And the other garbage?"

I do not know who he is referring to, but I can guess. What he calls me is appropriate, because I look like I am down in the dumps.

The beard starts to wag.

"I wish to report that I make contact with the man Pfeiffer and his companion tonight at nine o'clock, in the sedan. No trouble picking them up. I bring them with me to the plane and here we are."

"Good, good." The beak is smiling. "Go outside to the tanks and refuel at once. You must leave immediately and deliver our guests to the proper authorities."

The beard smiles and heils, then ducks out to refuel the plane. Meanwhile, the beak gives us the old eye.

"Sit down," he says, gesturing with the gun in a way that is too careless to suit me. "You seem cold, Pfeiffer."

Pfeiffer is sniffling and shivering again.

"Yes," he whispers.

The beak smiles. "Too bad you are so cold, but it will not be for long. Soon your journey will be over, and then I am sure they will make it hot enough for you."

This does not strike either me or Pfeiffer as so funny.

But the beak laughs.

"Yes, they are waiting anxiously for you, Pfeiffer. The Pied Piper is quite a catch, even for the Gestapo. It is well worth the risk we are taking to maintain a plane service when we can handle such passengers as yourselves." He grins very wide. "You are going for a ride."

"Achoo!" says Pfeiffer.

"Gesundheit," says the beak, very polite.

I study the situation. There is nothing in the old cabin but the table, some chairs and a couple bunks. Nothing to throw or hide behind. And the beak has a Luger. In a couple minutes we will be back on the plane, headed for Germany. I wish very sincerely to get my hands on that gun—but my hands are tied. I begin to feel a trifle depressed.

And Pfeiffer just sits there and sneezes. He has a terrific cold.

The beak notices it. "It is too bad I cannot light a fire," he remarks. "But sparks fly up from a chimney, and this is Canada. One must be very careful, you understand."

Pfeiffer shakes his head. And then a kind of gleam comes into his eye.

"Perhaps I can make myself warm," he suggests. "If you do not mind, I will my pipe play the time to pass."

The beak chuckles.

"A serenade? *Wunderschön!* It is not every man who can hear the Pied Piper play."

Pfeiffer reaches into his coat with his bound hands. And the beak's Luger follows every move, in case Pfeiffer springs a gat or something. But nothing comes out except the clarinet from inside the overcoat pocket. It is pretty beat-up, but Pfeiffer puts it up to his lips and lets out a blat. The squeaking starts.

The beak doesn't care. Out here in the wilderness there is nobody to hear. So Pfeiffer begins to dig in. He smiles a little and wrestles with the cold pipe. It doesn't seem to work right, somehow. The cold air makes the notes lower. And Pfeiffer's cold does something to his breathing, so that the tones are all screwy. They carry a long wail, a sort of echo from far away.

Somehow it is all kind of impressive—Pfeiffer sitting there tied up in this cabin in the woods at night, with a guy pointing a gun at his head—playing like one of those statues of Pan, or whatever they call him. His long fingers tug at the pipe and his lips pucker up, and the big squeals run up and down the air.

Now the door opens and the beard comes in. The plane is refueled and he is ready. He sits down for a minute when he hears Pfeiffer tooting away. He tries to get the beak's attention, but the beak is watching Pfeiffer.

And then I hear it. Far away. That rustling sound. That padding sound. It seems to be coming nearer, getting louder. More like a clumping noise. It sort of moves in rhythm to the piping. I look around, quick, but I don't see anything.

From the look in Pfeiffer's eyes, I know he hears it too. And all at once he pulls out the stops and gets loud on the clarinet. He rides to town. And over it comes the running sound, nearer and nearer.

Then the beak gets it too. He stands up all at once.

"Stop that!" he yells. But it is too late. All of a sudden there is a cracking sound, the walls of the cabin start to bend in, and the side of the door breaks down with a crash.

Pfeiffer's tune blares out louder, and there is a hell-splitting bang. The table spins into the corner.

"*Himmel!*" gasps the beak, turning around to face the door.

This is my chance. I throw myself across the room and grab the gun out of his hands. The beard falls down when the door topples over on him.

"Come on, Pfeiffer!" I advise him. For a minute or two there is nothing but confusion when the cabin is filled with what Pfeiffer calls on his pipes.

Then we are running down the trail, keeping the gun in the beak's ribs, and climbing in the plane. In three minutes we are off, making the beak pilot the ship.

So there is not much more to tell. When we return, we hand the beak over to the FBI, along with the plane. They get all the details on this Gestapo ring from the beak, and that is that.

"Naturally, Pfeiffer is a hero. I guess he will be doing sound effects for Walt Disney pretty soon. But right now he is working with the Coordinator of Information's office. You know, the babies that broadcast short-wave radio to the Axis.

"He is doing just what he does back in Germany—playing request numbers for the mice over there. He is trying to get the mice to revolt by using his pipe over the radio. Maybe he can get a bunch of them to tunnel under Berchtesgarden and kill Hitler. Perhaps the mice will get the rat.

"So that is why I come in here and order all this cheese. I take some down to the headquarters where the Pied Piper makes his broadcasts from, and feed it to the mice and rats that sneak into the studio when he starts to play.

"It is better to feed them than bump them off, because they do us such a good turn."

Lefty Feep sat back and folded his hands.

"Does this answer your questions?" he asked.

I stared him straight in the eye. "Listen, Feep. When you started this wild story of yours, I warned you. About holes in the story, wasn't it? And there is something you haven't managed to explain. Thought you'd get away with it—but I've caught you."

"To what do you refer, Bob?" asked Feep, pleasantly.

"To that little matter of Pfeiffer playing in the cabin. You said he did something which caused an awful commotion; started some kind of row that you took advantage of in overpowering the Gestapo men and escaping."

"Of course," Feeped answered me. "I can set you straight on that."

"Just a minute." I raised my hand. "I think I know what you're going to tell me. You're going to tell me that Pfeiffer played his pipe and a lot of mice started to tunnel under the cabin and eat away the foundations so that the door fell in. And I tell you right now, I won't believe it!"

"You don't have to believe it," Feep grinned. "That is not what happens. Pfeiffer has such an idea when he starts to play, but it is lucky for us that he also has a bad cold."

"What's that got to do with breaking the door down?" I snapped.

"I tell you before, Pfeiffer has a bad cold and it makes his music sound different."

"I know that," I replied. "And I also know that you won't find mice running around in the wilds of Canada."

"Sure," Feep agreed. "It is not mice that break down the cabin door. Pfeiffer plays music for a mouse to come, but his cold causes a slight mistake. And he does not get a mouse."

"What does he get to break the door down?"

"A moose," said Lefty Feep.

CONTRIBUTORS' BIOGRAPHIES

WILLIAM PETER BLATTY
William Peter Blatty is best know as the author of the best-seller *The Exorcist* and its sequel *Legion*. He wrote and produced the Oscar-winning script for the film *The Exorcist* (1973), which was also nominated for Best Picture, and wrote and directed *The Ninth Configuration* (1980), based on his novel *Twinkle, Twinkle, "Killer" Kane* (1966), and *Exorcist III* (1990) adapted from *Legion*. He collaborated with Blake Edwards on such films as the inspector Clouseau comedy *A Shot in the Dark* (1964), *What Did You Do in the War, Daddy?* (1966), *Gunn* (1967), and *Darling Lili* (1970).

RAY BRADBURY
Ray Bradbury is the author of *The Martian Chronicles, The Illustrated Man,* and *Fahrenheit 451*. He screenplayed *Moby Dick* for John Huston's film in 1954. He is now screenplaying his *The Wonderful Ice Cream Suit* for Disney and working on an IMAX film with Doug Trumbull (*2001*) and astronaut Buzz Aldrin. Nuff said.

RAMSEY CAMPBELL
Ramsey Campbell has been given more awards for horror fiction than any other writer. His novels include *Incarnate, Midnight Sun, The Count of Eleven* and *The One Safe Place. Alone With the Horrors* collects many of his best short stories from his first thirty years of publication and won both the Stoker Award and the World Fantasy Award. His latest novel is *Nazarell*.

HUGH B. CAVE
Hugh B. Cave, author of 30 books, first wrote over 800 stories for the pulps, then another 350 for the slicks, including 43 for *The Saturday Evening Post*. He has won a World Fantasy Award, the Phoenix Award for distinguished writing, and,

like Robert Bloch, the Lifetime Achievement Award of the Horror Writers Association. He is still writing.

ARTHUR C. CLARKE, C.B.E.

Dr. Clarke was nominated for the 1994 Nobel Peace Prize for his theories and invention of communications satellites. He was made a commander of the British Empire by H.M. Queen Elizabeth in 1989. He has written over 70 books and shared an Oscar nomination with Stanley Kubrick for the movie *2001: A Space Odyssey*. He wrote the script and the novel. His *Mysterious World* and *Strange Powers* TV series have been shown worldwide, and he is currently filming the 26-part *Mysterious Universe* for the Discovery Channel. His many honors include the Marconi and Lindbergh awards as well as 3 Hugos and 3 Nebulas for his science fiction.

HARLAN ELLISON

Harlan Ellison received the International Horror Critics' first annual Living Legend Award in 1995. In 1994 he received the World Fantasy Lifetime Achievement Award. The year before that he became the latest of a small handful of fantasists ever to be included in *The Best American Short Stories*. Forty years, 62 books, more than 1700 stories, essays, articles, screen- and teleplays. His closest friends have included Howard Fast, Lenny Bruce, Robin Williams, Isaac Asimov and, for forty-three years, Robert Bloch. He is a helluva writer.

PHILIP JOSÉ FARMER

Philip José Farmer has lived most of his life in Peoria, Illinois, which he considers to be as exotic as the Land of Oz. He's chiefly known for his Riverworld and World of Tiers series and for his recurring themes of religion, sex, absurdity, irrationality, and tricksterism. He loathes hypocrites and broccoli.

NEIL GAIMAN

Neil Gaiman is a writer of prose fiction and poetry (he's had stories in the last three *Year's Best Fantasy and Horror* collections, he cowrote the best-selling novel *Good Omens,* and his miscellany *Angels and Visitations* won the 1994 International Horror Critics Guild Award as best collection), and of comics (such as *Sandman* and *Mister Punch,* for which he's won Best Writer awards from places as diverse as Finland, Austria, England, and each year since 1991, America). He is working on a TV series for the BBC.

MICK GARRIS

Mick Garris was dubbed "chillmeister" by *TV Guide*. While story editor for the TV series *Amazing Stories,* he won an Image Award from the NAACP for his script "The Sitter" and an Edgar for his script of "The Amazing Falsworth." He won a special award at the Paris Film Festival as director of *Critters 2: The Main Course*. He has collaborated with Stephen King on "Stephen King's *Sleepwalkers*" and directed *The Stand* and *Is This Scary?,* a short film starring Michael Jackson. He created the syndicated TV show "She-Wolf of London." He is preparing to direct a new version of *The Mummy* and write short fiction.

SHELDON JAFFERY

Sheldon Jaffery is counsel for and on the board of trustees of the Horror Writer's Association. He has authored the bibliographical books *Horrors and Unpleasantries, The Arkham House Companion, Future and Fantastic Worlds* and *Double Trouble*. He edited and compiled *Sensuous Science Fiction, Selected Tales of Grim and Grue, The Weirds,* Hugh B. Cave's *The Corpse Maker,* Henry Kuttner's *Secret of the Earth Star* and Theodore Roscoes's *Toughest in the Legion.* He is currently working on a bibliography of pulp magazines and a book about book collecting.

STEPHEN JONES

Stephen Jones is the winner of 2 World Fantasy awards and 2 Horror Writers Association Bram Stoker awards, as well as being a ten-time recipient of the British Fantasy Award and a Hugo Award nominee. A full-time columnist, television producer/director, and genre movie publicist and consultant, he has written and edited more than 40 books.

STEPHEN KING

Stephen King is the author of more than 30 international best-selling books. More than 30 feature films, miniseries, television episodes, short films and TV movies have been written by him and/or based on his work, including the recent films *The Shawshank Redemption* and *Dolores Claiborne* and the ABC-TV miniseries *The Langoliers.* His next novel, *Desperation,* will be published in 1996.

JOE R. LANSDALE

Joe R. Lansdale is the author of *Cold in July, Mucho MoJo,* and the forthcoming *Two Bear Mambo,* all from Mysterious Press. He is also the author of numerous short stories and has edited or coedited several volumes of fiction and nonfiction. His most recent project is as coeditor with Rick Klaw of *Weird Business,* the most ambitious and exciting comic anthology ever.

RANDALL D. LARSON

Randall D. Larson is the author of 9 books of nonfiction as well as articles in books and magazines relating to the fields of horror in film and books. He compiled *The Complete Robert Bloch,* a bibliography of Bloch's books, stories, articles, and scripts. He also compiled *The Robert Bloch Companion: Collected Interviews.*

CHRISTOPHER LEE

Christopher Lee, a British-born actor, starred in countless horror films in Britain, Europe, and America. He is best known for his legendary portrayals of Dracula in dozens of Hammer films. He brought modern film villainy to new heights in the James Bond film *The Man with the Golden Gun.* He is host on the CD-ROM *Ghosts.*

BRIAN LUMLEY

Brian Lumley is the author of the internationally best-selling 5-volume *Necroscope* series and its spin-off *Vampire World* trilogy. Lumley is by no means finished with the hero of the *Necroscope* series; the eponymous necroscope Harry Keogh, who talks to dead people, teleports through the mathematical *mobius continuum,* and has an ongoing love-hate relationship with the monstrously alien bloodsucking Waphirie, will soon be back in the 2-volume *Necroscope: The Lost Years.*

RICIA MAINHARDT

Ricia Mainhardt is an independent literary agent and a popular lecturer. She coedited *Superheroes* with John Varley.

RICHARD MATHESON

Richard Matheson is one of the world's most diverse and respected writers of imaginative fiction. His 16 novels run the gamut from science fiction, fantasy, and horror to mysteries, suspense, westerns, and mainstream, as well as 7 short story collections and a multiple award-winning *Collected Stories*. He has more than 30 feature-length screenplays and teleplays to his credit, plus countless episodes of TV series. He has won the Bram Stoker, Hugo, Edgar, Golden Spur, World Fantasy, and Writer's Guild awards, as well as being named Grand Master by both World Fantasy and Horror Writers Association.

WILLIAM F. NOLAN

William F. Nolan is best known for writing the novel *Logan's Run,* which spawned a movie and TV series. He has written more than 60 other books as well as more than 700 articles and 40 TV and film scripts. Nolan has twice won the mystery writers' Edgar Allan Poe Award.

ANDRE NORTON

Andre Norton is the acknowledged grande dame of science fiction and fantasy. She is the sole author of 117 books and the collaborator of 21 books. She has 7 short story collections and has edited 20 anthologies. She is translated into eighteen languages around the world. She is a Grand Master of the Science Fiction Writers of America, and a member of Ohioana-Women Hall of Fame. She has received the World Fantasy Life Achievement Award and countless international awards. She is currently involved in establishing a writers' retreat for genre writers, as well as continuing her own writing.

FREDERIK POHL

Frederik Pohl has been a critic, agent, teacher, editor, and writer. He has won most of the awards science fiction has to offer. He has also received the American Book Award, United Nations Society of Writers Award, Popular Culture Association Award, and is a fellow to the British Interplanetary Society and the American Association for the Advancement of Science. His 1977 novel *Gateway* has been adapted for theater and a computer game. His books and stories adapted for film include *The Space Merchants,* "The Midas Plague," "The Clonemaster," and "The Tunnel Under the World."

DAVID J. SCHOW

David J. Schow tied with Robert Bloch for the Twilight Zone Magazine Dimension Award (1985) and won a World Fantasy Award (1987). He wrote a survey book on *The Outer Limits* TV series. His other credits include novels, short stories, collections, screenplays, and teleplays. His film credits include *The Crow,* Brandon Lee's last film. He has also written for Leatherface, Freddy Krueger, and Critters. His recent work includes scripts for the TV series *The Outer Limits* and *The Hunger.*

JULIUS SCHWARTZ

Julius Schwartz, a living legend in science fiction and comics, was Robert Bloch's first agent. His other clients included Ray Bradbury, Otto Binder, Alfred Bester, Leigh Brackett, and those were just the B's. For the past fifty-two years, he has been an editor with DC Comics. He is credited with creating the silver age of comics. He edited *Superman, The Batman, Flash,* and *Green Lantern.*

MELISSA ANN SINGER

Melissa Ann Singer is a Senior Editor at Tom Doherty Associates. She has published a number of articles on editing and on the publishing business.

PETER STRAUB

Peter Straub is the author of 13 novels, among them *Ghost Story, Shadowland, The Talisman* (with Stephen King), *Koko, Mystery*, and *The Throat,* and a collection of stories and novellas, *Houses Without Doors.* He has won the British Fantasy Award, the Bram Stoker Award of the Horror Writers Association, and 2 World Fantasy awards.

WILLIAM TENN

Philip Klass, under his pen name of William Tenn, has been writing and publishing satirical science fiction since 1946. He has published 6 collections of short stories and 2 novels (*Of Men and Monsters* and *A Lamp for Medusa*); and his 1953 anthology, *Children of Wonder,* was the first selection of the Science Fiction Book Club. He holds the title of Professor Emeritus of English and Comparative Literature at Pennsylvania State University. Do not confuse him with the other Philip Klass, who writes "I-refuse-to-believe-it" articles about flying saucers.

JEFF WALKER

Jeff Walker is a marketing consultant specializing in science fiction, fantasy, and animation films and TV. His efforts contributed to the success of such films as *Blade Runner, Jurassic Park, Interview with the Vampire,* and the *Batman* movies. He has written and/or produced films, including *The Flight of Dragons* and *The Gladiator* and documentaries, including "making of . . ." featurettes. He has acted in many films and TV shows. He has been a journalist, film and music critic and/or editor for magazines, including *Rolling Stone* and *Crawdaddy*.

BILL WARREN

Bill Warren writes about science fiction and horror films, mostly; he's the author of *Keep Watching the Skies* (two obsessive volumes on the SF movies of the 1950s) and has written for most of the magazines in the field. He's also the sysop of the Showbiz Round Table on GEnie, and a reporter for a French TV show. He is available for convention speeches and is fond of Hawaiian shirts.

GAHAN WILSON

Gahan Wilson is known primarily as a cartoonist (his drawings appear mostly in *Playboy* and *The New Yorker*) whose humor has a decided bent toward the grotesque and downright macabre. Besides his numerous cartoon anthologies (the latest being *Still Weird*), he also wrote some bizarre novels (*Eddy Deco's Last Caper* and *Everybody's Favorite Duck*), drew an animated cartoon (*Gahan Wilson's Diner*), a CD-ROM game (*Gahan Wilson's Ultimate Haunted House*), and wrote numerous short stories, which explore either the darkly humorous or the just plain dark.

DOUGLAS E. WINTER

Douglas E. Winter is a Washington, D.C.-based lawyer, writer, and critic. His reviews and essays appear regularly in *The Washington Post* and other major metropolitan newspapers and in magazines as diverse as *Harper's Bazaar, Gallery,* and *Fangoria*. His books include *Stephen King: The Art of Darkness, Faces of Fear,* and a forthcoming critical biography of Clive Barker. He edited the best-selling anthology *Prime Evil*. His own fiction has been collected in *American Zombie*.